*My homage to the creator of horror-crime,
and the best to ever do it. Thank you, T.H.
— S.C.*

For Ema & Henry

THE TAXIDERMY KILLER

STEWART CLYDE

HUNT PRESS

"Whoever fights monsters should see to it that in the process he does not become a monster."
—Friedrich Nietzsche

1

DEATH WAS HIS MISTRESS. He made an art out of her. He knew her and loved her, of course, but hated her just as much. In the same way as he lusted after—and so despised —the pictures of the girls stuck to his wall.

Above his head, in a neat row of square portraits were the faces of ten women. His girls. One was violently crossed out in harsh streaks of red and black marker pen. The others would soon follow. They were patiently waiting their turns, looking down on him with their perfect features and cold, distant stares.

Each was the face of a model. Each beautiful. Smiling, or showing no emotion at all. They had full, shiny, pretty hair. White teeth. Full lips. Everything he was not, but all he desired. He wanted it. Power over them. Control over them. He wanted to own them. To have them. Forever and always.

In front of him on his worktop was a round make-up mirror, some beauty products; a red lipstick, eyeshadow, moisturizer, and to his right, his open manuscript. He was applying the make-up to his face. Puckering his lips and blinking his eyelids. Same way he'd watched his mother do it. It was his ritual. His guilty pleasure. To look and feel like they did.

Open on the worktop was a very old book. His manuscript. It was embroidered with gold leaf and bound in leather. The hide was thinning and coming away and he knew he'd repair it one day. Perhaps with their flesh. Mmm, he liked the idea. Using their skin. How fitting. How serene. How majestic. He could cure it and treat it and make it malleable and pull it into shape.

Inside this book was what was really important. There were myths and legends of great deeds. Gods and demigods. Stories of vileness and beauty, of hatred and love, and violence and revenge. And he was adding to its stained yellow pages with deeds of his own.

He looked into the round mirror and didn't recognize himself now. He'd changed once again. He liked that too. He looked up at the portrait of the second girl on the wall. She was looking down on him like they all did, and he was looking back at her now, almost as if they shared the same skin. They would soon. If only she could see her own face now. How it looked. Where it was.

His other ritual was something he watched over and over on an old portable black and white television. He played a grainy VHS home movie of a preacher delivering a sermon. He was standing in front of the congregation of tent revival giving an Evangelical sermon. It was something to behold.

He'd watched the tape so many times he knew every note, every incantation, every tonal shift and inflection of the minister's voice. He knew the sermon by rote. And knew the messages Father Zimmer had hidden for him too, like so many breadcrumbs in a forest marking the trail. A way to help him find his way to the truth.

Inside him, the Black Dog stirred. That's what he called

it. The urge. He looked at the images on the screen. He knew his voice was naturally high-pitched so adjusted it deeper and repeated aloud the words he'd heard so many times as if he was reciting the Lord's Prayer in Sunday school.

He mimicked Father Zimmer's voice as he intoned, "In the labyrinth of the human psyche we find ourselves at a devilish crossroads."

In the background, he could hear the congregation shouting affirmations and agreeing with their leader.

"There's a fork in the path and we must choose between the fire of *damnation* and joyousness of glorious *salvation*. Each day—in every way—the path before us is filled with torment and meaning.

"Signs left for us to divine. Signs to help and hinder. Signs to believe and guide. To see these signs, first, we must ask ourselves, what is our nature? What is our true calling?

"Consider the eternal dance. The deadly game of chance. The pitched battle between the hunter and the hunted.

"The moth does not fear the flame, nor does the silent lamb shy from the slaughter. What of us, my children? Are we not also called to this immortal tragedy?

"Inside our actions, our choices, our very existence there lies a message, hidden, a cipher waiting to be unlocked like a bank vault filled with gold.

"Nothing on this plane is arbitrary; every piece part of a larger and larger more incomprehensible puzzle. Our deeds are a silent sermon, preached not from the pulpit, but from the core of God himself!

"What message, then, shall we send forth? It will be one of chaos and darkness. Behold! Await thee the moment of revelation. All things are subject to eternal change ..."

He'd listened to tape so often it was worn thin. He'd

studied it. And in turn, he knew Father Zimmer studied him.

Click. He heard a noise outside and turned his head to listen. The sound of tin rolling on concrete. Soda can. The wind outside. A scrape of dried leaves swirling. The heavy roll-up garage door rattled. He had a hypersensitivity to sounds and noises.

He went back to looking at himself in the mirror. The preacher's voice fell into the background. He would heed the signs. He would *create* the signs. He would be a torch bearer lighting the path for the followers.

He was the anointed one. Father Zimmer was preaching about him. To him. For him. And he was open to the signs. He saw them everywhere and let the lightness and profoundness wash over him like waves breaking on the shore. His was a continuation of the Ripper's legacy. He knew Father Zimmer would be looking out for signs too.

The Black Dog would not be tamed. Only quieted. And only for a short time. It was always hungry. He looked up at the pictures of his beautiful young women on the wall. The next in line was one he liked to watch. He liked to follow. And couldn't wait to caress with a scalpel. He would slowly remove her skin and take it home. He would treasure her face and treat it with care. And leave his own trail of symbols for others to follow. Breadcrumbs in the forest. So that Father Zimmer might find him.

He took the cap off a marker pen and stood up. He put the tip of the pen on the second picture and drew lines across it. Slowly at first, then building until it was vigorous and violent until she was no more. When it was done he breathed hard, wiped his forehead with the back of his hand, and looked down at a clear ziplock bag filled with melted ice water and the face and hair of Savannah Proctor.

2

PORTLAND, MAINE

THE GRAY OCEAN reminded her of Augustine Carver. The hiss and spray of the cold Atlantic. The waves smashed into the craggy outcrop below. It was how she thought of him. How she imagined he was inside.

She shivered against the wind. The waves were like barbarians at the ramparts. Angry. Ferocious. This was a war, she was certain. A war they were losing. A war against an unseen enemy. But perhaps there was still to be one defining battle. A chance to swing the tide in their favor.

She folded and tucked the *Portland Press Herald* under her arm and watched Carver come walking out of the icy-cold water toward her. She waited for him, leaning against a car in the asphalt parking lot that overlooked Ship Cove. She put her hands in her pockets and leaned back and tried not to smirk.

His body shivered in the cold morning air. His skin was patches of purple and red and the hair on his chest was wet.

There was a mist over the ocean behind him and she lifted herself off the hood of the car as he approached.

He put a hand under his dive mask and pulled the wetsuit hood off his head.

His teeth chattered. "It's a little early, isn't it, Deputy Director?" Carver said.

"Don't you *Deputy Director* me, Gust."

He made his way past her and she saw the scars. Thick around the side of his torso the color and texture of jerky. He bent down and reached for the keys he'd stowed under the rear wheel.

"It's dangerous to dive by yourself, isn't it?" she asked as he toweled off.

"You don't mind if I change before we chat, do you?"

He turned and stepped out of the wetsuit shorts and Bronwyn Gibson was left looking at his smooth purplish-white buttocks.

"Nothing I haven't seen before," she said and raised her eyebrow. Then, "Bit cold, isn't it?"

"About two inches," Carver said and half-looked back.

"You're looking a little thin, Gust. You eating?"

"What can I do for you, Bronwyn?"

It came out a bit sharp. His jaw was locked tight from the cold. He was talking through his teeth. Should let it go, she thought. Sharper than he'd meant it, she decided.

"Is there somewhere we can talk?"

"Is it that bad?"

"It sure ain't good," she said. He pulled on his pants and a shirt and glanced up at her as he fastened his belt. "Where're you headed?" she asked.

"The university, I have a dawn patrol starting in about ..." he glanced at his watch and swore silently, "I'm already late."

"Community college, you mean. Mind if I tag along?"

She went to the passenger door and lifted the handle.

"Do they still call you Bronwyn Barnacle?"

"Only to my face."

"You always were too clingy."

"Thanks," she said and pulled the door open and got in.

He climbed into the driver's seat and started up an old navy-blue German convertible. He drove off leaving a trail of whitish-gray smoke trailing behind. She glanced over her shoulder.

"Your engine's burning oil."

Carver checked the rearview and said, "It's charming."

"It's ... something," she said looking at him. She still liked his eyes. The cut of his jaw. She remembered his sand-paper-like stubble. He glanced across at her.

"How's Bethany?"

Carver didn't respond, instead, he changed the subject and said, "You're looking smart, dressed for court?"

"Thought I'd try for a good first impression," Gibson said.

"You could have called, you know?" Carver said as he accelerated through the quiet of Portland still in the embrace of soft morning fog. He looked at her out of the corner of his eye. And she looked out of the window, like a cat ignoring attention. She didn't respond.

"You look tired," he said.

Thanks very much, she thought and kept looking away. She unconsciously touched her fingertips to the bags under her eyes. Gibson knew him well enough to know that he didn't mean anything by it. It was just that brutal honesty was the way he worked. The only way he worked. It was one of the reasons he'd never kept a partner. Always worked alone. Never trusted anyone. Maybe couldn't. That had its advantages and disadvantages. She knew it was only his way of showing concern. Most people misread his intent and thought he was just being an ass. The truth was she did feel tired. She felt thin, like too little butter on too much toast.

"You would've said no," she said under her breath.

"I'm still married," he said, finally answering her question about his wife, Bethany. She turned and saw his iceberg-blue eyes cutting into hers. "But we're going through a rocky patch. Are *still* going through a rocky patch."

She could almost feel the weight he was carrying. The weight he'd be dragging around with him for a long time yet. It had put a strain on his relationships. His ability to do his job. It wasn't something the Bureau liked but it needed people like Augustine Carver. That was, until they get too close to the fire and end up burned out and washed up. Driftwood they called them. People who'd given more of themselves to the job than was good for them. Carver was one of those.

HE ACCELERATED hard under the thick-leafy trees along Preble Street. Went past the baseball diamond and headed toward the college. He pulled into the parking spot outside the Brightspace building and stopped the car with a jolt. Same old Carver, Gibson thought.

She opened the door and stepped out, looking at the low, white buildings of Southern Maine Community College. There was a view over the ocean. All green grass and neat angles. She shut the car door and hurried after Carver who was already making his way up the stairs two at a time.

"Mind if I sit in?" Gibson called from behind him.

"Sure," Carver said, "Just sit in the back."

They pushed through a pair of innately carved faded oak doors that swung on a noisy hinge and opened into a lecture hall lined with rows of students. It was an intimate auditorium of benches in a half-moon amphitheater style around a central desk and lectern. It was already full of students. Gibson slid into an empty seat at the back. Carver made his way down the stairs to the chalkboard and wrote his name in thin white letters.

Augustine Carver. Criminal Psychology 101.

He turned from the board and the students quietened down. He scanned the room and the faces. The last few conversations ended and Gibson watched the lecturer silently observe his class. She wondered what he was thinking.

ONLY WHEN THERE was perfect silence did Carver open his mouth to speak.

"You can call me Gust, or Mr. Carver," he said and waved a hand over his shoulder at the board. He put his hands in his pockets and spun on his heel like he was pivoting away from a jab. He smiled then looked up at Bronwyn and lifted his chin toward her.

"We have a special guest with us today, class, it's not every day your lecture is observed by one of the directors of the Federal Bureau of Investigation. BAU to be specific." He paused. There was a murmur and some of the students whispered behind their hands.

"Does anyone know what a BAU is?"

Hands went up. They were eager. She could see he liked that. They were interested. Carver pointed to one.

"The FBI's Behavioral Analysis Unit?"

"That's right," Carver said and smiled a little broader. Smart too. He lifted his arm and pointed to the back of the lecture hall. The young faces followed his gaze and turned to see. Gibson leaned on the side of her chair with her hand over her mouth and her legs crossed. She lifted her hand away from her mouth and gave a half-wave and an uncomfortable smile. Carver gave her a wink. Payback for accosting him during his morning ritual. His daily dance with death.

"I suppose that must either mean I am really good at what we're discussing today or a really bad person. Maybe subject to an ongoing investigation? You'll have to listen in to find out and weigh the evidence to decide for yourselves." The class laughed politely as they turned back to face their lecturer. "Now, what do we mean by criminology?"

———

AFTER THE LECTURE, the students filed out. The wooden floor creaked and bowed with each step they took. Gibson felt their eyes on her as they passed, but she looked to the front and avoided contact. She didn't want to be drawn into any inane conversations with children. She saw Carver disappear through the back of the lecture hall into an anteroom and Gibson stood and made her way past the stragglers. She followed Carver into the professor's chambers. Carver was bent over at the desk packing a leather briefcase with documents.

"Can we talk?"

"Sure," he said and gestured to a chair.

Gibson put her hands into the pockets of her pantsuit and browsed the floor-to-ceiling bookshelf instead.

"What did you think of the lecture?" Carver asked. It was an absentminded question as he packed the papers.

"I think it was good."

Gibson heard the packing stop and turned her head over her shoulder to see. Carver stood straight up, looking at her.

"What do you mean, good?"

She turned to face him and raised her eyebrows to

profess her innocence. Lifted her hands from her pockets and said, "It was really good, Gust, but—"

"But what?"

"But you're wasted here. Those kids maybe understood five percent of what you were saying. Maybe. Hell, I only *think* I get what you're saying. Nobody has been as close as you have. They know they like it. They know the legend. Most of them are probably there out of the weird sexual excitement they get from it. They know you're off-the-scale smart, but they don't have any idea what you're talking about, not really. They just know they like the way it sounds. The way it makes them feel. All tingly inside."

Carver shook his head and said, "So?" and went back to packing the briefcase.

"It's not Harvard, is it?" He'd be chewing on that, she thought. "How's Bethany dealing with it?" Gibson asked, she knew not to ask about Madeleine.

"We separated, Bron. I stayed here. She can't get over it. She can't forgive me."

Gibson shook her head sadly and said, "Sorry."

She knew he wasn't talking about their one-night thing. That was a mistake. Caught up in the pain and loss of a brutal case. Just a deeply human need for human closeness.

He was talking about the way they lost their daughter.

Carver shrugged as if to say 'what can you do', and said, "What can I do for you, Bron?"

"We need you, Gust," she said and took photographs from her pocket. Carver glanced at her and saw what she was holding.

"I don't want to see any pictures. We can talk about it but I don't want to see any pictures."

"Okay," Gibson said and slid the images into her pocket, "How much do you know?"

Carver shook his head again and shrugged silently.

"Only what I read in the paper. Not much. A murdered woman. Looked similar to Augusta."

"Not similar, Gust. Georgia was identical."

"Okay. What else don't I know?"

"He ties them up. They're naked when we find them. He leaves the curtains open so the neighbors can see. He cuts them, really bad."

"How?"

"Read the file."

"What do you know about him?"

She sighed. "Not enough. Likely left-handed. Meticulous. Not too clean. Good at knots. Probably a Boy Scout."

"A psychotic Boy Scout," Carver said.

"Look, I don't want to influence your thinking. I won't say anymore. Read the file. Please."

Carver sat on the edge of the desk and crossed his arms. He was silent. He stared at the floorboards. Gibson watched him. She knew this was him thinking. She'd learned to leave him alone when he went deep into his mind. They used to call it the Carver-trance. Drop into a half-consciousness, self-induced hypnosis-like state. Couldn't get him to respond. Finally—as anyone would—Gibson got uncomfortable and said loud enough to snap him out of it, "So, what do you think?"

Carver looked up. Blank stare.

"Um, about?"

"Coming back, consulting for me."

Carver shook his head and exhaled and looked at the floorboards again.

"Ah, you've got all the help you need," he said.

She gave a quick grin at his use of a typical Scottish throaty expression. Not bad for an American who'd spent time in Scotland, she thought.

"Plenty of good people. There's nothing there for me, Bron. My life is this now and starting the shop."

"The little shop of horrors?"

"That's just the clients. I'm getting better. Getting over it."

She sensed he was lying.

"I can see that, that's why we need you ... I need you. You can't just waste your time as a private investigator to the rich and famous chasing housewives with a zoom lens."

Carver shook his head, still looking at the floor. "I don't do divorces ..."

Gibson stepped forward. She flung the photographs to the floor in front of his gaze. Frustrated, she said, "There is something there for you, goddammit. Look at them, just look." Gibson's voice was hoarse. Her fatigue showed. Carver looked taken back by the display of anger. Gibson knew it wasn't like her to react like that.

"Your family, Gust, for Christ's sake. Come back with me, fight for them, and help me find this bastard. We need you."

Carver chewed the inside of his cheek and stared at the pictures and Gibson sensed he was nibbling at the bait.

"Don't you care?" Gibson asked him and pointed to the pictures scattered on the floor. Each one of a corpse. Bloody. Tied up. Teeth protruding through lipless mouths. Scenes of extreme and controlled violence. Women. Children. All naked.

"None of them stood a chance."

Carver was quiet.

"Can I ask you something?" Gibson said. "You saw it in the news. You knew what it was. Why didn't you come and help us?"

"I didn't know what it was," Carver said, almost too quiet for her to hear.

"What?"

Carver looked up at her, dead in the eyes, "I didn't know what it was," he said. "Okay? I didn't know."

It was forceful again. That was the man she remembered. So where'd he gone? He was traumatized.

"Hell, Bronwyn. You got rid of me. The agency."

"You shot a suspect, Gust," Gibson said.

"Yeah, and I'd do it again."

"Please don't say that to anyone but me ever again."

Carver shook his head.

"Look," Gibson said. "You took it hard. Okay. I get that."

"They don't want me back ..."

"I have a little assignment for you. Might be a way back in. That's what you want isn't it?"

Carver wasn't listening to her. Willfully ignoring her maybe, she thought.

"We've seen it before ..." Carver said, staring at the photos.

Gibson furrowed her eyebrows. "That's why I need you ..."

"He's improving and he's moving," Carver said.

"You'll need to prove it."

"He's in control. Demands control. He's going to be very hard to catch," Carver said, eyes still fixed, vacant.

"So help me catch him," Gibson said. She was pleading with him and Carver looked at her with pity.

He scoffed. "What am I going to do, Bron? You've got the best guys on this already. The labs. The manpower. You don't need some washed-up wanna-be academic stepping on toes and making life difficult for you, I promise."

"Better than to stay here, impressing some damn community college girls with your brains, Gust. Nobody thinks about this stuff like you. Sees this stuff like you. I haven't met anyone who can. You can."

"Plenty of them can," Carver said and shook his head.

The pictures were still there staring at him. Gibson could see them searing into his mind's eye. Never able to forget them. Her blessing, and his curse.

"No one else can do what I need you to do. You helped us catch the last one."

"And see how much good that did me?" He checked his watch. "I have a meeting," Carver said.

She gave him a look.

"Faculty," he uncrossed his arms and threw his hands up defensively.

"Bill Riley has retired."

She saw Carver processing.

"Basement Bill?" he asked. She nodded. "And you want me to take over from Backlog Bill?"

"It's a way back in."

"It's a punishment."

"It's an opportunity to be part of the show again."

"Cold cases in the basement …"

"They're not in the basement *anymore*. When Bill retired they moved them. Management thought having them on campus sent the wrong message. They wanted them further away from the action."

"That means you wanted them further away," Carver said. Gibson held his gaze. "The local police are starting to whisper about iconography and satanic verses. Come back. Consult on the case. Give them some reassurance, Gust."

"You mean talk to Zimmer and tell them, 'the Ripper said it isn't linked'."

Still just as sharp as a tack, old Carver, she thought and tried not to react. He knew he was right, she could see it on his face and he could probably read it on hers too.

"They'll trust you. The great Gust Carver. You can put it to bed," she said softly.

"You want me to speak to Zimmer so I can boost morale

in the state police? That's a hell of a reason to come. What's next? A wet T-shirt car wash for the veterans parade?"

"It's not charity, Gust. You've still got something to offer."

"When did coming out of retirement ever work out? Even Jordan couldn't do it."

Maybe he was right, she thought. But what choice did she have? "Let's be honest about what each of us wants out of this, shall we?" Gibson said.

"Please, some honesty would be nice for a change."

"You want back in the show," she said. "And I want to squeeze the last ounce of goodness you have left in you. Let's do that."

"You sure there's something left?"

"I'm not interested in the agent you were before, I'm interested in what you bring to being an agent now, Gust." Now he looked intrigued.

"Which field office?" he asked.

"Manassas."

Carver's face crumpled. It was confusion and disbelief. "Mannas—that's not even a field office, it's a—"

"Resident agency."

"—backwater of one."

"It was a one-person resident agency—that's right—until recently, now it has a staff of five. Six, if their new supervisory special agent decides to show up."

"It even comes with a promotion. You want me to be the new Backwater Bill in charge of a team of backlogs that badly?"

"If the shoe fits."

"It doesn't."

"Think of it like BAU-six but with your own team. You can do your own investigating—"

"With a team of screw-ups."

"Yes—okay—they made mistakes. Haven't we all, Gust,

hmm?" He was silent. Gave the slightest shake of his head. "Think about it. You'd be back in the fold. You can work cases—"

"Cold cases."

"They have a backlog of cold cases, yes—" Gibson said.

"Do you know that they used to call them—back at the academy—Bill's bad bunch?" She shook her head. "They called them dead cold cases, the *dead* case team. They were no-hopers, Bron. The cases ... *and* the team. Now that I think about it I'm not sure which they meant ... Probably both. Their careers had hit a dead end too."

"You can work any case you want, you have my word. As long as the backlog is cleared, or I can report on it being cleared, you'll be back in the circus again. Not the main act but—"

"I'll be the guy shoveling the big cats' shit, you mean."

"This is a gift, Gust. I'm doing you a favor. Coming back on promotion. Working cases again ... I mean c'mon."

Carver looked at her blankly. "You want me at arm's length."

"I want you to consult on cases again. This is the only way I've figured I can get you back in. Think of it as a chance at redemption. Hell, maybe you could even try and help the poor dead-enders." They stood looking at one another for a moment. Carver didn't say anything. Was he thinking, or blanking her? "God! You're so infuriating," Gibson said and smiled.

She gave him a light shove in the chest. "Meet me for dinner tonight," Gibson said, more command than an invitation, "I'm lonely and you're the only sorry *sonofabitch* I can talk to in this damned town."

3

IT WAS dark outside and late. There was mist in the air and it created halos around the streetlights.

Carver sat in an old leather armchair, the armrests all cracked and peeling from years of use, and it'd lost its puff. Some time ago he'd told himself he needed to buy more furniture. The truth was, he hadn't thought about doing any furniture shopping in months.

The apartment was dark except for a small lamp on the floor in the corner of the room. Carver's armchair was directly in front of the window facing the Atlantic Ocean. He never slept. Not really. He picked up the corded house phone from the floor and put it on his lap. He dialed his old home phone number. The phone rang once and connected.

His wife's voice whispered, "I had a feeling you might call."

Carver was quiet. "You were asleep ..." he said and felt a pang of remorse. He shouldn't have called. It wasn't fair on her, or the boy.

"It's okay," Bethany said softly.

"Is he already sleeping?" Carver asked.

"Ryan went to sleep around an hour ago," she said.

"Is he with you?" Carver knew that Bethany hadn't been able to let their son out of her sight since Madeleine died.

"Yes, he is ..."

Carver was quiet. "I'll just listen to you sleep."

Carver heard her soft breathing down the line. He wanted to feel it on his neck.

"There's another one, isn't there?" Bethany said.

Carver closed his eyes and then squeezed them shut. She still knew him to the core. It hurt him to have her so far away but, deep down, he knew it was best for her. For Ryan. To be far away from him. Nothing good ever happened after midnight.

"Yes," Carver said. There was finality in his tone. It felt like a moment of reckoning. This one would either kill him or set him free. Was there a difference, he wondered.

"I have the experience."

"We all do, Gust."

"I know, Beth. I'm so sorry —"

"What do they want you to do?"

"Help catch him."

"Maybe you should do it?"

That surprised him. Then again, maybe it didn't. He didn't know anymore. There was a time when he thought he was born to it but feeling obligated was the worst thing.

The unspoken truth they both knew; he had to do it to be happy. It was a hell of a disease to be born with. The disease was slowly killing him, that he knew too. He was like an addict. The worst part was—he liked to do it—which turned it from a disease into a vice. Then he realized he was exceptional at it and it became an obsession. Something he had to do. Obsession wasn't healthy.

"You've never ever told me what you're thinking, Gust. It's like you expect me to be able to get inside your head and crawl around in there. Like you do with them—"

"Don't," he said. Then, "Sorry."

"If you missed it—your old life—I'd have thought you'd mention it. You haven't though. You never mention it. If you can't let it go ... I mean—we'll never be able to—but if you think it might help? Stop some of the pain ..."

"What if I cause more pain?" Carver said, barely above a whisper.

"If you stop this one, you'll have helped all those people who might be next. Isn't that what we do? Kind of absorb their suffering so they don't have to feel it."

"Maybe," Carver said and sighed deeply.

"What was it you always told me, Gust? You said someone needs to stand for the dead."

Carver held the phone tight to his ear and watched the dark ocean waves roll in.

"Aren't you also the one who told me you have to be able to take those tiny bits of evidence and really, what was the word?"

"Envision."

"Envision what they're doing, their patterns of behavior to try and build a —"

"It's about reconstructing his thinking, Beth. The thinking of a violent sociopath. I don't know if I can go through that again ..."

There was a beat of silence. Carver knew he'd lost her.

"I've got to get up early, Gust. I miss you ..."

Carver choked back the lump in his throat.

"I miss you too," he garbled.

Carver heard rustling as Bethany laid the receiver on the pillow next to her. Carver wiped his eye with the back of his hand.

"Sweet dreams," she whispered.

Carver laid his head back on the cold leather and closed his eyes. He listened to her breathing. He heard the waves crash and roll back. He heard the wind shake the trees. He knew he wouldn't sleep. Not really. He doubted he'd ever sleep again. Too many faces appeared in his mind's eye. Just the heads rising up. Blending one into the other.

People he couldn't save. People he'd lost. People he'd killed. And one face to rule them all.

The man who murdered his daughter in front of his eyes.

4

CARVER HAD a long insomniatic night thinking about the terrors of the past, and what he wanted to do to change them for the future. Now he sat and watched the sun rise over the Atlantic Ocean and felt the warmth of the new day's rays on his face. He saw the dawn seabirds swooping and diving around the craggy outcrops of rock and felt some sense of renewal. Of rebirth.

Deep down he just flat out couldn't stand the thought of there being a form of insanity stalking around in the darkness, taking people's lives, and destroying those that were left behind. He knew the way it went all too well. Families ripped apart and destroyed for nothing. Just because the violent insatiable appetite of a mentally disturbed, criminally insane individual willed it. He wouldn't put up with it.

He had a duty to stand up for and protect those that were left. And someone, he decided, needed to stand for the dead too.

He had a wry smile on his face knowing it was too early for Gibson and that she'd be annoyed. He picked up the phone and dialed her number. It rang for ten seconds and just when he was about to hang up, she answered. She croaked, "Hello?" then said, "Deputy Gibson speaking."

Carver said, "I've been thinking about it, Bronwyn, and you're on … I'll take a look at the crime scene."

"You bastard, you were supposed to meet me last night! Never mind. I thought you'd flake. I'll arrange transport to Charleston."

"Doesn't need to be too early, Bron. I'm going to walk the scene at the same time the killer did."

"I thought you might. I'd say, 'get some sleep', but I know you won't."

"*Can't*," he said. "Maybe I'll get a few hours on the plane."

"I'll talk to you about Charleston PD once you've seen the file and been through the scene."

"Alright," Carver said and hung up.

He wasn't one for long goodbyes.

5

CHARLESTON

HE SLOWED when he saw the house. Carver drove past and leaned close to the car window and craned his neck to look at it. The sky was a crisp black, the windows were dark, and thick trees overhung the houses and the road. The American flag still hung from a white pole in a flower bed at the base of the driveway.

He checked the number to make sure—that was it—and decided to keep driving. He'd park some way away and walk back. Didn't want to scare the neighbors. One of them might pull a gun. People get jumpy when there's been a murder.

The houses here were all spaced far apart. Big lots. Lots of money.

Paradise lost.

Driving down Third Avenue in Mount Pleasant actually made him envious. The houses looked like castles next to Molasses Creek, which was their moat. Didn't protect the occupants from a particular kind of disturbed mind though, he thought. It was unintentionally begrudging.

He climbed out of his car. He held a thick leather folder. The Charleston Homicide Investigations' crime scene report. He'd spent most of the previous evening and some of the day studying it. Trying to get the details right in his head. He set it on the roof and hiked up his pants at the belt. It was a warm night. He could hear the water flowing in the creek and the insects were chirping in the grass. Carver was glad he'd come alone. Nothing worse than inane small talk people used to distract themselves from their fears. This way he could sniff the air and get in sync with his surroundings. He wondered how long the killer had stared at this house. How many nights he'd stood out here in the shadows watching the windows. Getting excited. Touching himself at the thought of going inside.

Carver wanted the freedom to feel fear. The kind of fear that the Michael Proctor family would have felt. He bent to pick up his flashlight. He took the folder from the roof and tucked it under his arm and walked along the gray sidewalk. His footsteps echoed as he walked. He checked over his shoulder more than once. He had the feeling of being watched. When he got to the house he stopped just inside the driveway and stood under the looming trees as they creaked and rustled above him. The killer had come at night. Carver felt nervous. He was aware of his breathing and tried to free himself from the onrush of thoughts and images in his mind. Fear heightened his senses. His brain was preparing to run but he needed it to concentrate. To think.

He stepped onto the covered porch that ran almost the whole length of it. He went to the front of the dark house and cupped his hands over his eyes and peered into the downstairs windows. It was too dark to see inside. He used his flashlight and shone the yellow beam through the glass. Living room and kitchen. They didn't seem homely. No fridge magnets. Everything was in its place. More model than a well-run-through boisterous family home.

Carver walked along the side of the house to the back-yard. He took careful steps and as he passed the windows had to remind himself that no one was inside. No one was watching him. As he rounded the house he got a sense of the space. The grass lawn ran all the way out to the water's edge. There was a long private dock leading up to the bank. No boat moored there though. He reached into his jacket pocket and spoke into his voice-activated recorder.

He whispered, "Is it possible the killer used a dock on his approach?" He put the voice recorder back. He looked up at the double-story wooden home. It was a good looking house. A pale yellow. There was a set of stairs running up to the second floor. Direct access to the garden. Carver climbed them. He held his breath and stopped to listen. The killer might have done the same. It takes calm nerves to enter someone's home when they're in it, he thought. The killer had easily jimmied the brass lock on the rear door. Carver flicked his flashlight on and shone the light on the worn brass handle. No obvious scratches or bending. He flicked the flashlight off and spoke into his voice recorder.

"Possible the killer had a key for entry? No sign of forced entry. Check with Charleston detectives."

He removed the police tape and pulled the door open. He felt the warm air coming from inside. The smell was stale. There was a weight in the air of the house where four people were forced to stop breathing. Just the facts, Carver, he thought. Focus on what you can control. Nothing he did now was going to bring them back but he could still speak for them. That was his job now. Stand up for them. Represent them. Find the insanity that took them.

Carver checked his watch. A few minutes past midnight. The pathologist said the family died sometime between midnight and two in the morning. Fear trickled down his spine. Carver forced himself to close his eyes. He took a few deep breaths through his nose and relaxed his jaw. The first step was to gain entry. He wanted to think about that. It'd been easy enough. Had that influenced the killer's choice of this family? Carver opened his eyes and stepped into the upstairs foyer. Hardwood floors. They didn't creak as he moved. There were two bedrooms off the corridor on this level. The master was on the other side of the house. Mrs. Proctor had decorated the upstairs foyer with two shiny wooden sitting chairs and a tall bureau. Fibers taken from the chair showed that the killer had taken a seat in one of the chairs.

Had he broken in and taken a seat? Carver did that now. He sat where the killer had sat. He put his hand on the smooth curve of the armrest and felt a jolt and removed it. He wanted to sanitize. It felt dirty. His eyes grew accustomed to the darkness. He wondered if Mrs. Proctor had done the interior design. The decor's style was confusing. The shine of modern black marble countertops and floor-to-ceiling tiles contrasted with the sense of antique furniture and polished dark-stained wood. Rich people without style. Carver stood.

The killer had gone to the master bedroom first. Mr. and Mrs. Proctor were asleep. Heavy curtains drawn. Mrs. Proctor in her eye mask. Carver made his way to the other side of the house now. He stood at the entrance to the master bedroom. Even with the curtains drawn he could see the outline of the king-sized bed. The mattress was bare now. A glowing white rectangle in an otherwise dark room. Carver walked into the room and stood at the foot of it. He raised his arm and pointed it at the bed. Mr. Proctor was rising when he was shot with a .22 caliber round. His body had slumped and come to rest over the edge of the mattress.

The gunshot didn't wake the rest of the house. The madman had used a suppressor. Why had Mr. Proctor woken up? He could have shot them from the doorway without ever entering the bedroom. Mrs. Proctor was found flat on her back, eye mask still in place. She hadn't even moved. With the patriarch immobilized the killer moved back to the other bedrooms. The Proctors had two children. Their son Jack was a sophomore in high school. Their daughter Savannah was home, visiting for the weekend.

The killer went into Jack's bedroom first. He'd pushed open the door and gone to the bedside. Carver stood in the doorway to the boy's room. He flicked the light on and his eyes popped at the brightness and the blood. The bare wall and mattress were streaked with dried blood. Carver heard a high-pitched whine in his left ear. Tinnitus brought on by stress. He took a deep breath. The killer used a knife to slice Jack's throat.

Carver closed his eyes and he saw Jack as he gargled and coughed and drowned in his own blood. He opened his eyes. There were long streaks of blood on the ceiling and down the wall from the arterial spray. It was a violent and quick attack. The boy bled out on his bed unaware that his parents were dead—or dying— on the other side of the house. Little consolation, Carver thought.

Now the insanity was free to take its time. It focused its full attention on the true target of the attack: Savannah Proctor. Local girl making it as a model in New York.

Charleston detectives believed the killer had entered her room before injecting her with some sort of neuromuscular-blocking agent. Something used to paralyze her.

The toxicology report was still trying to identify the

nature and origin of the paralyzing agent found in her soft tissue and lymph nodes near the puncture site.

In forty-five seconds or so, from when the insanity had administered the agent her vocal cords would've frozen, and her skeletal muscles would've relaxed. She couldn't scream for help and she couldn't fight back.

The detectives had found her with her wrists tied to the bed with a rough twine and her shoulders and neck secured against the headboard.

It was the sheer amount of blood that caused Carver to swallow hard and contemplate.

He'd never spilled a gallon of *anything* before. Once, his grandmother had left a large pot of strawberry compote on too high a heat. The whole thing boiled over onto the floor. A sticky, lava-like spillage.

Savannah bled out all over the bed and floor. Official cause of death was cardiac arrest. She died of a heart attack. Her body, perhaps her mind, simply couldn't take the torment anymore. Carver tried to imagine how the killer did it. He stepped into the room. He wasn't going to climb onto the mattress. The metallic tang of the victim's blood was thick in the air. He felt it clinging to the back of his throat.

Carver could see it in his mind's eye, though. How the killer straddled her. Her eyes wide with shock and terror. Unable to move, unable to scream, trussed up the bedpost like a crucifixion. The killer used a surgeon's tools. He was only after one thing. He started making lacerations around her neck, not deep enough to cut her throat or arteries, and got to work removing the skin covering her skull.

Carver didn't want to think about it, but his conscience wouldn't let him leave Savannah Proctor all alone. Someone had to stand up for the dead. He never slept and when he did he was repulsed by his dreams. He knew there would be more nightmares now. The sound of the killer tearing the skin from her bones—skinning her alive— would make sure of that.

6

CARVER CHECKED HIS WATCH. Three A.M. The Proctors were all dead by now. The killer had already made good his escape. Blood stains showed that he'd walked down the stairs and into Mrs. Proctor's kitchen carrying Savannah's dripping hair and face skin. Had he hurried or run? The precision and placement of the dripping blood said not. From the rest of his behavior, Carver doubted it.

Sure, he'd fumbled around, pulling open drawers and cabinets, and then taken one of Mrs. Proctor's freezer bags. He used it to store Savannah's skinned face. Then he helped himself to the fridge. Blood smears were on plastic-wrapped leftover chicken casserole and slices of cold meats. He'd worn gloves. Made himself a snack. This was not a person in a rush, Carver thought. He didn't bother retracing the steps downstairs. He'd seen enough. It was time to go.

THE COLUMBIA FIELD office booked Carver a motel room. A *motel* room. Either it was the budget cuts, or when Carver's name came up on the system someone thought it would be a nice little screw you. Carver didn't have many fans inside the Bureau. Partly because of how Carver himself did things. If anyone wanted a reason to dislike him they could find one easy enough. Not that he cared. To him, people's opinions were as if someone had turned the stereo volume right down. It hardly registered and if it did it was background noise.

Carver wasn't planning on staying in the motel anyway. He never slept. He thought better in the car. He liked the cold calculating calmness of the night. Headlights winding down black asphalt concentrated the mind. Focused his thoughts on a tunnel of light in a void of black.

He moved into a hotel in Manassas. Something temporary. It wasn't hard. Everything he owned fit in his car. There's a certain liberty with being able to pick up and go whenever he had to. It meant he was always on the run though. He didn't sleep in a bed. He had a comfortable armchair. Sometimes he dozed off. Grief always brought him back pretty quick. Carver liked to sit looking out at the water. The waves drifted in. Sucked back. Crashed again. A rhythm. It helped him doze.

The killer sat too. He broke in and took a seat. Strange, Carver thought. "Not that any of it wasn't strange," he said to himself.

Mr. Proctor had sat up too. What was happening ... the killer broke in and then—what—decided to relax.

He listened to the house breathe. The stillness. Making sure he hadn't disturbed anyone. Mr. Proctor couldn't have heard him. If madness took a seat, Mr. Proctor wasn't woken by the noise. Why'd he shoot them from the foot of the bed, and not the doorway? He didn't like to rush. He liked to feel the stillness. He had power over them in their sleep. Did he invade their dreams? Did they know he was there even when they didn't know? A subconscious realization. Like the feeling of being watched. Why had Mr. Proctor sat up? You waited, didn't you, Carver thought. You waited for him to become aware of you. You stood there at the foot of the bed watching Mr. and Mrs. Proctor sleep. Admiring them. Feeling superiority over them. Knowing you could do anything you want to them. Mr. Proctor startled awake, his subconscious aware of something watching him, didn't he? Something off. A different smell in the room and as he rose he was shot. His body slumped to the side. Mrs. Proctor, with half a Xanax in her system and an eye mask over her face, didn't react. She died where she lay. You couldn't shoot the boy. Too close to Savannah's room. Had he woken too? Was that the struggle?

Silence him quickly and hold him until he stopped struggling. Jack wasn't small. High school wrestling team. He could've fought back. That would explain the arterial spray on the ceiling and walls. If the killer immobilized the boy, did that make him a large man? Not necessarily. If he was small, it meant he might be technically proficient at self-defense. No doubt this homicide was planned.

It was organized. Had he just forgotten to bring a freezer bag? Or did he know that Mrs. Proctor had them in her kitchen? And, if he knew, how did he know?

Carver could imagine the insanity walking out of the house, clothes covered in blood, carrying a see-through freezer bag filled with the scalp, hair, and face of its victim. He felt sick. This person—this killer—walked around in society too. Bags filled with groceries. Bags filled with clothes. Bags filled with surgical tools.

Where'd he learned to use it? Dissection was part of the curriculum. At least it was back when Carver went through school. And why the face?

Carver shook his head. He was deep into it now.

There was no audience for the killer. That was his

trophy. His reminder. What did he do with them? The faces of his victims.

Carver chewed the inside of his mouth and watched the yellow lines on the road. Darkness swept out in front of him. Another set of headlights in the distance. He'd prefer to stop thinking about it now. He doubted he could. The light turned to purple on the horizon. Sunlight wasn't far behind it. He still had hours to drive. Why'd you take her face, Carver wondered, over and over again.

———

THE BRAKES SQUEALED as Carver pulled up outside a three-story red brick building in the middle of the Old Town Manassas. This was his first day. He gave his armpit a quick sniff and turned his head away. He smelled like he felt. Wired on roadside coffee. Bad breath, bad hair, bad feeling about this.

Carver got out and checked the brass plaque next to the entrance to the building. The Northern Virginia resident agency offices shared it with Chris A. Brown, Personal Injury Lawyer, and Set You Free Bail Bonds. Carver shook his head and pulled the door open.

When he got to the top, he stopped and listened. He heard a woman's voice coming from the office: "District of Columbia license applications, addresses, property tax records to cross-check." A thud of paperwork landing on a desk.

Another woman's voice. "Wait, these are from seven years ago."

"Library book lending from the past year. They need all the data on anything that might look like how to make a bomb."

"At least yours is recent," another voice said.

"I doubt anyone looking to make a bomb is going to be stupid enough to take a book out of the library called *The Terrorist's Toolkit*."

Carver had heard enough. He turned the handle and pulled the door open. All of the faces turned to look at him. A moment of awkward silence.

The woman holding all of the files dropped them on her desk and wiped her hands on her skirt as she said, "Special Agent Carver?" She put out her hand and walked up to him. "I'm Penny. Penny Maudmont. It's so nice to finally meet you!" He shook her hand lightly and forced a smile. "We were expecting you this morning. We're usually at our desks by nine A.M." she said and beamed.

She was a short, chubby woman. Jolly, Carver thought. He knew already she'd get on his nerves. "I'll give you the tour," she said and indicated the two women sitting at the prefab wall-mounted shelving they were using for desks. "This is Special Agent Lisa Chung. She prefers to be called by her Americanized name, Rachel Fox."

Fox was sitting in front of six screens mounted one on top of the other. She wasn't looking him in the eyes, she was watching his chin. She had short hair, like a schoolboy's, gelled and combed over. Carver nodded hello and she stifled a shy smile.

"And this is Special Agent Caitlin Sandling." She had a pretty face, straight nose, short-ish brunette hair pulled back in a ponytail. "And, as I said, I'm Penny I'm sort of the *unofficial* office manager. I take the tasks from Quantico and dish them out etcetera."

"They let you guys keep the special agent tags, huh?" Carver said. Maudmont flushed pink-cheeked. "What're you guys doing here, as in, what're you in for?" Carver asked.

He saw three pairs of big eyes looking at him. Maudmont was quiet for once. She put her hands together and looked at her shoes.

"We were hoping you'd be able to tell us that, sir," Fox said. She was looking at the ceiling. "I mean, we have an idea, an inkling, a suspicion—if you will—"

"None of you know why you're here?" Carver asked.

They shook their heads.

Fox spoke up, "You're the only one we have a good handle on, sir, a reasonable guess, beyond most probabilities. Killing that suspect, wasn't it?"

"*Shhh*," Maudmont said and waved her hand at Fox like she was swatting a fly.

"I think you're mistaken," Carver said.

"I'm pretty certain of it," Fox continued as Maudmont tried to shush her and wave her words away, "I remember it. It was all anyone would talk about for a while at the Bureau. All the chatter. How super agent Carver shot a suspect *etcetera*."

"That's enough Rachel, stop it!" Maudmont said. She was horrified.

"What, it's true!"

"Ignore her, sir," Sandling said. "Rachel has no filter. She says whatever pops into her mind out loud. You'll get used to it."

"Maybe I do know why you're part of the dead case team, Fox," Carver said.

"Oh, what is it, sir?"

Carver looked at Sandling. "She serious?"

"Never mind," Maudmont said. "Let me introduce you to the rest of the team and show you to your office."

"There's more of them?" Carver said.

"The boys are in the kitchenette."

A tall, older-looking guy stood up from a small coffee

table. Suited at least, Carver thought. He held a bony hand with skin so thin it looked like it would tear.

"Special Agent Frank Hornigen, sir."

Carver said, "You don't need to call me sir."

"Okay ... *Um*, what should we call you?"

"Gust, or boss."

"Okay, Gus," Hornigen said.

"Gust with a *tee*," Maudmont said.

"Oh, Gust, I see. Okay. Sorry—used to be in the Secret Service" Hornigen said. "Lots of loud bangs right close to my damn ears."

Carver looked at his coffee mate. Younger, good-looking guy. Smart suit. Clean white shirt. Carver liked what he was seeing. Professional. Could get used to it. Young guy also stood up.

"Toby Underwood, sir. Mr. Carver. Special Agent."

"Don't be nervous, kid. I'm not going to steal your lunch money."

"Ha—sorry, sir. We've just heard a lot about you. It's a pleasure to finally meet you."

"Thanks," Carver said quietly and glanced down at Maudmont. She was smiling away at the two men. He caught her eye.

"Right! The rest of your tour. Come on, *Gust*," she said and looked up at him and gave him an exaggerated wink.

"Not you, Penny ... you can call me Special Agent Carver."

Her face dropped and Carver gave her a big wink back. The two in the kitchen chuckled politely. As they walked, Carver said, "Only joking Maudmont, you can call me Gust too."

She started smiling again.

"This is your office, Gust," she said and indicated it proudly like a stewardess showing him to his seat.

"Thanks, Penny. Ah, tell the others I'll be right out. I need to make a phone call first."

"Yes, sir, Gust, sir."

"No need to call me sir, Penny. Certainly no need to call me sir twice in one sentence."

She looked sheepish.

"Anything you want me to tell them to get on with in the meantime?" Maudmont asked.

"I'll take care of that."

She stepped out of the office and pulled his door closed. Carver sat down heavily in his new chair and picked up the phone. He needed to speak to Deputy Director Bronwyn Gibson.

7

CHARLESTON

CARVER SAT in the back row of the Charleston Police Department auditorium. After speaking to Gibson, he'd flown in the night before. She'd asked him to be there—to support her—she said. There were two other FBI special agents already assisting the local police with their investigation. He felt like a fifth wheel. The other four were busy, which left him spinning in the breeze.

Something Carver had been thinking about was, why was he slicing their faces off. And what was he doing with them? He couldn't stop himself from thinking about it. On the plane. On his bed. In the car. It gnawed at him. He caught himself chewing the edge of his nail as he watched the local police detectives file in carrying their coffees.

They were interspersed with a few uniformed officers. They gave the standard issue sideways glances at the supervising detective. He stood with his hands on his hips and radiated annoyance at their poor punctuality. Carver checked his watch. 8:03. Supposed to start at 8 A.M.

"All right, come on. Hurry up. Take your seats," the detective said. Once everyone settled, he started, "Right, good morning. We have some guests here this morning, so for those of you who don't know me, I'm Detective Jim Chase. Welcome. If you do know me then you know you should have read the bulletin this morning—which you all have no doubt—you'll see there is an update on the forensics. We'll get to that in a sec. Situation so far: continuing to canvass the neighborhood. House-to-house interviews and we're setting up a tip line. We don't anticipate anything useful but you know how the public likes to feel involved in these kinds of cases. We're coordinating with Augusta for any unusual cross-matches on airline or rental car reservations. Hotels, motels, diners, cafes are all still on the list. Speak to everyone. Maids. Gardeners. Porters. Taxi drivers. They might remember a mess he left. The way he behaved. Something strange. Something out of place. Anything, 'cause the Lord knows nothing about this is as it should be."

Carver closed his eyes tight and massaged his eyeballs with the meaty bit under his thumbs. Waste of time, this. They'd have better luck throwing darts at names in a phone book.

"The press got wind of this. I spoke to the funeral home. Photographers are hiding in the bushes. Telescopic paparazzi lenses all over the place. Nobody leaks *anything*. If I see confidential information in so much as a tabloid I'll have internal investigations down here before you can wave goodbye to your pensions, do you understand?"

A ripple of nods went through the assembled troops.

"Okay, as I've said, we've had some interesting forensics come back. I'm going to hand over to chief of forensic services here in Charleston, Dr. Stacy Kelly."

The head of forensics stood up from the front row and went behind the lectern. She fiddled with a pointer and checked the screen behind her.

"Okay, good morning," Dr. Kelly said.

"Louder please," one of the detectives said.

"Oh, okay, is … is that better?" she said, lifting her chin. An affirmative murmur from the room. "As you know, we had a delay in processing some of the elements from the crime scene. We've been through a thorough process now and have some updates for you. Firstly, all the blood at the scene relates to the victims. We haven't found any saliva or any other secretions. The bullets were fired from a .22 caliber pistol. We believe he used a suppressor so as not to wake the neighborhood. The ballistics we found were from common ammunition, too common to trace."

"What about fibers, Dr., DNA?" someone asked.

"I'm coming to that, thank you. We have had one significant breakthrough. It happened in the second male victim's room. Lacerations to his throat. We took scrapings from under his fingernails and found DNA from what we believe is the perpetrator." She made her hands into claws and raised them behind her ears like she was trying to hug someone behind her head. "We believe the victim managed to scratch the suspect's face as they struggled."

Carver covered his mouth and he saw Gibson glance at him out the corner of her eye.

"What?" she whispered.

He shook his head. Nothing. Doesn't matter.

"That's a big break," Detective Chase said. He clapped his hands, "Come on guys, that's a really big break. Have we got a match?"

"Not yet," Dr. Kelly said. "If we had you'd have been the first to know, Detective."

Detective Chase's enthusiasm drained. He sighed.

Carver could tell that these deaths were affecting the local police. They just wanted it over. This wasn't something they were used to. Hell, it wasn't something anyone except the killer was used to. Carver closed his eyes again and tried to picture him. The killer.

He could see an outline but it was hazy. A silhouette in the shadows. He couldn't see him yet. Something was obscuring his view. He opened them. Why was there no match to the DNA, he wondered. It didn't make sense.

"Anything else, Doc?" Detective Chase asked.

"You all have the details of the partial shoe prints—size nine—when anything else comes up I will let you know."

She pursed her lips and nodded to Detective Chase.

"Any questions for Dr. Kelly?" Chase asked and looked around the briefing room. Carver looked down at the thinning, graying heads. Some chewing pens, some taking notes. Family men, to a man. Even if they wanted to, they didn't know the right questions to ask.

A few of them shook their heads. No questions.

"Anything to add from the FBI?" Detective Chase said to the black-suited pair of special agents in the front row. They shook their heads. Detective Chase looked at Bronwyn Gibson in the back row.

"You're up," she whispered to Carver out the corner of her mouth.

"Deputy Gibson, do you have anything to add?"

A few of the heads turned to see. Gibson moved to stand and walked to the front.

Detective Chase addressed the audience, "Deputy Director Gibson heads up the FBI's Behavioral Analysis Unit. You had one of your agents walk the crime scene, Director Gibson. Did he spot anything we missed?"

"Thanks, Detective. Just to be clear, we aren't here to step on any toes or make any changes. We want to supplement the fine job you and your detectives—and the FBI special agents—are doing on this case. We aren't going to be getting in your way. We want this maniac off the streets as much as you do—"

"Is that what he is, Director, a maniac?"

Gibson looked for the officer who'd spoken but it was a sea of blank faces.

"I don't think Special Agent Carver or myself are in a position to give you a diagnosis." She looked at Carver. Detective Chase followed her eyes. "But both of us have worked on cases like this before. In fact, Detective Carver caught the last one. And the one before that, Hermann Zimmer."

The whole room turned to look. Carver didn't know what to do. He just kept staring at Gibson. He wished she hadn't done that.

"You've worked this kind of thing before, Special Agent Carver?" Detective Chase asked.

"Yes, sir," Carver said.

"Won't you come down and give us your view, me and the boys'd sure appreciate it. Any and all thoughts you might have."

Gibson nodded to him. Carver put his hand over the back of the chair in front and pulled himself up. His left hand twitched a little and he shook it once, hard, to calm it. He didn't like all the eyes on him. Any opportunity to have that many people decide they disliked you all at once was always tough.

He stood at the front and took a deep breath. Carver waited. Detective Chase watched him. Then looked at the crowd. Carver was looking at each man in turn. The faces weren't hostile but they weren't friendly. None held his gaze.

"Um, he's a maniac, you say?" the same detective asked, prodding him.

Carver put his hands in his pockets to stop himself moving his hands. "Look—none of this is vetted— it's just my opinion. Is he a madman? Sane people don't do this type of thing. Do we know what's wrong with him? No. Frankly, it doesn't matter. Diagnosing him isn't gonna help us catch him. What *will* help us catch him is working out how he thinks and why he's doing what he's doing," Carver said and glanced at Gibson and Chase.

"He's doing it 'cause he's mad," one of the detectives said loudly. A few of the others laughed.

Carver forced a grin and touched the back of his hand to his mouth. He wanted to choose his words carefully.

"I think there's a big chance he does have some kind of criminal record. I could be wrong but—"

"What're you basing this on?" Detective Chase asked, interrupting him. His eyebrows pressed tightly together. Mouth open, the shape of a zero. It was meant as a challenge.

Gibson stepped forward almost in front of Carver. The peacemaker.

"Detective Carver has some insights from the scene and the autopsy. We'll get those over to you in a report. For now, let's just listen to what he has to say," she looked at Detective Chase who nodded and stepped back. "Carry on, Gust."

Carver was looking at Dr. Kelly. She was trying to avoid his stare. He tried to picture the scene. They had DNA from Jack Proctor's fingernails, but no match. Carver was sure the killer would have a criminal record, so his profile should have shown up in the system under analysis. But it hadn't. Why? How could that be? The only option open, at least to Carver's way of thinking was that it wasn't the killer's DNA. So it couldn't have been the killer's skin. But then whose was it?

"Is anyone from Augusta here?" Carver asked. A hand went up.

"Lieutenant Art Davies is our Augusta liaison," Detective Chase said.

Carver lifted his chin toward Davies, "Have you got the DNA from the Augusta victim, Freya Silvstedt? Her DNA, not the scrapings."

"Of course," Davies said. "Why?"

Carver didn't really know why he was asking. He was piecing it together as he stood there. Why was he cutting their faces off? What was the purpose? Carver turned and looked at Dr. Kelly again. This time she held his gaze. He knew he was about to say something outrageous. He couldn't stop himself though.

"I think you'll find the DNA from under Jack Proctor's fingernails is a match with the first victim, Freya Silvstedt."

A murmur went through the crowd. Detective Chase looked at Gibson, now even more confused. Dr. Kelly furrowed her brow.

"How could that be?" Dr. Kelly asked. "Are you saying that Jack Proctor was the killer in Augusta and then—what —sliced his own neck and has his first victim's skin under his fingernails?" She searched Carver's face.

"No," Carver said. "I'm not saying that so let's ask the question. Why is he cutting their faces off, have you asked yourselves?"

The room was silent. They didn't know what to say. Then Carver saw it, clear as day. What he was doing with the faces. They were masks. He was wearing them. He could hear the killer's stifled breathing obstructed by the skin of his previous victim.

"When the Proctor kid reached back and tried to defend himself he got skin under his fingernails. Except it won't turn out to be the killer's DNA. Why not?" Carver asked. It was rhetorical.

"How can you know that?" a voice asked. Carver didn't see who said it.

"We'll know for certain when Lieutenant Davies gets the DNA samples from Augusta." Carver scanned the faces. "But I'm fairly confident when I say he's turning their faces into masks and wearing them to his rituals."

There was a buzz of quick conversation. His words were drowned out by the rising volume of whispers and hushed laughter. Carver talked over them.

"If he's wearing the skin of his victims. He'll be wearing them again when he breaks in to kill the next one too. Next time it'll be Savannah Proctor. That's why we haven't got a positive ID on the DNA. It's not in the system, and it should be, 'cause no way this guy doesn't have a record," Carver said.

The assembled police started murmuring more loudly.

8

WHILE THE DIN FROM THE DETECTIVES' chatter died down Gibson walked up and leaned into his ear.

"Hell of a bombshell to drop, Carver. Why couldn't you have told me that on the phone yesterday?"

His face turned to stone. He didn't know yesterday. It only occurred to him this morning.

"All right, settle down," Detective Chase said. The detectives quieted down. A hand went up.

"Any thoughts on whether it might be a female suspect?"

"Special Agent Carver?" Detective Chase said and gestured to him.

"Sure, I've thought about it and dismissed it. Does it really matter if the suspect is male or female? Categorization like that is old-school science. You can't categorize insanity. They find it hard enough to categorize them once they catch them. They don't have names for what these guys have. Could it be a female? Sure. It could. It's incredibly unlikely given the nature of the crimes. Will it help us catch him? No. To be frank—"

"Oh, *now* you're being frank," Detective Chase said a little too loudly. The room gave a chuckle.

"If I was being Frank I'd do three bars of *Fly Me to the Moon* as I walked out," Carver said, then grinned at his own joke. No one else seemed to get it.

He cleared his throat.

"Frankly, I'd say, it's not my job to educate you. The more time we waste going round and round discussing possibilities without assessing the mindset and thought patterns—behaviors—of the individual, the more time it takes for us to catch him. First, we learn how he thinks. Then we get inside his thought *patterns*. Not his thoughts. His thought patterns. If we understand him, we can outthink him."

"You make it sound like a game," another detective from the audience said. Carver gave a nod and said, "It *is* a game. That's exactly what it is. Not a very nice one. And not a game you want to lose either. This guy is smart. He's mobile. He's thinking about it like it's a game. And at the moment he has the jump on us—"

Gibson put her hand on Carver's bicep and he stopped talking and looked at her.

"Right, gentlemen," Detective Chase said. "And lady. We'll get back to you on the DNA theory."

The detectives got ready to leave. Carver stayed standing. A big burly uniformed man walked into the briefing room. Carver recognized him as the captain.

"One more thing," the captain in charge of the Charleston Central Investigations Division said as he walked into the briefing. "You talked about the press?" He asked Detective Chase. Chase shook his head. The room settled back in their chairs. "I don't want any nicknames going around about this killer. Don't talk to any press. Don't give them any ammunition. The last thing we want is to glamorize what he's doing." The captain said and stared intently at each man.

"The beauty killer!" one of the detectives shouted out

48

and laughed. The others joined in. "The face-*off* killer," another one said. "Get it?"

"All right. Knock it off you morons," the captain said. "We don't even know for sure he's a serial killer at the moment."

"Anything else, sir?" Detective Chase asked. The captain shook his head. "Okay, dismissed."

CARVER STAYED at the front while the detectives filed out the same way they'd come in. They gave him the evil eye as they passed. He gave it right back. Poor fools. Gibson sidled up to him. Chase also appeared.

"Agent Carver?" Detective Chase said. "Come with me. My office. I'd like to talk."

"I'm heading back to Washington," Gibson told him. "I'll call you when I land."

"Wait for me," Carver said.

Gibson half-rolled her eyes but nodded to tell him she would.

Carver followed Chase through the corridors and he walked into an office, Chase holding the door open.

"This place's been crazy," Chase said and closed the door. "Gust, right?" he asked and pointed his fingers at Carver like a pistol.

"Yeah."

Chase went and sat heavily behind his desk.

"Yep, I tell you, boy, we don't know nothin' 'bout nothin'."

"I wasn't implying—"

"No, I mean it, we don't got diddly and we know it. Oh, sure, we'll get his height from his footprints. You staying in town a while?"

"My team is out of Manassas, I'll be heading back."

"I tell you what, stay a night, will ya? There's a witness says she saw something suspicious a few days before the murder. I'd really appreciate your help."

Carver didn't respond. He was thinking. Guy probably wants to check him out at close range. See what he was like in the field. Get a feel for him, see if he could be trusted.

"I'll think about it."

"You do that." Chase looked at a file on his desk and lifted the corner. As he did he said, "So, you think he's wearing their skin, huh?"

"It's a possibility."

"Possibility?"

Chase glanced at him and Carver nodded.

"You seemed pretty sure in the briefing ..."

"I am sure."

"Why is he doing that, huh?"

"That's a very good question, Detective Chase."

Chase didn't offer for him to call him by his first name. Instead, he leaned far back in his chair and watched Carver. Was he trying to intimidate him?

"No other possibilities?"

"There could be, maybe there was evidence I overlooked—"

"Like what?"

"I don't know."

"You seemed pretty—"

"I know how I seemed. Listen, we'll get him. One way or another. He'll make a mistake, or we'll find evidence we didn't *see* properly the first time. Maybe he'll get careless and one of the victims draws a gun in time ... this guy'll keep killing until we stop him, or someone else does. He will not stop."

"How can you be so sure?"

"You still think it's different unsubs in Augusta and here?"

Chase shrugged and said, "He killed a little girl in Augusta. Hung her from the pipes in the basement. He didn't do that here. Plus he went in during the day. Worked on her all afternoon and into the night ..."

"It's a compulsion, detective. Even if he wanted to stop— and he might want to—he can't. But you know what?"

"What?"

"I think he'll keep going 'cause he likes it."

"And that's it, huh?"

"That's it," Carver said.

There was a knock at the door. It opened. It was Lieutenant Art Davies, the Augusta liaison officer. He was a shortish ginger man with short hair and round face.

"Sorry to interrupt, gentlemen. I was wondering if I could have a word with Agent Carver."

Davies stepped into the office and quietly closed the door behind him.

"What's up, Art?" Chase asked.

"I was hoping you'd come to Augusta with me and inspect the crime scene there," Davies said, directing his words at Carver.

"Sure—why—what have you got?"

"We have a witness of sorts. She's an old woman. One of the only ones on the street without a fence. Seems she spends a lot of time spying on her neighbors. Thinks she saw something but can't be sure. I was thinking, maybe you'd like to walk through the Augusta crime scene and perhaps have another crack at the old woman. I hear you're quite a people person," Davies grinned and glanced at Chase but he wasn't fast enough. Carver caught the look and the glint in Davies' eye.

"You're insulting the person you're asking for help?" Carver asked.

"No, no. Nothing like that," Davies said. His apologetic act seemed genuine. "We—I—genuinely heard that; how you used to be able to get people to talk. Convictions from confessions. How you'd get in their heads ..."

Carver pressed his lips together. "That's Bureau gossip, Davies. Part tall tale, part exaggeration."

"Well, anyway, I was really hoping you might be able to come out and give us a hand, our boys are really dying out there ..."

9

CARVER SAW Gibson leaning against the hallway wall and silently mouthing words as she typed them into her phone. When she saw him, she put her phone away and watched him as he approached her.

They walked out of the Charleston Police Station together and into the warm-white sunlight. Carver noticed another woman out there. Red ball cap with a pen behind her ear. Hack, Carver thought as Gibson debriefed him.

"What you said in there, Gust, about him *wearing* their faces—"

"Yeah, hold on," Carver put his hand up to stop her.

"We need to discuss this, Gust," Gibson said.

"Yeah, just hold on," Carver said as the girl in the ball cap walked up to them. She chewed gum and smiled.

"You're Agent Carver, right? Agent Augustus Carver—like the Roman emperor—right?"

"Augustine," Carver said. Then, "Oh! Never mind. No press," Carver said as he pushed past her.

"Hey! Hold on. I just want to introduce myself and ask you a few questions."

The girl ran ahead and turned around, walking backward as Carver and Gibson tried to evade her. She stuck out her hand. "I'm Jessica Webb, call me Spider. No handshake? Okay, no handshake," Webb said.

"Listen, Jessica they-call-me-Spider, no press, okay?"

"Yeah, but you're out of retirement, man. Right? I mean, come on! That's a big story for people who follow anything to do with what you guys do. Hey listen, I'm a friend of Isabelle Thompson, up in Washington? She said I should find you. Good girl. *Great* reporter. You can tell her I said that ..."

Carver stopped. Webb gave him a wide white-toothed smile as she chewed gum with her mouth open.

"Should have mentioned her sooner, huh?" Webb said.

"How old are you, kid?" Carver asked.

"Twenty-eight."

"God, you're a child," Gibson said. "Come on, Carver."

"It's a serial killer, isn't it?" Webb said. The smile dropped from her face. "They wouldn't have called you in if it wasn't, right?"

Carver didn't respond. He looked past Webb and tried to move around her. Webb put her hand up to Carver's chest to slow him down. Carver looked down at the manicured hand and said, "Don't do that."

"Sorry," Webb said. "It's just that you're *the* serial killer king, you know? I'd love to get a few words from you for my article. Maybe an exclusive interview? For my book."

"Who do you write for?" Gibson asked.

Carver gave her a sideways look. She was sounding her out to see if it would be good exposure for herself, he thought.

"I'm freelance, right now. I've written for the *Times*, the *Journal*. I'm gonna really be somebody ..."

Gibson scoffed and walked on. "Come on, Gust," she called over her shoulder.

"Go'n get the details from the guys you're paying off in there," Carver said. "I'm not one of those guys."

"Can I quote you on that?" Webb asked. She was chewing her gum and smiling again.

"Print one word of that and I'll—"

"You'll what? Shoot me like that meth head in Atlanta?" Carver pushed past her. "You think I didn't know about that? I know all about you, Gust."

Carver walked down the police station steps and crossed the parking lot. Behind him, Webb stood on the stop steps and hollered, "They're calling him the Skinwalker Killer, Carver. The Skinwalker! Is that what he does to them?"

"WHO THE HELL WAS THAT?" Gibson asked as Carver approached her.

"No idea, some reporter. Said she knows Thompson in D.C."

"The woman who covered the Zimmer case?"

Carver nodded.

"How'd she get an intro from someone like her I wonder."

Carver shrugged. "I need to get back into the Proctor house."

"Do what you need to do," Gibson said and checked her phone. "I need to catch this flight to Washington."

"Say 'hi' to everyone for me," Carver said. Gibson smiled at the sarcasm.

"You play nice with others, Gust. You did good in there. Just go easy on 'em. They're trying their best with what they have, knowledge-wise."

"Sure," Carver said and gave her a single nod. "Except, I don't work and play well with others …"

"No, you just *think* you don't work and play well with others," Gibson said.

"What's the difference?"

"The difference is one is self-fulfilling. You convince yourself you can't, and then you don't. It's not rocket science. Read a book for Christ's sake."

"Any recommendations?"

"Anything in the I'm messed up as hell self-help section."

"I only work alone."

Gibson scoffed. "That's your problem, Carver."

"Who said I have a problem?"

"I did, just now. And your problem is you think you're better without people, well, I've seen you—I know you—" Gibson stopped herself. She smiled.

"I'm outta here," Carver said and turned to go.

"Gust," Gibson called out as he walked away.

"Yeah," Carver called out.

"Try and get some sleep, will ya? You look like a hobo."

"Love you too," Carver called out over his shoulder.

It was late afternoon when Carver stepped under the police tape and entered the Proctor household through the front door. He felt the neighbors' eyes on him. He didn't know where. Just felt watched.

What was he doing there? He wondered. He'd seen the death scene. Maybe he was after some life. Something that might give him any indication as to why they were chosen. Really, why *she* was chosen. There were four murders but only one significant in breaking the case. The girl whose face skin was sliced off.

He tried to imagine the Proctors at home. Children

running through the house when they were young. Parents hugging and looking on fondly. How happy they must have been to have their teenage daughter back from the big city for the weekend. This kind of home life felt alien to Carver.

Pictures of happy times were on the walls. Picnics in the garden. Philip Proctor and his son, Jack, out on the water in their kayaks. Savannah Proctor was everywhere. Her flowing brunette hair and striking blue eyes. She looked the opposite of Freya Silvstedt, the Augusta victim. She had blonde hair. Dyed to be lighter but a natural blonde with brown eyes. He wasn't picking them for their distinctive features. He wasn't a blonde *or* a brunette man. Their hair color, eye color, didn't matter. They were both models. Could just be coincidence, Carver thought. After all, anyone with a cell phone was a model these days. One was young in her career, Freya, a tall, leggy blonde just sixteen years old. The other, Savannah, was also tall. Strikingly beautiful. Established. Had an agent, an agency. New York Fashion Week experience and only home to visit her parents. How did he know she was going to be back?

Carver leaned against the window frame and looked out over the lawn and out to the Proctor's private dock. He sucked his cheek while he thought. Why'd he felt the need to come back? He'd missed something. He must have. What was that feeling? Two things still puzzled Carver. First, the unknown subject—the unsub—spent a few hours in the house alone with the Proctors, yet he arrived and departed without a single soul seeing him. How did he do that? Second, Carver had noticed it before. Last night. A strange smell. That was one thing he'd always had, a nose like a shorthaired pointer.

Carver walked around thinking. Strange how he'd sometimes catch the scent of someone on the air. You can tell a lot about a person by how they smell. Human beings had lost the ability. Go into the jungles and spend time with the tribes there. They could hear aircraft long before non-natives and smell a grub in the bark of a dead tree at ten feet. Carver walked around a different kind of jungle. He'd taken his shoes off at the door. Partly respect for the dead. He didn't want to be messing up Mrs. Proctor's Moroccan rugs. Also, he thought better in his socks. He padded around the house. He was detecting some other kind of smell. At first, he'd put it down to entering a home for the first time. How when you enter a strange house, the smell is so strong, until you become used to it. Maybe it was that? But he should have been used to the smell by now. This was something different. He just couldn't put his mind on it.

He walked around taking deep sniffs. There was a scent. Like a garden salad. What the hell was that? It was strongest in Savannah's room.

He entered the remnants of the scene and Carver tried to not look at the blood stains. They screamed out at him and flashed in his mind's eye like a morbid Rorschach test. There was a built-in wardrobe along one wall opposite the bed.

He shivered like someone stepped on his grave. There was this metallic twinge in the stale air of her bedroom. The iron in her dried blood. He could taste it. There was something else too. Something fresh. He shook his head. He couldn't see it.

He decided to look at Savannah's things. In the daylight, everything looked different. Her mother had kept her daughter's room—seemingly—just as it was before she left home, just waiting for her, whenever she might return.

A mother's buried hopes and dreams. Carver wanted to see pictures of her room before it was a crime scene. He had a feeling it was neat, tidy, everything in its place. The room had been searched, interrogated, and asked to divulge anything that might be of importance. But how do you know what's important when you don't understand the crime? Carver wanted to understand something about Savannah Proctor from before she was a faceless corpse. She had an antique dressing table. It was finished to a high-shine resin and lined with lotions, creams, and nice-smelling bottles of colorful liquids. Carver never was any good with women's cosmetics. He liked how they smelled. He twisted and moved a few bottles and tubs to check the labels. French names with fancy, classic-looking fonts. They were all arranged but also looked like they'd been moved. Fat-fingered policemen's hands had inspected them and put them back, just, not *quite* right. Something seemed off. Carver's mind was only projecting what he could intuit from what he knew: caring, doting mother, beautiful, successful woman in her chosen field. A sense of how things are from building out of the bits he could imagine. Like only having three pieces of a hundred-piece jigsaw and still being able to envision the whole image from the few particles of information he'd sifted and collected.

Carver took a closer look at the positioning and placement of the tubs and jars. There was a faint white ring on the polished resin of the dresser. Had the forensics team moved her things and not put them back properly, or was something missing?

"Doubt anyone is alive to tell us," he said to himself. Just then he spun around. There was a thump from behind him. He reached for the holster on his hip and his hand touched his belt. He wasn't wearing a firearm. The FBI hadn't reissued him one yet. Carver held his breath and listened. All was quiet. Not a mouse ...

Thump. He heard it again, this time his eyes darted upward. Was something in the ceiling? Something was in the ceiling. If Carver had a weapon he would've raised it toward the ceiling and yelled out to whoever was crawling around up there: "FBI! Drop your weapon. Come out." He was empty-handed, standing on the carpet in his socks, his big toe poking through a newly discovered hole. *Thump.* Carver leaned out of the bedroom door and glanced at the ceiling. He was looking for the square access panel that would get him up there. Nothing. He couldn't see it.

He climbed on the mattress, tried not to step in Savannah Proctor's dried and caked blood and leaned his ear up toward the ceiling. Something was definitely moving around up there. Carver leaned forward on his tip-toes and pulled open the top wardrobe cupboard door. Once neatly folded knitwear and sweatshirts were strewn where the search team had looked in the cupboard. Carver's sense of smell was hit by a new wave of the smell of cucumber. He furrowed his eyebrows. What the hell was that? *Thump.*

He quickly realized it was coming from inside the wardrobe. In an instant there was a brown and pink blur coming straight at his face. He turned away instinctively and yelled out. The scream of a wild animal. He stumbled backward and heard a heavy thud. Out the corner of his eye, he saw a large brown and black snake disappear out of the room in a flash.

Carver stood holding his hand over his heart and panting. He couldn't believe it.

"What the hell," he said as he sucked in air. He put two fingers to his neck to feel his pulse and checked his watch. His heartbeat felt like he'd sprinted fifty yards.

"Phew! Ah!" Par for the course, he thought. He got up. Standing there moaning and groaning like an old man, he thought. You are an old man. It was a rueful realization. He needed to get out of this house and on the phone with Charleston and Augusta.

He'd found something. This could be big.

Carver teetered on the edge of the mattress swaying and trying to keep his balance as he inspected the floor around him. He wanted to be sure the serpent was gone. The thought of stepping on it in his socks sent shivers down his spine. He hated snakes. If he didn't know it before, now he was certain. He always thought of Carl Jung's collective unconscious and the archetype of the snake. It explained his own fear. The collective, human, unconscious fear of snakes.

Carver didn't know who to believe but he knew enough that this very inherent, very human fear was thought to come from the same place as the human fear of the dark. Sleeping in trees kept you safe from predators on the ground. Snakes climb trees. They might only be looking for small primates or birds' nests but if you scared one, it could strike. Like the snake in the cupboard had just done to him. The thought flashed in Carver's mind that he was essentially in the same position as human beings a hundred thousand years ago. Not much had changed. Except perhaps his clothing. Haircut. He shook his head to rid it of these inane thoughts. He needed to concentrate. He needed to get out of here. No weapon, he thought. The FBI. Joke. Just try not to step on it, he told himself.

CARVER SAT on the white wooden rail of the Proctor's front porch with his pale big toe wagging in the fading sun. If he hadn't been waiting outside the scene of a massacre it would be pleasant. The neighborhood was quiet. Carver held his phone to his ear and spoke first to Detective Chase.

"Jim, it's Gust. Yeah, listen. Did the crime scene guys remove anything from the victim's room?"

"Which victim, Savannah Proctor?"

"The daughter. Yeah. She was the primary target, Jim."

Carver waited. Chase said he didn't know.

"Get me a list of all evidence seized from the scene, will ya? I think he may have taken something."

"What?" Chase asked.

"I don't know yet," Carver said. "Just get me the list, all right? I don't want to theorize without evidence."

"Sure no problem," Chase said. "Anything else?"

"Yeah," Carver said. "One more thing. Get animal control and our forensic guys back to the house."

"Animal control, why? The Proctors didn't have any pets."

"Confirm that?"

"Why?"

Carver swallowed. "I was attacked by a hell of a big snake right now." Chase was quiet. "My shoes are still inside."

"Your shoes?"

"They slipped off while I was getting out of the house," Carver said. He lied. He didn't want to admit that he thought better—by which he meant absorbed the crime scene better—in his thinned-out cotton socks. "It's locked in there right now."

"What kind?"

"I don't know. That's why we need animal control down here. It's still slithering around in there. Tell them to be careful."

"You think they had a snake as a pet?" Chased asked.

Carver shook his head. "Didn't see a terrarium."

"A what?"

"The glass box you keep snakes in. It's called a terrarium. Reptiles are cold-blooded. They need everything to be just so ..."

"Okay, okay," Chase said. He sounded annoyed. Maybe

because they'd missed it in the search. This out-of-towner coming around here ... Carver thought.

Carver saw a movement in his peripheral vision and glanced to his right. There was an old guy sauntering up the sidewalk with an even older-looking golden retriever. The dog's head drooped and his tongue was out to the side. He was panting.

"Anything else?" Chase asked.

"Yeah, ask them to collect my shoes too."

He hung up and called Gibson's phone. It rang, then switched to voicemail. Carver heard the beep.

"Get them to issue me a sidearm, Bron. ASAP," Carver said and hung up.

The old boy wasn't just going for a walk. He was walking up to Carver, who closed his eyes and felt the sun on his face. When he opened them the old man in a faded golf shirt was standing on the overgrown front lawn smiling up at him.

"Afternoon," Carver said.

"Howdy. You the police?"

Carver nodded.

"This'll be the murder house then, ain't it?"

"Mm-hmm," Carver said.

The old man felt in the pocket of his baggy shorts and pulled out a soft pack of smokes. He tapped the pack and pulled one out. He offered it to Carver. A smoke, God, he hadn't smoked in years. After being chased by a snake he felt he deserved one. Needed one. Calm the nerves. Carver took it and said, "Thanks."

After they'd lit them, Carver asked as he exhaled, "You see anything?"

The old man touched his chin and looked down. He looked up and kept glancing at Carver's shoeless feet.

"Um, hard to say, never can tell," he said. "Terrible what

happened to them. Terrible." He shook his head and the flabby skin under his chin shook back and forth. "Makes you wonder, how in the hell ... 'scuse my French ... they just had a new alarm system installed last week."

Carver kept watching him.

"Hope you find the *sonofabitch*, whoever did this ..." the old man said and turned to go. Carver stood up.

"Sir! Hold on. Sir? What'd you just say?"

"Eh?" he turned back and faced Carver. "I hope you find 'em."

"Before that. You said alarm system?"

"*Yessir*, that's right. Saw a security company van parked up on the street a few days ago. Assumed they were getting the alarm upgraded. Lord knows, Julia—that's Mrs. Proctor—Lord rest her soul." The old man crossed himself. "She'd been talking about it for long enough, and I thought to myself, I thought, 'Oh, at last, they've gotten 'round to it'. Never can be too careful, is what I always say."

Carver hopped off the wooden railing and went down to the old man. The graying-round-the-mouth golden sniffed his pant leg. Carver pulled out a notepad. The old man was taken a little aback.

"What's your name, sir?" Carver asked.

The old man stood to his full height and pushed his chest out. "Williams. Frank Williams, Senior," he said. His watery eyes stared directly into Carver's. He ashed his cigarette down at his side. He looked at Carver's socks again.

Carver watched Mr. Williams closely. Nothing you need to be more careful of than a stranger offering help to the police. He looked proud. Proud to be helping the investigation. Carver could see he was the type who took being a good neighbor seriously.

"Do you happen to remember the name of the security company? Or maybe a logo of some kind?"

Mr. Williams furrowed his brow. He was recollecting. He gave a slow nod and said, "I can't be too sure."

"Well, what gave you the impression it was a security company?"

Mr. Williams smiled widely. "Well now, say. That's a good question. I suppose, thinking about it, it could've been any old utility van. It had a, a, you know, emblem on the side. A big blue shield. Can't remember if it said a name. Or, in any case, if it did, I don't remember it."

Carver wrote the information down. "Okay, thanks. Mr. Williams, we may need to contact you to get some more details on what you saw; you're good to help us?"

"Why, *yessir*, of course. Anything I can do to assist."

"Okay," Carver said. "Thanks for the cigarette and thanks for the time."

"You'll be in touch?" Williams asked.

"Sure will," Carver said and watched the old man. He said, "Come girl," to the hound and nodded goodbye. Carver watched him go.

"Say, Mr. Williams, now that I think about it."

The old man turned slowly toward him again. "Yessir?"

"What made you think Mrs. Proctor wanted a new alarm system?"

He made his way back toward Carver and said, "Well, you know, there were some strange goings on. Julia said she thought there was a stalker after her. Everyone thought she was imagining it, she said so herself, she was being paranoid. I says to her, I says, get a good alarm system. I figured she took me up on the advice when I saw the van."

Carver stood looking at him tapping the notepad on his palm. He was staring past Mr. Williams. The old man grew uncomfortable and mumbled something about finding the man and good luck and turned to wander off with his old dog.

When he snapped back from his Carver-trance, the man was gone. His cigarette had burned itself down to the filter. Carver threw the barely smoked cigarette down and went to step on it. Then remembered he was shoeless. Carver put the notepad away and dialed Detective Chase again.

"Jim, it's Gust again," he said. "Look into any security companies that the Proctors may have called. They had a new alarm system installed in the last few weeks."

Carver was going to scour every inch of their lives. The sun was setting and cast shadows and an orange glow across the front of the Proctor residence. For now, shadows were all he had.

10

Caitlin Sandling liked to get to the office early and before anyone else. It made her feel like she'd accomplished something before the workday had properly started. It also made her feel like she'd secretly won this private competition she was having. She'd gotten there before them, so she had done something better than the rest of them already, even if they didn't know it.

She suspected they knew it though.

She was used to unlocking the office when she arrived, but this morning it was already unlocked. That'd never happened before and she became hesitant and wary. Was someone inside or had they forgotten to lock up? No. She was sure they'd locked up. She opened the door and peeked around the corner, holding her handbag in front of her like a shield.

"Hello?" she said.

No answer. She stepped in.

"Hello?" she said again. "Is anybody here?"

She put her things on her desk and unconsciously collected the mail from the floor then went to inspect the rest of the office. The boys' desks—Frank and Toby—were empty but she saw a light on in Special Agent Carver's office.

Had he really beaten her in? She felt taken aback and went to see. It was a matter of personal pride that she was first in and last out. After all, all she could offer was hard work. His door was ajar and she pushed it open.

Argh, Carver. He seemed so uptight and uncomfortable to be here. She heard a snore. Carver's feet—wearing only socks—were on the desk. His head was lolled back and to the side. He was breathing through his mouth.

Oops. She didn't want to wake him so leaned forward to close the door. The handle jangled as she touched it and he sat bolt upright and took his feet off the desk. His eyes were wide and unseeing and his hair was stuck up on one side.

"I-I'm sorry, sir, I didn't know it was you in here."

"Who the hell else would it be in my office?"

"Yes, sir, I meant in the building, erm, in the office."

"No need to call me sir," Carver said and leaned forward on his elbows. He rubbed his face.

"Did you sleep here last night?"

He looked at her all bleary-eyed. "Left late from Charleston, came straight here," he said. "Must've fallen asleep."

"What were you doing in Charleston, sir? I mean, Special Agent Carver."

"Gust ..."

"Gust," Sandling said.

"Who're you again?" Carver asked.

"Um, Caitlin? Caitlin Sandling. We met—" she looked up and counted in the air with her finger, "—day before yesterday?"

"Caitlin Sandling? Someone said you were Braddock," Carver said.

"I took my mother's maiden name. You know how it is - around the academy."

"I remember meeting you, Caitlin—sorry—I meant, what's your role, what did you do before you landed in Grant Avenue?"

"Oh, I was a profiler." She looked down. "Still am a profiler, actually."

"Profiler. Hmm. You look a little young, aren't you? Most profilers I know have done—I don't know—seven, ten years in the field before they sit behind the desk. How long've you been out of the academy?"

"Two years," She said. And immediately felt a pang. It was her self-confidence. Carver looked at her for a moment, a bit like he was trying to guess her weight. "I have a PhD from Berkeley," she said. And felt jilted again. No excuse. Didn't make up for anything.

"Big shoes to fill, I guess?" Carver asked, meaning her father's.

"I guess ..."

"Okay," Carver said and sat back.

He hadn't offered her a chair. She was still standing in the doorway. She could see his things lying around in boxes. On the floor in front of her was one filled with books. She could see part of their spines. *Sex Crimes*, *Homicide Investigations Handbook*, *Serial Killers*. Light reading then, she thought.

"But why didn't you become an agent before becoming a profiler?" Carver asked.

She felt her jaw clench. It was involuntary. Happened whenever she felt embarrassed. The deep kind of shame one felt at failing. Being a failure. Not living up to her father's expectations. Or, whatever she imagined his expectations might be.

"I'd rather not talk about it right now," she tried to say. The words came out quiet and got stuck.

"Excuse me?"

She cleared her throat.

"I mean, um, can I get you a cup of coffee, boss?"

Carver smiled.

He was going to let her get away with it, she thought. Maybe he wasn't so bad after all. She could do with getting out of the office. It smelled bad.

"*Oh*, I nearly forgot, there's a letter for you here." Sandling stepped into the office and held out the official-looking envelope for Carver. He leaned forward and took it, glanced at the address on it and frowned. He dropped it on his desk.

"Sure, coffee'd be great. Black, please. I like my coffee like I like my soul."

She turned quickly and headed for the kitchen, fists clenched against her sides.

"Stupid, stupid," she said through gritted teeth over and over. Why couldn't she just be honest and tell him? God, she would die from embarrassment. Telling *him*. Practically a legend in the service.

Carver got up from his chair and stretched. He made a half-assed attempt to tuck his shirt in and then gave up.

He caught a glimpse of himself in the glass of a picture frame. God, he really needed to find a bathroom and get cleaned up. His desk phone rang.

He picked it up but said nothing. He only listened. He could hear breathing on the other end.

"Hello?" Carver said

"Agent Carver? Agent Augustine Carver?"

"Depends. Who's calling?"

"Oh, good. It's you. My name is Bob Woodbrand, I'm an associate partner at Heckler, Lowe, and Rubinstein. We're a law firm out of Philadelphia. *Anywho* — the reason I'm calling ..."

"I got your letter. I assume it's yours. Official stationary ...." While he was talking Carver reached for the letter Sandling gave him. He tore it open and scanned it as Woodbrand spoke.

"Oh! You did? That's great, just great. So ... you'll do it?"

"You don't get away that easy Mr. Wood —"

"Woodbrand."

"Uh-huh. You don't get anything that easy in this life, *Bob*. Tell me what exactly is happening ..."

"Well, sir, Mr. Carver —"

"Special agent."

"Mr. Special Agent Carver, sir, ah, the partners here have decided to represent Hermann Zimmer."

"Represent him in regards to what?"

"Well, Agent Carver, as you yourself know all too well, Mr. Zimmer —"

"Aka Zimmer the Ripper, serial murderer, the person you're choosing to represent, but go on ..."

"—Yes, quite, as you know, Mr. Zimmer received an indeterminate sentence —"

"He received a life sentence."

"—Yes, he received an indeterminate sentence, sometimes called a life sentence, so we're applying—on his behalf—for a psychiatric evaluation and mental health tribunal to be held."

Carver felt his heart rate jump and the artery in his neck pulsate. He squeezed his hand into a fist and held it firm. As calmly as he could through gritted teeth, Carver said, "And what's the purpose of this tribunal?"

"Well, that's a good question, sir, actually. As Mr. Zimmer was tried under diminished capacity he received the lower culpability sentence."

"Come again?"

"He was never found guilty of murder, Mr. Carver. It was manslaughter due to his diminished capacity. He's what they call a mentally disordered offender."

"Right ..."

"Basically, sir—and feel free to say no—Mr. Zimmer has requested that you testify at his mental health tribunal."

Carver took a beat.

"For what purpose?"

"It's just the first step ... but if we can establish that Mr. Zimmer is no longer mentally disordered, at some point, he will be eligible for parole."

"Parole? Are *you* crazy? You'd willingly have a hand in getting a—literally a monster—released? Do you even *know* with whom you're speaking, do you have—*any*—any idea what he did?"

"I do, Agent Carver, I do, and I'm so sorry. You know, this part of the job ... It's something I'm obliged to ask of you."

"Why are you representing him?"

"Sir, to be honest, it's so high profile."

"He sells newspapers?"

"Essentially, sir, yes. He's a hell of a lot of free publicity. Talk shows. Interviews. You name it." Woodbrand's voice lowered. "And, between you and me, I think he may have threatened one of the partners ..."

"And now you're trying to get him released?"

"No-no-no-no. Don't misunderstand. It's only the first step in the process, sir. It's highly unlikely that he will get through, I mean, that's *if* he manages to convince the medical board."

"Why the hell would he request me?"

Woodbrand was silent for a moment, then said, "I'm afraid I don't know, sir, he never confided that in me. He actually wanted to represent himself, you know? Be a lawyer. Apparently thought he'd be pretty good at it."

"So you speak to him?"

"Occasionally, sir, yes."

"You know what he did to those men, right?"

"Unfortunately, yes. I do."

"Be careful what you wish for, *Bob*. You might just be his type when he next gets out. Be very careful, y'hear?"

"I will."

"I'm going to go now. Don't call here again."

Carver hung up. This day was just getting better and better. Carver knew exactly why Zimmer wanted to represent himself. He'd have access to Carver's information. Zimmer wanted his address so he could subpoena him, himself. Find out where he worked, maybe even where he lived. Carver, deep down, knew more about how Zimmer the Ripper's mind worked than he cared to admit, even to himself.

WHILE HE WAS MASSAGING his temples there was a light tap on the glass of his office door. He glanced up and saw Sandling balancing two cups of coffee in one hand and trying not to spill.

"Sorry, they're a bit full," she said as she came in and handed Carver his coffee.

"Thanks, Caitlin."

"Actually, I prefer Cate."

"Cat?"

"No, like Cate, short for Catherine, but Cat is fine too."

"Ah, Cate, sorry, I'm a bit tired and distracted."

"Why, what is it, sir?"

Carver gave her a look.

"Sorry, I mean Gus ... *Gust*."

Carver stared at her with a blank expression, then said, "Where would you learn to surgically remove a human face?"

Her mouth dropped open but before she could answer, Carver's phone rang again.

"Ugh, sorry," he said. "It's this damn lawyer for—" Carver picked the receiver up before he finished his sentence. "Listen, Wood*burn*, stop calling here."

A woman's voice said, "Who's Woodburn?"

Sandling made a face and pointed a finger pistol at the door.

"I'm gonna go," she mouthed.

Carver nodded. "Oh, nobody. Never mind. Who's this?"

"Carver? You remember me, don't you? It's Isabelle Thompson from the *Post*. We talked a lot during the Zimmer case."

Carver held back a groan and rubbed his forehead. "Hi, Isabelle. Yes, I remember. How'd you find me?"

"Little birdie told me you were back, don't worry though, this is just a courtesy call."

"All right, 'bout what?"

"There's a kid I want you to meet. She has some interesting research and ideas on serial murderers. Her name's Jess Webb. Jessica Webb. I'll let her tell you but she's convinced her sister was attacked by a serial killer. I thought it might be useful for her to talk to you ..."

"Oh, yeah? What do I get out of this little liaison you've cooked up, Isabelle?"

Carver sat back and leaned his head over the back of his office chair while he waited for the journalist to come up with something interesting. She didn't need to know that Carver had already bumped into They-call-me-spider Webb yesterday in Charleston.

"What do you want?" Thompson asked.

"For you damned people to leave me the hell alone. That's it."

"*That* I can't promise you, Carver. How about you meet the kid, listen to what she has to say, and I give you a fore-warning about any hatchet jobs coming your way for the next—mmm—say six months."

"Three years."

"One year. Don't pretend you'll still be around in three years."

"Hatchet jobs? You reporters are deadlier with a hatchet than some of the psychos we put away."

"Ah, flattery, Carver. Don't think it'll buy you any special favors now."

"I won't. One year."

Carver hung up before she could say anything else. He pulled open the top drawer of his desk and sifted some things around looking for an Aspirin. He slammed the drawer shut and pulled open another. He had a splitting headache. He stood and put the base of his palms into his temples and applied pressure.

"Maudmont!" Carver yelled. He heard a scuffle and a cup being knocked over. Maudmont, while brushing the front of her dress flat, arrived at Carver's office door. She stood there in her flowery dress and matching pumps and gave him the sweetest smile on the roundest face.

"Find me something for my headache, please. It's killing me." She hurried off to find something to help him with the pain. "Wait! Maudmont." She stopped and turned back.

"Also, please get me the number for whoever is in charge at Patton State Psychiatric Hospital. Seems like there's someone I need to talk to."

11

CARVER SAT ALONE in his office, blinds down, he was stewed in the ripe smell of his airless office. He slipped his feet off his desk and stood up. Tucked his shirt in and yanked a blind open.

"Argh! Damn this thing," Carver said and turned his head away from the disinfectant glare of the sunlight. Carver tilted his ear toward the voices.

"Count Dracula is up!" he heard one of the guys say. He thought it was Underwood but could've been Hornigen, the old codger. There was humor out there. Giggling. Laughter. The odd chuckle. This wasn't the Girl Scouts. Carver was going to put a stop to it.

He walked out into the middle of the bullpen. The hubbub quieted down as he moved past each workstation. Only Chung—Rachel Fox—kept up her high-pitched reverse laugh. She laughed on the inhale and hiccup-guffawed awkwardly. Then tried to stifle it when she saw Carver coming.

"That sounds exhausting, Fox. Cut it out."

"No, sir, it's actually—"

"*Shush*," Maudmont said and primly stood to attention

with a smile plastered on her face. She was giving him the go-ahead to speak.

"Thanks, Penny." She was thrilled.

Carver looked at the eager faces staring back at him. Christ, he didn't have the heart. Those little expressions of hope and wonder.

"Listen—ah—we aren't the best individuals," Carver said. Maudmont's face dropped and she looked around at the others in confusion. "But we could be the best *team*."

Maudmont relaxed a little.

"You know? I'm not really one for speeches ... but—um —we all come here with flaws, right? Each of us—myself included—did something that got us sent to the backwater of Grant Ave."

Maudmont dropped the corners of her mouth and, nodding, said, "I really like it myself, mmhmm—"

"No, Penny! Nobody likes it. This is the place you come just so you can get back to the other place, you got it? I don't know who of us deserves to be here—that doesn't matter— all that matters is we have a chance to show that we can get back to the big show, eh?"

They stared back at him with blank expressions. Maudmont raised her hand. Carver raised his own and said, "Not now, Penny, please."

"Questions at the end, got it boss," Maudmont said and gave a single nod and double thumbs up.

"Do you guys get what I am saying?" He scanned the faces. "You really wanna sit around back checking parking fines and cross-referencing overdue library books? We are part of the FBI. Maybe—as individuals—we're screw-ups. Maybe. But we sure as hell can't be worse as a team, can we?"

Underwood raised his hand, "We might make up for each other's deficits when we work together?"

"I thought it was questions at the end," Maudmont said quietly, and muttered, "but okay then."

"Don't think I didn't hear the vampire wisecrack, Toby," Carver said. "Listen, I'm working on a case—"

"A dead case?"

"—No, Penny. A living one."

"The Cape Fear killings?" Sandling asked. Carver half turned to her and nodded. "The press are calling him the Skinwalker Killer. It's a tough one. Cops have very little to go on. No real forensics at either crime scene, although we do know he stopped to make himself a ham sandwich after dissecting Savannah Proctor's face."

The team stared blankly back at Carver. This was too much for them.

"What does that mean?" Fox asked.

"Any of you guys ever worked serial homicides before?" Carver asked.

They shook their heads. Hornigen raised his long bony hand and said, "I worked a case that involved a homicide with the Secret Service once but that—"

"Drug and gang violence is totally different," Carver said.

"And you know because ...?" Fox asked.

"Let's just say I know," Carver said.

"I don't understand," Fox said. She was talking rapidly. "Was that an answer to the question? The question was really direct and easy—" She kept speaking very quickly. Her hand movements conveying the roundabout way she was talking.

Fox seemed like she had a bit of a problem in that she didn't like problems, Carver thought. He could see that she had a very low tolerance for uncertainty. And being uncomfortable with unknowns was a leading cause of anxiety. Anxiety led to stress and that's why she spoke so much faster when something was uncertain. Carver read it in her behavior.

"He knows because he used to work as an undercover drugs operative!" Sandling yelled. She seemed frustrated. Carver glanced at her. She shrugged, "Well, weren't you?"

Underwood cleared his throat and half-raised his hand.

"I worked a serial case before ..." he said.

"Okay, good. What about you, Sandling?" Carver asked.

"Me?" she said pointing to herself. "Um, I assisted on a couple of the profile write-ups on a few cases but nothing—"

"Okay," Carver said.

"I want you to come to the crime scene in Augusta with me," Carver said to Sandling.

She shook her head, "I don't know, sir. I'm a profiler. I don't go in the field. I mean, I haven't—"

"Fine, suit yourself," Carver said. "Stay here then."

"Listen, sir," Underwood said, on behalf of Sandling like he sensed the awkwardness in the room. He was saying what everyone was thinking. "Erm, you know what they call us, don't you? Back at Quantico?"

A beat and Fox said, "Sofa Squad."

"Team Turkey," Hornigen said.

"Thromboses Brown-noses," Sandling said.

"Slouch Force," Maudmont said, resigned, barely above a whisper.

Carver cut in: "Listen—ah—I don't care what they call us. It doesn't matter. Slouch forces, blue tortoise, grim noises. Whatever it is—we deserve it—right?" He looked at them in turn. "We *effed* up, didn't we? So we deserve it ... until we don't. Most of you aren't even willing to admit what you did. Some of you might not even know. Wear it with pride or wear it with shame but make sure—damn sure—

you put your own meaning to it." They looked back at him and he asked, "So, are we in, or are we out?"

Maudmont raised her hand and perked up, "What about all the work from Washington, the backlog of cases we have to clear."

They all groaned.

"We'll do that too ..." Carver said. "Listen, Penny, I know it's hard to take but—honestly—headquarters don't care about you, or anything you do. *You*, plural. And they won't—until—you give them something of value."

"Can we take some time to think about it?" Sandling asked. She sounded afraid.

"This is all good and well," Fox said, "but where do we even start? If we knew what we were looking for I could build an algorithm to automatically search all the ViCAP data we have on file—most of which I am supposed to be manually uploading," she checked her watch, "And, I'm losing valuable time to run a data dump, so any direction ... We need tasks. Task-oriented ..."

Carver put up his hand to stop her and she crossed her arms and frowned.

"Okay," Carver said. "Message received, loud and clear. So the bullshit artists were right." Carver walked toward his office. "Sofa Squad is right!" he said loudly over his shoulder.

He heard Underwood say to Hornigen, "You believe this crap?"

Carver stopped and turned around.

"Underwood," Carver called.

The smooth-faced special agent turned toward him.

"You're coming to Augusta with me."

12

CARVER GLANCED AT UNDERWOOD, who was unfolding a large road atlas of downtown Augusta in the passenger seat. Carver changed the position of his hand on the wheel, shifted in his seat, and said, "Don't worry about that, I know the way."

"You been 'round here much before?"

"Some," Carver said and left it at that.

"We brought the weather with us," Underwood said and lifted his chin toward the bright sunlight. Carver felt it warm on his hands and chest. "Are we going straight there?"

"Need to get the keys first," Carver said.

The artificially cheerful Toby Underwood sat quietly for a time drumming his fingers on his knees and looking out of the passenger side window. As they pulled into the parking lot of a small complex of shops and offices, Underwood asked, "What're we hoping to find, Gust?" Carver furrowed his brow and glanced at him and pulled into a parking space in front of Cannon Realty. "I mean it's been a few weeks since they were—um—killed, you know? There won't be much to see."

"Won't there?" Carver said and unclipped his belt and opened the door. "Well, we'll just have to see, won't we?"

Underwood hopped out and said from across the car, "What I mean is, what are we going there for? What're we hoping to find?"

He jogged to catch up to Carver who didn't answer him, instead, Carver pushed open the realtor's front door. Underwood fell in behind him. A woman wearing reading glasses glanced up from her desk. She took her glasses off and stood and hurried over to them.

"Agent Carver?" she asked.

Carver nodded and flipped open his identification. She barely looked at it before he put it away.

"Sally-Anne Cannon. My father's shop," she said and stuck out her hand.

"That's okay, thanks," Carver said and looked at her open hand. She dropped it to her side, unshaken, and said, "You want the keys to the York residence?"

"We do," Carver said.

"Okay," she said and went to fetch them. Carver took a few steps toward her desk where she bent down to pull the keys from her drawer.

"What's happening with the property?" Carver asked.

"Not much right now. Why, you in the market?" She looked up and smiled. Carver couldn't tell if she was making a bad realtor's joke or whether she thought he might actually be interested in buying the murder house.

"No, I mean—ah—what's happening with the property at the moment in terms of —"

"Oh, well, we've had painters and decorators there to, you know, spruce things up a bit. It took a lot of elbow grease and soapy water and more than one coat of paint, let me tell you!"

"Uh-huh," Carver grunted.

"And, um, the family's *stuff*," she said. "Well, they're waiting on direction from the police to know what to do with it all. So really very sad, isn't it? You don't know what we should do, do you?" She looked at him hopefully.

"No, I don't," Carver said and held out his hand for the keys. She put them gently into his palm.

"The parents, as I'm sure you can imagine, are totally broken up about it. I mean, their little girl! They can't bear to look at the house, let alone live in it."

Carver's hand closed around the bunch and he said, "So the child's parents won't be there? Anything else I should know?"

"No, I don't think so. There's an awful smell though," she said. Carver raised his eyebrows.

"Truly awful. My contractors tried to find it but they think a rat might be dead inside the walls." She shrugged. "Maybe attracted by all the blood?" and shook her head.

"Okay, thanks," Carver said and turned to go. "My colleague Agent Underwood will be by later to drop them off."

As they walked to the car Underwood said, "Maybe we should speak to the parents, Gust?"

"Why?" Carver asked and glanced at Underwood before he climbed into the vehicle.

"Why?" Underwood repeated. "Because maybe they have something that might help us?"

"They already spoke to the Richmond County Sheriff."

"Yeah, but I mean—local police—come on."

Carver frowned. "You got something against local law enforcement?"

"No, but, sir, you really think they questioned them properly?"

"To find out what exactly, Underwood?"

"You can call me Toby, Gust. And—I don't know—like if they had any enemies or anything."

Carver shook his head and looked out the corner of his eye at Underwood as he pulled out of the lot. "Enemies? Underwood, please. You think someone they had a disagreement with about money did this? Did you look at the crime scene pictures?"

Underwood turned and looked out of the window. Carver would take that as a 'no'. Part of him didn't blame him. Who wanted to see images of a little girl hanging from a pipe by her neck. Another part of him lost respect for the special agent sitting next to him. It's part of the job. We look so other people don't end up like that. We look because we have a duty to look. Carver was having his doubts about Special Agent Underwood.

After a time, Carver said, "No, we're here to find out information the local PD may have missed. Something they might not have seen. And give them a hand in confirming it's the same killer. I have no doubt, but some of them do. We can put their unease to rest."

Underwood didn't respond. Carver asked him as he turned the wheel off the freeway and onto Lakemont Drive, "You said you'd worked serial homicide before?"

"Yeah, I did ..." Underwood said.

"How come you ended up in Slouch Squad?"

Underwood glanced at him. "Sofa Squad," he said.

Carver felt like Toby didn't like the nickname.

"I'll be honest with you, Gust, my last foray into serial killings got me sent to Grant Avenue."

Carver waited. He knew Underwood wanted to tell him,

so why not let him talk? Never interrupt a man admitting his feelings.

"I was on a task force, tracking this serial killer. Dumping bodies—escorts—you know? Prostitutes on the highway. The Trash Bag Killer they called him. Anyway, I'd gone undercover. Met him a few times at the same truck stop-come-nightclub, you know how it is ..."

As Underwood talked Carver was glancing up at the houses. Big lawns. No fences. Lakemont Drive ran right along the water of Lake Olmstead.

"So we're all in this motel room, the whole team, I was on the phone with the guy arranging our next meet. There's this state bureau of investigation chick there, an undercover hooker. The whole shebang. I get off the phone with the guy and we're talking to the team, you know, planning the next move. Talking about how we're setting him up and all. Something inside me feels off, so I check the phone. I don't know if I butt-dialed him or didn't hang up—I swear I hung up that phone—anyway, he heard everything. Was the last we heard from him. He skipped the state. We never caught him."

Carver suddenly felt very hot under the collar. The air conditioner was on full but he felt himself start to sweat and bit his tongue. Rage. Rage is what he was feeling. He was sure of it. He forced himself to breathe through his nose and try to calm down. Through gritted teeth, Carver said, "And you think that's the reason you landed up here?"

Carver felt Underwood watching him. He couldn't bring himself to look at the guy.

"I mean, they never tell you, explicitly," Underwood said. "But I have a pretty good idea."

"A pretty good idea? So you reckon letting a suspected serial killer listen to an operational briefing—about himself

—thereby allowing him to vanish into the wind would do it?"

Underwood was silent.

Carver decided to let it go, for now.

The last thing he said was, "You think he is still out there, active, killing in another state though, the guy you let go ...?"

CARVER TURNED past a silver mailbox and up a winding gray concrete drive. The house sat on the top of a ridge over-looking the lake. Carver climbed out and shaded his eyes from the sun and looked out over the area. Tall trees all around. Lots of grass and open spaces. An affluent area.

"Listen, I feel really bad about what I did, okay?"

Carver waved him away.

"We'll talk about it another time, Agent Underwood. We've got work to do now and I want to concentrate."

"Call me Toby, Gust."

Carver looked at him for a second longer than he should have and turned and walked toward the house. Why was he so annoyed? He knew that each of the Sofa Squad had reasons—none of them positive—for being assigned to a former one-man resident agency outpost. Carver knocked on the front door. He felt Underwood's eyes on him. He didn't know why he knocked. He always did it. Maybe he felt like it was a mark of respect. Even though he knew no one was home, asking permission to enter a place where the dead had died was showing respect, in some weird way, it made him feel better.

"No one's home," Underwood said. "We have the only keys."

"I know," Carver said. "I just wanted to let them know we were coming."

"Who?" Underwood asked. Sounded confused.

Carver twisted the knob and pushed the door open. He stepped into the gloom. The chemical smell of fresh paint was the first thing he noticed. Underwood stepped in behind him.

"Close the door and lock it," Carver said without turning around and he heard Underwood come in and shut the door.

"Where were you?" Carver asked Underwood without looking at him. They were walking through the house, getting a feel for it.

"What?"

"Three weeks ago, when they were killed, what were you doing back then?" Carver asked.

Carver knew instinctively that he'd been sitting in that beat-up old recliner with a sealed bottle of single malt, a crystal tumbler, and a .38 revolver with a single bullet in the cylinder. He was sat staring at the bottle of booze. He hadn't had a drink since after Madeleine was taken by Zimmer.

He'd managed to avoid the depths of alcohol as a crutch to cope. He'd gone somewhere much deeper. Somewhere much darker. Alcohol couldn't help him cope anyhow. His solution was to throw himself into his work. He became obsessed and, if the only tool you have is a hammer, every situation starts looking like something you want to smash.

After he shot the junkie, they wanted him out of the Bureau. Slouch Force hadn't been an option for Carver. He'd gone too far over to the other side.

Instead of kicking him out, they made him do his penance. The powers that be gave him some sympathy—what with his daughter being murdered and all. They made him go into an undercover narcotics detail. Several years of hard, grueling undercover work.

He might not have drunk alcohol but the underworld

was a platter of narcotics and other vices and he'd treated it like an all-you-can-eat buffet. He was sober now. He still got acid flashbacks and occasionally the world looked like the shiny surface of a pool of water with a sheen of oil on the surface to him. He'd retired before it killed him.

"Boss?"

"Huh?"

"I said should we go down and check out the basement, you know … where it happened?" Underwood asked.

"Sure," Carver said back in reality. "Lead the way."

"God, is this where that smell is coming from?" Underwood asked as he made his way down into the basement.

It opened up into what would have been a den. Now it was bare walls and newly laid carpet but the photos Carver had seen were of a hunting cabin-style man cave. They were hit with the stench and Underwood tried to cover his nose.

Carver walked behind Underwood.

"I can't see anything," Underwood said and half looked back. Underwood sounded nervous, Carver thought.

"There should be a light switch on the right-hand side."

Underwood stepped down and ran his hand along the wall. He found the switch and flicked it. The basement was filled with white fluorescent light. There were lamps dotted all around, Carver thought they must not use the ceiling light much.

"How'd you know the switch was there?" Underwood asked.

"Lucky guess," Carver said.

"What are we looking for anyhow?" Underwood asked.

Won't know until we find it, Carver thought.

"Not sure," Carver said and stepped forward.

Underwood, who was taller than Carver, felt the need to duck his head but he probably would have been fine.

Walking at his full height, Carver went over to the bookcase and ran his fingers along the edge of it and scanned the book spines.

"Anything interesting?" Underwood asked.

Carver didn't respond. He could feel Underwood watching from behind. He wasn't in the mood for light-heartedness. A little girl had died down here. Hung from the exposed pipework. At least she didn't suffer, Carver thought. Underwood cleared his throat. Carver bet he felt sheepish. Underwood was trying too hard to get back on Carver's good side, if he'd ever been on his good side.

THERE WAS a full set of Encyclopedia Britannica including the children's edition. Lots of National Geographic magazines stacked up next to one another. And what was Mrs. York's collection of Danielle Steele novels.

"What're we looking for again, boss?" Underwood asked. Carver glanced back at him. "I mean, sir," Underwood said.

"You don't have to call me, sir."

Carver turned back to the bookshelf. It had been almost a month since the murder. Carver wasn't expecting anything significant but he was wondering if maybe the killer left them a similar surprise as the Proctor house.

"God, the smell down here is atrocious," Underwood said. He sounded like he might spew.

"I said let's find the source of it," Carver said.

Underwood blocked his nose.

"Where do we even start?" Underwood said.

To Carver, he sounded like a man who was purposely being ignorant so that he didn't have to do his job. Maybe this man wasn't an investigator after all. Maybe the Bureau had it right, sending him to the Sofa Squad.

"I'm going to go and look at the other room," Carver said. "Stay here and look for anything out of the ordinary."

"But I don't know what out of the ordinary looks like!" Underwood said.

"You will when you see it," Carver said and went into the adjoining room. He followed the exposed pipe along the ceiling. That's where the little York girl, Abigail, was strung up like a deer carcass.

There was nothing in the room besides bare walls, a storage cupboard, and industrial-style carpet. Maybe this is where Mrs. York did the laundry. It was also where her daughter took her last breath. Carver's throat got hard and closed up and he couldn't bring himself to imagine her last moments. The pressure on her soft small slender neck, the veins in her head bulging under the pressure. The pain that made her squeal and writhe. Until finally, the blackness overtook her.

"Think I might have found something!" Underwood called and snapped Carver out of his malaise.

Carver cleared his throat and said, "I'll be right there." He took a moment to steady himself. He inhaled deeply, stuck his shoulders back, and walked through to the den.

He saw Underwood on his knees next to a built-in wooden bench, pulling a trunk out from underneath. It was one of those metal ones that had Jeremy York Esq. written on top.

"It's padlocked but––oh my God––I think the smell is coming from inside.

Just then there was a knock and shuffling upstairs. The special agents looked at one another. Underwood looked shocked. Carver could tell he felt like he'd messed up.

"What was that?" Underwood asked.

"I thought I told you to lock the front door."

Underwood looked flustered. Carver could tell that he hadn't locked it.

"Why didn't you do it?" Carver asked.

"I–I–I didn't think there would be a need, no one was coming. We were alone here. I was a bit in the ..."

"You mean you decided not to do your job? You decided not to do what I told you," Carver said.

Underwood stood up and pulled his firearm.

"Give me your weapon."

"Sir?" Underwood whispered.

Someone was in the house. They can hear them walking around upstairs.

"Could it be the killer returning to the scene of the crime?" Underwood whispered.

Carver said, "Could be. Stranger things have happened. Now, give me a weapon," and stuck out his hand.

Underwood hesitated.

Carver gave him a hard look and Underwood relented and put the gun in his hand.

"It's loaded."

"No shit," Carver said and checked the weapon.

He hadn't held a pistol in his hand since after he'd last shot someone. Carver climbed the stairs carefully, one step at a time, his weapon pointed at the open door. He had a sudden regret about having a weapon in his hand again. He'd worked hard to move from this part of his life.

"Hello, anybody here?" he heard a man call from above.

Carver made it safe and secured the pistol in his waistband.

"I know that voice," Carver said to Underwood and climbed the stairs.

"Can I have my gun back?" Carver heard Underwood say from behind.

13

"CARVER! HELLO?" he heard Lieutenant Davies call out from above.

"Art, it's Carver. We're down here, coming up! For Christ's sake don't shoot ..."

"Ah! There you are. Damn. You had me worried for a second ..."

Davies looked uncomfortable, Carver thought. Either that, or the way his face was scrunched up into a half-smile half-grimace meant he was holding onto his mid-morning sabbatical.

"You okay, Art?" Carver asked and shook his hand.

"Yeah, why?"

"Your guts all right?"

Davies glanced down at his waistline and shook his head. Seemed confused.

"Who's this?" Davies asked and pointed at Underwood.

"That's Toby Underwood ... Special Agent. He's very pleased to meet you," Carver said.

Davies lifted his chin toward Underwood, eyeing him up. Could just be the constipation, Carver thought and handed Underwood back his weapon. Underwood put it in his holster.

"You're not going to make it safe?" Davies asked him.

Underwood shook his head once and said, "I just saw Special Agent Carver make safe downstairs."

"And you trust him, do you?" Davies asked and looked at Carver. He shrugged. "*Special Agent*," Davies said. "Where does the Bureau find these guys."

"Never mind," Carver said. "Come on," and headed for the door.

"Wait, aren't you going to tell me what you were doing down there?"

"We found something alright, God awful smell, sir!" Underwood said. Carver stopped him with a look.

Underwood closed his mouth mid-sentence like a goldfish. He didn't speak again. Davies laughed.

"What'd you find?" Davies asked, getting all serious now.

"A connection," Carver said.

Davies' eyes widened and he picked up the pace to walk next to Carver. They stepped into the bright sunlight and Davies covered his eyes.

"What connection?"

Carver stopped and stood square to him.

"Listen, Art, it's unconfirmed. We need to get some lab guys down here ..."

"But they've been, swept the whole house—"

"Look, I'm not saying your guys didn't do their job. They did. Murder scene's always a mess. Things get missed. And —I'm telling you—they missed something. It's not going to help us catch the killer but it's confirmed we're dealing with the same guy."

"Are you gonna tell me what it is?" Davies asked.

Carver held his stare. Davies broke off and looked at Underwood.

"You gonna get moving and spill the beans, Toby, you tall drink of water you?"

Underwood pushed his lips together and put his hands deep in his pockets.

"Oh, so you've decided to learn your lesson all of a sudden?" Davies said. "You're not gonna tell me?" he asked and turned back to Carver.

"This can't leak, Art," Carver said. "Understand?"

Davies nodded.

"Killer has a thing for snakes, all right?"

"Snakes?"

"Yeah. You know, little slithery things about yay long. He leaves them in the house. A little screw you to the police."

"Poisonous?"

"Venomous," Carver said.

"Huh?"

"It's definitely a signature of our killer," Underwood said. "He's sending us a message." His voice belied the confidence of his words.

"Ah-ha," Davies said. "And what message is that Big Nose?"

"Just process the scene and send the snake to the lab for analysis," Carver said. He was done with this conversation. "Let's go."

They walked out into the road and Carver turned back to look at the house. Single story under the shade of the trees swaying above it. The other two turned to look too. The property already looked neglected. Carver imagined the family there. Kids playing out front. Riding their bikes. Running in the trees.

He turned away.

Davies pointed up the street. "That's Mrs. Henderson, from across the road. Says she thinks she saw something.

We didn't get much out of it but may be worth speaking to her again."

They walked up the drive to Mrs. Henderson's front door. Carver turned and squinted down the road toward the York house while Davies pressed the bell.

He glanced at them and said, "Rumor is dear Mrs. Henderson's husband ran off. She's in denial. Children stopped calling her. We think it might be—"

Door opened just a crack. Davies cut himself short and bent forward a little from the waist and smiled.

"Hello Mrs. Henderson, it's Art Davies, from the police. Do you remember me?"

The door opened a bit wider and Mrs. Henderson stood there in her nightgown, thick glasses, oxygen tank hissing quietly by her side.

"Can we come in?" Davies asked.

"May we ..." she said in a croak.

"Excuse me?"

She cleared her throat.

"It's 'may we come in', officer," Mrs. Henderson said and stepped aside. "If you're barging into someone's home unannounced I'd at least expect you to be polite about it ..." They filed in and walked past her.

The house had an unpleasant smell. Like someone left a meatloaf in the oven and forgot about it for a couple of weeks. They stood in her dusty living room and waited for her to join them. She ambled up and stood in front of them.

Carver got straight to the point. "Mrs. Henderson, we understand you might have seen something on the day of the murders."

She looked flustered, "What? Oh no ..."

"Are you sure Mrs. Henderson," Davies said, stepping forward. "You told the police—."

Carver put his hand up to stop Davies talking.

"Can you tell us what you saw?" Carver asked.

She coughed and lifted the back of her hand to her mouth. "I need to sit …" her voice trailed off as she made her way to her ratty recliner next to a large single-pane window overlooking the street. Underwood went to help her and she waved him away and sat down with a *huff*.

"Mrs. Henderson …?"

She looked up at Carver with her watery eyes.

"Is this about the murder?" she asked.

Carver nodded.

"Have you caught him yet?"

Carver went over and got on his haunches next to Mrs. Henderson. She looked surprised.

"We're doing everything we can."

"I don't feel safe!" she wheezed. "All day I look out this window and I never see any of you people. No patrol cars. No one looking out for people—" She raised her hand to her mouth and hacked a rasping phlegmy cough.

"That's why we're here Mrs. Henderson, to catch him but we need your help."

"I told you I didn't see anything."

"You told the police—"

"I told the police I *heard* something," she said.

"Okay," Carver said. "When exactly did you hear something?"

She looked out the window. "I-I-I'm not sure, I need to think."

"Take your time."

"I don't …"

"Was it in the morning, afternoon?"

She turned and stared blankly at Carver. Then her face twisted and hardened. "What are you doing standing here in my living room when you should be out there trying to catch him!"

"We're—" Carver started to say.

"You're wasting my damn time! Wasting everyone's time. Do yourselves a favor, will ya?"

"Mrs. Henderson—"

"In fact, how do I know you are who you say you are? Show me some identification this instant or get the hell out of my house."

Carver glanced up at Davies and groaned as he got off his haunches. He reached into his pocket and flipped open his ID and held it under Mrs. Henderson's nose. She looked down at it and squinted. He doubted she could make anything out.

"I'm Augustine Carver. This is Toby Underwood. We're both special agents with the FBI."

"FBI? Oh my," Mrs. Henderson said and looked up at Carver. "Aren't you all meant to be in black suit and tie?"

Carver got down to her eye level again.

"Where were you when you heard something, Mrs. Henderson?"

"It was loud," she said. "Like a gunshot. I was right here. I pulled the net curtain back. I stood up to see."

"What did you see?"

"I thought it must have come from next door. Then I saw him. A man walking up the road toward me. I don't think he saw me. Or, maybe he did." She started to shake. "I'm so scared," she gasped. "What if he wants to kill me?"

Carver put his hand on her shoulder and she turned to look at him. Her face was drawn and her mouth was open. Then she recognized him and started to come back.

"You're safe, Mrs. Henderson. You said you heard a loud noise ..."

"It was a gunshot."

"Yes. Are you sure it was a gunshot? Could it have been something else?"

"I damn well know a gunshot when I hear one," she said.

Carver stared at Mrs. Henderson for a long time. "Can I take a look at your glasses for a moment?"

She furrowed her brow and took them off her face with a shaking hand. Carver saw the liver spots on her flabby arm as she held them out to him. Carver took them and put them on. He went to the window and pulled the net curtain aside and looked down the street.

"The man you saw," he said. "Did you see his face?"

He looked down at Mrs. Henderson. She was blurred and he started to get a headache. He could barely make out that she was shaking her head.

"How'd ya know it was a man?" Carver asked.

She looked into the distance as she thought about it.

"Well, he was dressed as a man," she said.

"What was he wearing?"

"Um, sort of, you know, workman's clothes. A uniform sort of like a ... one of those delivery drivers."

"Was it just the mailman you saw?"

She shook her head.

"How can you be sure?"

She glared up at him. "Listen, Mr.—"

"Carver."

"Mr. Carver. Give me my spectacles back please." Carver did as he was told. "I'm eighty-something years old. I've lived in this house, in this neighborhood, for fifty-something years. I brought children up on this street." She took two deep inhales of oxygen and wheezed. Carver thought her chest might explode with phlegm. "I think I'd know what the postman looks like. Okay?"

"Was he tall? Short?"

"He was tall, *grainy*-looking."

"Grainy?" Carver asked.

"No, *graingy*, you know, like gangly-looking. The way he walked."

"How old was he?"

She shook her head. "I dunno. You young people all look the same age to me. He had facial hair and a ball cap - it was hard to see."

"Young people?" Carver said. "Was he more like me or more like Toby?" He asked and indicated his partner.

"More like him," she said.

"And he was caucasian, like Toby?"

"Eh, what?"

"White, Mrs. Henderson, was he white?" Davies asked.

"Yes, he was white all right. Had blond hair coming down out of his baseball cap. It was long. Too long for my taste. Men ought to dress like men and leave the long hair to the women."

Carver glanced at Davies. He saw Underwood's eyes wide in his peripheral vision.

"What about his face?" Carver asked.

"Didn't get a look at his face. He had his head down. That's why I don't think he saw me."

"Was he carrying anything?"

She looked up at him suddenly. "Yes!" She said and raised her index finger to the ceiling. "He had a black bag in his hand."

"Which hand?"

"Ah, his right! In his right hand he was carrying a black case like builders use."

"And that's when you heard the gunshot?" Carver asked.

"Yes, I—" she furrowed her brow and lifted her hand to her mouth. "No, I ... yes, that's it. I was standing here watching the birds. Yes, I was watching the birds in the feeder and then ... I saw this man walking up the street. I ...

he was ... then ... and there was a loud *bang* like a gunshot. I heard a gunshot."

"Thank you, Mrs. Henderson. You've been real helpful," Carver said. "If you don't mind, we'll send someone over here to draw what you saw. A sketch artist. It'll be a big help to us."

"I don't want anyone to know my name or what I saw," she said.

"They won't," Carver said. "Come on Art, let's get going. Leave Mrs. Henderson in peace." He smiled at her.

She had a worried look, staring out of the window. They turned to go. As they stepped out of the front door, Underwood caught up with Carver.

"She's crazy," Underwood said.

"She's just old," Carver replied. He stopped at the bottom of the drive. "Art, you need a ride?"

"No, I have my car here," he said as he walked up to them. "Caucasian male, tall, thin, long blond hair, mid- to late-twenties wearing overalls and carrying a black case. Sounds like our guy," Davies said.

"Think you can trust a word she says?" Underwood asked. "We didn't find any shell casings here, no slugs in the walls. There was no gunshot."

"Yeah," Carver said, staring off into the distance. "So the question becomes, what *did* she hear?"

"First she said she was looking out because she heard the gunshot, then she said she was looking out 'cause she heard the birds, so which is it?"

"Yeah, she's confused," Carver admitted, eyes locked on the trees but seeing nothing. "But that doesn't mean she didn't hear something. My bet is it wasn't a gunshot she heard. It was a car backfiring. And I think it might have been the killer's van."

"Van?" Davies asked.

"Yeah," Carver said. "I think our killer was dressed as some sort of workman and was driving some old model van. That would fit with Mrs. Henderson's version."

"Hell," Davies said.

"How'd you figure that?" Underwood asked.

"I read the initial report, Underwood."

Underwood didn't say anything.

"Drop me at a motel," Carver said. "I'm going to California in the morning. Someone I have to see."

14

CARVER SAT on a faux leather chair outside Dr. Edward Forsmith's office. Magnolia walls and rough industrial blue carpet reminded him of being in a retirement home, or cheap hotel.

Anything but an insane asylum.

The fluorescent light on the ceiling hummed and flickered.

Carver blinked hard and fluttered his eyes.

Something about being near crazy people made him feel crazy himself like he was sliding into it somehow.

The white door to the office opened and Dr. Forsmith stood there in a white coat and thick gold-rimmed spectacles and beckoned Carver in. Carver stood up.

"Mr. Carver," Forsmith said and gave him a single nod as he passed. He didn't offer his hand. Neither did Carver. "We spoke on the phone. You sounded quite frantic then. Have things calmed down since?" Forsmith asked and went and sat behind his desk.

Frantic, Carver thought, hell. Forsmith left Carver standing. When no seat was offered, Carver sat anyway. Forsmith looked over the top of his spectacles at him and his eye twitched.

"You've had a stay in a state psychiatric hospital before, Detective Carver, as a patient, I understand?"

He smelled of mentos and mothballs, Carver thought.

"For a time—a short time."

Carver didn't bother saying he wasn't a detective. Forsmith kept on staring at him over his spectacles. He wiped the back of his hand under his nostrils and glanced at it. "After your daughter was killed?" he asked.

"Yes."

"Ward Twenty—the maximum security ward—is a bit different from what you experienced. Takes some getting used to." Forsmith looked at him over the top of his glasses again.

Carver didn't respond. He had this knot in his stomach and his brain felt like it was being squeezed in some circus strongman's grip.

"Zimmer doesn't receive visitors—rarely in any case—so you must be prepared for the worst."

Carver nodded and asked, "What's the worst?"

"Are you acquainted with him?" Forsmith asked. He raised to a higher pitch on the end at the same moment as he ever so slightly raised an eyebrow. Forsmith knew full well that he was, Carver thought. And he would've at least appreciated the professional courtesy of not being subject to a psychiatric inquiry before his meeting with Hermann Zimmer. "I mean, other than ... your daughter," Forsmith said. "Tell you the truth I'm surprised he agreed to take this meeting." Being coy now. "Of course, he still receives lots of fan mail, letters from all over the world. Women mostly. We read all of them, of course. Censor the filth. Them telling him what they want him to do to them. Truly disturbing. I suppose they treat him like some sort of confessional, some sort of cathartic release for their own depravity. Yes, that must be it. Are you surprised, detective?"

"That he took the meeting? I'm not surprised at all," Carver said.

Forsmith blinked curiously.

"He killed—" Carver felt a knot in his throat and put his fist in front of his mouth as he cleared it. "*Ahem.* He killed her to taunt me. Now he gets the chance to relive it every time I see him." Carver changed tack. "What exactly have you been doing with him all this time?"

"Would you like a glass of water?"

"I'm fine."

"Are you certain?"

Carver glared at him.

Forsmith sat patiently and interlocked his fingers. He rested his elbows on his desk and waited for Carver to formulate a response.

Did he really expect a response? This doctor should better understand his patients' motives if he considered them patients at all.

Finally, Forsmith spoke. "We study him, detective, but most of my time is spent simply keeping my staff safe. He managed to brutalize several of my orderlies when he first got here. One lost an eye. One nearly died. He's vicious. Truly vicious."

"I know," Carver said dryly and managed to avoid following it up with a scoff.

"He's calmed down now that he's applying for a mental health review board. We discussed it," Forsmith said. "Why'd you suppose they do it?"

"Do what?"

"Send him their secrets and their desires," Forsmith said.

"The women?" Carver asked.

Forsmith nodded.

Carver shrugged and shook his head. Odd change of subject. "It's a kind of power. People like danger, doctor. The feeling of being close to someone dangerous. Dangerous and insane. Someone who could kill them, probably *would* kill them. It's a thrill, I imagine. And the idea of being chosen. Being selected. Being somehow *special*—"

"Is that why you're here?"

Carver didn't respond. Enough of the psychiatry.

"I really need to see Zimmer in private, Dr. Forsmith."

"I don't have the staff to move him, detective. Even if I did, as I told you on the phone, the risk analysis report *simply* to do so wouldn't be worth the time it took to write it. You can see him in his cell. His natural environment—if you will—since you can't see him in the wild." Then, before Carver could respond. "You are going to be all right, aren't you, detective? You know he's psychotic. Truly disturbed. I wouldn't expect a lucid conversation. He will probably start fantasizing about the night he murdered your daughter, hmm?"

The raised eyebrow again. The slightly cocked head. Carver felt his skin get hot.

"Are you testing me, doctor, see if I can handle it, is that it?"

"Possibly." Forsmith's expression made it seem like the thought just occurred to him.

"Well, I'd appreciate it if you didn't bring up my daughter again. Is that clear?"

"Yes," Forsmith said. "But I wouldn't get so *tetchy* with Zimmer if I were you. He'll smell the fear on you like a snake senses a mouse *and* he'll use it. While we're on the subject of do's and don'ts, please, don't pass him anything through the bars. He used a rolled-up glossy magazine to put one of my staff in a coma. Nearly killed her. He's softly spoken. Calm. Even charming when he wants to be. But beware. Behind those glassy eyes is the mind of a serpent. He'll strike at a moment's notice. I warn you—"

"So warned," Carver said.

"You'll have to sign this release form, detective. It removes liability from the hospital in case of injury or death." Forsmith slid a single-sided piece of dusty paper over to him and Carver slid a blue ballpoint pen over it.

"Not going to read it?"

"Read it a thousand times."

Forsmith took the paper and, looking at it, said, "Curious how they trusted him, isn't it? All those years, people telling him their pains—confession after confession—only to have him tear their tongues out, hmm?"

"I'm not interested in that," Carver said.

"Oh? What, may I ask, is your interest in the killer priest?"

"It's federal business, doctor. You mentioned Zimmer's medical review board. What sort of treatment has he had?"

"Is that not protected?" Forsmith asked, being cute.

"I could subpoena the information, or you could just tell me ..."

"Okay," Forsmith said carefully and thought for a second. "Did you know he's received clinical drug trials on the effectiveness of hallucinogenics—psilocybin and LSD— for his psychopathy?"

Carver shook his head. "No, I didn't. What was the result?"

"For the general population, very positive, it seems. For Zimmer specifically, well, he must've had something like close to fifteen trips, as many as Manson. Unaffected by any of them. Brain chemistry didn't change. He seems impervious to psychological examination. Unintelligible."

"I thought it was the Irish who were impervious."

"I see you know your Freud. Yes, well, quite but this is something different. We've never seen anything like it. Nobody has."

"Have you had any sessions with him?"

"Personally? Oh yes, in the early days. When he wasn't so worried about trying for good behavior. We spoke. Your name came up, naturally," Forsmith said.

"Naturally. What did you make of him?"

"Some things in life, Detective Carver, there simply aren't explanations for. A man who believes he is a god? Delusion. Grandiosity. A pure psychopath of the highest order. The purest one I've seen, certainly. Of that, there is no doubt. He was a surgeon of sorts, I gather. It's difficult to feel, a sense of—" he searched for the word by rubbing his forefinger and thumb together and licking his thin lips.

"Superiority?" Carver suggested.

"—when he's so articulate." Forsmith stopped and looked at Carver and held his gaze. He didn't continue. Instead, he stood up.

That touched a nerve.

"I must warn you, again, Detective. Ward Twenty—the black hole—has been deemed unfit for human use. Nothing has yet come of it, of course. They say it's a violation of human rights—*human*—rights. You understand? Adrian!" Forsmith called out. A big orderly with a shaved head appeared in the doorway. "Take Detective Carver to Ward Twenty please, Adrian."

"I told you when we spoke, Doctor. With all due respect, you simply can't expect me to meet Zimmer in the cell block."

"And why not?"

"Well, it's unfit for human habitation—for a start—but I'm on official Bureau business. I need an interview room. I need Zimmer feeling distanced from his familiar surroundings where he's the one in control. It would be absurd for me to wander down to his cell alone with no chaperone and no recording equipment. I need a record of our conversation. I might need to record this one too—"

"As I explained, Detective—"

"It's supervisory special agent ... but, please, call me sir."

Carver saw Forsmith's eye twitch again. Seemed a little warm under the collar.

"As I explained—"

"Listen—sorry to interrupt—I traveled across the country. I'm in the middle of a serial homicide investigation on behalf of the Federal Bureau of Investigation." Carver pulled out his cell phone and held it up for Forsmith to see. "I'm a federal agent. I will have a *federal* judge on the phone and get a subpoena so fast that you'll still be wondering how I did it a year from now. Look at my face, Doctor. You're supposed to be good at reading people? Do I look like someone you want to mess around with? You want to test me, see how far I am willing to take this. I almost want you to. But I'm in somewhat of a hurry."

Forsmith blushed pink.

"I need an answer," Carver said and shook his phone.

The orderly was still standing in the doorway. Without missing a beat, Dr. Forsmith looked at him and in a measured tone said, "Adrian, change of plan. Please put all the necessary steps together and get patient Zimmer from his cell into one of the interview rooms. Better make it interview room 'B', it's got the one-way glass and the digital recorder."

Forsmith looked at Carver.

"That'll be all, I expect? Please show yourself out. I have a busy schedule."

Carver stood. Forsmith didn't look up. He shuffled some papers and tried to look busy.

CARVER FOLLOWED Adrian down the corridor.

The orderly half-turned his head as they strode and said, "I'm gonna take you past Ward Twenty on our way."

They wound their way, turning left and right around long brightly lit corridors. A heavy iron gate crashed somewhere behind him and Carver got his first whiff of Ward Twenty.

Human feces and urine. The stink hit the back of his throat and he retched. He turned quickly put his arm on the wall and dry heaved. A thick bile taste. He spat it out, stood up, and wiped his hand across his mouth. Better to do it out here where Zimmer couldn't see.

The orderly waited for him to finish.

"I'll send a cleaner to fix that," Adrian said when Carver rejoined him.

The orderly unlocked another heavy gate.

"No toilets down here," Adrian said. "That's the reason for the smell. They shit in bedpans. Stick close to the far wall. They shouldn't throw anything at you, but if they do, you wanna be far as away as you can get."

"Charming."

Adrian pulled the gate open.

"We go this way."

Carver started walking. He heard shuffling and voices in the darkness behind the bars to his left. Water dripping from the ceiling. He glanced out of the corner of his eyes. Thought he saw shadows. Things moving in the dimness. His footsteps sounded heavy. His heartbeat made the blood *whoosh* in his ears. The closer he got the more he felt Hermann Zimmer's madness in his own mind.

"Just down here," Adrian said and led Carver into another brightly lit passageway. This reminded Carver more of a hospital than a prison. "Wait in here," the orderly said and showed Carver into the observation room behind the one-way glass.

Prison hadn't been kind to Hermann Zimmer.

Carver watched from behind the glass as they shuffled him into the interview room. He was shackled and blindfolded with an eye mask. The three orderlies were constantly speaking to him and one another, hyperaware and vigilant, explaining what they were doing and what would happen next. They locked his shackles to the floor beneath his chair and, when they were ready, one of the orderlies stood behind Zimmer and put his fingertips on the eye mask. He whipped it off like he was releasing a snake from a sack and moved away from the patient.

Zimmer shook his head violently from side to side, as a wet dog would, and let out a growl and bark of a disturbed man.

The orderlies hurried out.

Zimmer stopped shaking the cobwebs from his head and turned to peer at the mirror's glass.

"Just got to give them a show! Something to talk about over their warm beers. Is that you, Special Agent Carver?"

The voice sent a shiver down Carver's spine.

The hair on the back of his neck stood on end. Tried to swallow. Mouth too dry. Breathing shallowed.

He sighed and said under his breath, "Now or never," and felt like throwing up again.

CARVER WALKED into the interview room. It was brightly lit. A red dot in the top right corner of the room blinked from below the lens of the video camera.

Even seated Zimmer was a tall man. He was thinner now, with the long delicate hands of a pianist. His shoulders lacked some of the power Carver remembered. Maybe he'd only been larger in his mind. Fear amplified things. The way a rodent grows massive fangs when it scuttles past you in the kitchen.

"Augustine," Zimmer said in his slight Austrian accent. "A saint's name for a man wrestling with his demons. How *apt*."

He held Carver's glare. Zimmer was an unblinking type of man. His eyes were glassy, like a reptile. Carver stepped toward the interview table and Zimmer made a sudden move to stand. His chains pulled tight against the locks. Carver jumped.

Zimmer, from his half-raised position, stuck out a hand and gave Carver a smile.

"No handshake for old friends? Pity we couldn't meet in my cage. Of course, you'd have to excuse the state of the place. The smell. God awful. I've petitioned the court. No response yet, I fear."

Carver couldn't tell if his accent had softened in prison or hardened. It was still that of an educated man. Someone bilingual but who speaks their first language at home or in the company of their closest relatives. Someone who considers themselves superior at their strong knowledge of both. Carver saw the same well-read pocket Bible in the top pocket of his jumpsuit.

"Aren't you going to sit with me, Augustine?" Zimmer asked.

"I think I'll stand," Carver said and cleared his throat.

Zimmer closed his eyes and sniffed the air like a dog

lifting its nose to the wind. "And what's this?" Zimmer asked. "Vomitus on your breath, Special Agent Carver. Are you so pleased to see me?"

"I am. You decided to talk without your council present?"

"Have I? You forced me down here, Carver. Carver. Carver. God, I love that name. Don't worry, special ... You can speak freely, I'm not going to say anything that'd get you in trouble," Zimmer said.

"Thank you," Carver said.

"*Oh*, I see you're on your best behavior," Zimmer said. "Have you come to confess to your sin?"

"My sin?"

"Oh, yes, Gust. Your *sins*. That is why we're here after all, isn't it? The things you did. The things you brought upon yourself. The things you brought upon your family. How did you do it, anyway?"

Carver said nothing. He had this high-pitched whine in his ear.

"Tell me, Augustine, how does a man like you find peace after all the darkness? Prayer, confession, or is something less ... sanctified? Do regale me, I'm so devoid of *stimuli*."

"A man like me ..."

"You know, a man with no faith. A man can't be without prayer, or void of confession. Or do you trawl the street whores in Washington seeking your salvation?"

"I'm not here for small talk, Hermann."

Zimmer continued as if he never heard him. "You weren't fast *enough*. She was so soft and so sweet, wasn't she? But you saved your darling wife. How's Bethany? I miss her. Her smell."

Carver swallowed. "We don't see one another."

"What a pity. What's the matter, couldn't handle the

remorse? Survivors' guilt. I'm sure. Unfortunate ... Do you suffer, my special agent?"

Carver watched Zimmer's eyes. His face, leaning forward. Dry mouth. Flecks of spit. Full of venom and anticipation.

"You wear your guilt like a second skin, Augustine. It's palpable. Does it keep you awake at night, the things you've seen, the choices you made?"

"I don't sleep."

Zimmer relaxed. Like the air had gone out of a balloon. Carver was giving him what he wanted.

"Your sins haunt you. I wonder, if you could do it all again, would you still come after me?"

Carver was silent.

"Do you regret what you've done?"

"No."

"Are you angry at God for what he took from you?"

"Was it God?"

"Did you ever ask yourself, '*Why me?*'" Zimmer said. "He made me, after all. He *told* me what to do. So you can assume it was him. I'm merely the instrument."

"That's what you believe?" Carver said and choked up a little. The whine in Carver's ear went to a new, higher frequency. Carver swallowed but his throat felt like glue. His voice croaky.

"My turn now. I'm not the one behind bars, Hermann. Let's focus on you, and why you're here. I need to ask you something about your days of killing people."

"Are they finished?"

"Tell me one thing. When you killed your victims, you'd rip out their tongues. Why?"

"No foreplay?"

"Not today."

"So there will be other days."

"Why did you do it?"

"Are you working on a case, my special agent?"

Zimmer stayed silent for a moment. Let the question linger.

"Did you always cut them, right from the beginning, or was it something you acquired? Did you do it before or after you tried to burn holes in their brains—"

Zimmer, serious now, amusement gone from his face.

"You're rambling, Augustine. Don't do that. Take a beat. This is no fun at all. My *victims*, you say? Who says? Who says they're even dead, hmm? Who says they didn't get exactly what *they* wanted? Longed for. I might have said: 'You didn't see their dying breaths' but that isn't true, is it? You've seen plenty. Too much, really. You saw little Madeleine's last. The peacefulness on her face, even though she'd suffered terribly, she still wanted it—willed it—at the end. You saw that, didn't you?"

Carver felt a pain in the base of his throat. It was sharp-edged like a piece of flint stuck there. He didn't have to answer. And the demon who killed his daughter could read it on his face.

"Was it from the start?" Carver asked again more quietly.

Regain some composure. Hide your feelings. Don't let him see.

Zimmer snapped his fingers. "It's the Skinwalker, isn't it?"

Carver furrowed his brow. "You've heard about that?"

"It's all over the wires. I have an 'in' with some of the guards. They bring the tabloids. Thrilling stuff. Is that why you came back? For atonement."

"Guards?"

"Friends."

"Be straight."

"So I might be useful? I might have insights, Augustine.

Mightn't I? But insights come at a price. A heavy price. You understand how it works."

"You haven't taken enough from me?"

"Not nearly enough."

"Let's skip the theatrics, Hermann. What can you tell me about your method?"

"Method? My *modus operandi*. Did you know your *kink* the first time you had sex? Did Bethany? Or does it develop over time? Was it always there, lying dormant, and then it— poof—*awoke* and *spoke* and walked around like a *joke*? Or did you create it, invent it, ruminate on it?" Zimmer's voice was a low hiss now as if he was speaking through the mesh in a confessional booth. "You might have created her but— deep down—you know she belongs to me now. Your precious little girl. They all do. They're waiting for me."

Carver refused to rise to the bait. Instead, he waited. He knew he could outwait a psychopath, especially one as narcissistic as Zimmer. Finally, Zimmer broke his gaze and slumped back.

"Now it's my turn," Zimmer said. "Tell me how you did it."

"Did what?" Carver asked.

"You know exactly what. How you got off the floor? Your spleen practically on it there next to you; you slipping through your syrupy black blood." Zimmer eyes glazed. He purred at the memory. "How'd you do it?"

Carver had an answer. He knew what it was: the instinct of a father. The love he felt for his daughter. To save her. To stop her pain. A love that an insane mind like Zimmer's could never comprehend, or—if he could—would simply see as weakness.

"Is that how you keep yourself occupied? Thinking about the moment I caught you."

"Caught me? You should have killed me. This is a

holiday camp, Carver. A holiday camp. You know I have the power in here. Our esteemed colleague Dr. Forsmith has even graciously reinstated my prayer group. A small congregation, but devoted. Even some of the orderlies are involved. Everyone is looking for salvation. He took some persuading though."

"Is that why it smells like a tannery in here?"

Zimmer waved his hand and dismissed the idea like Carver was thinking too small. "Barely a thing," Zimmer said.

"I'll tell you if you help me ..."

"Help you?" Zimmer asked. "In these walls, Carver, every word, every gesture carries weight. You'd be surprised. Even the faintest whisper echoes through the halls and out into the world beyond these bars. Be careful what you wish for because there's another one, isn't there? Another one ... another one. Another one of us."

"Of you ... yes."

"*Oh*, come now. Dear Augustine. You think you're so different from me. You know perfectly well what you are. You can't fool me. I've seen too many." Carver furrowed his brow. "Please, don't look confused, or try to feign it. You too killed a man. Didn't you? Judge Carver. Executioner Carver. You shot a man in cold blood, didn't you?"

Carver shook his head. "You and I are nothing—"

"Have you begged the Lord's forgiveness? You haven't, have you. You feel no conscience about it; why? I'll tell you. Because he *deserved* it. Didn't he? Who are you to judge me?"

Carver wasn't going to get into a debate on morals from a convicted serial murderer. If it helped him get more information, he was going to play the game. And this was a game he was all-in on now.

"If you help with this, I'll tell you how I did it," Carver said.

"No."

"What then?"

"You already know. My lawyer has by now been in touch, no doubt. In fact, it's what I assumed this meeting was about, otherwise, I'd never have taken it."

"You want me to testify at your parole hearing?"

"My psychiatric evaluation. Yes. See if I'm better, cured by the loving hand of Lord Jesus Christ ... all sinners deserve redemption, don't they, Augustine? Our demons are in our minds. Let's wash our minds clean and start with divine souls."

"So you can soil it again?"

"Tell them I'm cured," Zimmer said.

"You think I'll say nice things?"

"Why wouldn't you? You're not still mad, are you?"

"Mad?" Carver asked. He nearly laughed. "No, Zimmer, I'm not mad." Carver looked into that deranged unblinking blue eye. Carver chewed the side of his cheek, thinking.

"Dangle me a carrot, why don't you?" Carver said. "Just tell me one thing. Have you heard about them?"

"Have they left anything out?" Zimmer asked.

"Yes."

"Like what?"

"What he does to them after they're dead. And, before."

"What does he do, special agent?"

Zimmer was getting hot now. Curious. He licked his lips. The facade Carver always knew was slipping.

"Why did you cut their faces?" Carver asked.

"Is that what he's doing?"

"In a manner of speaking."

"Is there a file?" Zimmer asked.

"Yes."

"May I see?"

"First tell me."

"Why? Why ... why." Zimmer sighed deeply. "Have you ever seen wolves toying with the carcass of their prey, Carver? Why would they do that? Who can say. I am as God made me." Carver waited. "If you let me see the file, maybe, I can shed some light on why *he's* doing it," Zimmer said. "I spoke to a lot of them, you know? The ones who came to see me. Drawn to a cure like moths to a flame."

"They're trophies."

"Yes, but it depends. What it is he's doing with them ... It's a wonderful thing that no one seems to understand. Once you kill them, they're yours. You should know ... You *own* them. Their essence. Their souls. And no one knows them quite like you do. Not as they *are* but as they *were*. Or how you made them. Forever. What better way than to keep a little bit of them with you. To remind you. To relive the moment. Again and again."

"You think he's—"

"Let me see the file."

"Why did you cut pieces out of them?"

"Like I cut lumps out of you?"

Zimmer smiled cruelly and showed Carver his stained-brown teeth.

"How's the eye?" Carver asked.

"In the land of the blind, the one-eyed man is God."

"I meant the other one. The one I ripped out with my fingers. The one that's mush. The one I scraped off with the heel of my boot."

The whole time Carver stared at the scarred pit in Zimmer's head. "You aren't going to be entering any beauty pageants anytime soon, you know?"

"That's the wrong question, Agent Carver. Isn't it ...?"

"Yeah, change the subject. What's the right question?"

"Surely the right question is; what is it about the victim? What is it about having a piece of them for himself? No discount-beer answers, please. In a logical way. This is about his specific fantasy. Have you considered his own appearance? Of course you have. You're no fun. No disfigurement or mutilation of the genital areas, no?

"No, nothing overtly sexual at all."

"I can't assume to speak for this type of savagery, Agent Carver. But," in a whisper now, "Could you imagine the terrified faces of all of the victims?"

Some grotesque face coming to take yours from you. Like each subsequent victim taking the place of the former one, Carver thought and tried to un-imagine it.

"Embodying them, becoming them, using them—as one does a vessel—to cover his own actions. Maybe have some sort of disassociation between owning them, owning a piece of them, and him being complicit in his little adventures," Zimmer said.

"So how is he choosing them?"

"The million dollar question, my special Carver. Now for mine. Would you help them come to understand they should release me, to save the *next* victim?"

Carver always quit while he was ahead. He had a headache. Still felt like he might be sick. He looked at Zimmer's bright blue expectant eye. Carver saw him for what he was. He hid it so well though. No wonder he got away with it for so long.

"Time's up," Carver said and tapped his watch.

Zimmer smirked. "Hurry back now, Augustine. You know where to find me."

Carver opened the door to the room and left it open. The orderlies stood up from their slouched positions. Carver was already walking down the hall as Zimmer's voice echoed behind him.

"Testify at my hearing and I'll help you catch him, Carver!"

Zimmer the Ripper. Carver burst outside and felt a wave of relief. He'd broken the surface and could breathe again. He'd been weighed down. Now he felt light. His head spinning. Walking on an inflatable mattress. Get you what you needed? He asked himself. He felt he might be sick and stopped and put his hands on his knees. He took some deep breaths.

"Maybe," he said.

15

IT WAS THE BOREDOM. The mundanity that got to him. Hurry up and wait. Waiting for guards. Idiot nurses. Waiting for dinner. Medicine. Books. God, the *waiting*.

Zimmer sat alone chained to the table, and waited. He pulled hard on the chains so they crashed against the metal legs and called out, "Oh, Julian!" He sang the vowels in lurid long and looping *basso profundo*. Then he waited.

An orderly arrived. He leaned in the open door and looked at Zimmer, assessing his mood. "We don't want any trouble now y'hear, Father Zimmer?"

Zimmer had given up telling them to stop calling him 'father'. It didn't matter to them. The orderlies. The staff. He was ordained and that still meant something. The Church has power.

To them, calling him 'father' was a sign of respect. A sign of his standing. He might've been the one in chains but they knew who had the real power. Didn't they? Didn't they just.

"Yes, I hear, Julian."

"Good," the orderly said and moved toward him.

"But I'm not moving."

Julian stopped and looked at him to see if he was joking.

Zimmer had a sense of humor, after all. He could find fun in the mundane. Sometimes. Julian was watching to see if this was one of those times. He glanced at his colleague. A fellow orderly named Kingsley. A white man with a nose that looked like it had been broken once too many times and short shaved black hair that he was always rubbing with the palm of his hand. Kingsley shrugged.

"I'm not playing, Julian," Zimmer said low and slow so they would understand. "Get Forsmith."

"Now hold on a minute," Julian was saying. "Now listen here ..." he said, flustered.

Zimmer calmed him. "I know you're afraid to listen to me and to go and bother Dr. Forsmith. I *do* understand that. You believe me, don't you?"

Julian thought for a moment and nodded.

"All right then. That's good. That means we understand one another, does it not?" Julian creased his brow, unsure. "Now, Julian. Part of an orderly's job is to look after the welfare and best interests of their patients, is it not?"

"Yes it is, mmhmm," Julian agreed.

"But one must also think of their own self-preservation, mustn't one?"

Julian looked unsure of where this was going. Kingsley began rubbing his head and looking worried. There was some unseen, unspoken, but knowable tension in the little room. Like it was suddenly getting hot. And Zimmer's calm, measured tone built and built, and becoming more forceful as he spoke.

"I only say this, Julian, because if we were to consider the discomfort you might feel, fleeting though it will be, when you inevitably interrupt Dr. Forsmith and contrast that with the unbearable agony and long-lasting suffering you will endure if you *don't* fetch him when I *goddamn* tell you too, well, I shouldn't have to make a vow but I will. By the eternal love of all that is Holy, I will—" Zimmer whispered the final words. That was enough for the orderly.

"Okay, okay, okay ..." Julian relented and cooled Zimmer down.

All the orderlies had heard the stories. Whether they were rumors that he'd started himself, or they were true, Zimmer ruled the psychiatric hospital by fear. He stared at the desk and didn't look up. His chest rose and fell. He had spittle dripping from his snarled-up mouth.

"Go on and get him then ..." Zimmer said through his clenched jaw. Both orderlies turned and left.

Zimmer waited.

HE HEARD the good doctor's footsteps from far away. He closed his eyes and listened as the echoes grew louder. To Zimmer, it was like some Buddhist gong chiming a frequency of rolling rings. And then—*poof*—like magic, Dr. Forsmith was standing before him blathering on about nothing important.

"This better be extremely important, Zimmer. I was in the middle of a very important phone call—right in the middle—you've dragged me down here—"

Zimmer looked up at him, blank-faced, and raised his hand so the restraints pulled against the desk.

"Stop. Talking."

Forsmith cleared his throat and said, "Yes, well ..."

"Julian!" Zimmer called. The orderly came in from the corridor and poked his head round the door. "Come here a moment, Julian."

He stepped into the room. "Tell me something," Zimmer said. "You saw what happened to the inmates in Ward Twenty. Why'd they do that with their stool?"

"Oh—ah—because you told them to, Father Zimmer, sir."

"And why do you think they did what I said?"

"Gosh, well, ah," Julian glanced at Forsmith and said, "I figure you got some kind of hold over them," Julian said.

"What sort of hold?"

Julian shook his head. "I don't know, Father."

"You do. Go on ... then you can leave."

"They say it's some kind of black magic. Voodoo or something. You control them with your thoughts."

Forsmith scoffed. Zimmer looked at him.

"And, Julian, the orderlies gossip about who is moving where and why, and who's screwing which nurse. Don't they?"

Julian swallowed.

"What are they saying about why they're moving me to the padded-wall ward?" Zimmer asked.

"Well, sir, they sayin' it's on account of the Feds coming down here. Not wanting 'em to find out about the stench down there."

"Thank you, Julian." Zimmer moved his hand again and said, "Now close the door."

Forsmith glanced at the restraints and then at the door.

"Yes, best to shut it," Forsmith said and swallowed.

"Thank you," Zimmer said. "Now *I* will talk. You may sit, if you wish, but I understand if you prefer to stand. You like to look down at people from on high. Then there's little old defenseless me. Chained. As you can see. Now. You may think you have very important business and that it is all terribly meaningful ... but it's not. Believe me. It isn't. None of it matters one jot. It's the furthest thing from it. Okay?"

Forsmith made some strange movements like he had a tic or some kind of spasm. But he got the message. Zimmer was telling him exactly who was in control.

"That's because, Doctor, while you may run this facility from outside, as you and I both know, I run it from the inside. And *you* tell *me*, Doctor. Which is more important?"

Forsmith cleared his throat and said, "What do you want?"

"You said it yourself, didn't you, *Doctor*? He has a demonic-like possession over the other patients, especially the violent or criminally insane. That's what you said, isn't it?"

Forsmith started winking one eye erratically and moved his head like his neck was sore and he was trying to relieve the pain. The truth hurt, it seemed.

"Let me put it this way," Zimmer said. "What is going to make your life here easier, hmm? Give you more control. That's what it's all about, this life after all, isn't it? Control. The illusion of it. The reality of it. The need for it. Would my *not* being here *not* give you lots and lots and *lots* more control?"

Forsmith stopped twitching and stared directly at Zimmer. Now he was getting on the same page.

"Ah, now you understand," Zimmer said. "That's what your grossly important phone call was about, wasn't it? You were on the phone to the body corporate to deny them access to me." Zimmer leaned forward until his chest was digging into the desk. "Weren't you?"

Forsmith swallowed and looked at the floor.

"They'll have access. Understand?"

"But it's too much, Hermann, please. Can't you see? We don't have the—"

"*Bap-bap-bap-bap*," Zimmer said and pushed his fingertips together like a mouth snapping shut. "They *shall* have access."

Forsmith's tic was back. He blinked like his vision had become blurred.

126

"Remember what happened last winter," Zimmer said. "How you had to move. How someone found out where you lived with your wife, Molly, and daughters, Nicola and Elizabeth, remember, hmm? How you were so scared you urinated in your trousers when you saw me, hmm? I remember. I remember well. How is your new house by the way? Have the children settled into their new school? I understood they had to be moved for their own safety."

"What do you want?"

"I want you to go back to the council of your superiors and convince them to approve access. I want what you want. You want rid of me from here. And, I want that too. You don't want the violent criminals attacking your orderlies at random. Without provocation. When they least expect it. At the most mundane moments of the day. Do you? I don't want to have to make that happen, but I will ..." Zimmer sat back. "What on earth would happen to your career then?"

Forsmith looked at the floor.

"And one last thing, Forsmith, I want you to reinstate my weekly prayer group for orderlies *and* inmates."

"You ... I can't—"

"I don't want to hear it, Doctor. Now I want you to leave. I want you to think about your family. And I want you to not force me to make them part of this. *Capito*?"

16

WHENEVER HE BREATHED out he made a high-pitched whistling sound from his nose. Inhale, *tweee*. Inhale, *tweee*.

Sometimes he wondered if it was one of the things that made him mad. Drove him insane. Driven to insanity. What a thought. His eyes and delicate fingers concentrated on the glinting point of the needle as he sewed.

He could see the individual hairs of the animal's fur through the magnifying glass. The animal fur was thick and the dried skin needed effort to puncture and pull the thread through. He wore his work goggles. His face was right up against the clear, thick magnifying glass.

It was on a mechanical arm, locked securely to his desk with a vice.

He was working on his art. That was his true desire. To be respected. Like Carl Akeley. They'd never be able to turn him down then. He'd be an equivalent, albeit in another medium, but so what? Desire. Desire. Desire. For recognition. For gratitude. For acknowledgement. No. It's about art. The art. The art. Art is all.

Listen to me, he heard a voice say. The voice inside his head. Those competing voices. Shouting over one another.

All the time. Only when I'm working are they quiet, he thought. All except one.

The first time he did it—well—now he just wished it wasn't his first time, is all. To him, it was just some girl. Just some girl walking in the fields at dusk. Alone. All alone.

As per usual, there were two parts of him. One part wanted to help her, guide her home, make sure she was safe. Tuck her in. The other wondered what her head would look like on a stake without a face. Then something inside just made him do it. He didn't know what it was. The Black Dog, he called it. It was in the shadows with red eyes. Breath that stank. It just breathed on his brain and he got the urge. The urge. Uncontrollable. He used to try—controlling it—now, he couldn't. It had been let loose. The Black Dog. No way of getting it back. It was wild and feral and on a mission of chaos.

It was rushed and ugly and exhausting. So terribly exhausting. His first time. Her last. It'd taken so long to strangle her with his hands. He wouldn't have guessed it would've taken so long or that his hands and arms would've burned so badly. She was writhing and looking up at him as she gagged. He liked the look on her face when she realized her life was slipping away. Then that look when she knew she was going to be his forever. The look of pleasantness and submission. The look of not caring. The look of willing it to happen. Welcoming it. Like slipping into a warm bath.

He couldn't enjoy it. He'd been so scared. Scared someone would find him. String him up like he'd seen on the news. He panicked. He knew he didn't want anyone else to see the peaceful look she'd given him. No one else could have it. She was his. He searched around and found a sharp-edged rock and picked it up out of the soil and used it to bash her head in. The sharp slate stone sliced her face up good. How he'd wished he could've kept it. That look. Her gift to him. She belonged to him now. Always. His gift to her. He thought of her often. She deserved more. So much more. He regretted not giving it to her.

He wished he could go back with what he knew now and do it again. He wondered if her look would be different. More fearful, like the second one. He'd seen her alone on the beach. He'd seen her before that. He'd followed her but she didn't know. She couldn't know. No one could. He could change. He was a master of changing. Shifting. He felt invisible. No one ever saw him. If they did, they looked right through him. Like he was made of glass. Like he was a chameleon. That's what his mother always called him. On account of him being thin and wiry, he was able to blend in. She said he was her little chameleon. He was always startling her. She never heard him enter a room. She could feel his presence though. She'd jump and holler.

The second time was better. Now he had his tools. Every artist needed their tools, he thought. Ever seen a sculptor without a chisel, a surgeon without a scalpel? Course you haven't. Think I'm stupid? You're stupid. You're all so stupid. Idiotic. Lazy. You people. I could *spit* I'm so mad, he thought. But I mustn't. Plaster on the smile. Keep them docile and locked into their listless lives. Think they're so smart. Not smart enough.

This was a smart neighborhood, he'd thought to himself then. Big houses, with big walls. Electric gates. Video cameras. Alarms. None of it mattered. He pulled his cap a little lower. It was a nice sunny day. People going about their business. He pressed the plastic button on the intercom and waited. Then he heard a *clunk*, and the electric motor pulled the big black gates open. They welcomed him. He stepped through. Through the gates of hell and turned. Turned to look back. The world as it was before. Before it all changed. Changed into something new.

He breathed through his nose and made his way up the drive, calmly. Glanced up at the cotton ball clouds still in the sky. He went to the side door. The servants' entrance led to the pantry and the kitchen. He heard excited shouting—I'll get it, I'll get it—and running, and then the door pulled open. She immediately put her finger in her mouth and crossed her legs like she needed the toilet. Don't be afraid, he wanted to say but he couldn't lie. He could tell she knew. Children were perceptive.

"Hello, little girl," he said. "Is your mommy and daddy home?" But he knew they weren't.

———

Ruth Minnesota climbed the rickety old wooden stairs to the attic, heart pounding like a drum in her chest. Was it the climb or her nerves, she wondered as she took deep breaths. She raised her hand, paused for a moment, then rapped her knuckles against the door. She didn't hear anything.

She pushed it open. Maybe he wasn't here. Granny said he would be. Maybe he was gone. Maybe she wouldn't have to deal with him. Granny said he was somewhat difficult. She didn't know what that meant in *old woman* speak. Her grandmother was of the subtle and delicate old-school of southern women. She never said exactly what she meant. It was simply inferred.

She saw a barely lit attic room. In the pallid glow, she saw him. Edward, the shop's enigmatic caretaker. He sat with his back to her, his frame almost blending in with the shadows. A halo framed his head, his eyewear glinted in the white work light.

"Edward?" she called out, trying to keep her voice steady. He didn't respond. The silence loomed large. Suddenly she was losing her nerve. Was she intruding? Should she leave him alone? No. She's promised her grandmother.

"Whatcha working on Eddie?" Minny asked louder.

She could see the back of Edward Derange as he hunched over his worktop. She had an eerie feeling. She had no idea what was in the dark corners of the attic. It had a putrid smell too. Like her teacher's old biology classroom. She could smell formaldehyde and turpentine. The man at the work desk spun around. She saw now that he was wearing thick work goggles. Edward now looked stickly thin and long to her. Different. She hadn't known what to expect but it wasn't that.

"I'll turn the light on—" Minny said and reached for the switch.

"No, don't do that!" Derange shouted and lurched forward with his arm outstretched. She was taken aback and retrieved her hand.

Derange looked like he was searching for what to say. He let out a long high-pitched whine.

"It-it-it's just that the bright lights affect my sights," and indicated the goggles on his face. He had a voice like a child.

"Granny said you'd be up here, thought I'd pop in to say 'hi'," she smiled. "So, 'hi'," she said and lifted her hand.

"Hi," Derange said back.

"She's sick you know?"

"Who?"

"My granny."

"Who are you?"

"Oh! Yes ... ah, I'm sorry. I'm *Ruth*. Minny. People call me Minny on account of my surname. Minnesota. Not Mouse."

She stood there smiling waiting for his reaction. There was none. Minny's smile faded. She felt very alone. There was a cold wind in the attic. "Mrs. Spritely's granddaughter," she said.

"Okay."

Minny waited for him to respond, perhaps introduce himself, say hello, show a hint of recognition and familiarity, and smile at her. He did none of those things. Maybe that's what Granny meant when she said he was 'kinda weird' but 'harmless'.

"Are you ... are you Eddie?" She tried again. Uncertainty had crept into her voice. She couldn't shake it.

"Edward," he said. "Yes."

He turned his back to his stitching.

"Whatcha working on there? Granny said you were good with your hands."

Derange looked back at her over his shoulder. Eyes more menacing this time. His words muffled into his collar he said, "Eleanor's been talking to you about me?"

Minny took a step toward him but stopped. She felt like she'd better go.

"I'm sorry—I see I'm disturbing you, I'm going to go, okay? We can talk another time."

His lack of interest was unsettling. He was curt and the lack of eye contact made her feel very uneasy. She was now aware that she was not welcome and started to feel a deep sense of unease. The attic felt even colder than before. She got scared. He lifted his head. Almost like he could sense her fear. Her heart raced. She needed to leave.

"I-I-I-I just wanted to let you know Mrs. Spritely—Eleanor—was very sick in the hospital ..." she said. She was rambling and turned toward the door, looking for a way out.

Derange didn't say anything. Then as she was about to duck out, more loudly than before, he said, "Is she going to be all right?"

"Huh?" she turned and looked at him again. "It's—ah—not looking, well, they don't quite know what is wrong with her. I came down only after she lost consciousness,

you know? They think it might be some sort of infection
..."

"Do they ..." He said and stood for the first time.

He was tall and very thin. It seemingly took him only two strides to get across the room. She cowered slightly, braced herself, and looked up at him. He was standing over her. His eyes distorted by the lenses of the goggles strapped to his head. She jumped as he raised his long, thin, fingers toward her and held out his hand toward her. She reached out and took just the tips of his fingers. They were remarkably soft.

He leaned forward and very quietly said, "Pleasure to make your acquaintance, Ruth."

It sounded like something he'd been trained to say, like someone who'd learned one sentence in English and repeated it by rote upon each new meeting.

"I'm sure we'll see more of one another but not here. Understand? Eleanor and I have an understanding. This is my studio, you understand? Private."

"Yes but—"

He raised his hand. "Private. Thank you. Goodbye."

He slammed the door behind her and she flinched and hurried down the creaky old stairs. She was in tears and said under her breath, "What've I got myself into, *God*, what've I got myself into."

She burst out the glass doors of the antique shop and into the cobbled street and the sunshine.

She gasped for air and closed her eyes and breathed and calmed down.

EDWARD DERANGE WENT BACK to his workstation. He adjusted the chair and got comfortable. He was hunched over the magnifying glass again looking down at his creation. The bright shiny-tinged shell of a Chesapeake blue crab lay on the worktop. In place of the head and eyes part of its shell he stitched a baby sloth head. It'd been quite some work. First, of course, sourcing these exotic animals and then the painstaking process of performing taxidermy on them. It was his creation. A kind of hybrid nightmare. For an imaginary gallery opening he'd invented called, Ixionidae. Or Hippocentaur. He hadn't decided. After the half-man, half-horse in Greek mythology. These were his nightmares. The sloth's expression was a gaping mouth open in a terrified-looking scream. Like he'd screamed. Like he'd looked when they turned him into a half-man. He lifted the needle to finish stitching the sloth head to the crab shell and touched the tip of it with his finger. It was sharp. That's where she'd touched him. On the tip of his hand. Who was that sad little person. Frumpy Minny Mouse Minnesota. *Frumpesota*. Who was she? The old witch's granddaughter. She'd never mentioned her. Not in the five years he lived in the attic. And why was that? Had she forgotten. No. She'd only started losing her mushy gray matter when he'd fed her the syrup of ipecac. God, what a slow process. Feeding her soups laced with ipecacuanha. Helping her as she weakened. Then she fell down the stairs. Finally, she was on her way out. But now this person. This Minny. What did she want? Aware of the voices echoing in his mind. Accusations, praise, threats, applause. Each wanted control. Burdens and inspiration. He also knew he was a *creator*. The power. An artist. Crafting a world from the remnants of reality.

There she'd gone, footsteps echoing away. Minny, the lively one. He was aware, suddenly, of the dark room. So quiet. So still. Wraps itself around me like an old friend, he thought. She'd left, a good thing, that. Poking around, snooping where she shouldn't. Too bold—that one—yet too naive, she doesn't understand. The world spins in such peculiar ways, and she ... she's just caught in the whirl. A force sucking her toward me. Like a leaf in the wind, her destiny isn't hers any longer. It's in the eye of the storm. And in my hands.

Her face. Her face was burned into his mind. That fleeting image. Would it look better with different eyes, perhaps? Blue ones? Gray ones? Ones that have seen more life—more death—than hers. Questions, questions. Swirling like a whirlwind. A madness. My madness. My reality.

She doesn't know, Minny doesn't. She doesn't know the size of the storm she's stepped into. Does she feel it, he wondered, the undercurrent, the threat lurking under this calm surface? She thinks she's in control. She thinks wrong. How fragile she is. Illusions shatter, *oh*, how they shatter.

She's in my world now, Minny, the bright-eyed one. She doesn't belong here, doesn't fit into my symphony of chaos and beauty. But could she? Her, in the attic, among my creatures.

She'll resist, she'll fight. Good, good, that's good. The struggle, the fear, the horror. Feeder of the chaos. They scream. They beg. They plead. Then they break. And silence, sweet silence. She'll be beautiful.

Oh, Minny, Minny, you opened the wrong door.

17

Augusta

"Ingrid! Where the fuck is this ..."

The boss was shouting from his stool. She brushed the skirt of her maid's uniform and her eyes darted uneasily.

She'd only been in the job for two weeks and was petrified. She was scared of losing the job—sure—but she was even more afraid of keeping it. Señor Dufresne was *loco*. Her sister Jasmin Martinez had told her so. Jasmin had been the maid in the Dufresne mansion for the past three years. Before she got pregnant. She said she didn't know who the father was but Ingrid thought she was lying. Why lie? She often wondered. Why lie. What did she have to hide?

"Ingrid, you bitch!" She heard Mr. Dufresne yelling. God, how she wished he would be silent.

"Coming, Mister," Ingrid called out and hurried to the kitchen. Bastien Dufresne was sitting on a high stool at the white marble kitchen counter.

"Bastard," he swore and scooped another mouthful of

the Venezuelan-style chili con carne into his mouth. He was sweating. "Oh, Christ!" Ingrid hated cooking hot food for him because he took the Lord's name in vain in a display of pleasure. She crossed herself and said a silent prayer. She felt somehow complicit. All the time she used to watch Señor Dufresne. He was a strange man. He was not old but his eyes were tired. They were always wet. Wet like he was full of emotion but also they stared, dull, looking all the time without seeing. He wiped his brow with a white silk napkin. Then blew his nose. "Goddamn! This is hot."

The buzzer for the front gate rang.

"Answer it!" Señor Dufresne shouted. "But for Christ's sake, I'm not here. Tell them we moved or something, not known at this address."

Ingrid ran to pick up the handset and answer the gate.

Mrs. Dufresne came down. She looked elegant as usual. A long white dress. She moved like a swan.

"Who is it?" Mrs. Dufresne asked. "Not the gardener, I saw him cleaning the pool again. I swear he does it just to look in my bedroom window."

Thank God, I am saved, Ingrid thought. Mrs. Dufresne will save me. Ingrid handed the phone to Mrs. Dufresne who removed her earring as she took the phone and said, "Yes, who is this please."

Ingrid stood watching her. They had both been married before, her sister told her. They'd only been together for a few years and already slept in different rooms. She was far more intelligent than him. See if he notices it. See if he can tell. Be careful, Jasmin had said. Mr. Dufresne thinks all women love him. Be careful late at night. Her sister had left the house to have her child. She didn't know who the father was, she said. Never tell a lie to Mrs. Dufresne. Never.

"Yes, okay," Mrs. Dufresne said into the receiver. She pressed the button to open the gates. She hung up the phone. "Ingrid, there will soon be someone at the door. Go and meet them please."

"Yes, missus," Ingrid said and did a small curtsy and hurried off. The front doorbell chimed. She lifted the heavy cast iron latch and used her weight to pull the heavy door open.

"Who is it?" she heard Mr. Dufresne yell.

She was looking at two people. A man and a woman. The woman's hair was pulled back and she was wearing dark sunglasses like a man. She was dressed in a suit like a man too. The man was tall and said, "Hi, how are you doing? We're here to see Mr. Dufresne."

"Can I say to him who is it you are? I suppose to ask your name."

———

CARVER TOOK out his identification and flipped it open for the maid to see.

"I'm Special Agent Carver, this is Special Agent Sandling, from the Federal Bureau of Investigation."

The maid pulled the door open wider and ushered them inside. Carver would never get used to being around rich people.

The special agents were taken along a long passageway to a sitting room that looked like it had never been sat in. Some of his friends' grandparents had rooms like that. Just for show. Something elegant that was never used. Sandling was inspecting the art on the walls. The maid disappeared and Carver and Sandling glanced at one another when they heard the neat *click-clack* of expensive shoes on the hardwood floor. A model-skinny woman entered the room with her bony arm extended in greeting. She smiled with movie star teeth and had gold jewelry hanging from every limb. It jangled like a cowbell as she moved. Her big brown eyes were calm and curious and open wide as she said, "Mr. Carver?" She shook his hand and held onto it just a bit longer than was necessary. She was sensual. "You must be Agent Sandling, welcome. How can we accommodate you?"

He liked how she sounded. Her voice soft. Demure tone. Like she'd never gotten riled up by anything before.

"We'd like to speak to you and your husband about your *au pair*, Freya Silvstedt."

"Oh, that poor girl," Mrs. Dufresne said. Her face suddenly creased in pain. "Of course! Anything we can do. Although, I believe we've told the investigating police what we know already. An unfortunate accident of timing and events. Only, my husband is unfortunately indisposed—for the moment."

"Indisposed," Sandling said and put her hand on her hips and her tongue in her cheek. The corners of Mrs. Dufresne's mouth lifted ever so slightly.

"Yes, my dear, you see, *my husband*—because he does his hobby for a living—doesn't feel that many of life's conventions apply to him. Do you understand?"

"No," Sandling said.

"Well, I'm afraid you've come at a bad time. You see, mid-afternoon is when he has Ingrid, our Venezuelan helper, blend him up *authentic* margaritas while he watches the racing from Hong Kong on his satellite dish. My husband doesn't realize Ingrid is not Mexican and that margaritas don't come from Venezuela but as long as he believes she is, and they do, we're *all* happier."

"Does your husband gamble on the horses too, Mrs. Dufresne?" Carver asked. She paused, thinking about the question. "You see, we're federal agents and tend to frown on that kind of thing, gambling being illegal n'all. And, since we're in your home voluntarily from yourselves—"

"You're within your rights," Mrs. Dufresne said, putting the rest of it together for herself.

"I think it might be best if you follow me to the pool house where we may catch Bastien before he sinks one too many tequilas. That okay with you?"

They followed Mrs. Dufresne's white flowing dress through the rooms. Her tight ponytail bounced as she walked. Sandling was looking up and spinning around taking in the modern art and billboard-sized black and white photographs on the enormously tall walls.

"What is it your husband does for a living, if you don't mind me asking?" Sandling asked.

Mrs. Dufresne half-turned and glanced at her as she walked. She looked bemused. "You don't know?"

"Famous photographer," Carver whispered to her under his breath.

"Quite famous," Mrs. Dufresne said. "He's worked for all the top designers at one time or another. They always come to him. He discovered many of the supermodels you see on television today."

"Impressive," Sandling said and dropped the corners of her mouth and nodded. "Not my world but impressive."

They walked out the back of the mansion and into the sunlight.

"Gosh, that's the biggest pool I've ever seen," Sandling said under her breath. It looked like the slow ride at a water-park. It meandered all around with little shaded sections and large ferns and overhanging palms. Turquoise water. Diamond clarity.

On the far side, Carver saw Bastien Dufresne sitting on his plush outdoor furniture. He sipped from a goldfish bowl filled with green margarita mix and slammed his fist on the tabletop as he swore at the television. He glanced over as he saw them coming.

"Oh, God. What now?" Dufresne said.

Out the corner of his eye, Carver saw their pool boy scooping leaves with a net on a long pole. He wore a trucker cap and watched the water. Dark hair and dark skin. He didn't look Latino though. He kept fishing for leaves.

"Do your servants have the necessary paperwork to be employed in this country, Mr. Dufresne?" Carver asked by way of a greeting.

Dufresne threw his head back and laughed. "Hell, throw them all out I say! Eh, Ingrid. You can go back to Tijuana, eh?" He laughed again.

"Yes, Mister," Ingrid said.

"What about your pool boy?"

Mrs. Dufresne went and touched Carver on the arm and said lightheartedly as she glanced over at the pool boy. "Oh, that's our gardener from our *gardening* service. Jefferey something or other." Then louder calling over and waving to him, "You're American aren't you Jeffery? American?" Carver followed her gaze as the gardener moved out of sight behind some big potted palms.

"He's American I think," Mrs. Dufresne said. "Anyway, there's something more serious to discuss, isn't there sweetheart? They want to know about Freya."

"Christ, we've told everything to the police already," Dufresne said. "Wasting taxpayer time and money."

"Don't scoff at the people, dear, they're just trying to help."

Sandling popped. "Excuse me, how dare—" Carver put out his hand to stop her and gave her a cautionary look. He saw her bite her tongue.

"Sit doggy," Dufresne said and picked up his drink. He took a long pull on it and smacked his lips.

"Mr. Dufresne, I'm Agent Carver, this is Agent Sandling.

We'd sure appreciate it if you could answer a few of our questions to the best of your ability."

"You sure would, huh?" Dufresne laughed and mocked Carver's way of talking.

"I sure would," Carver said and smiled.

Dufresne smiled and looked up at Carver and said, "You know what? I like you. Don't know why. I just do. Just then you made me like you ... pull up a chair. Ask your questions. We feel terrible about what happened to Freya."

They both sat down. Ingrid had made herself scarce.

"Do you? Why's that?" Sandling asked. It was harsh and accusatory and Carver stepped in.

"What my partner means is, besides what you've already told the police, perhaps there's something you remember about the day or the night before the incident that you think may, or may not, be of help?"

Carver heard Mrs. Dufresne's gold jewelry making a *tink-tink-tink* sound. He looked up at her and she stopped tapping her foot and took her thumbnail out of her mouth. Dufresne followed Carver's eyes and glanced up at her too.

"Why don't you go inside and make sure they're getting things ready for dinner?"

His wife nodded. "If you'll excuse me," she said and moved like she was floating away.

"Sorry," Dufresne said and looked at the horse racing on TV. "What were you saying?"

"Anything suspicious? About the day?" Sandling prompted him.

"Listen, you say *au pair*, right? I say babysitter. My wife is the fancy-faced bitch, all right? She's the one comes from money. Not me. I made everything I have, all right? Freya was a nice kid. She used to model for me sometimes. Teen fashion. Fast fashion, you understand? When she needed a little extra money she used to babysit for us too."

"If she used to work for you, what was she doing at the York house?"

Dufresne picked up the remote, turned the volume down, and faced Carver square on, resting on his elbows. "I didn't say she worked for me, I said she used to babysit."

"Where are your kids?" Sandling asked.

"With their mother. My first wife. She don't want them hanging around here right now, what with all that's happened."

"What all's that?" Sandling asked.

"You know, the murders. All that." Dufresne's face looked like he'd tasted something bad and was ready to spit it out. "It's disgusting. Horrible."

"Yes," Carver said. "Why was she at the Yorks?"

"Like I said, she needed money and they needed a babysitter. We know them from the club. *Knew* them."

"Golf?" Sandling asked.

Dufresne gave her a sideways look. "Yacht, okay?"

"The yacht club. All right," Carver said. "Think of anyone that would want to hurt her? Any reason they targeted her?"

"Hey, another little girl died there too, you know? What makes you think it had anything to do with Freya?"

"Gee, I don't know, Mr. Dufresne," Sandling said, lifting her hand to her chin. "Perhaps it's the fact that she was the only one brutalized by the killer; how about that?"

"You don't call being hung by a belt from a basement pipe brutal?"

"Who said it was a belt?" Carver said.

"I did, just then," Dufresne picked a newspaper up from the chair beside him and slapped it down on the glass table-top. "And they say so, right there," and jabbed his finger at the paper. Carver turned his head and spun the paper a little to see.

The byline was from Jessica Webb. Damn her.

"It's all anybody's talking about, okay? People are scared out of their minds. Everybody's buying guns. Some poor S.O.B. is liable to get shot walking his dog."

"Yeah, well," Carver said, "It wasn't a belt. It was a piece of twine. The killer went there prepared to deal with the people that were in the house. He knew what to expect. Now how do you suppose that's possible?"

Dufresne shrugged and looked around like he was feigning being struck dumb. "The fuck you asking me for? You seriously think I had something to do with this?" He jabbed his finger into the newspaper again. "You guys are breaking my balls. I was in Miami when all this was going down. Check my plane tickets. Speak to the models I shot down there. They'll tell you."

"We're not accusing you, Mr. Dufresne," Carver said. "But we followed up on your alibi—"

"Watertight," Dufresne said and sipped his cocktail.

"That's interesting because we checked with the airline. You never boarded your flight to Miami," Sandling said.

Dufresne sat looking at her for a few seconds. Did he know he was caught? Carver wondered.

"That's right, Mr. Dufresne. Turns out you weren't in Miami at all. So what we want to know is, where were you on the day of the murders?"

"Look," Dufresne said. He looked around and lowered his voice. "You think I had something to do with those girls? Are you out of your *goddamn* minds? I never killed anyone in my life—"

"Where were you?"

"Look, okay—"

"Okay?"

"Okay, just—*shhh*—I don't need Daphne finding out about any of this, all right? She'll go ballistic."

"Find out about what?"

"The reason I didn't get on that plane. I was—I had—another engagement. A photoshoot, all right? With a model. A young one. Okay?"

Sandling shook her head. She furrowed her brow and sat forward and said, "Wait, what do you—"

Dufresne looked at Carver and made a 'would you tell her please' face.

"All right," Carver said and put his hand up to stop Sandling digging. "I think what Mr. Dufresne is trying to say is that he was engaging in extracurricular activities with one of his models, and doesn't want his wife to find out."

"He gets it," Dufresne said to Sandling and cocked his head.

Carver took Sandling's notepad and pen and put it down in front of Dufresne.

"The name and number of the girl. Write it down."

Dufresne picked up the pen and started writing it down. He slid the notepad back toward Carver.

"What about her parents, Freya's parents?" Sandling asked.

"They've been informed. Her father is coming over here. They're not wealthy people so we're helping out where we can."

"That's decent of you," Sandling said.

"We'll follow up on this, Dufresne. I better not find out she's underage. If I do, I'm coming back and this time I'll bring a warrant. You'll have a lot more explaining to do."

Dufresne was looking at his drink. Beads of sweat collected on his forehead. His jaw pulsed. Carver stood up and put the notepad in his jacket pocket. Dufresne was looking down.

"We'll show ourselves out," Carver said. "Say goodbye to your charming wife for us."

As they walked to the car, Sandling said, "What did you think?"

Carver glanced back at the imposing home and saw Mrs. Dufresne standing in the glass outer stairwell, watching them leave.

"Bit too modern for my tastes."

"Not the decor, Carver, the *alibi*."

"Let's wait and see," Carver said and opened the car door. "If it turns out Dufresne's wealth wasn't so honestly gained, we might have to look into it. He came clean about Miami. That's something."

He got in and closed the door.

18

MANASSAS

THE NEXT DAY, Carver sat with his elbows on his desk and his head in his hands. He had a pounding headache. His phone rang and without opening his eyes dropped his left hand and let it hit the receiver. He lifted it to his ear. Didn't say anything, just waited. The person on the other end eventually said, "Hello?"

A woman's voice.

"Hello, Bronwyn," Carver said. He opened his eyes.

"That's Deputy Gibson to you, Carver, *geez-Louise* is that how you answer the phone? I should've listened to them."

"What can I do for you, Bronwyn?"

"I'm serious, Gust, I've just had the director on the phone chewing my ass out for the last four minutes straight."

"Chewing your ass out?"

"You know what I mean, pervert. That little house call you paid to Bastien Dufresne hasn't gone down well in the department. His lawyers have been getting hold of anyone who'll listen, saying you were overly aggressive in questioning him at his home."

"Oh, yeah, well that's good."

"No, it's not good. It's not good when I vouched for you and you're taking liberties."

He let her catch her breath.

"Why is it good?" Gibson asked.

"It means we made an impression. It means he's scared."

"Of course he's damn well scared, he thinks you're going to pin the murder on him."

"If he didn't do it then he has nothing to worry about."

"Yeah, well, he is worried. His lawyer said he made some false statements under duress and would like to come clean about his alibi."

"So he was lying."

"Nobody said anything about *lying*," Gibson said. "I just told you he wants to press charges for attacking him in his home."

"Attacking is a bit strong when we were invited in."

"He says you forced your way in, past the maid, and she'll testify to it."

"There's no need. We know he didn't do it. We just need to know where he was and what he was doing there."

"If he didn't do it then why are you pressing the issue when I'm asking you to drop it?"

"You haven't asked me to drop and, even if you do, there's no way I can do that."

"Why the hell not?"

"Bastien Dufresne knew one of the victims," Carver said. "Freya—a barely of legal age *au pair* and part-time model for Daphne and Bastien. Dufresne has a link to this case."

Gibson was quiet for a moment. Carver thought he might be winning her over.

"It's circumstantial," Gibson said.

"Until we prove the link."

"That's what I am telling you, Carver, there is not going to be an investigation into this line of questioning."

"I see," Carver said. "Dufresne has some friends in powerful places."

"His wife, actually."

"And she knows what he is?"

"No, I don't think so and Mr. Dufresne would like to keep it that way, and we're going to let him."

"Listen, Bronwyn, maybe you can live with yourself safe and secure in the knowledge that your 401k is protected but I can't. We're trying to solve a serial homicide here."

"Do me a favor, all right?"

"You think I owe you?"

"You do owe me and I am asking you to leave it alone."

"He's connected to this somehow, Bronwyn."

"It's not a conspiracy, Gust."

"We don't know what it is yet because you are impeding an investigation."

"Local PD is confirming his revised statement and will carry out the necessary checks on the girl or girls. This isn't something to concern yourself with. I brought you back to run the psychological angle and look for forensics that we might've overlooked. Let's concentrate on that, shall we? If it turns out that there is more to it than a simple coincidence then you will be the first to know. You have my word."

God, Carver resented her. He knew the real her. The scared little girl she really was inside. Not this bureaucratic bully hiding behind management speak to cover her true feelings about it. Sometimes he simply didn't understand people. Were they so basic in their instinct for self-preservation, even at the expense of innocent victims? Now he wondered why he ever thought it would be different coming back.

"The Bureau booked you a flight."

"Much obliged. Where to?"

"California."

"I hear it's nice this time of year."

"Not where you're going."

Carver immediately felt that familiar feeling of dread. Somehow his stomach felt like it was incredibly empty and full to bloating at the same time. People say 'butterflies' but it was more than that. It was the feeling of a nine-inch blade being pushed into his liver.

"I need two—" Carver's voice croaked and he coughed. It was violent. He put his hand over the mouthpiece.

"What? I couldn't hear you."

"God, ah, sorry. Something in my throat. I said, I need *two* tickets."

"*Oh*, I see, you're taking young Miss *Thang* out there with you."

"She's a Berkley PhD for Christ's sake," Carver said.

"In what? How to climb the ladder by sucking off the boss?"

Carver was stunned to silence. He scoffed and said, "Some things never—"

"Don't get so defensive, Carver. *Jesus*. I was only a—"

"I know what you were *only,* Bronwyn. I ought to wash your mouth out with soap ... thanks for keeping tabs on me, okay? I'll take it from here."

He hung up while she was still talking back to him. He put the palms of his hands back over his eyes and groaned.

"Sandling!" he called out.

She appeared in his doorway. "Yes, boss?"

"Get your go-bag, we're going on a little trip."

"When?"

"Five minutes."

19

SAN BERNARDINO

CARVER WAS LOOKING through the windshield into the far distance at nothing in particular and Sandling started feeling awkward, or nervous; she couldn't decide which. So she jumped a little when he abruptly said, "Hunting serial killers is a lot like divorce when you have a child."

"Don't you mean marriage?"

Carver turned his head and looked at her. His expression blank. He shook his head and calmly said, "No ... divorce."

"How so?"

"Well, you think when you catch 'em that's the end of it. Like when you divorce. You do it to get *away* from them. But then—you realize—your lives are intertwined forever. No matter what, and in the cruelest way. This person you now hate. You'll never be rid of them."

Carver looked out into the distance again.

"Like you and Zimmer?"

"I'll never be rid of this bastard. He's always there. Parent-teacher conferences. After-school pick-ups. Visits to the principal." He shook his head. Sandling didn't know how to read him yet. She thought him strange but at the same time someone to be admired. Why? She didn't know. She felt herself frown, then saw Carver look at her again.

"Do you see what I mean?" Carver asked.

"Yes, I think I do—" Sandling began to say then stopped herself. "Sorry," she shook her head. "No, I don't understand."

"As long as Zimmer and I are locked in this devil-dance we may as well use him as much as we can, right? He might not have anything useful, you understand? He's certifiable. But you never know, by analyzing him, what he says, what he thinks. The *way* he thinks. Maybe it'll help us ..."

"So you got the house in the divorce and now you're wanting alimony to pay for the maintenance?" Sandling said and tried to smile.

Carver gave her a grin back. It came out more like a grimace.

"What do you know about him?" Carver asked.

"Zimmer?"

Carver nodded.

Sandling thought.

"He was a neurosurgeon," she said.

"Yeah, a common misconception," Carver said.

She didn't like him correcting her. She furrowed her brow again.

"But I thought —" she started to say.

"He worked as a neurosurgeon—a supposed neurosurgeon—but Zimmer has no medical qualifications, no surgical training of any kind, as far we can tell."

"Hmm," she said and thought on it. "He operated on people though?"

Carver nodded. "That's right. He had a very particular kind of clientele."

"Particular, strange, or particular, specific?"

"Specific," Carver said. "Throw out the dates and data you read in the file and try to think about Zimmer's life as it would have happened to him."

"Okay," Sandling said.

"Zimmer was born here, in California," Carver said. "Son of a maladjusted Vietnam vet. The usual alcohol-fueled beatings of his mother and siblings. In one of his more lucid moments, Zimmer once told me that he was left in the stairwell of a fire station, abandoned by his father—who was by now a Christian missionary to Japan of all things. He never forgave his father for trying to get rid of him. His mother—an Austrian woman—found him though, and took him back. She was apparently very promiscuous while her husband was away. A new lover every night to hear Zimmer tell it. The start of his hatred of women. She was from a good family—his mother—and she eventually got sick of the beatings, which continued when her husband came back from Japan. She left him and took the family, including young Hermann, back to Austria. Very Catholic country, Austria."

"Mm-hmm," Sandling agreed, not knowing whether it was or not.

"Zimmer started acting out, cutting up animals into various piles of limbs and leaving them outside the front doors of people who he disliked, or said they disliked him. They never proved it was him. Safe to say, he never fit in and got sent away to Catholic boarding school."

Her eyes were wide, listening now.

"No wonder," Sandling said.

"Zimmer found God in the church and became a missionary for one of the fundamentalist Catholic sects.

Like his father, he also worked as a missionary for many years, mostly sub-Saharan Africa. You know, real poor folks, desperate situations. Trying to be like his daddy—maybe a little too much—and do good by the Lord. Anyway, these people had no money. No clothes. No shoes. No money for medical expenses. That's where young Zimmer comes in. He starts off doing minor surgeries."

"How minor?"

"Who knows." Carver shrugged. "Only Zimmer and God, probably. He claims he was helping people but I wonder how many of those wretched souls went the way of those Austrian pets?"

Carver looked at Sandling. He talked with his hands.

"Zimmer grows in proficiency and starts doing larger and more complex surgeries. God's work, he called it. His calling. He would do complex operations on people in mud huts, no sanitation, not a sterile environment, you understand? Those who didn't die from complications with the surgeries died from Zimmer's untrained hand. Perhaps intentionally. After all, if you accept free healthcare from a missionary with no means to pay for it and your child dies, who are you going to tell?"

"So that's where he got a taste for it?"

"I think so," Carver said.

"What happened then?"

"Zimmer comes back to the States. Starts preaching at those roving tent revival meetings. You know the ones I mean? Evangelical rattlesnake-waving healing crusades. He was very popular. Drew people in from all around. Meanwhile, he's looking for his father."

"Did he find him?"

"Not before we did," Carver said.

Sandling looked confused. "Who was his father?"

"Zimmer claims it was Ray Ridgeway-Kraft."

"The Peninsula Killer?"

"Yep."

"Like father, like son."

"Supposedly."

"You don't believe it?"

Carver looked away and into the distance once more. "I don't believe or not believe. Just the way it is. There is no right and wrong."

"My father caught the Peninsula Killer," Sandling said, absentmindedly.

"Jim Braddock caught the Peninsula Killer," Carver blurted.

Sandling's eyes went wide and fixed on him. Carver looked tense and wouldn't look at her. She was shocked.

"You knew him?" she asked.

"Jim Braddock's your father?" Carver asked.

"Alexander James Braddock, yes, he was my father."

"Some people called him Jim," Carver said.

Then he was quiet like he was weighing something. After a moment he said, "No, wish I had, though. Sounded like a *helluva* guy ... from reputation."

"Which was?"

"Something to be proud of," Carver said. Sandling got the impression he wanted to change the subject. "Right, should we—"

"Wait," Sandling said and put her hand on his knee. They both looked down at it and she removed it slowly. She wanted to say 'sorry' but didn't.

"What is it?"

"Why are we asking for Zimmer's help? He's insane, right? What do we hope to learn from him?"

"Yeah, he's insane. I mean—he's lucid—but yes. Evil as the devil and twice as clever."

"Well then?"

"Zimmer had a very particular kind of clientele ..."

"Particular, weird, or particular, specific?"

"Both, actually," Carver said. "Being the son of a famous serial killer—or believing you're the son of a famous serial killer—made a lot of sense to Zimmer. What confused him, though, was how to marry the idea of his Catholic God with the idea of his father being a murderer. No doubt by this time Zimmer had also—during his surgeries—maimed or murdered dozens, perhaps hundreds, of people—"

"And, he was just getting started," Sandling said. Now it was her turn to stare at nothing in the distance.

"When he started operating as a neurosurgeon again—they get a craving for it—serial killers can't stop even if they want to and some want to. It's an addiction. A rush like no other. And Zimmer believed he'd stumbled onto an affliction that all sociopathic killers suffered from."

"Migraines."

"Migraines and stomach problems," Carver said. "Zimmer started an unlicensed neurosurgery specializing in treating untreatable headaches. But he was very selective about his clientele."

"Why would he do that?" Sandling asked and immediately regretted letting her mouth work before her brain.

As she said the words she realized why. And before Carver could answer, she said, "He wanted to weed out the serial killers. He had this revenge fantasy against his father, for leaving him in a stairwell, and so through his newly acquired trial and error neurosurgery skills, he put the word out that there was a practice that would treat those that couldn't—or wouldn't—be welcome anywhere else. Killers."

"Serial killers," Carver nodded. "He was still experimenting. After all, if he messed up, who was going to complain?"

"So he spoke to these people?" Sandling asked.

"There's something else," Carver said. "He was still looking for his father. Perhaps he wanted his father to find him. He was a killer, after all."

"Moth to a flame," Sandling said.

"But yes," Carver said. "I believe he did speak to them, I mean, he must have, right?" Carver said. "He had sessions with them, often multiple sessions. Zimmer is homosexual, you know. Or, anyway—at a minimum—bisexual. "

"No, I didn't know."

"He had control fantasies. Typical abandonment issues. He was so afraid that people would leave him that he often tried to leave them first—or in Zimmer's case—kill them first."

Sandling put her hands to her face and said, "He wanted to keep hold of them ..."

"Yes. Zimmer's experiments were with the human brain. As a lay neurosurgeon, he wasn't just killing these people. He was trying to keep them alive. He was trying to zombify them. We found cadavers with holes drilled into their brains. He'd kept some of those men alive for days—weeks even—they had acid and glue poured into the holes in their heads. They'd be walking around talking, according to some witnesses. But you knew they were gone. He was trying to create biological robots. Men beholden to him. Men that would—"

"Never leave," Sandling said, finishing Carver's sentence. Now she understood.

"Well, let's do this then, shall we?" Carver said and opened his door and went to climb out.

"Wait," Sandling said and put her hand on his arm. Carver looked at her. "Maybe I should meet with him alone?"

Carver settled back into his seat.

"What did you mean?"

"Well, it's just that, given your history ... it *might* be better if I speak to him alone."

Carver thought about it for one second. "No, we'll see him together."

"I'll be all right," she said. "If that's what you're worried about."

"It's not."

"Will he make the connection between me and my father?"

She saw Carver's eyes fix on her. He was breathing more heavily now. His mind working. Finally, he shook his head.

"No, he shouldn't make the connection. And, I wouldn't mention it to him, either."

Sandling almost laughed.

"Don't worry. It's one of the reasons I don't use his surname. Too much attention on him from the FBI already."

"Let's go," Carver said and stepped out.

"Who's this?" Dr. Forsmith asked as they walked down the corridor followed by two orderlies.

"Agent Sandling, meet Dr. Forsmith, the preeminent Zimmer the Ripper expert in the country," Carver said as they walked.

"*Oh*, hardly, Mr. Carver."

"*Special Agent* Carver," Sandling said and held out her identification. It sounded defensive and Carver gave her a silent shake of the head. Telling her: don't bother, he's not worth it. They were making their way deep down into the psychiatric hospital.

"*Oh*, that won't be necessary, sweetheart," Forsmith said and rejected her identification. "I'll brief you while walk," Forsmith said. "After your last visit, I spoke to my regional director. We were of the opinion that if you'd like to keep studying Zimmer, you must do it in his cell. He's been moved now. Into one of our psychiatric treatment rooms. He's restrained. You'll have privacy. We don't evade the tendency of those considered to be helping the police forces from being considered traitors by the criminal underclass."

Sandling glanced at Carver. "He means Zimmer is worried about being a rat."

"Indeed," Forsmith said. "What's the matter, Agent Carver? You were sitting in your car an awfully long time?"

Carver stopped and looked Forsmith up and down.

"So, you're telling me you moved Zimmer for our benefit? Not because he has a medical review board coming up and you don't want it to come out that he's been swimming in his own feces for the past few years?"

"Pardon your French," Forsmith said and laughed nervously. Carver squinted at him. "Don't talk down to me you white-coated wannabe."

"I beg your pardon!"

"You moved Zimmer because you don't want it to come out that Ward Twenty is unsafe for human habitation, not because the FBI is interested in questioning Zimmer, isn't that right, Doctor?"

Forsmith lifted his chin and looked down his nose at Carver. He turned. He wasn't going to dignify him with an answer. Forsmith started to walk and regained his composure. Carver looked at Sandling and gave her a wink.

"It's not padded but you will find the room has a soft, rounded feel to it. It wasn't by design, mind you, simply decades upon decades of heavy lead paint added layer after layer. There's a video camera. No privacy in these psychiatric treatment rooms, I'm afraid. Zimmer even seems to have been taking his medication. Of course, if he refuses, he's fed liquid through a tube until he complies. The whole process of getting the tube down his throat and into his stomach is unpleasant for him and for my orderlies. He's in room twelve—"

"Yes, I'm sure it's as unpleasant for the staff as it is for your patient," Sandling said.

"You sound like an idealist, Miss ..."

"Special Agent Sandling."

"You sound like an idealist, Miss Sandling. I was one too, once upon a time but somehow the depravity of the depths of the human condition seems to have drummed it right out of me. But, as they say ... inside every cynic there's just a disappointed idealist." He gave her a polite, trite smile. His leather-soled shoes snapped against the freshly polished floor.

Forsmith pulled up abruptly mid-stride. "This is where I must leave you, I'm afraid." He checked his watch. "I have another engagement. I'd appreciate it if you could share any of your—less confidential—findings with me, Miss Sandling. I doubt you'll make much progress but if you do, I'd appreciate being consulted on your breakthroughs. I've been studying Zimmer's mind for years now and find him incomprehensible."

"That won't be necessary, Doctor," Sandling said.

"I see." Forsmith said, "Good day," and turned. He didn't bother shaking Carver's hand. The orderlies stayed behind. Sandling and Carver glanced at one another. The long fluorescent tubes lined the long corridor. The doors were painted blue with round porthole-like windows peering out like unseeing eyes.

20

WONDER if she's feeling as nervous as I am, Carver thought.

He glanced at Sandling and then stood close to the port-hole window and looked into Zimmer's room.

He saw his child's killer sitting at a metal table. He was in a white overall and had leather straps restraining him. Carver stepped away as Zimmer looked up. Carver was apprehensive. He knew he'd have to make a bargain with the devil to get the information they needed. His hand was shaking.

"Maybe it would be better if you wait outside?" Sandling suggested. Carver thought about it. Longer than a second this time.

"And let the cat toy with its dinner?"

"Something like that," Sandling said before quickly asking, "Wait, who's supposed to be the mouse in this situation?"

"My question exactly," Carver gave her a grimace-smile.

"At least let me try," Sandling said. It sounded like plead-ing. What man is strong enough not to bow to a pleading woman?

"If it doesn't go well, or I can't handle it, you can come in and save me." She stuck out her hand to shake on the deal like she'd just sold him a used car. Why did he feel like he was getting screwed over?

Carver shook his head in resignation. He didn't shake her hand but he said, "Fine, listen to me though, be polite. Mind your manners. Keep your cool, okay? Nothing personal. Ever. And listen, just remember ... He's glib and he'll be charming. It's the way he's wired. Okay?" She nodded. "But never forget he's like a cold-blooded serpent, waiting, tasting the air, looking for the body heat of a mouse. He will get very hot-blooded once there is an opportune moment to strike, so don't give him one. Stay frosty. Remember you've got something he wants too so he shouldn't get violent." She nodded again. *Shouldn't.* She was watching Carver closely. "I'll wait in the cafeteria but if you so much as feel a teardrop brewing you get one of the orderlies to call me." He turned to look at them. "I mean it guys, stay alert, please. Call me if anything happens. *Anything.*"

"Yessir," one of the orderlies said.

"And, Caitlin," Carver said. "He may be a pastor, but he's also a killer."

Hermann Zimmer must've heard her come in but he wasn't showing it.

He sat with his back to her hunched at a metal table. How long had he been waiting, she wondered.

She'd have to walk past him to sit down and then he'd be between her and the door. The door would be locked from the outside. She lifted her chin and held her handbag tightly and walked past him. She heard him *sniff* and she glanced at him. He was looking down.

"Hello," Sandling said and then cleared the lump in her throat. Zimmer didn't move.

"Excuse me, Mr. Zimmer—ah—I'm Caitlin Sandling from the Federal Bureau—the FBI. May I call you, Hermann?"

Zimmer slowly sat back and, as he did, raised his eye to meet hers. Sparks flew in his glassy eye. It was the first time she felt trepidation and they'd only just met. The scarred tissue where his other eye was supposed to be was disturbing. She tried to hold his glare but found herself searching the corners of the rectangular white room instead. She'd lost the first confrontation.

"Black," he mumbled, then said, "You have the loveliest black eyes," Zimmer said.

They're blue, she thought but resisted the urge to correct him. He was *mad* after all.

"Do you carry evidence of your trials?" he asked.

"Evidence?"

"Proof."

"I'm sorry, I'm—"

"Your badge," he said. "Show it to me."

Her hand went to her pocket instinctively. His voice was softer than she'd imagined from the type of man in front of her. She presented it to him.

He snatched it with a swiftness that surprised her. "May I?" Zimmer said as he took her ID.

She felt uncomfortable as he scrutinized her credentials. He smirked and slid it back across the table.

"It's a temple of trust, isn't it?" Zimmer said. He had a sly grin on his face. She furrowed her brow and looked away.

"What do you mean?"

"Who to trust, when, and by how much," Zimmer said.

"Beg your pardon?"

"A pardon? No, I doubt it," Zimmer said. "But I do like when you beg."

She ignored him. A bolt on a door slammed home loudly, making her jump.

"Where's Augustine? I was expecting another revenant," Zimmer said and checked over his shoulder.

She hesitated, "He thought I should—"

"Why you?"

"I'm sorry—"

"Don't be sorry. Answer the question, simply."

"Why me?" she said.

"Yes."

"Because he—"

"No, why *you*, my child?" Zimmer pushed her as if he was peering into her soul. "What special qualities did you bring to this house?"

She was finding it hard to maintain her composure. She didn't know how she felt. Flushed. Uncomfortable. Like she didn't want to be there. She tried to redirect the conversation. "Mr. Zimmer—"

"What happened to Hermann?"

"May I record our—"

"I've so missed the company of women," he said, speaking over her. It was quiet, wistful, and threatening all at the same time, and she didn't know how he achieved that with his voice. She could barely keep hers *gruff* enough to sound authoritative. Zimmer's unsettling mix of clarity and delusion was making her feel disoriented.

"They think you prefer men," she said and held her breath for some reason. Was it a step too far too soon?

"Do labels fascinate you?" he asked.

She breathed again. "I'm only here for any insights you might offer."

"To dissect my mind, you mean?" he said.

She could see his amusement.

"It's not an interrogation."

"All the same," he said. "You understand my concerns." He was intense. "What do you want, special agent?" Zimmer's voice lowered, drawing her in. "I'm busy."

"Help with a profile," she said and sat more prim and proper.

"A killer's profile? The Skinwalker, yes? How does this information eke out in your world, I wonder?" She opened her mouth but hesitated. "Just a fishing expedition, then?" He said. It was sarcastic. "Using me as bait?"

"No—"

"Is that what this is, Agent Sandling, a fishing expedition? Has Saint Augustine sent you here to tempt me and torture me and test me like some sort of devil?"

"No, I—"

"Don't lie to me," Zimmer said. "Don't you dare lie to me. You know what they did with witches, don't you?"

The switch from seemingly serene to full of spite was as quick as it was sharp. Her heart was pounding. Everything in her being was telling her to get out of there. She couldn't breathe. Zimmer had spittle on his lip and left it there.

She heard the latch to the cell door slam out of the lock and the heavy door opened.

The orderly put his head around and looked in.

"She's fine," Zimmer said over his shoulder. "Or she will be soon. Tell Jiminy Cricket and his pals to leave," he said to her.

"It's okay. Thank you," Sandling said, her voice higher pitched than she'd hoped.

"You sure, ma'am?"

"Run along now," Zimmer said over his shoulder.

Sandling nodded to the orderly and he gave her a single

nod back. The door closed again. Her heart was still racing. He was testing her.

"I think it's time for me to leave."

"Stay where you are." She was too scared to breathe. "You haven't got what you came for yet."

She wasn't sure she could go through with it. She wanted to quit. She wanted to leave before she suffered any more stress and anxiety.

"You want a profile of a killer?"

She nodded. "I want you to help me understand his impulses."

Zimmer's face relaxed and his shoulders sagged. He breathed normally through his mouth.

"I won't tolerate lies," he said. "I won't tolerate it and I *will* know."

She nodded dumbly.

"I can practically smell it on you. I could always tell a murderer in the confessional. They reek of it. Their sweat." Zimmer squinted his eyes at her. "Why does any of this even matter to you?" he asked and observed her like a chimp in a cage.

She hesitated, "It's crucial to the investigation."

"And you want to do a good job for Augustine and your flourishing career. Are you a daddy's girl, Caitlin?"

She looked away. Something lodged in her throat and she swallowed. Used to be, she thought and looked up at the killer opposite her.

"Tell me, Caitlin, does faith still hold you in its embrace? Or did it too abandon you, like a father leaving his child crying all alone in the dark?" She stared at him.

"My faith isn't on trial."

Zimmer leaned in.

"You ever been thirsty, Miss Agent? So thirsty you'd do anything for a swig?"

She took a moment, trying to work out his intent, and nodded slowly, cautiously.

"Then understand the compulsion like crawling on all fours on hot sand toward an oasis in the desert. When you crave something; when it consumes you from inside. That's our peregrine."

He spoke about the serial killer with a warmth she'd rarely heard in the world. They were building a rapport, she felt. She cleared her throat and asked, "What did the men tell you in the confessional?"

"You like the attention of men," Zimmer said. "The way they look at you. Leery eyes undressing you." She was unimpressed. He was trying to find a weakness and she was bored by it. "You sometimes wish they'd just grab you and use you."

She didn't say anything. And waited. Zimmer smirked, then said, "People don't confess in a confessional, that's one thing you learn. It's not what they say that's important. It's what they don't say. There's a secret language, like a *sect*. It's like the spiritual side of religion. Why do you ask? Have you something to confess?"

She swallowed. "No, this isn't about me."

"Oh, isn't it? Then why are you here? Running from something?"

"Aren't we all?"

"No," Zimmer said.

"Tell me your theory," she said.

"We don't want theories, Caitlin. Do we? We want truth. Let's speak truth to power."

"I don't understand—"

"Why are you here?" Zimmer asked.

"To ask you for help."

"Help with what? And don't say creating a profile. Tell

me your desires. Undress them for me and show me your nakedness and openness to change."

"I need help ..." she felt like he'd succeeded in making her feel stupid.

"I know you do," Zimmer said. His voice was laced with pity. "We are all God's children. We're all weakest at the inflection between good and evil. So easy to tip into sin. What is it, my child, pride, lust, and conceitedness?"

She looked up at him. How had he had this effect on her? She felt like she might cry. Keep it together, she told herself.

"If you knew me you'd know I'm none of those things," she sniffed and wiped her hand on her lip.

"But I do know you. I see your soul. I've spoken to Our Father in Heaven about you many times. Our fate is intertwined, you see? There are a multitude of universes where this interaction has been playing out for eternity already. And here we are again."

The thought of sitting opposite Zimmer for eternity was worse than hell.

"What do you think he's doing?" Sandling asked.

"Communicating," Zimmer said.

"What is he trying to tell us?"

"His innermost desires."

"And wha—"

"You understand how this works, Miss Sandling, don't you?" Zimmer asked, cutting her off.

She nodded but was unsure what he meant. "You're making a Faustian bargain; are you prepared to trade your soul for my favor?"

"I'm ready."

"The first one is always free," Zimmer said. "Life, death, rebirth. What if the light people see when they die is them being reborn from their new mother's vaginal opening?" He watched her reaction intently. She blushed and wished she hadn't. "That word makes you uncomfortable?"

She shook her head.

"You were born Catholic, weren't you?" Zimmer said and looked deep into her soul.

She nodded and cleared her throat and said, "Yes. Non-practicing."

"The altar isn't where the practice happens," Zimmer corrected her.

"His crimes are non-sexual," Sandling said.

Zimmer raised an eyebrow. "And what makes you so sure?"

"Forensic evidence. Or lack thereof, to be more precise."

"Ah, science. Yes. The science indicates that he didn't ejaculate in or on his obsessions *ergo* he's not driven by lust."

It sounded sarcastic.

"You disagree?"

"Let me ask you this, it's a narrow prism—forensics and logic—but if they are right, then why haven't you caught him yet? Why are you even here? I don't offer any of those things."

"I don't know."

"Is there anything logical about these rituals?" Zimmer asked.

"Is that what they are?"

"What would you call them? They're too complex to be mere games. Too practiced to be play. This is serious business with heavy consequences. Darwin was right about one thing, we all want to survive. Killing is hard work, Miss Sandling. If it was easy, we'd be overrun. It takes a special kind of creature to accomplish this calling."

He looked at it like a vocation, she thought. His matter-of-fact way of assessing something so horrible left her stunned.

"So what does it mean?" she asked.

"Death, desire, and temptation," Zimmer said. "Just as the serpent sheds its skin, so we continue our dance."

"How did you lose your virginity?"

"Excuse me."

"I see no wedding band," Zimmer said. His eye turned darker as if storm clouds had appeared overhead. "You're no doubt living in sin. So when did it happen, who'd you let desecrate your holy hole?"

She couldn't hide her surprise.

"That's none of your business."

"Isn't it? And yet here you sit. All made up and dangling your dripping snatch at me like some kind of Mexican *piñata*." Scorn and contempt were written all over his face.

"It was taken from you, wasn't it? Is that how you lost your faith and became a heathen? Not so *katharos* then are you?"

She was confused.

"Don't tell me you're ignorant of meaning in your own denomination. Your Greek roots. *Katharos* means pure— something you certainly are not—you're the type of woman who should be stoned to death."

"This isn't about me—"

"Oh, yes it is. That's *all* it's about."

"I don't speak in riddles."

"Only because you're hearing my answers but not listening to them."

"Tell me how to catch him."

"First you must confess your sins to me. Each and every one. You're living in sin, going through hell, but like that newborn baby—and through God himself—I can show you the path to light. You just need to give over your ego to me."

They sat staring at one another for a moment. Sandling's head was spinning. She tried to stay composed but she wanted to run. She felt like a little girl scared of the dark, wanting her daddy to come and protect her.

"Time's up," she said and stood up. Zimmer didn't move. She felt like he'd got what he wanted.

"Come and see me again soon," Zimmer said as she walked past him. "And remember dear Caitlin, he said 'I am the light, I am the way'. Every confession, every sin, every fear ... leads us to the truth we seek, in the end."

21

Sandling slumped down in the car seat and inhaled deeply and closed her eyes. She wanted to scream and shout and let it all out. The tension, the intensity, she'd never felt a thrill like it. Just like Zimmer had said. If one thing was clear, it's that he understood the human condition. Maybe it meant he could be sincere about his depth of understanding of a serial killer's condition too.

She let out a husky groan and reached across and dug her nails into Carver's forearm. She opened her eyes and said with a glint in them, "I need a dripping double cheeseburger and a beer."

Carver grinned and nodded and started the car, "I know just the place."

They didn't speak during the drive. Sandling was too deep in her own thoughts. She stared out the window and watched the blur of the bushes and tarmac go by. When they pulled into the parking lot she followed behind Carver and sat down in a booth. After they'd been there a minute, she noticed Carver looking at the menu.

"You're back," he said.

"Yeah, was I away?"

"With the fairies."

"Nuckelavee and Dullahan," she said. Carver looked up at her from his menu, his face blank. "You know, dark fairies. Evil fairies."

Carver shrugged and looked back at the menu. The waitress came over.

"I'd like a cheeseburger," Sandling said looking up at her. "Medium rare. Lots of onion rings. Extra greasy."

"I don't know about the extra greasy but I can try," the waitress said and jotted it down. Sandling looked past her toward the kitchen and saw the grill chef's stained apron and gap-toothed smile.

"I think you'll manage. I'd also like a beer. A big one. Ice cold."

"Anything else?"

They both looked at Carver.

"Oh—ah—nothing for me."

"Oh, come on, Gust! You can't leave me here with a mouthful of burger all alone."

"Fine," he said and looked at the menu again. "Tuna melt. Extra cheese and a Pepsi."

"We got Coke."

"Coke then, whatever."

"Thank you," Sandling said.

The waitress slid the menus off the table and went to place their orders. Sandling grinned in anticipation of her cheeseburger and fries.

"God, Gust, I wish you'd been there ..."

He raised the sides of his mouth slightly. He's thinking 'Me too', she thought. He didn't say anything.

"You don't want to know how it went?"

He sighed. And looked at the table. Then, said, "No," and shook his head. "I don't actually."

"You're right. We need to blow off some steam. It was

exhilarating though. I've never been so ... I don't know, worked up. Tense. You know?"

He knew, she thought. Of course he knows. He'd been doing this for years. Not to mention. He'd seen Zimmer out in the wild. His psychosis out in the wild. Like having a black jaguar loose in a city.

"Just be careful," Carver said. He was glancing at her now and then, watching her closely. Closely for what? She wondered. Signs. Signs of having been near Zimmer?

"Tell me about you, Gust. Please? I feel like this is one of those 'what goes on the road, stays on the road moments'. You know?"

He leaned back and relented.

"Like what?"

Shit. He was actually going to let her question him. "Um," she said and glanced out of the window at the parking lot. "What do you do for fun?"

Carver let out a loud burst of laughter. She was shocked. It was the first time she'd heard him laugh. It was nice. He sounded like he'd forgotten how to do it.

"For fun?" Carver said and took a deep breath again. "I like to dive."

"What, like scuba?"

"Well, yeah, but without the tank. Free diving."

"Where do you do that?"

"In the Atlantic, mostly. Around the rocky outcrops. Where the seaweed is."

"Huh," she said and searched his face. "Why do you do it?"

"Why?" Carver said and looked up at the ceiling. "Why. It's simpler down there."

"Simpler?"

"Yeah."

"Like how?"

"Like, an intense and effortless focus."

"On what?"

"How long a single breath is going to last you before you black out ten feet underwater."

She raised her eyebrows.

"Yeah," he said. "It's the weightlessness. Zero gravity. Your whole body becomes attuned to your environment. An alien world. And you drift along with the swaying current and ..."

"And what?"

"Never mind."

"No, I want to hear it. Please."

"And ... nothing. That's it. You know? Life becomes real simple when you only have one thing to worry about. How long this single breath of air is going to last me before the ocean crushes me."

"Is that like a metaphor for how you feel about life too?"

He gave a single laugh this time.

"I'm not on your sofa."

"No, but I am trying to understand."

"You'll understand it one day. I hope you won't have to but I fear you might."

The waitress came back over. "One burger—extra greasy—with lots of onion rings for the young lady. And, a tuna melt for the gentleman. And, I'll just go'n grab your drinks."

She came back and placed the beer in front of Sandling and the soda in front of Carver. "Enjoy," she said.

Sandling was smiling. She picked up her beer and said, "Cheers!" and touched her glass to Carver's. She took a couple of big chugs and lifted the back of her hand to her mouth and coughed.

"So cold but so good ..." she said and slumped back in the booth. "I feel exhausted. It was like he was testing me the whole time," she said.

Carver nodded and cut the edge off his tuna melt. "That's one thing about Zimmer," Carver said. It was absent-minded like he was talking more to himself than to her. "Maybe sociopaths in general. They spend so much time trying to learn what it is to be human by observing humans —they look at us like we're an alien species they're trying to understand so they can infiltrate our world—they become social anthropologists. They understand the wiring of the human brain better than we do, much better in some cases. Even if they don't realize it."

"Like a game," Sandling said and took a big bite of her burger. It spat juice and it ran down her chin. "God," she said and grabbed a napkin to wipe her chin. "Sorry."

"Such a lady," Carver said.

"It's *so* good. I haven't had a burger in forever."

"I bet Zimmer would tell us where the bodies are buried for a juicy burger like that," Carver said. "All that gruel he's been eating for years."

"Do you?" Sandling said and studied her burger. "I don't. I think that is a man—if you can call him a man—who's so singularly focused that he doesn't even differentiate tastes. Nothing matters to him other than ..." she hesitated.

"Than what?"

Sandling put her burger down and left her greasy hand hovering above the plate. She watched Carver for a second.

"Well, *you*, of course," she said. "I could practically smell it on him. It just hung in the air like a bad odor. I think Zimmer wanted to play it cool like he wasn't interested, but he has an obsession. A compulsion. His only focus and motivation in life is to get one over on you, Gust."

Carver sat silent. He looked long at his tuna melt. She could see he'd lost his appetite.

"Maybe we can use that," Carver said.

"How's everything?" the waitress came over and asked.

Carver and Sandling were staring at one another. Neither replied. Eventually, when it got awkward, the waitress stuck her pencil into her permed black hair, scoffed, and walked away.

Carver picked up a napkin and wiped his mouth and pushed the plate away.

"No good?" Sandling asked.

"Lost my appetite."

"There's more to life than food," she said. "Like—"

"Catching serial killers," Carver said. He had a glint in his eye.

"Like *using* serial killers to catch serial killers," she said. They clinked their glasses. "Cheers to that."

"Come on," Carver said. "Let's get back to Grant Avenue."

22

Carver and Sandling walked into the office on Grant Avenue. Maudmont was leaning over Fox's desk and stood up as they walked in. She couldn't help but glance at her small gold wristwatch. She was the timekeeper and made a face to indicate her displeasure at their lateness.

"Yeah, we're late, Penny, put a dollar in the swear jar for us."

"It's a dollar a minute, Gust," Maudmont said. She was as prim and proper and as persnickety as usual.

"Where have you two been?" Underwood asked. Carver noted the tinge of jealousy underlying the curiosity in his voice. Sandling missed it and enthusiastically answered, "Oh goodness, you should have been there, Toby, we went to see Hermann Zimmer in California."

That pricked up everyone's ears. Even old Frank Hornigen came out of the back office and leaned against the doorframe.

"That's enough," Carver said under his breath to Sandling. She stopped and glanced around. Everyone was looking at her.

"Actually, I'm glad that everybody's here for this," Carver said.

"Here for what?" Fox asked.

"Well, I'm getting there, if you'll give me a chance," Carver said and cleared his throat. "Sorry. What I mean is, I'm glad that we're all together, because we've got something to share with you."

"Go on," Maudmont said. "You went to visit Zimmer."

"Who's Zimmer?" Fox asked.

"Zimmer the Ripper; haven't you heard of him?" Underwood asked. She shook her head.

"Okay, gather round *team*," Carver said. It sounded awkward like they were a motley crew of failed agents. Everyone moved in a little closer.

"We're actually in the middle of something, Mr. Carver, do you think we can put in a proper appointment and get together at a more convenient time?" Maudmont said.

"Listen, Penny, I appreciate this may not be the way you always do things but this is important, okay. We've been to see Zimmer to help with a case I've been working on. *We've* been working on. Toby and Caitlin have helped too but this thing is big. Bigger than any one of us can manage. So, I'd appreciate it if you could just let us have this briefing, you know?"

Maudmont had her hand in front of her mouth. She looked shocked. "You mean a *serial killer* is out there," she said.

"We're the Slouch Force, remember," Fox said. "We can't do anything to help."

"Listen guys, just hear him out, *please*?" They all turned

to look at Sandling. Carver could feel himself getting frustrated. He tried not to show it.

"Go on," Hornigen said from the back of the room. "We're listening. Tell us what you've got. We'd like to hear."

"Okay," Carver said and then looked at the ground. "Actually, I don't know where to begin." He searched his mind for a few seconds and tapped his finger on his lips as he thought.

"We've got a serial killer out there," Sandling blurted out. "And he's murdering whole families and removing the faces of the women."

Maudmont gasped. Fox had a curious look on her face like she was going to sneeze or bust out laughing.

"Thank you, Caitlin," Carver said.

"It's true," Toby said. "I went to one of the murder houses with the boss."

"What do we know so far?" Hornigen asked. "What's the nature of the investigation?"

"The nature ..." Carver repeated. "The nature. Um, we've got two murder scenes, so far, one in Augusta and one in Charleston."

"What does that suggest?" Maudmont asked.

Carver shrugged. "It suggests he can move around. It suggests planning and motive."

"How so?"

"Because you wouldn't drive somewhere and kill someone unless you knew who they were and how you were going to get away, would you," Sandling said.

"The local police are working together with the FBI and BAU," Carver said. "Charleston is employing a wide range of tactics including neighborhood canvassing, setting up a tip line, and coordination with Augusta for any unusual patterns in airline or rental car reservations. It won't do any good ..."

"Can I just ask," Underwood interrupted.

"Go on," Carver said and sighed.

"If local PD, the FBI and BAU are all involved in this, then how do you two fit in?" Underwood asked.

"It's not just the two of us," Carver said. "We're all going to be working on this."

He paused. No more questions. They waited now, with anticipation.

"Forensics say all the blood at the scenes belongs to the victims. The killer used a .22 caliber pistol with a suppressor, ammunition too common to trace. No foreign saliva or secretions were found, but skin DNA was discovered under the nails of the second male victim, suggesting a struggle. The brother of the victim whose face was removed. Partial shoe prints of size nine were also found—"

"Wait," Hornigen jumped in. "You said DNA under the fingerprints, from the suspect?"

Carver glanced at Sandling. "No," he said. "The DNA was from the first victim, Freya Silvstedt, in Augusta. She was an *au pair* at a wealthy family in town and was babysitting for a little extra pocket money."

Hornigen furrowed his brow.

"The killer was wearing her face," Carver said.

Maudmont dry heaved and lifted her hand to her mouth. "Excuse me," she said and hurried out of the room.

"Oh my god," Fox said.

"The killer is creating masks from the victims' faces and wearing them while committing his subsequent murders."

Penny came silently back into the room holding a handkerchief to her mouth. "Sorry," she said.

"It's okay," Carver said. He acknowledged her and looked at Underwood. "What else, Toby? You were in the York home."

"Snakes," Underwood said. "He leaves snakes at the scene."

"Cottonmouths," Carver said. "Lab confirmed it. Pretty common around where the murders have happened. They're venomous and extremely aggressive. One attacked me when I was in the Charleston scene."

"Why do that?" Fox asked. "Why leave a snake behind?"

"It's a good question," Carver said, his answer measured. He had his own opinion. "The Bureau thinks it's a kind of calling card or that he leaves them there to scare the police when they show up."

"Calling card," Maudmont said. "Surely that's the faceless victim."

"I tend to agree," Carver said. "So, that is one of our questions; we need to think critically about *why* he's leaving cottonmouths at the scenes."

"Any other theories?" Maudmont asked.

"It could be meta," Carver said. "You know, theological or mystical. The killer might attach some meaning to snakes in a way we don't understand yet."

"Sounds thin," Hornigen said.

"Thanks, Frank," Carver said.

Fox spun around and started tapping on her keyboard. "What's the address in Charleston?" The tips of her fingers moved quickly over the keys. "Never mind, found it."

"Right," Carver said and they turned back to focus on him. Fox kept tapping away.

"Any other questions?" Carver asked.

"Are there any suspects or persons of interest?"

"Not so far, Underwood," Carver said. "Bastien Dufresne knew both victims. He's a fashion photographer and has photographed both girls at one time or another in the past. That's the only connection we have between them. Local

PDs are following up on his whereabouts and confirming his version of events. We've been tasked to cast the net a bit wider and come at it from another angle."

"I have a question," Hornigen said. "Why'd you guys go and visit Zimmer the Ripper?"

Sandling glanced at Carver. His eyes were fixed on Hornigen. The skin beneath his left eye twitched. It was like the whole room held their breath.

The only sound was the rapid-fire tapping.

"Well, it's complicated Frank, but I guess people need to know, especially if you're going to help me out on this one. Zimmer and I go back, *way* back. Back to the first serial homicide case I worked. He was a minister of some description at that time. Took a strange interest in the case, made himself involved, offered his services. Turned out he was the one we were after the whole time. When he realized we were on to him, he killed my daughter."

There was stunned silence.

Sandling looked at her shoes. Hornigen looked like he was searching for something to say. The right words. But they must've escaped him. Instead, Maudmont, ever reliable blurted out, "And you still go and ask him for help?"

"It's not quite like that, Penny. Yes, we are using him for help, but you have to know about the background in his case to be able to understand where he could be involved. He was working as a lay brain surgeon and his clientele were mostly psychopaths suffering from migraines. Horrible migraines. He offered them a cure—the ones he didn't kill—and I think that Zimmer's hiding more secrets than he'll ever let anybody know."

"So you're using him?"

"In a way," Carver said.

"And how's he using you?" Maudmont asked.

Carver was silent. Sandling opened her mouth but he got her to close it with a stern look. Maudmont was on a roll.

"You've hardly said a word to us since you've been here and now you're trying to get us to forgo the work the agency gave us and help you on this crusade?"

"It's hardly a crusade, Penny, innocent people are being slaughtered out there."

"And the FBI is working on it, BAU is working on it, they don't need the Manassas, Grant Avenue outpost here—out there—fumbling around like drunks in a bar."

"I understand if you're frightened," Carver said.

"Frightened? I'm not frightened," Maudmont said. Her voice went up in pitch.

Carver saw a glint in Sandling's eye.

She said, "Yes, you are, Penny. Yes you are. Gust is right. You're scared but guess what, so are all of us, right? You're lying if you say it isn't a risk. We might be made to look like fools. *Again*. God knows I'm more afraid of that than anyone. I can't even hold a gun without spasming with fear. But that just means we have something to prove."

"She's right," Underwood said. "Caitlin is right. It's not even that I'm afraid of failing again. It's like I expect not to succeed. I let a serial killer escape once—"

"You can redeem yourself," Carver said. "I was a little hard on you at the crime scene, Underwood, I'm sorry."

"Wait a second," Maudmont said. "We all know why we're here, and you know why we're here Gust, but none of us know why you're here."

"That's true," Hornigen said. "Fair is fair."

Fox spun around in her chair. "He killed someone."

"Excuse me!" Maudmont said.

"Yeah," Fox said. "He killed someone, a suspect. That's what his record says, anyway."

"I thought those were sealed," Carver said.

Fox gave him a look that said '*Oh, please*'.

"FBI cyber security is a joke," she said. "I hacked your file in under three minutes. I timed it. I hacked all your files."

"Not cool, Rachel," Sandling said. "Not cool at all."

"But Deputy Director Gibson put in a good word for you," Fox said. "That's in there."

"Stop going through my stuff, Fox," Carver said. "I don't care how good you are at getting into places, exercise some self-restraint, will you?"

"Is that why you're here?" Maudmont asked.

"Not exactly," Carver sighed. "Look, I'm not proud of some of the things I've done, and some of the things I've seen in this job but I'm in too deep now, all right? All I know how to do is catch killers. I'm not a people person. I'm not a manager. I'm not a hugger. All I know is there's a killer out there right now and they brought me back and put me here to find him and stop him. Now call it fate, or call it dumb luck, but either way here I am, and here you all are too. Right now, we're like this little island of misfit toys. But, if we work together and use the skills that we have, I *know* we can catch this guy. I also know I can't do it alone ..."

There was a pause.

"What do you say, guys?" Sandling asked.

"You're on his side now," Maudmont said accusingly.

"I'm not on anyone's side, Penny, I just want us to help stop him."

"And what makes you think we can?"

"We're all FBI agents for one thing," Carver said. "Sofa Squad or not, you're all carrying a badge." He turned to Fox. "We've got one of the best computer specialists in the whole Bureau sitting here."

"Not one of," Fox said. "The best. And not just in the Bureau."

"See? And here, Frank Hornigen, didn't you used to work in the Secret Service? He's a currency specialist. That's a unique skill. Toby has worked serial killers before. Sandling is the youngest profiler in agency history. And Penny ..." She crossed her arms. "You're one of the best planners and organizers I've come across. Investigations are a mess and we'll only win this thing by crunching the data. Now we have no one better. Come on guys, what did you say?"

"He made a 911 call," Fox called out. She leaned closer to her computer monitor and spoke to them with her face almost touching the screen. "The bastard made a call to the emergency services while he was still in the house."

The team crowded around her desk. Carver stayed where he was. He had a stupid look on his face but he was confused.

"Couldn't have," Carver said to himself. "Local PD ..."

"It says so right here." Fox touched the screen with her finger. "Approximately *three-oh-three* they received a call from the crime scene. No one spoke. He only pushed numbers on the phone then left the phone off the hook. They sent a black and white to do a drive-by. Non-urgent. Saw nothing out of the ordinary, so left."

"Bastard was probably still in the house. He was probably watching them," Carver said. "I need a copy of that 911 call and I need the number for Charleston. I need to chew out some—"

"Idiots," Sandling said.

"Morons," Penny added.

"Nitwits," Underwood said.

"Knuckleheads," Hornigen chimed in.

"Jokers," Fox said.

"—out," Carver said. "All of the above. Get a recording of

it, analyze it. Find out what the dial tones mean, if anything. Tell me what you make of it, Foxy, okay?"

"Isn't this nice," Sandling said. "All working together, like a *team*."

"Yeah? Let's not get our hopes up. One step at a time," Carver said. "Get to it."

23

RED EARTH and pools of water. That's what Derange remembered.

The clay and puddles surrounded their tiny box home. He always thought about it while he worked. How the clay wouldn't let the water seep into the ground and so it stayed in these murky, shiny, twirling puddles. Stagnant. Waiting.

They lived between a railway line and a main road. When the trains would go by in the night it'd shake the windows so that Edward, as a young boy, thought the glass would come crashing down onto his face and hands and cover his skin in tiny cuts.

He worried about who would pay for the doctors. They had no money. He remembered standing beside a huge wooden chopping block on the kitchen table and watching his mother's hands covered in blood as she cut the brown and gray parts off a chuck steak they'd fished out of the trash. She'd told him it was called 'chuck steak' 'cause they'd chucked it out.

He liked to think of her bloody fingers. He would watch her hands and wonder, 'Where's my daddy? Did she kill him with those bloody fingers? The other children have one. So where is mine?'

"Soon", she would tell him. "I'll speak to him soon and he'll change his mind, visit us, and take care of us. You'll see."

But he never came.

"Where's my daddy?" he always asked. She always said the same thing. Instead, he came up with stories. Fantasies about the shapeless, figureless man and the void not knowing left in his life.

"Where's my daddy?" Derange said as he stroked the head of a ferret he was busy attaching to the body of an iguana. The ferret was one of the first animals he taxidermied. He'd kept her all this time. Through so much. He only went back and unpicked her stitches and removed her skin when he needed to think. Or when he needed a change. Something new. The Black Dog was stirring. He knew he'd have to put it to sleep again soon. He sat alone in the dark. Except he wasn't really alone, was he? All around him were moments. Elements of the things he had done. He didn't like people. You can't trust people. That's what mummy had always said. He'd always called her mummy. She was from Jamaica, she'd explained. And there, people, when they spoke properly, spoke like the King and Queen of England. She's always insisted he call her mummy, and he still did.

Sometimes, as he worked, his mind would run away from him and he would imagine how he and his idol, Hermann Zimmer, could be friends. Maybe even more than friends.

He fantasized that perhaps indeed the priest, infamous surgeon, and shining example for all people who plied his trade and carried out his God-given gifts of hunting men, could, in fact, be his father. Likely *was* his father, Edward told himself. And part of that ideation and fantasy was that he, mummy, and Hermann would be able to live together. He knew that Hermann would accept his relationship, and his mother's current condition because of how he was, and who he was, and what his fascinations were. Hermann Zimmer was the only man who understood him. He was sure of it.

Other people didn't. His mother was one of the main reasons why he was so brutally picked on while in juvenile detention.

He thought about his time there a lot. He thought about how he got there and what it made him. And he burned with hate. He hated the boys who'd beaten him. He hated the masters who'd let it happen. He hated the lawyer who'd sent him there. And mostly, he hated the woman who'd let it happen. He loved her. He loved her with all his heart. That's why it hurt. But he hated her. He had to. There was no other way.

He remembered standing in front of the judge and thinking, 'You can't judge me, how dare you try and judge me.' He still felt like that.

"I wasn't playing by their rules, even when I was," he said to the ferret head. They were poor. They were helpless. He didn't know any better. The first he knew of what was happening was when the policeman tapped on the foggy sedan windows with his flashlight. He would never forget that sound. He was naked in the back seat with a stranger. He was only young. He didn't know any better. She'd said she'd always look after him. She said she'd never be too far away. She said if he did this it would help her be able to buy a ticket to see his daddy. "You were so beautiful. You said you'd always protect me but you didn't, did you, mummy?"

· · ·

As the policeman pulled him out of the car and pushed him against the cold metal door he saw the silhouette of his mummy running away. He was crying. He didn't understand. Solicitation and resisting arrest. That's what the judge said. What did it mean? He'd looked around for her in the courtroom but there were no faces he recognized. Only the looks of shame and pity from the people present. He didn't feel ashamed. Why should he?

The detention center was hell. Hell on earth. Torment and suffering around the clock. Everywhere he went. They all knew, all the boys in the place knew why he was there. They called him *bitch*, they called him *faggot*, they called him *pillow biter*. He was terrorized and he was terrified. Still was. Started wetting the bed. That made it worse. He'd be dragged by the duty matron to the ablutions and thrown under a freezing shower.

The other boys stood around and mocked him. Sneered. Shouted abuse. Some nights they'd stand over him and piss on his head and in his face. They told him that if he ever told they'd slit his throat in the night. He would wail for his mummy.

He learned where to hide. He learned how to lie. He slipped out of view and stayed in the shadows. One day it was very hot. The type of stale, stagnant, oppressive heat that makes crazy people do crazy things. There was a commotion by the fence. Everyone went to see. A boy named Angel had caught a snake. What kind? Nobody knew. But it was a venomous one alright. Very venomous. Everybody wanted to see it.

Except Edward. "I don't want to see it," he said.

That night he was sneaking to the toilets. He'd gotten good at hiding his night waters and rinsing his underpants out so no one would know. He heard a strange noise in the bathroom. Boys whispering and giggling and shadows dancing against the white tiles in candlelight.

"Hey look, it's piss head," one of the boys said. "He's wet himself again." God, he stinks. Come on, let's fix him. Let's teach him how to behave. Let's scare his little snake with a big snake so it doesn't wet the bed anymore. Angel held the viper out to him. "Quick, grab him so he can see."

He'd tried to run but they pinned him down. They were making it up on the fly. Excitedly coming up with new and novel ways to scare him straight and stop him wetting the bed. "I know," Angel said. "Let's see if the snake recognizes its friend. If not, we know he's a cocksucker." What about if it does recognize him, one of them asked.

"Then he might want to say hello."

Writhing and howling to get free the boys pulled down his urine-soaked underpants and set the snake on him. The bite was sharp and vicious. The pain indescribable. His violent screaming made the boys drop the snake and run. They were terrified of the sound coming out of him.

"And where were you, mummy? You weren't there."

The doctor told him that he'd managed to save his penis. Save it from what? He said he'd saved what he could but that the venom was very strong. Luckily they'd found the snake and could tell what kind it was. The anti-venom had saved his life. But they hadn't been able to save his genitalia. "I don't think it'll work properly again, son," the doctor said. "After that, you came to visit me, didn't you mummy?"

The boys had been right about one thing. He no longer wet himself. Lying there, in his hospital bed. Snake venom coursing through his veins, he no longer felt the same. He no longer looked at life the same. People weren't to be trusted. Snakes could be trusted. They were simple to understand. They were quiet. Everyone was afraid of them and everyone left them alone. That's how he was. How he wanted to be. He'd asked to see the snake. They brought it to him. He asked to sit with it for a while. Soon they left it in his hospital room. He didn't sleep much anymore. One of the reasons he stopped pissing in the sheets.

Snakes didn't need to sleep, did they?

"Then they let me out, they said it was because I'd changed—I'd reformed—but it was because of my scars. They were scared of how I looked and what I was. They were worried about a lawsuit. Or worried I would hurt someone, weren't they? Instead, you let them pay you off, didn't you mummy?"

The police found his mummy's body where she'd fallen. Lying face down in one of the mosquito-covered pools of water. Clay on her cheeks and hands. And a snake bite on her wrist. The state took care of the burial. But the thought of her rotting in the ground didn't seem right to him. He wanted her with him. He was sorry for what he'd done but he couldn't help himself. He spent most of the night digging her up. He dragged her body away in a tarpaulin. He got used to the smell after a while. And he salvaged what he could of her best features. Her face. Her eyes. Her hair. He looked across at the glass case containing his snakes. There lying in her own false bottom was his mummy. He could see her eye still staring, all glassy and dull, like a fish eye that'd started to turn.

"Now we'll always be together, won't we mummy?" Derange said and put the final stitch into the ferret's neck fur.

24

MANASSAS

SANDLING SAT at her desk and stared at the cursor blinking on and off on her computer screen and thought about Zimmer. She hadn't stopped thinking about the tall, blond, ferociously insane Austrian since she'd left him sitting shackled to that metal table.

"Sandling," Underwood said.

"Mmm," she said and looked at him, pulled from her daydream.

"Do you not hear that?"

"What?"

Then she heard Carver yelling, "Agent Sandling!"

She jumped to her feet. "Coming!" she called back. She walked around the desk and Underwood said to Hornigen, "Reminds me of this joke about the pilot and the stewardess."

"Yeah," Sandling said as she breezed past, "We've all heard that *one* joke you know, Underwood."

He started telling Hornigen the joke anyway. "So the pilot gives his usual 'welcome aboard' speech to the passengers ..."

The voices tailed off as she approached the beast's lair.

Before she entered she turned and called out, "Don't forget the coffee!" Then Underwood saying, "Oh, *jeez*, thanks Caitlin, ruin the punchline why don't you."

She went into Carver's office. Carver told her to close the door by lifting his chin and looking toward it. She pushed the door shut and it clicked closed. Carver had his shoes off and his feet on the desk and he leaned all the way back. He looked tired.

"What's all that about?" Carver asked.

"Oh, nothing. Underwood just telling the *one* sexist, lazy stereotype of a joke he knows. A swipe at women in the workplace."

Carver said nothing.

"Are you still sleeping in here?" she asked and looked around.

"Nope, I'm in a motel just out of town. Moving into a little apartment next week."

"Just all your stuff is in here?"

"Yeah. Listen, there's something I wanted to ask you. Tell you. Talk to you about ..."

"Are you okay, Gust?"

"Yeah, sit down," he said.

She did. Hands on her lap. Perched on the edge. Showing attentiveness and concern.

"I've been thinking about Zimmer," Carver said. "Have you?"

"Um, not really. No, I wouldn't say thinking about him. No. How come? Why do you ask?"

She was worried that it was written on her forehead. Everyone could tell she couldn't get him off her mind.

"Listen, don't tell the others—they wouldn't understand —but you've met him so you know how it is with him, right?"

She nodded but wasn't sure where he was going with it.

"I've had Zimmer's lawyers on the phone to me pretty much non-stop. He just won't give up on this idea of me appearing at his medical review board. You know, periodically they have these reviews because of the type of sentence he was given and they need to assess his condition and find out if he's reformed and fit for reintegration, of all things. Anyway, for some reason Zimmer wants me to appear and I don't know what to do."

"Hmm," she lifted her hand to her mouth and looked down and nodded slowly like she was considering what to say.

"Zimmer says he'll help us with the profile in return for my presenting myself—so to speak—at his hearing."

"Hmm, yeah," Sandling said.

"Well?"

"Well, what?"

"Well, do you think I should do it?"

"I mean, Gust, Zimmer said he'll only help if you turn up ..."

"Yeah, I know, but is it worth it?"

"What do you mean?"

"I mean, do you not think that it's kind of odd for me to turn up and testify on his behalf considering I'm the one who put him away and was on the stand pointing the finger at him about his insanity and the murders he committed? Don't you think it'll undermine what we're trying to do here if I end up defending him or going back on my word?"

"Forget what it *looks* like, Gust. I mean, you need to do what *feels* right, don't you?"

"How do you mean?"

"Well, can you live with yourself, you know, with your history with him?"

"You mean as the killer of my daughter?"

Sandling didn't respond. Then said, "He never actually said what he wants you to say, right?"

Carver's face was blank and his eyes unblinking. They were bloodshot. Stubble on his face.

"Gust?"

"Yeah," he said. "I'm thinking."

"He never actually said he wants you to defend him, right?"

"Right."

"You're thinking it was implied, though?"

"Yeah."

"Well, you get up there and you tell the truth, how you see it—"

"How it is."

"How it is, and you ... you—you know—you keep him in jail, where he belongs."

"Psychiatric hospital."

"Yeah."

"It's too good for him."

"Sure is," Sandling said. She was chewing the inside of her cheek.

"You okay? You seem nervous."

"Me? Oh, yeah, no, I'm fine. Just thinking."

"About?"

"Blowback."

"You think we get the press involved?" Carver asked.

"Yeah, potentially? I don't know."

"That could be an option," Carver said. "Get out in front of it. You know how the press loves anything about Zimmer the Ripper."

"The tabloid press, yeah."

"Well, this is where this game is fought, kid. Down in the trenches. In the sewers and the rainwater ditches. You gotta get right down in there and pull them out of their holes in the ground like they do with catfishing down in the Everglades," Carver said.

"I don't know what you're talking about but it sounds dirty."

"How do you think the team will take it?"

"Hell, Gust, have you turned over a new leaf? You're suddenly concerned about how it's gonna affect morale?"

"Yeah, you're right. Screw it."

She stood up.

"Okay, get out of here," Carver said. She closed the door behind her and walked back to her desk. Underwood was still talking to Hornigen.

He looked up at her and said, "So, what did the captain want?"

"Blowjob and coffee."

"Huh?" Maudmont grunted, confused.

"Haven't you heard Toby's *one* joke that he knows?"

"No," Maudmont said.

"Captain says, 'Man, I could really use a blowjob and coffee'. Stewardess goes bombing it down the aisle to tell him that his microphone is still on, and a passenger—in this case Toby, because the joke works better if you tell it in the first person—yells out, 'Don't forget the coffee!'"

"Oh! Now I get it," Hornigen said. "*Ha*! That's a good one."

Underwood gave him a pained look.

"What?" Hornigen asked. "Worked better when she told it."

"Right, that's enough, y'all," Maudmont said. "Ya'll might all be working this exciting case but this backlog of boxes isn't going to upload itself. Get cracking."

They all groaned. Sandling hid behind her screen and bit her thumbnail and fretted about whether she'd said the right thing. There was a general *hubbub*. They were all facing Maudmont when her face dropped. The conversation died down and they followed her eyes.

Carver had come out of his office and was standing in his socks, hands on hips, moving his jaw from side to side.

"What are you doing, sir? Carver. Gust. Sorry," Maudmont said.

"Thinking," Carver said, absentmindedly. Carver trance.

"Anything in particular?"

Carver shook his head. He was staring into the distance. "The case, Penny, always the case."

"Anything we can help with?"

He started nodding, slowly, still with a thousand-yard stare. "Yeah," Carver said. "I've been thinking, we don't have many leads but the few we do have are at least— something—and we need to follow up. It's more than I can do alone."

"What can we do to help?" Sandling asked. "Well, for starters, Toby, Frank, you could do me a favor and follow up on Bastien Dufresne - any connection between the two victims."

"I thought HQ told us to leave that alone," Underwood said.

Carver furrowed his brow and cocked his head and glared at Underwood for a moment.

"What else?" Maudmont asked.

"Caitlin, Penny, maybe you two can work together to try and build a profile of the victims. We only have two victims, but we need something to help local PD. Who were they? Why is he targeting them? And how can we use whatever's distinctive to try and build a profile of his victim preferences?"

"There are more than two victims though, boss, aren't there?" Hornigen said.

"Yeah, thanks, of course, Frank but what I mean is the *main* victims. We're working under the premise that the girls with their faces taken were the intended targets and the others just got in the way. That's a bit blunt but—"

"Wouldn't expect anything less," Underwood said under his breath.

"Is there anything I can do?" Fox asked.

"Foxy—" Carver said and his voice trailed off.

"Don't call me Foxy."

"Right," Carver said. "Maybe you can use your computer magic to somehow find out if there are any connections between the victims. Doesn't matter how tenuous. Both of them were models. One part-time, but still. Is there something there? Anything? Is there some way that we can get the system to analyze the data and pull connections we can't see?"

"Easy," Fox said. "I can write an algorithm to analyze any and all online behavior, mentions, and connections in the matrix and we'll make a—"

"Sounds good," Carver said. "Let's get on it. This guy is going to be planning his next face-peeling session any day now. And, in my experience, the hotter they get the shorter the time is between killings."

There was silence. Carver stood for an awkward moment looking at them.

"Okay," he said. "Go get 'em." And gave a half-hearted air punch. He turned and went back into his office and closed the door. The team sat and looked at one another for a moment in silence.

"Well, don't just sit there y'all. You heard the man. Hop to it!" Maudmont said.

25

TOBY UNDERWOOD and Frank Hornigen made an odd couple. They were each like younger and older versions of themselves. Both tall and wiry. Looked like they could each go the distance in the ring, or finish comfortably in the top ten of a half-marathon.

They stepped out of the black sedan at the same time. The car doors slammed shut simultaneously and Underwood glanced across at Hornigen just as they each straightened their ties.

"Why do you always gotta dress like me?" Underwood asked.

"Not this again," Hornigen looked over at his partner. "Dress code says white or cream shirts, charcoal or navy suits. Stands to reason on the occasional day we'll be wearing the same shirt."

"Yeah, that, or you're just trying to be like me."

"Son, the day I want to be more like you is the day I

check myself into the psychiatric ward and they ain't never letting me go."

Underwood grinned and raised his chin. "This the building?" he asked and looked up at a squat apartment block.

Hornigen took a bit of paper out of his pocket and held it out under the street light.

"Seems to be."

"Remind me, why in the hell are we doing this again?"

Hornigen buttoned his suit jacket and said, "Lisa—Rachel Fox—Chung ... wait a second, are you just trying to get some old timer to try and badly explain computer mumbo-jumbo to a young'un?"

"No," Underwood said and laughed as they crossed the street. "I'm genuinely asking."

"This girl knew Savannah Proctor," Hornigen said. "Far as I can tell. And we're following up on it. Got it?"

"Sure," Underwood said and pressed the buzzer for apartment two-twelve. "That, and because Penny Two-puddings Maudmont told us to, right?"

"That's right. Gotta do as the good office manager says."

"Asks," Underwood said. "Good one. What's this one's name?"

"Van-es-sa Har-ris," Hornigen said, emphasizing every syllable so that *maybe* Underwood would remember it this time. "She's five-nine, twenty-three years old. Green eyes. Light brown hair. Wavy. She has a small crescent moon tattoo on her left wrist."

"Hell man, how do you know all this?"

"I read the damn report, you idiot. You didn't though did you?"

"There were like fifty of 'em."

"There were seventeen and I thought Foxy Chung did a real good job on them, if I'm honest. You wouldn't know though, I suppose? I am starting to see why you ended up where you did."

"That's harsh. That's what I have you for, Frank. That's why I have you." Underwood balled up his fist and gave Hornigen a light tap on the shoulder. "Now if I could just get you to stop dressing like me, we might actually make some real progress in this flourishing partnership."

"Sure ..."

"How'd she do it anyway?" Underwood asked.

"Said she wrote an algorithm—like a search code—that matched key characteristics from Proctor's contacts."

"Like?"

"Age, profession, looks, I don't know; the usual stuff you'd assess to try and match traits, I guess."

"Uh-huh, and she did this on a computer?"

"Yup."

"Well, what about the 911 calls?" Underwood asked.

"What about 'em?"

"She was supposed to analyze them too."

"Yeah and she did," Hornigen said.

"What did she come up with?"

"*Jeez*, do you want me to wipe your ass too?"

"I'm an auditory learner, Frank, you know that. I prefer when you tell it to me."

Hornigen *huffed* and said, "No recognizable pattern. No Fibonacci scale or prime numbers."

"What was the sequence again?"

"Why, you gonna solve it in your head?"

"No, I just—"

"One-zero-one-nine-five-three," Hornigen said.

Underwood touched his chin. "What does it mean?"

Hornigen laughed. "Are you serious?" He laughed again. "I just told you we don't know!"

"Maybe it doesn't mean anything," Underwood said.

Hornigen shrugged. "Maybe, yeah, maybe not. Only one person knows right now."

"Who?" Underwood asked.

Hornigen shook his head.

"Never mind."

INSIDE HER APARTMENT, Vanessa Harris was setting up the camera in her room. There was a light tap on the door.

"Hi, *Vee*." Carina Ellington said and stepped in.

"Hey, Ellie. *Oh!* You look sexy; are you going out?" Vanessa asked, looking at her out the corner of her eye while applying mascara.

"Oh, thank you! Yeah, I'm meeting Bobby."

"Again! Wow - you guys are getting serious. Careful out there, kid."

Carina flopped on the bed and spread her arms and asked, "What are *you* doing?"

"Oh, you know me, gonna hang out with my lovely followers and do a make-up tutorial. I've got so many people now since the last one! It's taken on a life of its own."

"That's amazing! You're such a business bitch, I love it. A bit *jelly* but I love it." There was silence as Ellie watched Vanessa in the mirror. She applied eyeliner then blinked and noticed Ellie watching her.

"What?" she asked and smiled.

"Oh, nothing, darling," Ellie said. "I just still can't believe that you did that to your hair. I mean, it looks lovely. I could never do it ... but looks lovely. You just used to have such long beautiful hair when I first met you and it's gotten shorter and shorter. What made you decide to shave it all off?"

"I just felt like a change," Vanessa said. "You know how it is ... Gotta change things up, right?"

Ellie sat up and looked at her watch and said, "Right, I'm gonna leave before I end up in the background of your tutorial and somebody recognizes me and becomes a stalker. You aren't worried about that, are you? Getting a stalker? Anyway, Bobby's on his way to pick me up. Actually, he's already late, so I'm just gonna go wait for him in the living room. But I'll see you later. So ..."

"Okay, bye-bye lovely. Have a great time." She put her eyeliner down and turned to look at her housemate. "Oh, hey lovely, before I forget, don't come home all blackout drunk and wasted like you did last weekend, please. You left the front door open again and I don't want to have to wake up to a cold draft at 4 A.M. with your new stalker in our living room every Saturday morning!"

Ellie smiled and said, "I'll try sweetheart but I can't make any promises. See you tomorrow!" She left Vanessa's room and closed the door.

"Hopefully," Vanessa said.

A knock on the front door. It sounded loud and threatening. Like it demanded attention. She heard Ellie pad over to the front door and open it.

Vanessa stopped breathing and sat very still and listened.

For some reason her heart was beating fast. She heard the bass of a man's voice and then Ellie's high-pitched replies.

She sounded worried. "I'd better go check," Vanessa said to herself.

EDWARD DERANGE SAT on the dirty fabric seat of his old van and watched the house from under the shadow of an overhanging tree. He liked shadows. He liked darkness. No one else seemed to. He wore a dark cap and dark sweatshirt. It was one of the things he liked about his skin. How it blended. How it *creeped*. How he was like a chameleon. He could fit in anywhere. No one could put him in a box.

He had the white glow of his phone on his lap waiting for Vanessa's tutorial to start. He always watched. It made him feel close to her. He felt like he knew her. Like maybe they could be friends if they gave each other a chance. He pushed those soft, reckless desires down and built up the fantasy of his night with her.

She was a special one.

He was ready and just about to step out of the van when he saw the two dark-suited gentlemen sidling over to Vanessa Harris's front door.

What the hell? He watched them. They were so busy chatting to one another that they hadn't been interested in who or what was around. They had no idea, did they? He imagined the different ways that he could have approached and executed them right there, getting in the way of his big moment, but he knew that those were just daydreams or—night-dreams and hellscapes as he called them—places his mind went but wasn't allowed to wallow in and enjoy.

The men pounded on the girls' front door and Derange watched as Vanessa's housemate, Carina Ellington, opened up. They'd been friends since college. Maybe before. Derange didn't know. He knew enough. He followed their every move. Pictures taken here. Videos taken there. Always looking drop-dead gorgeous. Champagne. Clubs. Runway shows. He loved it. He wanted it.

Ellington looked bemused at first, then afraid. He recognized the look of fear on a woman's face. He liked it. It thrilled him. He didn't know why. The way their eyes glowed with horror. He wished he could feel what they felt. Then Derange got excited.

The men pulled out black leather wallets which he couldn't see properly but he assumed they were police. Could they be? Maybe they were Jehovah's Witnesses. Does the Church of the Latter-Day Saints carry leather wallets? He didn't know. They had to be police, but how? How could they have known? Were they watching him? Were they tracking him? If they were, surely they would know he was there. No. He was in the shadows. His mind spun out of control in some kind of paranoid frenzy. His thoughts were like piranhas charging at a dead carcass and spinning away with chunks of meat in their mouths. He felt the taste of vomitus in the back of his throat. He wasn't going to throw up, but he knew that something was wrong.

VANESSA CAME out of her room and cautiously peered around the corner.

She saw Ellie standing in front of two tall men. They both looked similar, with similar haircuts, and similar suits. Ellie turned toward her and said, "Here she is now ..."

The older man looked directly at her and said as if he was delivering somber news, "Miss Harris, we're from the Federal Bureau of Investigation. We're investigating the murder of somebody we think you might have known. Do you have a few moments to speak with us, please?"

She had an immediate feeling of dread and emptiness in the pit of her stomach. She simultaneously wanted to find out everything and ask all the questions she could think of but at the same time wanted to go and hide under the covers and pretend like nothing bad had happened and nobody wanted to speak to her.

They always joked about stalkers and over-exuberant fans, people they looked down on as wanting their lives, but she never really worried about it, she never thought it was serious and she never thought anything bad would ever happen to them.

So why was the FBI standing on her front doorstep and asking questions of her and her housemate? This must be some kind of bad dream.

"Is this real?" Vanessa asked and gave a single laugh. "Is it April Fool's Day today or Halloween or something? Are you guys dressing up as the FBI to just impress us?" She said in a please-tell-me-you're-joking way. It was the only thing she could think of to say that wouldn't give the fear and pain a way out.

"I'm sorry, Miss Harris—" the younger one started to say.

"Please call me Vanessa," she interrupted. "We don't go by formal names in this house."

"—Okay. Excuse me, *Vanessa*, but unfortunately we aren't joking. It's quite serious. And we wanted to ask you if you knew Savannah Proctor."

All of a sudden, Vanessa couldn't hide her emotions. She stepped forward to the door, almost in-between Ellie and the federal agents. Vanessa turned to Ellie as she said, "Do you need to speak to Carina too, or is this just me?"

The older agent looked at Carina and asked, "Did you know Savannah Proctor?"

Carina shook her head.

"Nope," the older guy said. "I guess it's just you then, Miss Harris."

"Bye, Ellie," Vanessa said and gave her housemate a look that said, *go away.*

"I'll be in the kitchen if you need me," Ellie said and gave a polite smile and nod to the federal agents.

"So how did you know Savannah Proctor?" the younger one asked. "How did you know her? When did you meet? Were you two friends? Did you keep in touch? When was the last time you spoke?"

"Easy tiger," the older guy said.

"Do you gentlemen want to come into the living room and sit down so that we don't give the neighbors even more to gossip about?" Vanessa asked.

They nodded and stepped in.

DERANGE WATCHED. Vanessa let the men into her home. She did a quick check of the street and shut the door. He licked his lips.

He was salivating. He could almost taste her. He couldn't wait to be in her bedroom and touch all of her, and all of her things, take the nicest bits and leave the rest.

He was sure it was going to be the most exhilarating experience of his life. He just had to wait. He checked his watch. There was still time to get things done the way he wanted. He just needed those official-looking men to leave so he could get on with his business.

He never felt as focused and in tune with the vibration of the universe as he did when he was sitting in his van waiting for the right moment. He felt tense and relaxed at the same time, like a sprinter at the starting line waiting for the gun. He needed to be released.

He was waiting for it. The anticipation was his oral stimulation. The kill, his ejaculation. Skinning them, his warm embrace.

He waited. His knee bounced. He drummed his fingers

on the steering wheel. He got ready. He wasn't going to wait. This might be his last chance. If the cops were onto him. The last place they'd expect him to be was the same place they'd just been. He'd always imagined them as incompetent but now he was sure.

Fifteen minutes. That's all they'd taken. How thorough, he thought. How reliably mundane. Even when he was right under their noses they couldn't get even a sniff. The front door opened. They stepped out and turned around and said their goodbyes and thank-you's. Derange watched them go. The cops sauntered across the street to their sedan. Cops. Scum of the earth, Derange thought. Know nothing. Understand nothing. Couldn't begin to grasp the importance of what he was doing. They opened their car door and got in. He saw the tail lights turn red, then white smoke from the exhaust. They pulled out without signaling. He scoffed and pulled Savannah Proctor's face skin over his own and tied it behind his head. Put his baseball cap back on and pulled it down over his eyes.

He stepped out of the van and closed the door without locking it. A quick scan up and down the street. It was quiet. He could hear himself breathing in the mask. It felt like wearing something rubber over his face. He could smell the moisturizer he lathered on the inside several times each day. Got to look after your things well, mummy always said. Derange walked up the stairs to the front door and tapped on the brass knocker. He heard a thud and stomping footsteps from inside. A voice started talking before the door opened.

"Jesus, finally. Bobby, you're *so* late!"

The door swung open. It was Carina Ellington. Her face dropped from a wide happy smile to confusion, and then recognition. She opened her mouth to scream and Derange swung his arm and hit her with a monkey wrench. Her head snapped to the side and her body dropped to the floor.

He stepped over it, into the hallway, and gently closed the door.

26

THE D'ARKE MODELING AGENCY was at the end of an industrial park. It had low square buildings and all kinds of different trucks and trailers parked around the place. It didn't look inviting. Open scrubland with a few trees dotted here and there. It was a concrete oasis in a remote wasteland on the outskirts of Charleston.

It didn't look like somewhere that teenage girls should find themselves. And Carver could tell that Sandling had the hairs on the back of her neck standing up. She was like a bloodhound for danger. They pulled the glass door open and walked straight past the reception counter and into the owner's office.

"Hey! Hey, what are you doing? I'm on the phone here." His name was Craig Smatten, "You can't just ..." Then into the receiver. "Hold on a second, Roy, I'm going to have to call you back. Two suited clowns just barged into my office."

Smatten went to stand. Before he could, Sandling flipped open her wallet and said, "I'm Agent Sandling. This is Agent Carver. We're with the Federal Bureau of Investigation. We'd like to ask you some questions about Savannah Proctor."

"Who?" Smatten blurted out then closed his mouth and dropped back into his swivel chair. He said quickly into the receiver, "Listen, Roy, I gotta go, okay," and dropped the phone into its cradle. "What's all this about?"

He leaned to look past them and out of his office and said in hushed tones, "This is a place of business, you can't just barge in."

"We can, Mr. Smatten," Carver said.

"What's this about?"

"Might we sit?" Carver asked. Smatten nodded. He was flustered. Sandling took a seat. Carver went over and looked at the black and white pictures hanging on the wall.

"How old is your clientele, Mr. Smatten?" Carver asked.

"Huh? Oh, ah, in their teens. Mostly teens. They're getting started in their modeling career. You know ... we have a range though. Older models. Plus size. We don't discriminate. You know how it is ..."

"No, we don't know, Mr. Smatten," Sandling said. "That's why we're talking to you."

"*Jeez* lady, all right. Calm down."

Carver knew that would rile Sandling up. She hated being told to *calm down*. She hated to be told to relax almost as much as she hated firing her service weapon. He saw her clench her jaw.

Carver turned back to the photographs.

"What is this about? I find it odd that I have to ask twice."

While browsing the pictures Carver asked, "Do you know who Savannah Proctor is?" Then he stopped in front of one.

"Savannah? Yes, I know Savannah. Only a long time ago, before, you know ..."

"Before what?" Sandling asked.

"Before she became all rich and famous and dropped

me for a high-end New York agency." A beat, then, "Wait, why are you asking me about her?"

Carver glanced at Sandling and gave her a solemn nod. Carver reached up and lifted a framed photograph off the wall.

"Savannah Proctor is dead," Sandling said and watched Smatten's face for a reaction.

His jaw dropped and he covered his mouth. His eyes darted. Carver could see he was thinking. He didn't look surprised. More like he was feigning surprise.

"What? Oh my God," he said. "Savannah's dead? When did this happen? How did this—" He stopped talking and thought. "I can't believe it," he said.

"Where were you on the night of the thirteenth?" Sandling asked.

Smatten furrowed his brow. "No idea," he said. "I can barely remember what I had for dinner last night. Wait ... Are you saying I'm a suspect?"

Carver turned from the pictures holding the one he'd removed in both hands. "No, Mr. Smatten. We're asking where you were. That's it. What I want to know now is, who's this a picture of?"

"Oh, um, marlin fishing, you know, down in the Gulf."

"He said 'who'," Sandling said.

"He's—ah—he's a photographer I used to work with. He'd give my girls work."

"What's his name?" Carver asked and tapped the frame's glass.

Smatten rubbed his head and looked down. "*Jeez*, ah, let me think, he's ah—"

"Don't mess around Mr. Smatten," Carver said quietly. Smatten glanced up at him. "We'll bring you in for obstruction and set the IRS on you."

"Are you threatening me?"

"Nope," Carver said. "Just letting you know how it's going to be."

Smatten took a deep breath and said, "His name's Dufresne. Bastien Dufresne. Working class prick with a fancy French name, okay?"

Carver nodded. "Good. Good. That's what I thought. You see, we talked to Mr. Dufresne a few days ago. At his home. He told us about you."

"Really? What did he say?"

"That's not how this game works, Mr. Smatten. Why don't you tell us what you think he said and I'll confirm or deny."

"What were you two doing on this boat together?"

"Marlin fishing, I told you."

"You did, but what I want to know is who goes Marlin fishing with a boat full of ..." Carver turned the picture and glanced at it. "They're blurred but it looks like teenage girls in bikinis behind you two. To me anyway."

Smatten sighed and slumped and went all floppy. "Look, I don't want any trouble, just tell me what this is about and I'll tell you whatever you need to know."

"You mean you'll tell us the truth," Sandling said.

"Yes, of course, the truth, whatever I know, whatever you need to know," Smatten said.

"You and Dufresne know each other personally as well as professionally?" Carver asked.

"No, that's a strictly professional relationship. I think he's a douchebag. I don't hang out with him outside of work."

"I see," Carver said. "So this little boat trip was for work?"

Smatten was quiet, eyes bouncing over Carver's face. He looked like he was trying to think what the next right move was. Think of the right thing to say before he compromised himself, Carver thought.

"How did you find me?" Smatten asked quietly.

"You have a small list of success stories on your website, Mr. Smatten. Savannah Proctor's details and a picture of her as a very young teenage girl are also on there. We're able to use computers too, Mr. Smatten," Sandling said. "And we're able to do addition. Two plus two equals moron."

"Answer my question," Carver said.

"Um, what was the question again?"

"Your relationship with Bastien Dufresne, was it outside of work as well as inside of work?" Sandling asked. "What we mean by that—to be crystal clear—is, were you and Bastien Dufresne in collusion to supply him with young talent, in exchange for favors outside of your day job?"

"We, um, we ..." Smatten was searching for an answer. Carver stepped forward and slammed the picture frame on the desk. Smatten jumped. He was shaken.

"You supplied Bastien Dufresne with young girls," Carver said. It was accusatory. It was hard. It was said with an edge. Don't try and mess with me. "Dufresne has a thing for young girls he's photographing doesn't he," Carver said. "What did you get in return?"

"You groomed them for him and gave them to him to do with as he liked," Sandling said.

"No," Smatten said.

"Yes," Carver said.

"No, I swear."

"Is that what happened to Savannah Proctor?" Carver demanded. "You offered her up to Dufresne as a tribute and he took her and damaged her. That's what happened isn't it?"

"No," Smatten searching now. Looking around. "I mean

—*yes*—but that's not how it happened. It wasn't forced. It was consensual. They had a relationship."

"It wasn't consensual," Sandling said.

"She was sixteen. It was," Smatten said.

"There's no way she was sixteen," Carver said.

"The paperwork she filled in said she was," Smatten said. "As far as we were concerned, she was. She'll tell you herself. If she lied then I don't know nothin' bout that."

"Not anymore, Mr. Smatten," Sandling said.

"You see how that looks, Craig, don't you?" Carver asked.

"No ..."

"The way we look at it, looks like you had motive and opportunity."

"Motive for what?"

"For killing Savannah Proctor."

"No!"

"Yes," Carver said and nodded. "It looks like an underage girl became famous; famous enough that if she decided that she wasn't happy about what had happened to her, she had the power to not only ruin the reputation of a famous fashion photographer, as wealthy and powerful as he is, and a small-time hustler at a talent agency but also put the two of you in jail." Carver looked around the room. "These walls are filled with pictures of girls that you fed to Dufresne like a big cat."

Smatten started trembling and shaking. He shook his head. "No, no, no..." he was saying over and over to himself.

Carver felt they were getting into muddy water with this interrogation now. He wanted to bring it back to where they wanted to go, not get down in the slop and argue semantics with Smatten.

The truth was they weren't interested—for the meantime—about his business practices, legal or illegal. They needed confirmation that Dufresne was a predator and Smatten was his pimp.

If there was some sort of discrepancy with his whereabouts on the night that any of the victims were killed, they might have enough to compel the FBI to look again at the famous fashion photographer. Gibson would have to listen to him then.

"Girls are dying, Craig," Carver's voice rose as he spoke. He slammed his hand on the table and Smatten jolted again. Carver leaned on the table and imposed himself in Smatten's space. "Girls are dying and you know something about it. Tell us what we need to know and we'll leave you alone. You had nothing to do with this, remember, Craig? You had nothing to do with this, you said. So tell us what we need to know. Tell us the truth!"

"Okay, okay, yes, yes, all right," Smatten said. "Savannah was one of the girls. Dufresne was a big name, you know, national news, national celebrity, and he was giving my girls a chance. He was putting food on the table. And did he take advantage of them from time to time? I mean, show me a photographer in the fashion world that doesn't, right? Show me a director of a film that doesn't."

Carver slammed his hand on the table again and Smatten jolted and recoiled and pulled his hand up to his chin to protect himself. He was scared. Sandling pursed her lips and shook her head from side to side while watching the specimen in front of her. Carver straightened up. He'd got what he needed and looked at Sandling. She took the cue like a pro. She'd make a hell of a field agent yet, Carver thought.

"Thank you for your cooperation, Mr. Smatten," Sandling said dryly. She sounded like she almost meant it, Carver thought.

"We're going to need access to a full list of your clientele.

We're going to need documentation about the clients that've worked with Bastien Dufresne from when your records began. We're going to need you to sign off on access to your telephone records. And we will send some blue and whites over to take a statement from you about what you've just told us. Mr. Smatten, you can of course have a lawyer present should you request it, but I wouldn't bother .... You're in such deep water that if we wanted we could drown you under the weight of felonies we'll dig up, and you know it. We'd also appreciate it if you refrained from contacting Bastien Dufresne until such time as we are finished with our investigation."

Smatten's eyes were wide. He looked like he might burst into tears.

"Is that clear, Mr. Smatten? Do you have any questions?" Carver asked.

JUST THEN, Carver's phone rang. He glanced at Sandling and she looked at him at the same time. They both felt the same bad feeling, he thought. He lifted the phone to his ear and said, "Hello," as he turned and walked out of the office. Sandling got up and followed him. It was Gibson with bad news. Carver heard Smatten call out from behind them, "Hey, what happens now?"

He ignored the creep and focused on the call. "When did this happen?" Carver asked and waited. He rubbed his forehead. "And you only thought to tell us now?"

He listened. Then said, "What do you mean *not* a priority?"

Carver leaned his head into the phone and bit his tongue. He closed his eyes and forced himself to have a measured tone. His blood was boiling.

"He said he'll only help if I testify at his hearing."

He opened his eyes and scanned the horizon.

"Okay, okay, enough Bronwyn. We'll be there as soon as we can. Have someone from forensics meet us."

He hung up and turned to Sandling.

"What's going on?" she asked.

"Found another victim," Carver said. "Same *modus operandi*."

Carver walked to the car. Sandling hurried along behind him.

"Where?"

"Savannah, near Forsyth Park."

"Georgia? Do you think they're connected? The names I mean, not the bodies."

"Savannah? Don't know. We're going there now."

"What else was that about?" Sandling asked.

"Deputy Gibson, our friendly foe," Carver said.

"How so?"

"We've got a new nickname, apparently," Carver said. "Yukon Club. The boys at Quantico are getting a real kick out of it."

"I don't get it—"

"On account of the remoteness."

"Ah, it's a backwater, like us," Sandling said. "Got it. Is that why we weren't informed about the murder?"

"She said we should be focussing on the Zimmer element, but let's go," Carver said and got into the car. "We're already late."

That would be the end of the conversation. He needed to think.

27

CARVER HADN'T SPOKEN during the whole journey. Sandling was watching him out of the corner of her eye as he drove and could tell he was distracted.

He moved his lips silently and made unconscious gestures with his hand, having an imaginary conversation with someone. Occasionally he would realize he was doing it, and in moments of self-awareness say, "Sorry, just a few things on my mind."

"Anything in particular?" Sandling would ask.

Carver never responded.

Most times he just berated another driver as a way of changing the subject.

He slowed down as they drove along the length of Forsyth Park. It was a clear day. A woman jogged along the path next to them. People were walking their dogs. Smiling. Enjoying the day. Sandling watched them with envy. Her eyes drifted to Carver. He looked tired. His eyes withdrawn.

She could feel how he was straining against this unseen obstacle.

He turned a corner and glanced at the torn bit of paper where he'd written the address. "Think it's around here," he said. They saw the street ahead full of cars and people. The local police had set up a perimeter around the front of the house and a tall African-American policeman was trying to calm down the crowd of onlookers and reporters.

"Turning into a feeding frenzy," Carver said as he spotted a parking spot and swung into it.

They'd have to walk up to the house. He stepped out of the car without a word and they walked shoulder-to-shoulder up the sidewalk. Carver pushed his way through the three-deep crowd and signaled for the attention of the policeman.

"Step back, sir," the policeman yelled over the rabble. Carver flipped open his ID and the policeman's attitude switched instantly. The uniformed cop lifted the yellow police tape. Carver and Sandling ducked under and made their way up the stairs to the front door.

They gave their names and badge numbers to another local cop holding a clipboard at the top of the stairs and went inside.

"The bodies are already on ice," a woman in a white hazmat suit and blue mask said as she approached them. "Erin Holtzclaw, forensics," she said. "I won't shake your hands," and indicated her nitrile gloves. "You must be Carver and Sandling. You're a bit late, we're just finishing up but I told Deputy Gibson I would wait for you. Don't worry about putting on personal protective equipment, we've already swept the scene. We'll need a swab before you leave though, just in case."

Sandling watched Holtzclaw closely. A little enviously. She seemed so on top of it. A real professional. They were rare. Sandling wanted to be the same way but knew she wasn't.

"Thanks," Carver said. "You said *bodies* ... how many were there?"

"This way, Agent Carver, let me walk you through what happened. I hear you think it might be a serial murderer. I wouldn't wish this crime scene on my noisiest neighbor." Holtzclaw looked at them and waited for a laugh and Sandling forced a smile. "Where you're standing now is where the first victim, one Miss Carina Ellington, died. Blunt force trauma and a bullet wound to the head. Point blank range. We think the killer came to the front door, victim answers, he dispatches her quickly with something heavy, she falls. Stands over her here, like this," Holtzclaw widened her stance and turned her hand into a finger pistol. "Fires a single round and leaves her where she falls."

Sandling was hearing the words but her mind wasn't processing it at all. So much detail she didn't want to imagine. She wanted to drift away. She felt like she was back at her divorce hearing. Lawyers talking. Ex-husband arguing. She knew she should try and fight for her position but all she could do was think of the good times they'd shared. She felt sad. She felt sad now. Standing there, looking at blood splatter patterns on the floor and walls. Bloody footprints of a serial killer who was invading her dreams and nightmares. She felt like she hadn't slept in weeks.

"The second victim we think was hiding under her bed. It's this way." Holtzclaw took them down a corridor and turned right into what Sandling thought looked like a typical girl's bedroom. Except for the gallons of blood that had been spilled all over the dresser, floor, and pink bedding.

"I've never seen anything like it," the forensics lead said.

"None of us have," Carver replied.

"Tell us what happened," Sandling said and swallowed. Her throat was dry and her tongue felt thick.

"Victim hears the commotion and gunshot. We think it was suppressed—as none of the neighbors heard the report. Killer comes in, victim hiding under the bed, grabs her and drags her out of the hiding spot. Doesn't immediately kill her, instead we found ligature marks on her neck which indicate strangulation. He subdues her, yet doesn't kill her. We also think he was interrupted."

"What makes you think that?" Sandling asked.

"I'm glad you asked. There was another victim, male, thirties—Robert Ford—we believe he was victim number one's boyfriend. He turned up at the house. He'd called Ellington's phone several times, and we think he possibly could have heard the phone ringing from outside. Peers in through the bedroom window and sees movement. Killer decides he needs to deal with the situation and leaves Vanessa Harris, the second victim, where she is; answers the front door, shoots Ford in the face, and brings his body in, leaving it lying next to victim number one."

"And nobody heard or saw anything?" Carver asked.

Holtzclaw shook her head. "We have uniforms going door to door, canvassing, haven't heard of any witnesses yet. Neighbor said she saw two men in black suits walking up to the front door but figured they were bible salesmen or somethin'. They don't fit the profile of the murderer."

"How so?" Sandling asked.

"It was one killer, not two," Carver said.

"Yes," Holtzclaw said. "And they were wearing suits."

"What happened then?" Carver asked.

"Well, if you know your boy, and know the red stains aren't spillage from a bottle of merlot, then I'm betting you can guess. He comes back. Harris, victim two, is waking up or has woken up. He gags her. Ties her head, hands, and feet to the bed. And—"

"Yeah, we know the rest," Carver said.

"—Proceeds to peel off her face."

"We *know*," Carver and Sandling said at the same time. "Don't need to imagine it again," Carver said.

"Tell us about the method," Sandling said.

"The method?"

"How he did it, was it measured, rushed; how was he?" Sandling said.

"It was hard to look at. I'll say that," Holtzclaw said. "I unfortunately spent quite a lot of time looking at the open wound where Vanessa Harris's face used to be. Just one eye, teeth, tongue, and stripped away blood vessels. If you ask me how he did it, given the tools and time he had, I'd say it was … *slick*. If I can use that word, I feel gross saying it, but he was competent. Proficient. He peeled it away without leaving any patches or bits pulled off if that's what you're asking."

"He's had enough practice," Carver said.

Sandling knew it was meant to be rueful but somehow it came out sarcastic.

"Sorry," Sandling said. "I'm just trying to get a feel for how he is as a person."

"Wait, you said just one eye," Carver said. "What do you mean?"

"Miss Harris only had one remaining eyeball," Holtzclaw said, confused. "He removed the other one. Why? Is that unusual behavior from this suspect?"

"Maybe," Carver said and glanced at Sandling. "Do you think she was still alive while he was cutting her?" Carver asked.

"Undoubtedly, yes," Holtzclaw said.

"So how did the neighbors not hear?" Sandling

wondered out loud. "She would have been screaming in agony."

"He did strangle her, perhaps he did it while she was passed out?" Holtzclaw said.

"The venom," Carver said. "Run a toxicity screen on Vanessa Harris's body. I'm betting you'll find cottonmouth venom in her body. It's hemotoxic."

Sandling furrowed her brow. She wasn't following. Carver noticed.

"Cottonmouth venom prevents blood from clotting and wreaks havoc with the red blood cells. It couldn't clot so she bled out. Hence all the blood."

"The full gallon by the looks of it," Holtzclaw said and looked around the room.

"Anything else?" Carver asked.

"One other thing," Holtzclaw said.

"What is it?" Carver asked.

"It seems like the second victim, Vanessa Harris, was filming on her desktop computer when the killer came in."

"Wait, what," Sandling said. "She recorded her own murder?"

"Not just recorded," Holtzclaw said, "Live streamed it to a few hundred thousand people—as far as we can tell—before they cut the feed."

"Who cut the feed, the killer?" Carver asked.

"No. The platform. Killer smashed the screen but the webcam stayed on. Judging by the angle could have captured the whole thing. Think you can identify him?"

"Killer wears a mask," Carver said.

"How do you know?" Holtzclaw asked.

Carver ignored the question. Sandling knew he wasn't allowed to answer it anyway and changed the subject. "And where's the video now? Have you seen it?" Carver asked.

"I believe we're trying to subpoena the video as

evidence, you'll have to check with the lead detective," Holtzclaw said. "It's a process but we aim to analyze it as soon as we get it so I can—"

Carver turned to Sandling and said, "We need to expedite getting hold of that video, Caitlin. Get hold of Penny and Fox and tell Penny to reach out to Judge Ambrose at the Department of Justice to subpoena the video as evidence. Let's do that now." Carver turned back to Holtzclaw. "What about the 911 call? Did they follow up on that yet?"

She looked stumped. "I didn't know there was an emergency services call. What makes you think there was one?"

"We'll check in with the investigating detectives on that. The suspect has been known to call the police from the scenes. It's just a series of dial tones to us right now, but we think it has some significance. Anything else?"

Holtzclaw shook her head.

"Thanks, Erin. We'll get back in touch if we need anything else. Here's my card," Carver said and held it out to her.

She took it and glanced at it and gave him a polite smile.

"I won't be shaking your hand either," Carver said. "I'll have enough trouble getting the smell of this crime scene off me as it is—no offense—but thank you for waiting for us. You've been really helpful."

"Happy to help," she said. "Hope you get him."

Sandling felt like she should give Holtzclaw a hug. The woman had a stiff upper lip, but she doubted the Savannah Police Department's Forensics Unit had ever dealt with anything like this.

Carver moved toward the door. Sandling was about to follow, then hesitated.

"Can I ask, what was it like?" Sandling asked. "Seeing the bodies."

Holtzclaw stayed composed and stared at her. Sandling

thought maybe she hadn't heard the question or didn't understand it. Sandling was about to leave when Holtzclaw's lip quivered. She cracked. "Horrible," she said. "Disturbing and horrible."

Carver came back in. "Wait, did you find the snake yet?" he asked. Holtzclaw looked confused. "Tell your people to be careful, there's bound to be a cottonmouth hidden around here somewhere. He did it at the last two scenes we worked. One nearly bit me in the face. Anyway," Carver said. "Good luck."

He turned and walked out. Sandling pursed her lips and gave Holtzclaw a sympathetic look. The forensics lead gave her a single knowing nod.

"Thanks for all your help, I gotta ..." she said and turned and followed Carver out.

THEY WALKED out through the front door to a barrage of clicking cameras and reporters shouting questions at them. Sandling lifted her hand to cover her eyes as the flashes went off. "What was it like—who were the victims—are there any suspects—any motives for these killings," the reporters shouted. Carver lifted the crime scene tape and Sandling ducked under it.

"We should have gone out the back," Sandling said breathlessly as she and Carver speed marched toward the car. "We're gonna be all over the nine o'clock news."

"Yeah but it's local," Carver said. "Wait 'til you make the national papers."

"You think we'll be in the paper?"

Carver didn't reply.

"We need a copy of that recording, Cate," he said instead and opened the driver's door.

"I'm calling Penny now," Sandling said and got in.

Carver sat down heavily beside her. He was perspiring and dragged the back of his hand along his forehead.

"We need a connection between the victims," Carver said, thinking out loud. "We need a connection and we need a break in this case."

He started the car. "We're gonna be in the papers anyway, right?" he said and glanced at Sandling.

"Are you asking me or telling me?" she said.

"Both," Carver said as he pulled out.

He glanced over his shoulder and slammed on the brakes. Sandling put her hands up and they hit the dash. A car honked loudly as it sped past.

"Bastard," Carver said and pulled out again. Then, "Sorry. You okay?"

"Yeah," Sandling said. "Just hungry again."

"Christ on a stick, you're worse than a teenage boy. What's it with you and crime scenes where you suddenly crave calories?"

"I don't know but now all I can think of is a corn dog for some reason."

"You're disgusting," Carver said and looked at her out of the corner of his eye. They both laughed.

"I came to the right place then," Sandling said. "What were you saying about the press?"

"Nothing," Carver said. "Just thinking I might need to call in a favor."

28

GOD, he was in such a rage. He was De-rage now. That's funny, he thought. He was witty, even if he was too shy to talk because of his stammer. But how'd he let this happen? How'd he been so stupid? Stupid, stupid, stupid! He was angry now, of course, it wasn't funny. It was ludicrous. Who did he think he was? Of course the FBI was on him. He was haphazard. He was lax. He wasn't paying attention to what he was doing. Did he want to get caught? Is that what he wanted? Go back to prison? Be amongst the general population?

Seen as a freak? No, he needed to stay out. He needed to finish his work. He needed to show these people who they were messing with, even if they would never be able to see him, even if they would never be able to tell exactly what he was.

That stupid boyfriend turning up. God, why hadn't I seen it? I should have known that dumb slut would have another guy over, he thought. Another jock, obviously. Well, I showed him. He wouldn't be running the quarter mile again any time soon.

Perhaps he'd overdone it with the venom this time. The

amount of blood. He'd done his best to clean himself in the bathroom. The coveralls he'd been wearing still stank of iron and that tinge of sweetness that comes with human blood.

The cloth was caked now and viscous. Almost dry.

He'd probably have to burn the van now too. Someone must have seen him. He turned the key in the ignition and the old engine stopped grumbling.

He arrived back—as he always did—in the early hours and parked around the back of the shop. Pulled an old, dirty tarpaulin over the vehicle, checked quickly over his shoulder that no one was looking, and went through the back door into the workshop and kitchen of the antique store. He had the only key for the back door. He could see from the base of the staircase that the chain was still on the front entrance. He knew it was locked and he knew he was safe. He climbed the stairs to his attic room. No one would bother him ... and if they did, well, they wouldn't bother anyone else again, ever.

The only problem with living in the attic of the shop was that there was no plumbing upstairs. There was only a small staff toilet cubicle downstairs, and the big metal kitchen sink that the old bat, Mrs. Spritely, would use to clean antiques that came in from deceased estates.

There were all sorts of chemicals and detergents back there. He never had to go shopping for anything. She'd add whatever he needed to the list. He thought he loved her once, like his own mother. That is, until she started to lose her marbles and said the feeling wasn't mutual. She had a family, she said. She didn't need any more family, she said. He was an employee and they should treat the relationship as such. Don't try and become something you're not, she said. So he fed her arsenic in her soup and in her coffee instead. It got so she was used to the taste. Then he pushed her down the stairs. Now she was gone.

Maybe he'd have to make do with the kitchen sink for now. Now it was time to save Vanessa's skin and make sure that it would be presentable and captivating for the next audience. It was long and delicate work. He'd spend hours pouring over every detail making sure it came out perfect. It was such an adrenaline rush for him. Some people went to clubs and took ecstasy. Some people jumped off bridges and pulled parachutes out of backpacks. Not him, not Edward Derange. The adrenaline would keep his mind focused and clear until well after the sun was up, not that he would know the time. He lived in perpetual darkness in the attic, every crack of sunlight cut off. Shunned. Chased out like vampires by fire-wielding villagers.

IT WAS SO EARLY in the morning she didn't think she'd see anyone. The sidewalk and road were slick with the night's rain and the morning's dew. A man who looked like he was on his way home from his night shift glanced sideways at Minny and then smiled at her. She was smiling back. She hadn't been this happy in quite some time. She was practically skipping down the sidewalk and full of gratefulness and hope for the future.

She felt like the Lord had heard her prayers. She had just come from the hospital where she was visiting her grandmother. She'd woken up from her induced coma the day before and Minny was so thankful she could be there. It was a stroke, they said. She'd collapsed.

Granny Spritely was weak. Her mouth was dry and she couldn't talk above a whisper. She didn't remember much about what happened, she'd said, but she remembered that her live-in employee, Edward, was there.

That was the other part of Minny's happiness. She'd confided in her grandmother that Edward gave her the creeps. The family had discussed it. Meaning that Minny had spoken to her mother and her mother had phoned her sisters. They'd all decided that it would be best for simplicity's sake and for her grandmother's health if Edward was no longer a part of the fabric of their lives.

Minny didn't quite know how to break the news to him, but she was happy that there'd been a decision.

The sun was barely up. She saw a delivery driver delivering fresh flowers to a shop.

She crossed the street and greeted the delivery man and leaned in and inhaled the fresh-smelling air. The flowers smelled that sweet fresh cut and fresh watered fragrance. She'd taken her grandmother a lovely bouquet of sunflowers, which were her favorite. Now she wanted something for herself. Something to embody the brightness and light-heartedness she felt. She stopped and bent down and smelled a bouquet and closed her eyes and felt happiness.

She opened her eyes and saw the shopkeeper looking at her as he trimmed roses before opening and they smiled at one another.

And then for some strange reason, she felt a pang deep down in her belly. Was she hungry? No, that wasn't it. But she sure would like something warm and runny for breakfast. Maybe pancakes. Then she felt a tingling on her neck. She was nervous now. She was thinking about how she was going to break the news to Edward. What his reaction might be and how she might be able to help him see that, while it might be hard for him at first, really, it was good news. Her grandmother was recovering.

She wasn't far from the antique shop and thought she

might as well go and see Edward now. What was the harm? She quickly chose a bouquet and paid the florist in cash. She didn't wait for her change. Instead, she sniffed them and daydreamed about what life would be like now, on the way to her family's shop. She'd decided she'd stay and help her grandmother, especially if Edward was no more.

When she got to the front door she saw that the thick chain was wrapped around the handles and it was padlocked. The shop should be opening soon, she thought. She put her hands to the glass and peered in. It was quiet and empty. Where was Edward, she wondered. Involuntarily, she looked up at the building but didn't see any signs of movement or life. She rapped on the glass but it was solid and hurt her knuckles. Nobody came.

Then she remembered that her grandmother had told her about the secret hiding place where she kept a spare key in case of emergencies.

She'd never been around the back but she went around the corner of the building and down the alleyway until she came up to a gravelly and potholed parking lot and storage area. There were puddles of stagnant water dotted around and she dodged them so as not to get her shoes wet. She remembered Granny Spritely's instructions and directions and lifted one of the bricks at the end of the wall near the back door. She reached up and felt with her fingers and touched the brass key. She guessed she'd go in the back way instead.

EDWARD DERANGE WAS DISTRACTED. He sat in the bright glow of his computer screen. Intense heavy metal roared out of the tinny-sounding speakers. He still wore nitrile gloves and was smearing Vanessa Harris' blood on his keyboard.

He had the day's papers open to stories about the murders on his desk in front of him. One had particularly caught his attention. A profile of Agent Carver and his family. Including an interview with his wife and a picture of their farmstead. Buried at the bottom of the page, it seemed something like an advertisement.

He'd finished the initial clean and the disposal of his clothes. But he kept the hazmat suit for the work he needed to do with the chemicals to treat her skin. Soon to be *his* skin. He leaned forward close to the screen like someone who needed reading glasses and pored over the news from the Savannah, Georgia crime beat.

It *was* the FBI! He knew it. How did he know it was them? Those fools thought that they could get one over on him. They'd known he was going to be there—how though? —he wondered. No one else knew. Did they have listening devices all over the place?

Were they watching his computer? Could they hear his thoughts? Were they listening now and watching, the sick bastards?

He felt a sudden panic and anxiety. His skin crawled and he dragged his gloved nails over his chest like he was tearing at his breast. He glanced at the dried, mummified corpse of his mother, looking at him with one eye glinting in the light from his screen. It wasn't her real eye, of course. He smiled.

It calmed him, knowing she was with him, watching his every move. "It's silly, isn't it, Mummy? I shouldn't worry, should I?" he said. "I'm probably just being paranoid."

As usual, he thought. Every time he worried that someone was onto him or smarter than him, they again and again proved themselves incompetent and incapable with their stupid actions. Dumb people made him angry. It made him want to put the world out of its misery by getting rid of them. They deserved it.

He was scanning for any information about the missing eyeball. He wanted a leak. He wanted to know that someone out there was feeding information of his impressions to the world. Something was *new*. Something was *different*. Why hadn't they written about it yet?

He scrolled through the article. There was a picture, not the same two FBI special agents he'd seen. Those were lanky, middle-aged men with square haircuts and badly fitted suits. Get a tailor, he thought. He could do it if they wanted, or just asked nicely. Juvie taught convicts all sorts of skills. Anything to do with your hands. And anything useful to the ruling class, like stuffing hunting trophies for hanging above their fireplace or setting above the mantle. Let the lessers of society do it. They needed something to keep them busy and out of the justice system.

He zoomed in on the picture. They were walking out of the Harris house, he could tell by the stairs. These two were strange. He checked the description under the photograph. "Special Agent Carver and Special Agent Sandling," Derange said out loud. "*Carver* and Sandling, *Carver* and Sandling," he said over and over, rolling the vowels around his mouth like he was tasting port. Sandling had her hand covering her face but Carver's was grimacing and taut, he looked like a man who'd worked in the mines.

"Who are you, Agent Carver?" Derange asked as he typed. The screen filled with lists of references to Special Agent Augustine Carver. Derange whistled. "I *knew* I knew that name. Look, Mummy," he twisted the screen so her dull eye could see, "Here, this guy that's after me, he's the one who caught Zimmer the Ripper. Do you remember we talked about it?"

He turned the screen away from his mother's corpse. Derange mouthed the words as he read, and mumbled some out loud. "Disgraced former ... abducted ... baby daughter ... survived by wife Bethany and son ..." He pushed himself back from the desk and stood up. He was suddenly filled with power and energy. His mind was focused. He knew what he had to do. It was time for a new message. He'd underestimated how stupid and uneducated the local police forces could be. But now that he knew that the Federal Bureau of Investigation had their best serial killer hunter on his trail, he hoped maybe they'd be able to decipher the cipher he used in his calls to the police. How they hadn't managed to track him down yet was beyond him. It's not like he hadn't left them any clues. He walked over to the book-shelf under the eaves and bent down to pull a large, weath-ered, ancient version of *The Metamorphoses* off the shelf.

IT WAS JUST as he was being taken in by Mrs. Spritely. He'd never heard of such a thing. A customer had brought it in wondering what it might be worth. And although the old bat bought it from them, she said it was too damaged to sell, but that treasures like this deserve to be kept someplace safe and warm, just like people.

He thought it sounded dumb. But then she explained that it was actually a poem, an epic poem all about transfor-mations. And that appealed to him. The poem had survived since ancient Rome and was written by the poet Ovid.

It all sounded so fantastic to him. Like nothing he'd ever heard of. Then he started to read, and something in those words spoke to him like they had to Dante, Chaucer, and Shakespeare.

It was a book of great stories and great deeds. Unlike anything he'd ever read, the Greeks knew about gods and men and demigods and prophets, Derange thought. And now it included new stories, photographs, news clippings, bits of hair and skin, perfumes that he'd collected; all interlaced amongst the pages of the great poem. There were stories of Medusa with snakes all over her head and Oedipus, the great Greek king of Thebes who unwittingly fulfilled the eternal prophecy by killing his father and marrying his mother and bringing disaster to his city and family. Now it also included other great myths and legends. It included details of Zimmer's trial, information from the scenes of his crimes, and types of forensic evidence used against him.

It was now part of the fascination and connection that Derange felt with the Ripper—as someone who truly understood him—and someone who proved that he was special. And there were other special people just like him.

It spoke to him like it spoke to them. He was one of them. An artist. A poet. A mighty person in the annals of history. If it spoke to him and showed him the path, surely he was adding to the great canons of the Western world. He thought he was. He knew he was. Time for a new message. He went back to the desk and dropped the book so papers flew up into the air and dust twirled in the white glow. Then there was a knock at the door ...

———

MINNY HAD WALKED in through the kitchen and seen lots of stains and dirty cloths and general mess. Someone had been busy, she thought and tutted. Never mind, it'll all soon be over. She looked down at the bouquet of flowers and thought maybe she should keep them for herself. But no, it was the right thing to do. A present and warm news to help Edward transition.

She climbed the narrow creaky staircase up to the attic and thought she would surprise him. She tapped on the door but could hear the raging music inside. She didn't like it and decided to get this over and done with quickly.

She swung the door open in an act full of confidence and bravado that she didn't feel inside. She saw Edward jump. She felt shocked too. He was standing next to his desk in white plastic coveralls that had dark stains streaked across it. She saw the light glinting off some clear liquid in a jar. She peered at it and saw what looked like a human eyeball with the nerve still attached just floating there. For a moment they were still and silent and looking at one another. She could see Edward's chest rising and falling.

Then she gasped, she couldn't help it. Edward started coming toward her and she dashed at the wall and pressed the light switch on. He was shouting, "No, don't do that!" as the fluorescent tubes flickered and groaned and then flicked on and buzzed.

Suddenly she saw it all and she screamed. In an instant she realized exactly what was going on here. All of her worst fears came true in a single moment. She flipped. The horror of sudden realization hit her and she ran like a startled doe.

Before she could get away, she felt the weight of the creep on top of her and dragging her down. She stumbled and fell on the stairs and tried to claw herself away but he was too strong. She was no match for him. He mounted her from behind and held her down and forced her face into the wooden stair and hissed, "*Shhh*, little Minny Mouse." He breathed on her ear. "You're now part of the Medusa House."

29

HE PINNED her arms and lifted her and forced her forward. He was pushing her back into the brightly lit attic. She was confronted with the horror she'd only glimpsed before. She could see the walls were lined with glass cases and in each one the writhing, slippery, slimy suggestion of snakes.

She was surrounded by reptiles.

Right next to Derange's desk was another terrarium and she could see a face or—what she thought was a face—before he grabbed the back of her hair and twisted her head away. He pushed her down to the floor and she quivered in the corner. He stood over her. Threatening and intimidating.

"Stop, you're hurting me," she said. "Please don't hurt me."

"Shut up, you stupid bitch. I'm gonna teach you to pry into other people's business. You wanted to see what I was doing, now you're gonna bear witness to my strangeness," Derange said.

"What's *wrong* with you Edward! Why are you doing this to me? We've been nothing but kind."

"Kind?" He scoffed. "You know nothing. You're getting

rid of me. Admit it. *Admit* it. I know all about you. I know all about your kind. You people *hate* people like me. I should have dealt with you before ..."

"What do you mean? I don't hate *anyone*."

"Stay here," he said. "I command you to stay. If you don't, I'll do you like I did that Spritely wench."

Minny's bottom lip shook. *You* did that, she thought. Of course he did. How stupid could she have been. She never trusted her instincts. She felt the anger and hate bubbling up inside of her. It made her calm. She acted meek. What did they teach in hostage situations? Don't antagonize them. Make them see you're a human being. Say your name. Make them see you as human.

Derange went over to a filing cabinet on the far wall. He kept checking over his shoulder as he ripped out one of the drawers and leaned over it and rummaged around. He found what he was looking for. He stomped back over to her. She watched his face. Looked at his features. She was studying him.

He pulled her wrists up violently and she felt a muscle tweak in her shoulder. She thought he'd rip her arms off.

"*Ouch*, you're hurting me!"

"Shut up," Derange said as he pulled a zip tie tight around her wrist. He grabbed her shoulder and pushed her down and forced her other arm behind her back. The restraints made a *zipping* sound and she felt the sharp plastic dig into her soft plump wrists. When he was done he shoved her hard into the wall and left her crumpled there. She stayed there with her head down. She was weeping. It hurt. She was hurt. She felt stupid for getting herself into this situation. And her grandmother, that poor woman. He'd nearly killed her. Now who was going to look after her? She felt like such a failure. No. No. No. You *always* do this to yourself, she thought. No more. Not this time. This monster isn't going to win. She started to sob.

"Shut your goddamn mouth, Minnesota. I swear," Derange said through gritted teeth. "I will choke you until you see a white light if you don't shut up *right* now."

She whimpered. She had his attention. She turned her face to look up at him. He was glaring at her.

"Please, Edward." His face relaxed when she said his name. She took it as a cue. "My grandfather's a judge."

Derange was taken aback. He straightened and looked down his nose at her. Then raised an eyebrow.

"No," he said. He felt superior, she could tell. "That bitch Spritely's husband is dead," Derange said. He thought he'd caught her in a lie.

"My other grandfather, Edward, on my mother's side. He's a judge here in Augusta. They'll give you whatever you need to make sure I'm safe, you know? It doesn't matter what you've done or what you're planning to do, they'll be able to help you. They'll be able to give you, like, a deal you know, right?"

"A deal?" Derange smiled. He had crooked discolored teeth. She doubted he brushed them, judging by how he lived. Like an animal. Worse. Animals lick themselves clean. Then the creep started to laugh. It wasn't the laugh she expected. It came through his nose and was like a squeaky toy. He opened his mouth and wheezed harder. He was enjoying this.

"A deal?" he said again. "Help me? You have no clue Minny Mouse. No idea. I've got a deal for them alright. I'm going to feed you to my snakes for supper." He shook his head. His babbling didn't make sense. She tried again.

"There's no hope for you, Edward," she said. "People know that I'm missing. People know that I'm here, and they're going to come look for me, and you're going to get caught and be put on trial for what you did. Otherwise, you can let me go and run away, and nobody will ever know. I won't tell a soul. I promise. I swear to you. Believe me. Today, to make friends, I brought you a bouquet. You are being asked to leave, Edward. People are coming here to get rid of your stuff any minute …"

He was watching her closely. Analyzing her expressions, her voice, her inflection. She felt the observation. She was a creature under his microscope. But all she could see was, past his right shoulder, the human eye looking at her dead and unblinking. Whose eye was it? Where had he gotten it? God, she prayed, please don't let that be me.

Then Edward grinned and said, "You know, they teach you all sorts of useful things in juvenile detention, Miss Mouse. One of the things they gave me to read was a book called The Power of Positive Thinking. It's where you imagine good things happening, and it says that they *do*. You should try it. You should try imagining that you aren't in the situation you're in. You should try imagining that everything's going to be fine. It'll help you. It'll help me. Look at everything I've accomplished," he said and swept his arm around the attic. He walked over to the wall and flicked off the fluorescent light. The whole room went dark and her eyes adjusted to the low white glow of the computer screen.

"I much prefer the darkness," he said, "and I much prefer the silence. Have you ever heard of the seven stages of grief? I think you must be at about number three. I'm not sure exactly which one it is, but one of them is bargaining. Making a bargain. Bargaining with yourself. You're bargaining with the devil. And if it helps you to get through it, you can bargain, but your fate is sealed. So you may as well imagine whatever it is that makes you feel better about this dark, dark place that you've gotten yourself into."

She started to sob quietly.

Derange sat back at his desk and said, "Now be quiet. I have work to do."

Minny cowered and cried silently to herself. He was going to kill her, she knew it.

30

As they got back to the office, Carver went straight to his desk and picked up his phone to call Jessica Webb.

They'd spent the night in some crap motel on the way back to Grant Avenue. Carver didn't sleep anyway, but now his hand was shaking from some sort of withdrawal or phantom halo of a trip he once went on. Residue, he called it, from his days as an undercover drugs enforcement officer. Hard days and hard times created the making of a hard man.

He dialed and the line rang. It went to an answering machine. Old school, he thought. He was just about to leave a message when Webb answered.

She was out of breath and panting. "Hello?" she said.

"Spider, it's Carver."

"Oh, hi, I guess ..."

"You sound like you were expecting my call."

"Well, yeah, I thought maybe you might check in."

"Why would you think that?" Carver asked. He was incredulous.

"Well, you know, nature of the business, how we play the game, I guess."

"A game, is it? Well, we saw the picture and the caption in the paper. Nice way to play the game, Webb." Carver said. "And now it's all over the media—apparently—so they tell me. Did you really have to do that to us?"

She was still breathing heavy. "What've you just come back from a run?" Carver asked.

"A run? Yeah, sure, why not. Yep - a run ..."

"Okay, well, while you're out there banging some bloke you met at a dive bar last night, there are real people from real families that are suffering here—you know—and you've just given the killer an insight into the people chasing him. Did you ever think that we might end up targets of this insanity running around out there?"

"It wasn't a dive bar," she said. Carver didn't say anything. "And just so you know, it wasn't my decision to put your names in the caption of the picture, Carver. I didn't know anything about it. It was my editor. He doesn't think these things through like we do. But maybe, just *maybe*, he thought it would be a good idea for the public to know that the man who caught the Ripper was also out there trying to catch the Skinwalker. Did you think about that?" Carver still didn't say anything. "So get off my back, why don't you, while I'm trying to keep my job and also find out how deep this thing goes," Webb said.

"Is that what you said to the hunk you humped?"

Webb laughed. Carver smiled. He wasn't actually angry with her. There were worse things that had happened to him during his career, and having his photo in the paper wasn't even in the top ten, serial killer or not.

He needed her to help him and so he needed her to owe him a favor, which she did now.

"I sure could use your help with something now that you exposed us," Carver said.

"Oh yeah? What is it?"

"I can't tell you over the phone but we could meet somewhere if that worked for you."

"Why? Are they listening?"

"Maybe," Carver said.

"And is it scandalous?"

"Yes."

"Why would I meet you, Carver? Why would I help you?"

"I know how you're always thinking about number one, Jess, and that's what I like about you ... I don't know, what do you want? Let's say there's an exclusive in it for you—"

Without hesitating, Webb said, "An exclusive interview with the man who caught Zimmer *and* the Skinwalker as soon as the case is over."

Sure, Carver thought ... but like a good hostage negotiator, he knew, never give them what they want until they've done the thing that you *need*.

"I'll think about it," Carver said.

"Oh, come on, Carver, you know you want it."

Sandling came to his office door, leaned in, and knocked lightly on the glass.

Carver held up a finger.

"Another thing you probably said last night," he said. "Listen, Jessica, meet me in an hour. Let's come up with something. I have to go..." Carver hung up. "What's up?" he asked.

"The Vanessa Harris scene, they just confirmed that a 911 call was placed from the property just after the time that she died. The patrol car never made it. They figured it was some hoax."

"And the dial tones?" Carver asked.

"Same pattern," Sandling said.

"Same pattern or similar pattern?"

"Same exact pattern."

"How can you tell?"

"Foxy ran it through some analysis gizmo on her workstation. Same exact pattern as at the Proctor scene."

Carver stood up. "This is big. It's a sequence, so he's trying to tell us something. Not only is it a sequence," Carver said, "It's a clue and it's also probably a cipher. But we have no idea what the decryption key is.

"So that's something we're going to have to figure out. And how do we do that?" Sandling asked.

"Good detective work," Carver said, "Crunch the data. We need to go and pore over every piece of evidence we have to try and make the link. I have a feeling that solving this riddle is our new top priority when it comes to finding this guy. Come on, let's brief the team."

SHE WENT BACK to her desk and Carver followed her out of his office. He surveyed the troops. He stood there like a headmaster giving an assembly. One that wasn't great at public speaking. The team turned to look at him.

"Guys, your attention please," Carver said. "We have a break in the Skinwalker case." Fox wasn't listening. "Foxy … Foxy? Foxy!"

She was plugged into her computer screen and not looking at him. Maudmont caught her attention and mouthed that they were having a meeting and Foxy took her headphones off and turned toward Carver. "Fox, you already analyzed the cipher from the 911 calls, right? Same exact pattern guys, so the killer's trying to tell us something. We need to get to work on decoding it."

Underwood was nodding along and Hornigen glanced at him. "Wait boss, what do you mean? If there was another 911 call, was there another murder?"

"You guys didn't know?" Sandling asked.

"No, we've just gotten here—just like you—and you've just gotten back from wherever the hell you were. We don't know anything," Underwood said.

Carver took a deep breath and said, "Okay, listen up. Yes, we got a call yesterday while we were in Charleston that there was another scene that was eerily similar to the Proctor house. Turns out that it was not eerily similar. It was —eerily—exactly the same ..."

"If a little more haphazard and out of control," Sandling added.

"Where did this happen?" Underwood asked.

"Savannah, Georgia, near Forsyth Park," Carver said.

Hornigen and Underwood looked at one another.

"What's the name?" Hornigen asked.

"Vanessa Harris was the main victim," Carver said,

"Holy shit, *holy shit*!" Underwood started saying over and over.

"What's going on?" Sandling asked.

"We were there—at the Harris house—day before last," Hornigen said.

"What the hell?" Carver said. He didn't understand. "What do you mean you were there?

"*Why* the hell were you there?" Sandling asked, getting to the point faster than Carver.

"We went to check it out. It was one of the names and addresses on the list that we got from Foxy," Hornigen said.

Underwood was still saying "holy shit" to himself.

"What list? What are you talking about?" Carver asked.

Maudmont stood up, just as Foxy was opening her mouth. "You know, we've got a bright little bulb here, Carver, and one of the first things that Foxy did—off her own initiative—was to write an algorithm which she ran through her little program thingy, and it made connections between followers of Sarah Proctor's accounts and her contacts list on her phone to overlay—"

Carver said, "What the hell are you talking about, Penny? Explain it to me like I'm five."

"You still wouldn't get it," Maudmont said under her breath.

"Pardon?"

Fox said, "We just made a simple link between likely victims via Savannah Proctor's closest contacts ... You did say that the killer might be following a pattern, and so I analyzed everyone she knew against a set of data points. That's what Frank was saying when he said they were following up on the list."

"How many names were on the list?" Carver asked.

"There were eighteen in total," Underwood said and stared into the distance.

"Okay," Carver said and furrowed his brow at Underwood's expression. "And it just so happened that you went to visit the victim on the same day that they were killed?"

Everyone was silent.

"It was a coincidence," Hornigen said.

"It doesn't matter," Carver said. "You know how that looks? It looks incompetent at best, and downright suspicious at worst. This information can *never, ever* get out there."

"You were the guys that the witness saw," Sandling said in sudden realization. "You were the suits selling Bibles that night."

"We went to speak to her to find out if she knew

anything or could help us in any way with the investigation," Underwood said.

"Oh yeah?" Carver replied. "And what did you find out?"

"Nothing really. She told us that she knew Savannah Proctor and she said she was feeling vulnerable and that she'd been getting some weird vibes—like she was being watched—lately."

"But she said that it was probably paranoia and we kind of agreed with her," Hornigen added. "She didn't have any more information except the fact that she confirmed that she'd also had a photo shoot with Bastien Dufresne."

"That's kind of big news, don't you think?" Carver said.

"Well yeah," Underwood said. "I mean, we wrote it in a report and sent it to you and we've been following up on the rest of the list too." Carver closed his eyes and took a deep breath again.

"Listen guys, it's okay," Carver said. He was visibly trying to stay calm. "I'm not *attacking* you. I'm just trying to take the information on board, all right?"

He felt like that was a good response while he was trying to grow as a manager, as well as catch a serial killer. "I'm just trying to understand where we're all at, right? Not used to this type of teamwork yet."

"Teamwork?" Underwood said loudly and stood up. He was upset. "What do you mean, 'teamwork'? You've barely said two words to any of us besides Caitlin over there since you arrived. Teamwork? You berated me when I told you why I was in this godforsaken redundancy operation—"

"You did let a serial killer go to be fair," Hornigen said.

"Oh, go to hell, Frank. Seriously? This guy comes in here acting like a big shot, clearly not wanting to get involved and now that the poop has hit the fan and the serial killer's running wild out there, now he wants us to come together; there's the team. What's that shit?"

"Language!" Maudmont said.

"Sorry, Penny," Underwood said and turned back to Carver. "Seriously man, do you even know I have daughters? Do you even care? Did you take the time to find out about my family life, how it is for us, or do you only care about yourself?

"I have daughters," Hornigen said wistfully, "Marlene and Darlene. They're all grown now, though, not like yours, Toby."

Carver was going to say something but bit his lip. He sighed. "Okay, okay. You're right, Toby. I admit it. I haven't been the most sociable person since I've arrived. What's gonna make this right?" Carver looked at the ceiling, thought about it for a second, tapped his foot, and put his finger to his chin. "How about we go round the room and we all say one thing that you'd really like me to know about your personal lives, hmm? Would that help?"

Underwood looked confused. They all looked at one another. Just as the silence grew uncomfortable, Maudmont said, "Um, well, I like to bake ..." She clasped her hands together and blushed, "And, well, I'd just love to know your favorite pie so I could make one for y'all sometime."

Everyone was quiet. Maudmont sat down.

"There you go, thanks, Penny," Carver said.

"I have access to each of your personnel files and know about each of you already," Fox said.

"Okay, thank you, Foxy," Carver said. "That does not surprise me—"

"Don't call me, Foxy."

"—but thank you for sharing. Anybody else?" He looked around the room.

"I have a phobia of guns," Sandling said faintly.

"No? Okay," Carver said. "Can we move on with solving this case before anyone else dies?"

Underwood bent to pull his chair under him and said, "It really would help if you were nicer to us," he said.

Carver was nodding and staring at Underwood. He felt like he might slide across the table and grab him by his tie and shake some sense into him. Instead, he said, "You're right, Toby. You're right. Let's call this step one of my twelve-step program of getting to know each of you better. Okay? Now, can we please get back to the case?"

"Holy shit snacks," Underwood said, and put his hands on his head, "I can't believe the killer ... He might have been there when we were visiting her."

"He might have seen us," Hornigen said.

"He probably did see you," Carver said.

"He probably enjoyed it," Sandling said.

"What do you mean?" Carver looked at Sandling.

"Well, it's exhibitionism, isn't it, guys? And he knows that we're looking for him. And now—thanks to our friends in the press—he also knows the *names* of the people who're looking for him. This is a game to them—serial killers—I mean, isn't it? It's 'run and hide' versus 'get caught and die.'"

"Get caught and live in infamy forever," Maudmont said.

"Okay, so what do we do now?" Fox asked.

"We need to work on that cipher," Carver answered. "We need to find out what the code's key is."

"And how are we supposed to do that?" Maudmont asked.

Carver looked at Fox. "Is there any way we can analyze the sounds to see if there's anything—anything—we can link the sequence to?"

She looked at the ceiling and she thought about it. Then shook her head and pressed her lips and said, "No, no way, Gust. The data set would be so huge we wouldn't be able to narrow it down. We don't have enough processing power for a query that wide. It could take years."

Everyone was silent. Carver was thinking.

"There's only two ways we're gonna catch this guy," Carver said.

"Which are?" Underwood asked.

Carver looked at Sandling. Her eyes went wide and she cleared her throat. The team looked at her. She could feel their anticipation.

"Criminals like this don't just start out killing people, especially not in the choreographed and systematic way that the Skinwalker does it. If anything he graduated to this from something else. You know the biggest predictor of serial killings, or people becoming serial killers, is an abusive childhood which leads to cruelty to small animals, you know, potentially killing cats and dogs or squirrels or birds, and then they graduate to bigger and bigger prey and their level of sadism increases."

"Right," Underwood said. "So what does that mean?"

"It means," Carver said, "that we need to try and work out his previous crimes. We need to try and analyze whether there are any links to previous sadistic behavior that potentially got recognized and is on file."

"So a needle in a haystack," Maudmont said.

"More like a needle in a haystack of needles," Carver said.

"So, hopeless ..."

"What's the other way," Hornigen asked.

"He makes a mistake," Carver replied. "And we can't just wait and hope for that to happen."

"So what are we going to do?" Underwood asked.

"I need you to work together as a team and to help Rachel come up with a way of finding that haystack so we can start searching for the needle. In the meantime, we're going to help him make a mistake."

"How?" Underwood asked.

"That's a good question, Toby. I'm thinking that there might just be one killer priest who has an idea about what our boy is playing at and what he's trying to tell us."

"You're gonna go and speak to the Ripper again," Maudmont said.

"I think we have to," Carver said and looked at Sandling. "Deputy Gibson's been pretty clear that's the one area of the investigation she wants us to focus on. And now that we have a new victim—and we've confirmed this potential code in the 911 calls—we have a good reason to go and ask Zimmer about it."

"Yeah, but he said that he won't help us unless you testify at his medical board," Sandling said.

"Yeah," Carver said, "the medical board is happening the day after tomorrow, so I figure we go speak to Zimmer. And maybe I'll tell the board what a nice guy he is."

"You aren't actually going to go through with it?" Sandling asked.

"I might not have a choice."

31

SPECIAL AGENT CAITLIN Sandling walked through the entrance to the Patton State Psychiatric Hospital a little after eleven o'clock at night. Carver sent her alone and she felt tired, wired, and a little jumpy. Not a good state to be in when questioning a serial murderer. She jolted as one of the inmates let out a horrific scream. Doors slammed and she heard shouting and something crashed. She hugged herself and leaned away from the noise.

"Sounds like a horror film in here," Sandling said to the orderly leading her through the hospital.

"This is a quiet night, Miss," the orderly said.

Their footsteps echoed down the hallways. It was like being in an abandoned high school at night. She always felt nervous in those long dark tunnels as a teenager.

"Uh-huh, quiet night," the orderly said as he unlocked one of the steel gates and held it open to let her through. He slammed it shut again and she heard the gate lock with a *scrape* and a *click*. She felt cold and rubbed her upper arms. "We had to move all 'em other inmates," he said. It was weary sounding. "He has some kind of effect on 'em. They all start screaming 'an hollering 'an rolling around on the ground. Saying they's cursed. That he done put a curse on 'em."

"Who?" Sandling asked.

"Who'd ya think? Him. *Father Zimmer*. The maddest bastard I ever seen. And I seen some, you understand?"

"Yes, I understand," Sandling said. She didn't. But she said she did. The corridor ahead of them was silent and dark. The orderly must have seen her face.

"Don't worry, Miss, he awake. He always awake at this time of night." Then the orderly whispered. "He likes to watch the preachers on the television."

"He has a television now?"

"Dr. Forsmith give it to him. Try to keep his mind occupied so he stop scheming ways to start a riot in here."

"Fair enough," Sandling said while thinking it unbelievable. She heard the *buzz* of the television and saw the light on in Zimmer's room. Her pulse jumped and she touched the artery in her neck. It was throbbing. She tried to breathe and to relax but it kept getting faster. When they got to the cell door, she heard him.

"Caitlin. A feeling of pure joy to see you. It's been so long, I feel like I hardly know you anymore," Zimmer said as he got up off his cot and turned around to put his hands behind his back and through the slot in his cell door.

The orderly took handcuffs from his belt and ratcheted them tight against Zimmer's wrists. "Step forward," the orderly said. Zimmer did as he was told. "Go sit on the bed." And he did.

The orderly unlocked the door and slid the bolt back. The heavy door swung open and Sandling felt the thick, humid air from the cell. Zimmer's breath warming the place.

"Yes," Sandling said to Zimmer as the orderly knelt in front of him and chained his ankles. "Turns out distance makes the heart grow fonder."

"Does it now. Well, to what do I owe the pleasure?"

The orderly straightened and turned to her. "You can go in and sit down now. I'll be right outside. This door stays open, you understand?"

She nodded and the orderly left. She went in and stayed standing. Looking down at him on the bed.

"We thought we'd ask again to see if you'd want to help."

"You think I want for anything?"

"I don't know Hermann, I've stopped trying to work you out."

"An enigma wrapped in a riddle hiding behind a mystery."

"So will you?"

"You know my conditions."

"Yes."

"And so you're going to play our little game and, in so doing, save the girls and your career?"

"I suppose. If you think you can help?"

"I don't know. Saint Augustine looks to me for guidance from time to time but then again, he and I do share an unbreakable bond," Zimmer said.

"What's that supposed to mean?"

"You know what it means. Trust is brittle and its foundations are shallow. I won't simply be disappointed if you lie. I'll be disappointed that I can't trust you again—and that may make me vengeful."

"You mean you and his daughter." Zimmer was silent. "I don't speak in riddles, Hermann. You know that."

"Just as well I do."

"Augustine is going to testify for you."

"Nice that he has come around to my way of thinking," Zimmer said. "And once he has—testified—I will share what I know."

"How about a compromise?"

"Such as?"

"If you're so good at puzzles, can I play you a riddle now? We can discuss it. It'll show me you can help."

"A game for me? How interesting," Zimmer said. "I'm intrigued. Play your riddle."

"It's a recording," Sandling said. "The Skinwalker has been calling 911 from the crime scene."

"How interesting," Zimmer said again. "How provocative. What's he been saying to them?"

"That's just it. He doesn't say anything. He is punching in numbers on the touch-tone telephone keypad."

"How interesting," Zimmer said. "So, it's a dual-tone multi-frequency code. Is it a sequence?"

"You're familiar with them?"

Zimmer shrugged. "My father and I used to play with ciphers when I was young. I really am *very* good at it."

Sandling was nodding, her mind buzzing. Always so modest, she thought. "Yes, it is a sequence," she said. "The same sequence. Every single time, the same tones."

"And you have it here?"

"I can play it for you."

"Please do. I'm *all* ears."

She pulled out a small handheld voice recorder and turned the volume button up on the side and pressed play. Zimmer closed his eye and listened. There was a shuffling sound and then the dispatcher saying, '911, fire, and police. This call is being recorded. What's your emergency?' There was a pause and then a sequence of very long tones. The call finished with the dispatcher saying, 'Hello? Is anyone there?' and Sandling pressed stop.

Zimmer said, "Play it again, Sam." He still had his one good eye closed. Sandling felt drawn to the gaping hole in his face. She pressed rewind and played the tape again. Zimmer was quiet and let the sounds penetrate his mind. She was too uncomfortable to look at him in the eye when it was open. Now she was staring at the crevasse. The one Carver put there when he removed Zimmer's eye with his hands the night his child was butchered. They each had a grizzly reminder from that night. He opened his eye and caught her looking. He smirked and watched her intently.

"And what do you make the dial tones out to be, number-wise?"

"It's one-zero-one-nine-five-three," Sandling said.

Zimmer's mouth moved as he silently repeated the numbers. Then she saw his face change. He was intense now, focused. His chin was down and he stared at her looking up from under his eyelid. His expression darkened and he asked her, "Has our peregrine left any iconography or symbolism behind?"

"Like what?" Sandling asked. It came out a bit defensive and Zimmer noticed. She knew that the Skinwalker had but didn't want to give the game away.

"Does he have a thing for reptiles?" Zimmer asked. "*Reptiles* that shed their skin?"

Sandling's heart started to race. She could feel a pulse in her neck throbbing now like it was about to jump out of her. "Maybe," Sandling said.

"Aha. Does your killer have a thing for snakes, by chance?" Zimmer asked.

Sandling was taken aback and not quite sure how to respond. "Let's say he does," Sandling said. "What then?"

"So defensive, my dear special agent ... here I am, giving

you my precious time and giving you my precious mind, and even though you've already shared this code with me, you're *still* being defensive. You'll forgive me if I don't know which gaps you need me to fill. Judging by your attitude, maybe you need more than one filled. Is it ... *sexual* frustration?"

"Sorry," Sandling said. She hated apologizing to a murderer.

"Perhaps you can help me color between the lines?" Zimmer asked politely.

"Okay," Sandling said. "Ask me again."

"Does our peregrine have a thing for snakes?"

"Yes."

Zimmer's eye glinted and narrowed into a slit and his mouth turned up in a snarl. Sandling was afraid now. She'd never seen this expression on Zimmer, or on anyone. She was staring and Zimmer noticed her noticing his face. He relaxed it now.

"Living or dead?"

"Living."

"What does he do with them? Does he leave them at the scene?"

Sandling nodded, "He leaves them there."

"And are they venomous?"

"Yes," she said. "Very"

"And are any of them posed in any way?"

"How do you mean?" she asked.

"Are they, umm, eating their own tails, for instance?"

"Not that I know of," Sandling said. "Why do you ask?"

"What did we say our traveler was doing, in our first meeting?" Zimmer asked.

"Communicating," Sandling answered.

"So you remember."

"Very well, Hermann. How could I forget?"

"And you're an eminent psychologist, are you not?"

"I wouldn't say that."

"Oh, yes, you are. It's the very first thing you told me about yourself when we met, and here you are delving into the mind of a convicted madman."

"Okay."

"Have you not read Jung's *Man and His Symbols*?" Zimmer asked.

She'd heard of it and studied Jung, but hadn't read the original text. "I know him, of course."

"Of course," Zimmer smirked and nodded. It was sarcastic.

"Jung wasn't a psychologist, though."

"No," Zimmer said.

"Why do you ask?"

"Given your interest in the working of the criminally insane mind, I would've thought a work by Jung that delves deep into symbolism, dreams, and the unconscious might be mandatory reading. It's complex and would offer plenty of scope for encoding a message. Have you looked into it?"

"We've tried to find the cipher, but no luck."

"I see."

"What do you think a posed snake eating its own tail might be trying to say?" Sandling asked.

"You really are fumbling around for a match in the dark, aren't you?"

She swallowed her pride and said, "Yes."

Zimmer's voice grew loud and he projected it like he was standing on stage and said, "All things are subject to eternal change. Thus I am changed, but I remain the same. Everything changes, nothing dies: the spirit wanders, arriving here or there, and occupying whatever body it pleases, passing from a wild beast into a human being, from our body into a beast, but is never destroyed. As wave is driven by wave, and each, pursued, pursues the wave ahead, so time flies on and follows, flies, and follows, always, forever and new."

She swallowed again. It was impressive but it went over her head. "I don't follow, Hermann."

"Ouroboros," Zimmer said. "Yes?"

"It's an ancient symbol … of a serpent eating its own tail," Sandling said.

"From Jung," Zimmer confirmed with a nod. "What else?"

Sandling thought about it. Her heart still racing. Her breathing shallow. "Isn't it often interpreted as a symbol for eternal cyclical renewal—the cycle of life, death, and rebirth?"

"Indeed. Anything else?"

Sandling shrugged.

"The snake's skin-sloughing symbolizes the transmigration of souls, young Sandling. The snake biting its own tail is a fertility symbol in most religions. The tail is phallic, wouldn't you say, and the mouth, well, the mouth is a womb-like representation."

She felt herself blush. Zimmer was enjoying it no doubt.

"There's more," Zimmer said. "We could go on all day but I am short on inspiration."

"Go on, Hermann, please." She knew she sounded desperate. She hoped he wouldn't despise her for it. She saw that glint in his eye again.

"I believe the earliest known ouroboros decoration is found in the *Enigmatic Book of the Netherworld*; do you know it?" She shook her head. "An ancient Egyptian funeral text that was found in the tomb of Tutankhamen more than two thousand years ago," Zimmer said.

"It could also be inverted libido," Sandling said.

"There, you see? What do you need me for," Zimmer said. "You *do* know your Jung."

"But what does it mean, Hermann?"

He smiled. "For now I have everything I need," Zimmer said.

"And what's that?"

"The one thing that you do not have ... time. I have all the time in the world. To think, to observe, to wait. I channel God's will without the sin and decay and deprivation that so distracts you out in the world. Good night, sweet Cate. Sleep on it. I will see you in the morning."

That was all she was going to get. Zimmer went back to looking at the television. She left the cell and the orderly nodded to her. She would have to call Carver. In the morning he was going to testify at Zimmer's medical review board hearing. There was no other choice. They needed to know what Zimmer knew.

32

THE NEXT DAY Carver walked up to the high barbed-wire fence that ran around the perimeter of Patton State Hospital and knew what he had to do. Supplicate yourself, he thought. "You have no ego. You do not exist. None of this matters," he said to himself.

It wasn't how he felt though. The truth was, it *did* matter. It mattered more to him than anything else in the world because this man took his child away. His joy. His happiness. His contentment. Carver knew he was a dope for believing in retribution through the system. To him, justice was just karma without the satisfaction. And he didn't believe in justice. The large wire gate in front of him rattled as it retracted and Carver reached into his jacket pocket and showed his ID to the security guard in the booth.

"Hello, sir," the guard said. "I must respectfully ask for your badge and firearm."

"Yes, sir," Carver said.

"In addition, I have some paperwork for you to sign. A disclaimer that states in the event of your death, or if you're taken hostage, attacked, assaulted, or otherwise abused within the correctional facility, the United States government forswears any and all liability."

"Oh, okay," Carver said and signed the paper. He handed over his badge and said, "I'm not carrying a weapon."

"This here's an escorted visitor tag, wear it at all times, please. If you go'n wait around inside this building to your left, a colleague of mine will be down shortly to escort you to the assigned location of your meeting."

Carver pursed his lips and gave the man a nod. Nothing like a glorified check-out assistant who took their job seriously.

CARVER WALKED into the waiting room.

A man in a suit looked up from a file he was reading. He kept looking at Carver, closed the file, uncrossed his legs, and stood up.

"You must be Special Agent Carver," the man said and stuck out his hand. "I'm Mr. Zimmer's legal representative, Robert Woodbrand the *third*, we spoke on the phone a few weeks ago, if you remember."

Carver looked at the guy's hand but didn't take it. He stood just inside the threshold holding the door open as he tried to decide whether he wanted to stay in this waiting room with this man or not.

"I'll wait outside," Carver said. "You stay in here, Woodbrand."

"I actually need to speak to you, Mr. Carver," Woodbrand said and followed him outside.

"Of course you do," Carver said and sighed. The sun was low and the air crisp and Carver squinted as he stepped into the sunlight.

"Listen, Woodbrand, I appreciate the candor, but I really don't want to speak to you right now."

"I understand how you feel, special agent, but I have a message from Zimmer for you."

Carver waited. "We wouldn't want to disappoint a murderer," he said.

"Zimmer said he expects you to put him in a positive light."

"I think that goes without saying," Carver said.

"Shining light is actually how he put it. A glorious shining light. He's more than willing to follow through on the arrangement and help you with this case you have out east. It's just that he wants to be sure you—"

Before Woodbrand could finish his sentence, Carver said, "Submit to emotional damage."

"No. Let them know how helpful he's been. And that you've forgiven him for what he did after he *asked* for your forgiveness, of course."

"Of course," Carver said, but thinking this slime ball needed to get out of his face before he tasted asphalt. Carver stood glaring at him and Woodbrand hesitated. Carver looked at the door to the waiting room and back at Woodbrand. And back at the waiting room. He got the message.

"See you in there," Woodbrand said. "And thanks for doing this, we sure appreciate it."

THE ROOM LOOKED like a very old boarding school dining hall that was being used as a conference room.

"Just so I understand this correctly, Special Agent Carver, you're appearing here today to testify—or provide a character witness—for Mr. Zimmer even though you're the arresting officer in his case. Is that correct?"

"Who are you again?" Carver asked.

He was set off to the side at a perpendicular angle to the medical review board of three white-suited physicians.

The room was cold, like a big Tuscan farmhouse in winter. The floor was of square pumpkin-colored tiles like you'd find in a classic Italian kitchen, and it had a drainage plug in the middle of the room.

Easy to clean when you needed to spray it down. Carver wondered if this room was chosen because of the tendency for inmates to exfiltrate their bodily fluids at inappropriate moments.

He was chewing the inside of his cheek and his foot bounced involuntarily. He knew what he had to do. He knew what he was supposed to say. He was supposed to suppress his real feelings and tell the medical board—against his better judgment—that, in his opinion, Zimmer not only felt regret for what he'd done but was also reformed. That their treatment had done what they'd promised the federal government it would do and had helped to fix whatever psychological instabilities Zimmer had.

It was common for people who'd been diagnosed as psychopathic, sociopathic, and sadomasochistic to be released on parole.

In fact, Carver knew it happened all the time. The justice system just wasn't interested in the nuances of mental health. They just needed to fulfill the criteria of the courts. These mental health issues were simply left up to the state to handle once these people were let back into society. And everyone knows how good those systems are, Carver thought dryly. Generally it's a tick-box exercise for people in charge. As long as they clock in and clock out, do they care what somebody does outside of hours? And so the circle turned. Like karma. What goes around comes around. Justice without the satisfaction. He didn't believe in justice.

"Mr. Carver?"

He must have missed the question.

"Sorry, can you say it again?"

"Yes, you seemed a little lost in thought. I'm Dr. Edmund Blackwood, as we stated. Independent member of this medical tribunal."

"Okay, thank you. Yes, sir, that's correct."

"I see. And what are the circumstances under which you are providing evidence on Mr. Zimmer's behalf? Has he promised you anything, or has offered something to exchange for your testimony?"

"It's true that Hermann requested I provide a character reference for him, and it's also true that we have been consulting with Mr. Zimmer during an ongoing criminal investigation."

"So let me get this straight, Special Agent Carver. Mr. Zimmer's helping you with an investigation and in return, you're testifying at his medical board. This is highly irregular Mr. Carver, you do know that, don't you?"

"I'm aware, yes."

Blackwood glared at Carver to transmit visually how *serious* and *unconventional* he found this before he checked his notes and said, "Before we begin, I would like to remind everybody, especially the witnesses providing testimony here today that this is not a legal hearing, this is purely a medical review of Mr. Zimmer's case to ascertain the extent to which his treatment has resolved his mental health issues. As you can see, we're recording and have a stenographer in case the finding is something that needs to be referred to the justice system. As such I will do a round of introductions of the people present for the benefit of those in attendance and those who may be listening to this recording at a later date. I am Dr. Blackwood, forensic psychologist, behavioral consultant, and adjunct professor at Johns Hopkins University. To my left, we have Dr. Amelia Harris, who is herself a seasoned psychiatrist and representing the institution here at Patton State Psychiatric Hospital." Dr. Harris nodded to those in the room. "We have retired judge Henry Watson here to observe and provide guidance on any findings, and Mrs. Lucinda Richardson who is a civilian parole expert and court-appointed safety officer."

The atmosphere was tense. Zimmer sat opposite the panel. He was expressionless and staring blankly with his one good eye at the wooden sculpture on the wall behind the panel.

"We have our first witness," Blackwood said, "Sitting over to my left, Special Agent Augustine James Carver, who has volunteered to provide testimony on Mr. Zimmer's behalf. Welcome Special Agent Carver to the proceedings."

Carver nodded and shuffled in his seat. It was wooden and hard and reminded him of detention at school. Dr. Harris addressed him with the first question.

"As you know, Mr. Carver, Hermann Zimmer, seated here before you was convicted under a diminished capacity ruling. You've spoken to Mr. Zimmer recently, I believe, do you think his punishment has fit his crime?" Harris asked.

Carver sat stone-faced and observed the judges on the panel. Even though this wasn't a courtroom, they were the judges and the jury of his opinion. He could feel Zimmer's black eye watching him. The tension was palpable. Almost as thick as trying to cut out a spleen with a dull blade.

"Mr. Carver?" Blackwood pressed him.

Carver took a deep breath. His mind was racing. All the answers he could give. Did the punishment fit the crime? He had to say 'yes', right? He had to placate Zimmer so he'd help with the case. Get a profile out to the cops. Reestablish the team's competence. Catch a killer. Watch Zimmer walk free. Hell no.

"Punishment?" Carver said. "No, I don't believe this is a punishment in the slightest, especially not for somebody like Zimmer."

"Could you elaborate?"

"Well, this is a holiday camp for him, don't you think?" Carver said.

"He's here for treatment," Harris said.

"Do you think his punishment has fitted the crime?" Blackwood said, reiterating the question.

"No, I don't," Carver said.

"Why not?"

"It's a little like slamming the barn door after the horse has already bolted, isn't it?"

"How do you think people like Mr. Zimmer should be punished?"

"Like Zimmer? Death by torture," Carver said. "Probably. Haven't given it enough thought."

The panel all looked at one another.

"You are here testifying on Mr. Zimmer's behalf?" Harris asked.

"That's correct," Carver said.

"You don't think that's a little harsh?"

"No," Carver shook his head. "In fact, not in the slightest."

"You don't believe that Zimmer has been treated?"

"According to Dr. Forsmith, they stopped treating Zimmer the Ripper after he injured several orderlies and they haven't tried since."

"I'll have you know, Mr. Carver," Blackwood said and lifted a thick manila folder off the table, "that Dr. Forsmith's notes are comprehensive and show that treatment has been ongoing and that Mr. Zimmer has been responding exceptionally well, better than could have been expected, to his regimen. Speaking of which, Mr. Carver, what do you think gives you the professional capacity to be a witness here today?"

It was a question Carver had been expecting. "Thank you, Dr. Blackwood, yes, I appreciate I don't have a PhD in psychology—or any PhD—but what I do have is decades of experience working to catch actual psychopathic and socio-pathic serial murderers," Carver said. "And I've been pretty successful at it. I caught Zimmer, and I paid for it, and I continue to pay for it, every day. So I believe that my experience hunting these depraved monsters gives me a unique insight into their mental state and their bloodlust."

There was an awkward silence. Blackwood cleared his throat and checked his notes. "Anything else?"

"Yes. In my experience of criminal behavior, Zimmer is uniquely manipulative. While he has a profound understanding of the human psyche through theology and his experiments on human brain anatomy, he is hell-bent on using his knowledge and narcissism in sadistic ways."

Zimmer started to laugh.

"Please, Mr. Woodbrand, control your client," Blackwood said. He was stern and Woodbrand glanced at Zimmer. No one dared say anything to the madman.

"Agent Carver," the retired judge Henry Watson said measuredly, "In your interactions with Mr. Zimmer, have you seen any signs—any at all—of remorse or a change in his behavior that might suggest some rehabilitation?"

It was Carver's turn to laugh.

"Remorse? I don't think this man could tell you what that emotion feels like. I don't think he's ever experienced empathy before. Zimmer is sick. Twisted. I wouldn't be surprised if he asked me here just so he could see me in this room talking about him with other people who *know* he murdered my child in front of my eyes."

It was the panel's turn to move uneasily in their seats and fidget with their stationery.

"He has actively tried to drive me insane. And he nearly succeeded. But luckily I'm sitting on this side of the desk and he's sitting on that side, where he belongs. No. Remorse would imply a desire to recognize his actions and make a change, but he wants to keep doing what he's always done. And that's ripping people's lives apart, ripping people's families apart, and ripping pieces of their faces off with his own teeth. I wouldn't be surprised if he's sitting there right now wondering what you'd taste like, Judge."

"That's quite enough of that," Blackwood said. "I believe that speaks more closely to your own state of mind than Mr. Zimmer's, so be careful."

Blackwood was starting to rile Carver up.

"Zimmer is not crazy," Carver said. "He understands exactly what he's done. He understands why he did it. He probably even understands that his ideological and fervent belief in the God of Abraham is something that allows him to justify his actions. This man is untreatable because he is sane. He is calculating. He's intelligent. And he thinks that you are stupid."

"I'll remind you that Mr. Zimmer was found to be of diminished capacity by the courts, and therefore is considered to be insane. And this hearing is about whether we have treated him, and he has recovered from his disease," Blackwood said.

"In that case, we're the ones who are insane," Carver said, "How can it be that the system allows somebody like this to escape from their horrendous crimes? We're the deranged ones."

Carver sounded subdued now. At a loss. He wanted to be

under the ocean, far away from these people. They were all tiny cogs in the churning, grinding machine of the criminal justice system. And so was he.

"Thank you, Special Agent Carver, you've certainly given us some food for thought. Do you mind me asking about your own psychological troubles? Have you recovered from your episode and is your family able to move on?"

"This isn't about me, Dr. Blackwood. You know that, but thanks for bringing it up. And if anything in my past is going to blemish my statements here, then that's something you need to think about," Carver said.

He turned and pointed at Zimmer, who looked furious. "My family will never recover from what that man did."

Zimmer looked like a man trying to keep a wasp in his mouth for fear of it escaping.

"My family now lives on a small farm in a small town in Tennessee. I never see them. It's just about all they can do to be safe and stay out of harm's way. God knows how many of Zimmer's disciples there are out there just waiting to pay homage to their murderous master and killer priest."

"Mr. Carver, that's quite enough of your soliloquy—"

"Just one thing Blackwood, before I go, I realize you can't wait to get me out of here, but I have to say this: On your heads be it! On your heads be it if you start this dice rolling and chance it that Zimmer might *actually* make parole. I would lock every door and every window and never let your children out of sight. If you let him walk out of those doors —even for a minute—you would be putting your family at terrible risk. The first thing I'd do if I were you is interrogate those notes from Forsmith. There is no doubt in my mind that Zimmer has him under some kind of influence—blackmail or worse—and has forced him to doctor those clinical reports."

"Maybe it's not Mr. Zimmer who should be being assessed, special agent."

Carver was stunned. "Excuse me, what's that supposed to mean?"

"That's all I'll say for now." Blackwood glanced at the rest of the panel. "Does anybody have anything further for the special agent?" They shook their heads. "Thank you, Mr. Carver. I think it's safe to say you're against this patient's release from the hospital. You're excused."

Carver glared at them. His hand trembling. He could feel Zimmer's eyeball burning a hole in the side of his head. He stood up and kept his own eyes on the panel as he left the room. He didn't even want to glance in Zimmer's direction. Carver heard Zimmer whisper, "You're dead," to his attorney.

CARVER PUSHED his way out of the building and back into the sunlight. He closed his eyes as he walked and took some deep breaths. He stumbled down the path and loosened his tie and undid the top button of his shirt to try and get some air.

He felt ragged and out of breath, like he'd just chased a car stereo thief down. He was a bit panicky. He tried to collect himself and fight the voice in his head that was telling him he'd done the wrong thing. He heard his name being called.

"Carver?" It was Sandling. He turned around.

"Gust! Are you okay?" She stood in front of him and put her hands on his shoulders and held onto him.

"I'll be fine, I'll be fine."

"Wait, stand here with me, where are you going?"

"They're gonna be a few hours yet, Caitlin. But, I've set Zimmer up for you. Wait until the hearing is finished and then go in and see him directly. Don't wait one second, he is going to be seething."

"Why? What did you do, Gust?"

"I did what we said. I provided evidence, but not the evidence that Zimmer was expecting. He is on the warpath now, and you need to get him to talk. Okay? I need to get out of here. Let's meet after."

33

IT WAS dusk when Sandling managed to see Zimmer again. He'd asked for her apparently.

She'd heard from Adrian, the orderly leading her down the cavernous passages, that Zimmer had spent most of the afternoon with his lawyers, pouring over paperwork, and working out the next steps in his quest for release.

"Too much excitement today, Miss Sandling. Much too much to let Hermann out of his cell. Doctor's orders. They agreed you can talk to him through the food tray opening."

"Okay," Sandling said, struggling to keep up with Adrian's large strides.

"But don't hand anything to him that might end up poking outta my neck, ya hear?"

"I won't," she said.

"And," Adrian said as he stopped and held open one of the metal gates for her, "If he grabs you and pulls you in, just try and resist as best you can. We'll do our best to get you outta there before he breaks your arm."

She pursed her lips and raised her eyebrows. She'd never get used to this place. They arrived outside his cell and she could see Zimmer's eye. He was hunched over, one hand against the wall of his cell, his head dipped to look through the thick magnifying glass-like hole. Adrian unlatched the food hatch and snapped it open. He nodded to Sandling and he moved away and stood to the side.

"WHAT IS IT, HERMANN?" Sandling asked.

"Here," Zimmer said and bent as he held a scrap bit of paper through the slot in his cell door. "Take it."

"What's this?" Sandling asked as she took the note, her fingertips accidentally brushed against his skin. It felt ice cold and she shivered.

"It's what you wanted," Zimmer said. "And it's what I said I would do. I made a promise. You were right ... Carver did testify." It was difficult for her to hear him clearly through the thick door. "And a deal is a deal, isn't it, Cate?"

"Yes, I suppose so," Sandling said. "What is it?" she asked.

"Read it," Zimmer said.

"I have and I don't understand," Sandling said.

"It's the way you're going to catch him. Bring him to justice. Too smart, isn't he? Too vicious and too ... vacuous. He's not complying with the rules of your game. But this way, you'll flush him out. Bring him to the surface like a mole escaping the water and drowning in his hole."

Not much clearer to me after that, Sandling thought and looked at Zimmer's scratchy handwriting on the bit of paper again.

"You'll put it out there. Put it over the airwaves and see if someone can help you solve it. The person—or people—who come forward—who present themselves—will undoubtedly have something to do with the case *and* it might even be enough to draw the Skinwalker out from his lair."

Sandling was dubious. "Lair? What do you mean?" Sandling asked.

Zimmer sounded annoyed and impatient. He sighed and said quietly, "Napoleon was a great emperor—a great commander—wasn't he?"

Sandling shrugged. She wasn't familiar with French revolutionary history. "I don't know," she said.

"He was," Zimmer replied. "He said this, 'Amateurs talk strategy. Professionals talk logistics.'" Sandling didn't know what to say, so she shrugged again. "Understand now?" Zimmer asked.

She shook her head. "Not following, Hermann."

"An army marches on its stomach, dear Caitlin. Think a little about the logistics of our outlander," he said. "He's the Minotaur or the Cyclops. Like a mythical beast; he hides. Either due to shame or torment, or both. He is in a dark cave, something that matches the dark place of his mind. He is, however, stealing and eating the king's sheep. Our heroes seek to destroy him. To do that, you must draw the monster from his cave. That's logistics. That's strategy. You want to catch him don't you?"

"Yes, I do."

"You want to redeem yourself and get back in the big time, don't you?"

She thought about her answer. "Yes, I do."

"You want to stop this man from killing innocent people, don't you?"

"Yes, Hermann, obviously I do."

"But mostly you want the recognition, don't you."

Sandling didn't respond. She had the uneasy feeling that Zimmer was right. Even though she could never admit as much to him. She glanced at Adrian standing against the wall. He tapped his watch.

"Okay, thanks, Hermann." She held up the note. "I'll take this to the Carver and see what he thinks."

"No, dear Caitlin, you don't understand, do you? This is between you and me. You need to be the one to deliver this message to the Skinwalker. And—if you do—it'll be his undoing and your homecoming."

She locked eyes with Hermann Zimmer through the glass. He held her gaze. She couldn't read any emotion on his distorted face. He was placid. Plain. Unintelligible.

"I have to go, Hermann."

"Think about it," he said. She turned. "Think about it!" she heard him call after her.

34

SANDLING SAT ALONE at her desk in the Grant Avenue offices. She'd had a long flight to think about it. What exactly was Zimmer after? She'd asked herself over and over. Carver wanted me in there, she thought. And Zimmer finally cracked. Carver kept his part of the deal. Was there some sort of honor amongst enemies here? The rules of warfare were strange to her.

'Get it out in the world', Zimmer said. Get it out in the world. Then it clicked for her. Carver had been talking about using the press. And now she had a decision to make. This was between her and Zimmer. If she could *just* do this. If she could just pull this off ... things would be different. She knew they would. She'd be on the road to redemption. But putting her faith in a murderer?

She tapped her teeth with her fingernail as the thoughts rolled around her head. All the lights were off except for the glow from her computer screen and her desk lamp. She stared at the number that she'd taken from Carver's desk drawer.

It was scrawled in his handwriting, spider, web, and a telephone number. Sandling didn't know what to do. She was in a quandary. On the one hand, she was going behind Carver's back. On the other hand, she was doing what she thought he'd asked her to do. Either way, she was helping the team by doing her job, which was to get a psychopath to help them. And now he had. Hadn't he?

Reluctantly she picked up the receiver and dialed the number. It rang and rang and just when she thought it was going to ring out, and just before she lost her nerve and hung up, a groggy voice answered, "Hello?"

"Hi, is this Jessica Webb, the reporter?"

"Who's calling?" Webb asked.

"It's Caitlin Sandling with the Manassas FBI. Special Agent Carver's team?" She raised the inflection at the end like she was asking a question.

"Yes?" Webb said and sounded more alert like she just sat up in bed.

"I know it's late. I'm not sure if it's too late for the print run, but ...." She shouldn't be doing this, she thought. She clenched her jaw, took a deep breath, and plunged. "Gust asked me to get in touch—urgently—to see if it was possible to get an addition into tomorrow's paper. You're running the story about his family tomorrow, aren't you?"

"He told you about that?"

"Yeah, he was quite upset but also said that it might help us. Do you think you could do it?"

"What sort of addition?"

"It's something to do with the case ..."

She felt like Jessica was checking her watch. "It's late but if I call the duty print team I might be able to catch them. What's the message?"

"You'll need a pen and paper, it's quite complicated and I'll have to talk you through it."

35

SANDLING WAS SITTING at her desk with her head in her hands when Penny Maudmont clattered through the office door. She was carrying a coffee with her purse in the crook of her elbow and inadvertently banged her forehead against the pane of glass in the door.

"Oh my goodness, gosh, dear me, I've spilled my coffee everywhere!" Maudmont cried. Then she saw Sandling. "Oh, you're here! I thought that I was the first one in, I tried to unlock the door and—ah—silly me," she said and looked down at her coat and shoes.

"Here let me help you," Sandling said and pulled some tissues from a box on her desk and went over to Maudmont.

"Oh, thank you, darling," Maudmont said and looked at her properly for the first time. "Are you okay?"

Sandling didn't know how to answer. She forced a smile and said, "Fine thanks."

"Can I ask?" Maudmont said. "Are you *still* here, or have you just come in early this morning?"

"No, I'm still here," Sandling said. "Just back from California. Had something urgent to take care of so came straight in."

"I know we have a lot going on but—seriously—why don't you go home and take a bath and take some time off?"

"I can't afford to do that," Sandling said. "There's just too much going on."

Maudmont went over to her desk, put her things down, took off her coat, and hung it on her chair.

"Well, in that case! I think we've got something exciting to talk to you about. Rachel Fox and I have been using her computer skills to try and help solve the puzzle."

Sandling felt suddenly tired. Her shoulders slumped and her expression contorted. Maudmont raised her eyebrows and immediately stopped talking.

"Listen here, Caitlin," Maudmont said as she walked up to her and put her hand on the small Sandling's back. She directed her toward the kitchenette. "Why don't we put on a strong pot of joe to get ourselves re-engaged and when Rachel's here, we can run through it all together. How about that?" Maudmont's voice was soothing, like a commercial for chamomile tea. Sandling nodded vaguely and allowed Maudmont to direct her toward the makeshift kitchen area, where they proceeded to make the strongest coffee she'd ever tasted.

WHEN EVERYONE WAS in the office and settled at their desks, working, morning conviviality and small talk over, Penny signaled to Sandling, beckoning her over to Rachel Fox's desk.

Fox was locked in. That was something that Fox had explained once: When she had her bucket headphones covering her ears, with the high tempo, trance beat coming out of them, she wasn't to be disturbed. Maudmont must not have gotten the memo.

Maudmont and Sandling stood next to Fox's desk

awkwardly waiting for her to look at them. She just kept tapping away some incomprehensible code into her computer screen.

Maudmont leaned forward and waved and said, "Foxy, we'd really like to talk to you, please. It's important. About the case."

But at the volume Maudmont spoke, and compared to the sound of the trance music coming out of her headphones, Sandling was pretty sure Fox couldn't hear a thing. Sandling, being as tired as she was, feeling as dirty as she did, still somewhere psychologically far away with the stench of Zimmer's foul breath in her nostrils, didn't have time to give people much space or consideration. She glanced at Maudmont, who looked apologetic, and leaned forward and yanked the headphone cable out of the computer.

Fox stopped typing and looked up at the two of them standing there smiling at her. Sandling was twirling the headphone cable. Fox looked sheepish and gave them a small awkward smile.

Maudmont smiled and clasped her hands in front of her and said, "Really sorry, Rachel, but I thought we should share what we were doing with Caitlin to see if she could help, or maybe it would help with the case."

Fox looked Sandling up and down and said, "Your new cologne smells like prison, Cate."

"Thanks very much, Foxy. That's much appreciated. "

"No problem," Fox said and looked at her computer. "Don't call me Foxy."

"I'll be sure to get a spray of deodorant from my desk."

"No, I like it," Fox said. "Suits you."

"Do you reckon you could just show us what you've got, please?" Maudmont asked.

"Give me a second," Fox said and pulled herself closer to the desk and started tapping the keys again.

WHILE FOX WAS TYPING she started to explain the process that she and Maudmont went through.

"So I was reading your reports," Fox said, "Well, actually I scanned them into the system and analyzed the reports for any points of interest."

"Wait, you can do that?" Sandling said.

Fox stopped typing and glanced at her with a look that said, *why are you interrupting me?* Sandling took the hint.

Fox went back to her keyboard. She talked as fast as she typed. "You said that you thought because of the proficiency of the first murder scene that we didn't think it was this killer's first time."

"It was actually my idea," Maudmont said, looking pleased with herself. "I was wondering whether we might be able to match any of the key traits or *modus operandi*, I suppose you'd call them, of the murders and see if they matched anything unsolved on the system."

"That's a good idea," Sandling said. "Did you come up with something?"

"Well that's the thing," Fox said and indicated the piles of boxes and files stacked up next to the workstation. "Most of the older paper-based reports and offender profiles are right here, not digitized."

Maudmont clarified for Sandling, "Part of Quantico's task for Sofa Squad is for Fox to upload the files to the ViCAP database."

Sandling shook her head. She couldn't believe it. Someone of Rachel Fox's obvious—while undoubtedly on some sort of spectrum—tech talent was being holed up in a Manassas field office doing data inputting. She just couldn't wrap her head around the resource allocation decisions by the higher-ups. The bureaucracy made her want to scream.

"Exactly," Maudmont said, reading Sandling's expression.

"Have you found anything?" Sandling asked.

"It was Penny's idea to look at all the data. So I set up a program that would help us scan the files …"

"And we've been up all night for the last three or four nights," Maudmont said.

"But then I wrote this algorithm to search through the documents," Fox said.

"It was really quite exciting," Maudmont added, unable to contain her excitement. "Because we had all this information but we didn't really know how to search through it. Like, what should we look for?"

Sandling thought about it for a second and said, "Well, based on the age of the killer from the footage and the eyewitness, if you did have something that we had a record of, you'd probably be looking at a juvenile."

Fox glanced at Maudmont and they both said, "Exactly."

"What if we're asking the wrong questions," Fox said. "Most files are sealed if the perpetrator is under sixteen."

"So they wouldn't be in the system anyway," Sandling said.

"I wrote this algorithm as a search query of all of the paper files we uploaded," Fox said.

Maudmont jumped in again, "And it was a hell of a job let me tell you because first we had to transfer all of the handwritten notes into text-based and …"

Sandling took a deep breath and they both got it. Tell me the solution, not the problem.

"Anyway," Fox said and swung a monitor so that Sandling could see. "I wrote this query checking against first names, last names, years, locations, representative incident

ID types, where it took place, between what years, and included the search terms ..."

Sandling read the queries to herself: rape, decapitation, dismemberment, murder, binding, torture, kill, hanging.

"Wow," Sandling said, "that would be quite a hit list for a juvenile. Did you find anything?"

"Maybe, but we needed to check with you first," Fox said.

"Those search terms are too narrow, we think," Maudmont said. "You're the profiler, we were thinking that maybe you could help us with some insight into the psychological profile of the killer."

"Yeah," Sandling agreed and held her breath and looked up at the ceiling as she considered the puzzle. She was thinking out loud when she said, "If he's a juvenile and we believe he's in his late twenties or early thirties now, then that means that this was twenty or so years ago, maybe more. And what sort of crimes would he have been sent to juvenile detention for? We need to cross reference this with something that would be evident in his records. I'd say probably an orphan, only child, or single-parent family."

Fox was typing as Sandling spoke.

"Something I've been thinking about a lot," Sandling said. "The crimes don't seem to have any sexual motive but the women he's picking are all successful, very well known, beautiful. How could they not be sexual?"

"Unless he has a thing for boys," Fox said.

Maudmont lifted her index finger to her lips, "This might sound silly but could have something wrong with him?"

"What do you mean?" Sandling asked. "Besides the desire to kill people?"

"Like, is there something wrong with him physically that he can't be intimate," Maudmont said.

"Could something have happened to him *sexually*," Fox whispered, "When he was a young age?"

"One way to find out," Sandling said, "Could we try and update the search terms to include orphan, single-parent family, some sort of sexual abuse?"

"Over four hundred hits," Fox said. She sounded despondent. Like the amount of time and effort they'd put into this was slipping away with nothing to show for it.

"What else is rarely depraved?" Sandling asked.

"Him leaving poisonous snakes at the scene ..." Fox said more to herself than either of the others. "*Eurgh*. Gives me the creeps."

"Venomous," Maudmont corrected.

"Put in something about snakes or reptiles in there," Sandling said.

"This sounds like a stretch."

"A hundred and twelve hits," Fox said.

Sandling suddenly felt optimistic. "I mean, this is a much narrower field than you could have ever hoped for before," Sandling said.

"What else can we try?" Fox asked.

Maudmont's eyes went wide and she blurted out, "Don't they usually offer loads of programs and courses for juvenile offenders when they're in prison?"

"Depends on the institution," Sandling said. "I think some are better than others."

"Well maybe if it wasn't that grievous of an offense and they thought that he could possibly be reformed, maybe he would have been at an institution where there were a variety of courses offered?"

"What's a list of courses that they give juveniles?" Fox asked.

"Actually, Penny, that's not a bad idea," Sandling said,

"But I think rather than a list of courses we need to look at the traits and methods of his murders, right?"

"Do they offer things like butchery or surgery?" Sandling asked. "Unlikely," she said answering her own question.

She saw the blur of Fox's fingers running over the keyboard and hit the enter button.

"What about taxidermy?" Fox asked.

36

Richmond County Sheriff patrolman, Jet Tenant, sat riding shotgun next to his partner, Wisdom Rowntree, and looked lackadaisically out of the window at the passers-by.

The dispatch radio crackled with static, and Debbie, the radio operator that Tenant thought he fancied should his wife ever die, came over the radio.

"Calling all units, we have a ten-forty-two, MISPER report at Treasured Relics Antique store on the corner of McDowell and Monte Sano."

Tenet and Rowntree glanced at one another.

They were just a few blocks away. Tenet shrugged, *what the hell*, and Rowntree picked up the handset.

"Dispatch, this is two-seventeen. We're nearby that location. Send details, over."

"Roger, two-seventeen. Missing person's report received for one Ruth Minnesota, nickname Minny, five foot six inches, brown hair, green eyes, usually wears glasses, no known medical issues. Heavy build. The property caretaker was a male, caucasian, named Edward Derange, no prior record. The missing person's grandmother confirmed that the family had no contact with Minny in several days and is concerned. You're to proceed to the property and give it a quick once over and see if you can have a word with the person of interest, Edward Derange."

"Unit two-seventeen en route for welfare check and question any individuals on the premises, confirmed. Will update with further in due course. Unit two-seventeen out."

"Slick," Tenant said and Rowntree started the engine.

"Only way I roll, boy-o"

THE PATROL CAR pulled up outside Treasured Relics Antiques.

"What are we doing here again?"

Rowntree sucked on the gap between his front teeth and said, "Looks abandoned, don't it?"

"Sure doesn't seem like much going on inside."

It looked dim inside and there was a thick, padlocked chain wrapped around a wooden-framed, pane-glass door.

"Check it out in any case," Rowntree said and stepped out of the car. He picked up his nightstick from the door and shoved it into his belt. Tenant dutifully got out into the sunshine and put on his sunglasses. He walked up to the front door of Treasured Relics and cupped his hands over his sunglasses and leaned close to get a look inside.

He didn't see anything out of the ordinary, just lots of glass display cases on antique tables scattered around the bottom of the shop.

"Nothing," he said.

"Go and take a look around back," Rowntree said. "I'll

get in touch with dispatch and send them a quick update. Let me know what you find."

Without saying anything, Tenant made his way to the alley and had a look down it. Looked clear, nothing too suspicious, nothing to be too wary of. He started walking at a leisurely pace and whistled a show tune that his daughter had been listening to at breakfast. It had been stuck in his head since. The alleyway opened up into a stone gravel parking lot. There were a few vehicles scattered about and some open scrubland at the back surrounded by buildings. He turned the corner to the back of the shop and was surprised. The back door was ajar. He touched his hand to his weapon and grabbed his flashlight.

"Hello?" he called out. "This is the county sheriff." He used the flashlight to push the back door open and shone the light onto the linoleum floor. It was streaked with something brown and rust-colored, and then he got the smell of chemicals, and saw what he recognized as blood splatter.

"How 'bout that," he said and took a step back. He leaned around the wall and called out to Rowntree. "Wisdom! You better come and check this out, man."

37

FOX TYPED '*I.TAXIDERMY, i.taxidermist, i.skinning, i.mounting, i.stuffing*' into the search field and hovered her finger above the enter key for a second longer than she usually did.

Then she pressed it. The database popped up and returned five possible hits.

"Five," Maudmont said. The excitement was palpable.

Fox flicked through the different electronic files as Sandling and Maudmont leaned a bit closer.

"Nope. Nope. No," Sandling said as Fox scrolled. "Fourth one ... no, fifth one..."

Fox's eyes scanned the page and said, "Wait a second, this guy's file was sealed. It's redacted but the medical report says he was maimed by a snake bite to his *penis*."

Sandling stood upright. She felt the blood drain from her face.

"Hey! What are you girls doing standing around there?" Underwood called out from behind them.

They ignored him.

"No," Sandling finally said. "That can't be him. One of the eyewitnesses at the Silvstedt *au pair* murder said she saw the suspect with curly blonde hair and *pale* skin. He was white. Well, actually, I don't know if she said pale skin, but she definitely said blonde hair, and often people would assume that they would have pale skin ..."

"What are you saying? It couldn't have been somebody wearing a wig?" Fox asked.

Sandling thought about it. "No, of course it could be."

"And that eyewitness," Maudmont said, "Wasn't it a woman in her eighties with glasses? I mean, how can she be sure what she saw? I keep seeing my dog Squeaky running into the living room and she's been dead for three years."

"Carver spoke to her," Sandling said. "We could ask him what he thought about her reliability. It's just that witnesses saw a white male, and this guy," she leaned forward and peered at the name again, "Ronald Jeffery Hyatt, it says African-American. He looks possibly mixed race, or maybe Latino? But he doesn't have the bone structure. It's kind of hard to tell from the picture."

"Hey," Underwood called again.

"Hell! We're busy," Sandling said and turned toward him, her face scrunched up in anger. "We're busy, could you leave us alone?"

Underwood was holding his desk phone.

"Agent Carver was on the line for you, Caitlin. He says it's urgent. You need to call him and get on a jet with him to a crime scene in Augusta right away. He's waiting for you at Marine Corps Air Station Quantico. You're welcome! *Jeez.*"

CARVER WAS TALKING to the first policeman on the scene, Jet Tenant, when he saw Sandling arrive and duck under the police tape.

"You said you'd gotten a call from the owner of the store?" Carver asked.

Sandling sidled up to them and stood there, silent. Carver indicated her to Officer Tenant and said, "This is my partner, Special Agent Sandling. She's helping me with the investigation. She's late."

"Missed my flight," she said apologetically to Carver. They both looked back at Tenant.

"Yes sir," Tenant said and nodded to Sandling. "Ma'am."

Tenant had those youthful good looks and square jaw. Carver glanced at Sandling, who was ogling him as he spoke.

"You were saying ..." Carver said.

"Yes, sir," Tenant said. "We received the dispatch from command to come and check out the scene. Missing persons case, family worried about their girl. Name of Ruth Minnesota. No lights or activity when we arrived. Carried out a check of the premises and I went around to the back door and found it open."

"Okay," Carver said. "What happened then?"

"I called my partner over," Tenant said and pointed to a large officer who was talking to someone else at the police cordon, "Corporal Rowntree, the big guy standing over there. We entered the building but something told us— immediately—that things were wrong. So we drew our service weapons, cleared the building, and called for forensics and backup."

"Was anyone inside?" Sandling asked.

"No, ma'am," Tenant said and flashed her a grin. Carver growled to himself.

"Is there a victim?" Sandling asked. Tenant glanced at Carver with a questioning expression.

"I haven't had a chance to brief Agent Sandling on the situation yet. Thank you very much for your time, officer," Carver said.

Tenant nodded and Carver guided Sandling to the side where he could bring her up to speed on what they'd found.

"Sorry I'm late," Sandling said and started to explain. "We found something quite exciting through the sealed juvenile documents that Foxy was working on ..."

"That's great," Carver said. "Listen, this is really important. They think they've found the Skinwalker's hideout. And they think there's a hostage situation. We don't know exactly what happened and I haven't been inside yet. We're going to take a walk-through and speak to forensics when they're finished with the crime scene.

"Why do they think they've found him?" Sandling asked. She looked excited. Things were moving fast.

"We can't be a hundred percent sure yet, obviously, and I haven't seen what's going on but from what I understand it's pretty horrific and this could very well be our guy."

Just then someone called out, "Special Agent Carver? Is there a Special Agent Carver here from the FBI?"

Sandling and Carver turned to see a white hazmat-suited man with blue nitrile gloves waving them toward the back door.

"Come on," Carver said. "Game faces. Let's do this one properly. A girl's life is counting on it and we don't know how long we have."

"How many of these have you done?" the head of forensics asked Carver as they stepped through the threshold. Too many, Carver thought, without answering. "It's a bit of a horror show up there," the guy said, "Watch your step."

"Oh God, the smell!" Sandling said and covered her nose.

"Yeah, you might want some of this." He held out a small tub of menthol camphor. "I'm Bob, by the way."

Carver and Sandling each dabbed a finger into it and rubbed underneath their nostrils to mask the smell of death.

"Gust, Caitlin," Carver said.

"Are there any bodies?" Sandling asked.

"No bodies," Bob said, "But there might be a few other things you're interested in. We found lots of blood splatter. We've got fingerprints, saliva, hair, and a full-on zoological reptilian display."

"Cottonmouths?" Carver asked.

"About twenty of 'em. I had to get animal control down here just in case 'cause they scared the skin off my team ... so to speak."

No one said anything.

"Excuse me," Bob said by way of apology. "That was in bad taste."

"We don't mind gallows humor," Carver said and winked at Sandling, knowing she did mind it.

"You already know about this guy, I take it," Bob said.

"A few bits and pieces here and there," Carver said.

Bob stood and stared at him, nodding as if he was trying to understand the subtle way Carver was downplaying his involvement in the case.

"Right, well, anyway, follow me up into the attic. Mind your step, it's a bit rickety."

As he entered the cavernous attic space, Carver was hit by a kaleidoscopic collage of what he thought insanity must look like. He didn't know where to start.

"What did you say this guy's name was?" Carver asked the head of forensics.

"Edward Derange," Bob said. "According to the old lady in the hospital. She swears she didn't make it up. That's what he's really called."

Or called himself, Carver thought.

"Wasn't the stroke talking," Bob added.

A few other forensic technicians were moving around in the background. Carver noticed them and Bob said, "Don't mind them, they're just finishing up. We're all good here."

What he meant was that neither Carver nor Sandling would contaminate the scene. Carver was looking at Sandling.

"What?" he asked her.

She was tapping her finger on her arm and chewing the inside of her cheek.

"No, it's just that we thought we'd narrowed down the list of suspects to five and—one in particular—but that name, Edward Derange, wasn't part of the files we isolated. The closest one we had was a Ronald Hyatt. Could be an alias."

"We'll know for sure when the fingerprints and DNA analysis comes back," Bob said. "Until then, let me take you on a little guided tour. You can see they left in a hurry."

The head of forensics indicated the desk and worktop where it looked like a laptop or computer terminal had been dragged and scraped through the dust, lots of pinned pictures and blue-tacked papers had been ripped haphazardly off the wall. Carver's eye was drawn to a newspaper open on the desk. He could see a large black-and-white picture of Bethany holding Ryan in front of the house in Tennessee. The bottom half of the profile piece looked like it had been torn off in a rush. Carver could imagine the killer stuffing all of his notes and recordings and memorabilia into a garbage bag. He looked at Sandling again.

She was staring at the newspaper. She saw him looking

at her and quickly switched focus. She didn't say anything about the paper open on the suspect's desk. They turned to Bob as he spoke.

"Over here you might see signs of a struggle, there's a wet patch on the floor. We think this might be where the hostage or kidnapped victim, Ruth Minnesota, was held. She peed herself. That's adding to the aroma."

"She's terrified," Sandling said.

"Wouldn't you be?" Carver asked.

"What about the drag marks here on the floor?" Sandling asked.

"He moved something," Bob said. "You might've seen the winch and pulley system for moving big antiques around. It looks like he got in here with some cables and took something down. It's around the size of a coffin, a small coffin, maybe. We don't know exactly what it was."

"Did you find anything else?" Sandling asked. "Personal belongings—anything like that—clothing?"

"Funny you should ask," Bob said. "Was there anything specific you were looking for?"

Sandling paused and looked directly at Carver. "How about a blond male wig?" she said.

Bob's mouth dropped open and then he smiled. "Interesting you should say that." He looked over his shoulder at one of his white hazmat-suited colleagues and said, "Cindy?" An Asian woman looked up at him. "Hand me that evidence bag."

She tossed him a clear bag with black pen markings on it. Bob held it up. Inside was a quite authentic-looking yellow-haired wig.

"What does this mean?" Carver asked Sandling.

She raised eyebrows. "It means that maybe—while your little old lady eyewitness testimony was correct—our suspect is actually darker-skinned, mixed race, or possibly

Latino unsub who likes to wear makeup and wigs as social camouflage."

"Got it. Do you have a picture?"

"Of what?" Sandling asked.

"Ronald Hyatt," Carver said. "The suspect you identified from the database."

"Back at the office," Sandling said.

Carver turned to the head of forensics.

"How soon will you have the fingerprint and DNA evidence analyzed?" Carver asked.

Bob shook his head and looked at the ceiling as he calculated. Cindy piped up from behind him and said, "We can have it over to you by tomorrow morning."

Bob pulled a face. "That'll be a stretch, but we'll do our best to get it over to you as soon as possible."

Carver wasn't sure if he needed to, but he thought he would take a stern line with them, and said, "You do know that a girl's life is at stake here, Bob, don't you? I mean, I'd pull whatever strings you've got to try and make sure that we find her safe. Who knows what sort of brick shithouse will come rolling downhill crushing whatever's in its path if we don't ..."

38

CARVER WAS AT HIS DESK. He was sitting in the dark managing a migraine when his phone buzzed in his pocket. He pulled it out and glanced at the screen, he recognized the number and answered.

"Hello Bronwyn."

"Hello Gust."

Carver thought she sounded downbeat and said, "I was just thinking about you and thinking about giving you a call. You must have read my mind and beaten me to it ..."

"Maybe," she said.

"You heard about our horror house in Augusta?" Carver asked. "I think we've identified our suspect."

Gibson, suddenly animated, cut him off, "That's why I'm calling you."

He could hear something strange in her tone.

"What is it?" he asked.

"The girl," Gibson said and he heard the rustling of paper as she checked her notes. "Ruth Minnesota."

"She's about to be the next victim," Carver said. "What about her?"

"Turns out she's somebody's daughter."

"Aren't they all?" Carver said.

"Yes, well, this one's somebody *important's* granddaughter, and he's not pulling any punches."

"Pulling any punches?" Carver said. "You make it sound like a prize fight."

"That's exactly what it is," Gibson said. Frustrated now.

"So what's going on, Bronwyn? Something that I need to know?"

He wondered if she was searching for the words or just for effect.

"You're taking us off the case," Carver said.

"Yes. I'm sorry."

"No you're not."

"Listen, Gust, this is a courtesy call, okay? Nothing official, but I'm giving you a heads-up. Ruth Minnesota is the granddaughter of the chief justice of the Georgia Supreme Court. It's all grown too high profile since her kidnapping. And I have it on good authority that the president has privately expressed very strong support in finding the perpetrator."

"Kidnapping?" Carver said. "I hate to break this to you, Bron, but that girl is about to be a cadaver if she isn't one already."

"You'd better pray you're wrong. We need to find her. And fast."

"Isn't that what we're trying to do?"

"Yeah, well, perhaps. But with the press already around this thing, like flies on shit, and with your history ... getting freaking *Zimmer* involved," Gibson said and left the sentence hanging.

"That was your idea," Carver said. "It's why you brought me in."

She didn't answer.

"I don't want to fight about this, Gust."

He did though.

"What's the real reason, Bronwyn? Is it that you can't be seen to have defective agents working on this case, now that the president is involved?"

"That's part of it."

Carver was fuming.

"Carver ..."

"Just say it."

"Say what?"

"Come on, just say it. This is about my record and your neck being on the chopping block."

"My neck, my reputation."

"Your career."

Gibson was quiet.

"A girl's life is on the line here, Bronwyn. My team led you straight to him. Who knows what would've happened to her if we didn't get involved and *now* you want to bench your best players? What the hell ..."

"I'm sorry, Special Agent Carver. The decision's about to be made. It's out of my hands."

Carver sighed. He was resigned now. Migraine was killing him.

"So what happens now?"

"A lot of actions and protocols, that's what," Gibson said. "Crisis response team has already been activated. You and your team could expect some calls from different government agencies. There'll be a coordinated effort. Interagency collaboration, domestic and international. They'll be assigning a liaison officer to keep up communication with the family and protect their privacy, and, speaking of which, manage media exposure to avoid compromising the investigation or the victim's safety."

"What're you trying to say?"

"That article," Gibson said.

"Oh, you saw that," Carver rubbed his forehead. His brain throbbed. He had a black spot in his vision.

"Yeah, I mean, full page spread and full bio on you. Interviewing Bethany. I mean, what the hell? They're the last people who I thought you'd want on this."

"Yeah, well, shit happens."

"Yes, indeed it does."

"Just for the record, I never agreed to it. I didn't sign off on it. Haven't even read it." Gibson didn't say anything. "So that's it," Carver said. "One too many embarrassments for the Bureau and we're off the case. That about sum it up?"

"Your team has done a sterling job up to this point, Gust, and once the dust is settled and the suspect is in custody, I'll make sure that you are not forgotten in the official report."

"Don't do me any favors," Carver said and hung up.

He rubbed his forehead. God, she was infuriating. These types of cases always dredged up unresolved tensions in their relationship. The cases they worked on brought up personal demons for both of them. The truth was it went back a long way, to a time before Carver even worked in the FBI. They had a shared history. It meant they could support one another. It also meant they were acutely aware of how easily the other could be wounded by the horrors they'd confront. They first crossed paths during an undercover drugs operation that led to the discovery of seventeen bodies dumped in a swamp. This was the very start of the Peninsula Killer case. Carver was still working narcotics back then. She said she recognized something in him that was unique. A blend of raw intuition and unorthodox methods. Skills she didn't possess but needed. Plus, it helped that he'd caught the guy.

Carver knew that Gibson's decision to recruit him into the Behavioral Analysis Unit and her subsequent doubling down on her support of his ailing career hadn't been without personal sacrifice. She advocated for him and it put her own position at risk. She was intensely career-focused. She hadn't risen as far as she had without knowing how to wield a dagger at the appropriate moment to stab someone in the back. It was strange for him because their relationship relied on the perfect blend of resentment and protectiveness she showed toward him.

SANDLING KNOCKED QUICKLY and poked a head around Carver's door. "You'll never guess who I've just spoken to," Sandling said, and then, "Gosh, it's dark in here. And smelly. Are you okay, Gust?"

Carver didn't respond. He just covered his eyes with the palms of his hands and said, "Who?"

"I just got off a call with forensics from the antique shop."

"Yeah?"

"Ronald Jeffery Hyatt, matches the suspect Foxy and Maudmont traced down using the system."

Carver nodded. The pain of his migraine was pushing needles down his neck. "That's good work from them," Carver said. "I'll make sure they get the recognition."

"What's the matter, Gust?" Sandling asked. "I thought you'd be more excited about the news. We've got him."

"Don't ask," Carver said. "Migraine. Just trying to push through here."

"There's something else," Sandling said.

"What is it?"

"There's a DNA match. Remember how Dufresne gave us a swab? The suspect, Hyatt, is a very close relative. Could potentially even be Dufresne's son."

"Bastien's bastard son?" Carver asked and opened his eyes and leaned forward.

"We've got the suspect's mugshot picture. If you want to see?"

Carver nodded. Sandling handed him a folder. He opened it and closed one eye and squinted at it.

Sandling leaned on the desk and turned his reading lamp on. Carver saw the picture of Ronald Jeffery Hyatt more clearly, faded mugshot though it was, and said, "Wait. I've seen this person before. Where?" He couldn't quite remember.

Carver looked up at Sandling. She was waiting patiently. He stood up.

"Is the team all out there?" Carver asked.

She nodded.

"There's something I need to ask them," he said.

39

"Do you know what this is?" Derange asked from the front seat of his van. He didn't seem like he was talking to her. He shouted it.

Minny jumped in fear. She was lying on her side on a plasterboard panel he'd put as a base in the back. Her body swayed and bounced as he drove fast and erratically through the night.

"Do you know what this is?" He was saying it loudly, over and over. He was frantic. Excited. Like he was on the upslope of a manic episode. He turned around and leaned over the seat while accelerating.

He held a scrunched-up bit of newspaper in his hand. It was something he'd ripped out and venerated and studied and walked around holding while muttering to himself.

Minny's mouth was taped shut but she let out a muffled cry trying to sound out, 'Watch the road!' She might be dead anyway but a car wreck wasn't the way she wanted to go. Not with a live snake in the back of the van. He paid her screams no attention. He liked to see her squirm and scared, she thought.

"Of course you don't. You're just a stupid *bitch*. Of course you don't. This. God, *this* is everything I worked for. Everything. This tells me the Ripper is something else. He knows my mind. He knows my thoughts. We're connected in an alternate plane of existence."

He was ranting loudly to himself over the road and engine noise. "He's talking to me. He's talking through me," he was saying.

She was uncomfortable lying on her side, elbow pressed into plasterboard; mouth, wrists, and ankles wrapped tightly with duct tape. A huge cottonmouth snake with a fat belly lying next to her. Behind her back—it didn't bear thinking about—was the mummified corpse of a shriveled-up human being that Derange had been calling *mummy*.

She closed her eyes and tried to concentrate on not sliding around in the back as he drove. The whole van stank of gasoline, snake feces, and Derange's insanely bad breath. Minny doubted he ever cleaned his teeth, something she couldn't abide was bad oral hygiene, forgetting everything else that he'd done. To her that was completely unforgivable. Anyway, she thought, she'd just try to control the nausea. Don't let yourself panic, she told herself. She took deep breaths.

She was surprised at how well she was dealing with it up 'til now. She'd often, while reading her novels, allow herself to fantasize about what it must be like to be the target of a killer's attention. Never in her wildest dreams did she think that it would happen to her, especially not by this wiry insect-looking borderline homeless person her grandmother had taken in against her better judgment.

Just then the brakes squealed and Minny's head hit the back of the seats. Derange started turning the van in somewhere. They went over a bump and her body lifted into the air and she slammed back down onto the hard flatbed with her hip. *Ouch!* It hurts, she thought. But refused to cry out.

"Sorry, Mummy. Sorry, Bess," Derange said from the front seat, talking to the withered and dry corpse of his mother and the pregnant snake in its terrarium next to her.

He wasn't concerned about my well-being at all, she thought. They pulled in, and rolling over to look up and outside, Minny saw they were under the bright lights of a gas station. The daylight was fading. *Help*, she thought. Derange got out and slammed the door. He obviously changed his mind because he climbed back in and leaned over the front seats. She was looking at his upside-down face. His mouth was open in a snarl.

"If you move, if you make a noise, if you bang, if you break the glass, if I come back and find anybody snooping around this van, whether you enticed them or not, I'm going to feed you to Bessey. She's full of about seventy brand new baby Cottonmouths and I will keep you alive until they hatch and let them crawl all over your body and pick you apart as their first measly, mousy morsel. Do you understand?"

She nodded affirmatively and whimpered and he was gone and slammed the door again. She jumped. She wanted to cry. She was definitely going to die. Her eyes were shut tight. She was too scared to move. She thought she would pee herself soon.

Then she heard the door open again and Derange climbed in. The whole vehicle rocked as he did. He put the key in the ignition and the engine struggled to turn over.

"Come on, come on," he said. "Damned thing."

Eventually, the engine started and the old Ford Transit kicked into gear. He pressed the accelerator a few times and the fan belt whined.

"Don't worry Mummy," Derange said loudly over his shoulder talking to the corpse. "One more stop and then we'll be on our road trip to visit Agent Carver."

40

CARVER WALKED out of his office.

The team was at their desks. Underwood leaning back in his chair and rolling his wrist under a toy basketball and catching it. Hornigen, looking serious, checked paperwork against whatever was on his screen. Fox—headphones on—completely zoned out. Maudmont busy tidying up.

He felt nervous. He never usually felt nervous but Carver was aware the situation had changed and was even more critical now than before the kidnapping. The other murders weren't preventable. This one was. But it was slipping away from them.

Carver glanced at Sandling. She looked nervous too but mouthed the word *smile* silently to him and forced one herself. He turned back to the team, grimaced, cleared his throat, and said, "Hey guys—listen up—there's something I need to discuss with you."

The team turned to look at him. Fox noticed Maudmont standing with her hands clasped in front of herself. Fox swiveled in her chair and took off her headphones at the same time. Carver cleared his throat again.

"Guys, I'm not usually one for speeches but I feel it's

important to say something, I guess. I've got good news and bad news and I need to share it, okay? So, do you want the good news or the bad news?"

"Good news," they all said.

"I think the first thing to say is—congratulations—to Fox and Maudmont for your stellar work in solving the problem of the juvenile files. The idea to go back to juvenile records to try and find the perpetrator was ingenious and you actually narrowed it down to something we could work with. The good news is, we've positively identified a suspect named—Ronald Jeffrey Hyatt—who you pulled out of a stack of needles. So well done."

There was an air of anticipation and hesitancy. The team looked around with solemn faces. Nobody said anything. All waiting for the bad news.

"So we caught him then?" Maudmont asked.

Carver winced. "Not exactly. And that's part of the bad news."

"Wait, there's more than one part?" Underwood asked.

"Maybe there's two parts to the bad news," Carver said.

He admittedly hadn't thought through what he was going to say and his splitting headache wasn't helping. He felt like he might fall over at any second.

"The suspect is in the wind," Sandling said, being helpful. Carver looked at her and nodded.

"That's right. And he has a hostage. It turns out the old woman who hired him and let him live in her attic was very nearly one of his victims. When her granddaughter didn't visit her in hospital, she got worried and called the police. We just missed them."

"Have there been any ransom demands or conditions?" Underwood asked.

Carver shook his head. "Nothing that I'm aware of—yet—and I wouldn't expect it."

He left an opening for Sandling and she said, "Based on his BAU profile, I think it's more likely that he'll try and use her as a human shield, and if he manages to escape the cordon ..."

"She'll likely be killed," Underwood said, finishing her sentence.

"That's right," Sandling said. "Unfortunately."

"So is that the good news then?" Underwood asked with a hint of sarcasm, "We've identified the killer but he's escaped. Is that right?"

"And he has a victim hostage," Carver said. "We presume alive, for now."

"Jesus," Underwood said and looked around the room at the others, "If that's the bad news, I'm starting to really worry about the good news."

"Right, yeah," Carver looked at his shoes and stuck his hands in his pockets. "I've just had a call from Deputy Gibson. The hostage is a prominent Supreme Court of Georgia judge's granddaughter. This is now national news and there's a multiple statewide manhunt on the go."

"Wait, what are you trying to say?" Sandling asked. She looked confused. They all did.

"It's become too high profile for us and ... we've been stood down."

"Lord, no," Maudmont said and took a step forward. The anxiousness was evident on her face.

"They've pulled us from the case," Carver said more bluntly. He didn't know any other way to break the news. Underwood looked at Hornigen and they both shook their heads. But they were used to this kind of disappointment, weren't they, Carver thought.

"So, what?" Fox asked. "That's it, it's all over? We're not on this any more?"

They all looked at Carver for an answer. "That's what we need to decide now, guys. You know, we can either follow orders and stand down—go back to filling in paperwork and scanning documents into the system—or ..." Carver hesitated.

"Or what?" Sandling asked.

"Or, we can risk it all."

"Meaning?"

"Keep working on it and keep trying to save at least one more girl's life."

Hornigen furrowed his brow, clearly not okay with disobeying direct orders.

"Look, I understand if you would prefer your pensions," Carver said. He was being genuine. "But I think it's important that we make a decision as a team about what our next steps are because we're gonna think about this moment—this decision—for the rest of our lives."

"But there's no decision," Hornigen said. "It's not up to us."

"Toby, I know you've got a family and two young daughters that you need to think about," Carver said, looking at Underwood.

His eyes turned to Hornigen. "And your wife, Frank, I know about her condition and your time spent by a bedside in hospital. I always meant to say, you know, anytime you need to go and be with her, go be there for her. I realize it's a huge ask."

He looked at Fox. "Rachel, your grandmother needs you. She's your only support and you're her only family."

He looked at Maudmont. "Penny, I realize this must be shocking for you and something that you and your husband would probably need to discuss. And," He looked at Sandling. "Caitlin, you've done an incredible job on this case, so far, and really shone by bringing Zimmer into the fold." There was silence. "I get it. You guys have got a lot riding on your careers here."

"And you don't?" Maudmont asked.

Carver shrugged. "My life was going nowhere fast before coming here. I've got a wife and a son who are holed up in a compound in Tennessee, too scared to leave the property. I was at a community college lecturing on criminology before I met all of you. I don't have a long way to fall to go back to where I was before."

Everyone was quiet.

"Neither do we, if we're being honest," Underwood said quietly and shrugged at Hornigen.

"That's it," Carver said. "That's all I wanted to say. I've told you the situation and presented the choice: follow orders and step away from the case, or, risk everything to save Ruth Minnesota's life."

Underwood opened his mouth to speak.

"Wait," Sandling said and put her hand up to stop him. She stood up and stepped forward. "I—, I can't hold this in anymore. I've got to say it."

She balled up her fists. There was a long pause while everybody waited to hear what Sandling was going to say.

"A few weeks ago we were discussing the reasons that we got sent to Sofa Squad." Sandling took a deep breath. "The real reason I'm here," she started to say, her voice cracked and her eyes welled up. "Is that—God, this is difficult. All I ever wanted to be was like my dad, you know? All I ever wanted to be was somebody who could make a difference, to keep people safe, to help them. Then he was killed—taken away from me—and I didn't know this about myself until I got to the academy but ... I can't fire a weapon."

Everybody was quiet. Carver could hear the wind blowing through the trees outside.

She said the last part like she was opening a twelve-step meeting. "I have a phobia of firearms."

Everyone was watching her. "I've never admitted that to anyone and I understand if you think less of me."

"God, no," Maudmont said. "We'd never think less of you, Caitlin, you're amazing at what you do. You helped us identify the killer."

Sandling thanked Maudmont for the words with her expression but turned to Carver. "The reason I'm telling you all this now is, that was the hardest thing I've ever had to say, so this next part is the second hardest because of how far we've come as a *team*."

Carver felt the blood drain from his face.

"I think I might've done something terrible and I don't know how to tell you but I'll try. Someone asked me to publish something in the paper that carried your profile and the interview with Bethany—with your family—I have a feeling that, well, I don't know what was meant by the poem but ..."

"What?" Underwood said. "I don't understand."

"I know! God, I'm so sorry," Sandling said and covered her eyes and broke down.

Carver was unmoved. Not completely sure what Sandling was trying to confess. He went to her and put his hands on her upper arms and said, "Caitlin, Caitlin, look at me. It's okay. It's okay. Really ..." She looked up at him. "It's okay."

Sandling looked confused. Carver swallowed. He felt compelled to tell her the truth he'd been hiding.

"If we're doing this," he said and looked at her earnestly and ignored the audience. "There's something I need to tell you too."

Caitlin sniffled, her big doe eyes staring back at him.

Maudmont came over with a box of tissues and Sandling took some and dabbed them under her eyelashes.

"What is it?" Sandling asked.

"Um, well, your dad wasn't a victim of the Peninsula Killer like they told you."

Sandling furrowed her brows. Her jaw clenched. Her face hardened. The mere mention of her dad brought out tough emotions.

"What? Wait, then who?" she asked.

Carver felt the room go black. He'd opened the cursed relic. There was no going back now. He had to tell her. All he could see was Caitlin's eyes staring at him and he was realizing that this was going to hurt her beyond his ability to understand her pain. Before he could answer her question, Carver saw the clarity of realization on her face.

"Zimmer," she said quietly. "No. Not Zimmer. Please."

Maudmont gasped.

Carver swallowed and nodded.

He was solemn. "We ... the *Bureau* suspect he was killed by Hermann Zimmer."

Her eyes welled up again. She had a look of utter disbelief on her face.

"Why would Zimmer have done that?"

"Because he believes Ray Kraft was his biological father."

Carver could see it etched on her face. The sudden glare of betrayal.

"Did Zimmer know who I was?" Sandling asked. Her voice barely above a whisper. "Did he know he'd killed my father?"

Carver looked as apologetic as he could. He'd agreed to send her into the interview alone while knowing not only that Zimmer had murdered her father but that he would probably work out who she was.

"Zimmer knew who I was, and what he'd done to my dad?"

The gravity of what he'd just told her started to dawn on him. He realized they were in a room full of people watching them. She looked like she was about to scream.

"You asked to go in alone, to be fair ..."

Suddenly she looked around the room at all of the eyes that were on her. She hesitated for a moment and then panic-bolted out of the room. Carver just stood there, looking helplessly after her. Maudmont squinted her eyes at him and glared at him before following Sandling out.

Meanwhile, Fox, who was the least socially conscious person Carver had ever met, spat venom at him when she said, "What did you go and do that for, Carver? Even I know that's not something you bring up in front of other people."

Underwood looked shocked. Hornigen shook his head.

Carver turned silently and went back into his office and closed the door. He locked it. His head ached even worse than before.

41

THIS IS IT, he thought. Rock bottom.

"If this isn't then what is," Carver mumbled to himself. Not a question. He knew he had hit it. Again. He was wallowing and yanked open his desk drawer.

What the hell had he just done? God, for someone so good at being an empath, so able to assimilate—even with someone insane—maybe it was only the killers he could connect with. And for good reason. What did that make him? Any better than them?

Hardly. Maybe worse.

"Talking to yourself again," Carver said out loud. "I sure have to hand it to you, *boy*." He whistled to himself like he was impressed. It was sarcastic. "What the hell was I thinking?"

The thought just rolled around his head. It was dark now. The lights in the office were off. The team had long gone home; or wherever they went when they weren't here. He checked his phone again. No returned call from Sandling.

There was a distant rumble of thunder and he heard drops of rain start to patter on his office window. A few at first, building up, until it was coming down in pelts. He glanced down at the open drawer and saw a fifth of Talisker, a snub nose .38 special, and a new box of ammunition.

Carver silently recited the lines from his favorite Robert Louis Stevenson poem,

"*At lack of a' sectarian fush'n, /An' cauld religious destitution. / He rins, puir man, frae place to place, /Tries a' their graceless means o' grace, / Preacher on preacher, kirk on kirk.*"

Off to the side of the bottle of whisky was a thick document entitled 'divorce agreement'.

42

_____

A DEAD DAUGHTER. A dead mind. Dead marriage. Dead friendship. Dead career.

What he was doing was hopeless and he knew it.

Carver reached for the bottle and put it on the desk in front of him and stared at it. The rain battered the window. He looked closely at the label. He could already taste it. He hadn't tasted this Scotch in a decade. Definitely not since he'd been sober. He knew every flavor and every peaty note. He could smell it without anything in his glass.

Carver pulled an empty coffee mug toward himself and leaned over and took the revolver out of the drawer. He placed it neatly on its side next to the auburn bottle. He opened the box of ammo and put a single bullet on the desk between the handgun and the liquor.

Three blind mice, he thought. No, what was it? In the land of the blind, the one-eyed man ... that was it. His breathing was shallow. He felt trepidation and nervousness in his stomach. His migraine meant thinking too much was impossible and next to useless. He took the heel of the bottle in hand and twisted off the cap. The satisfying _crisp_ of the seal breaking. He got a nose full of the notes.

Without ceremony he sloshed a quarter of a mug full into the coffee cup, picked it up, and tipped it back down his throat. His brain exploded in white light and flashes of color. He leaned his head backwards and let the taste, texture, and tone strum through him like a bass guitar. He opened his eyes and stared at the bullet. He picked it up and inspected it. Held it close to his eyes and looked at the little piece of metal that would penetrate his brain, mushroom, splinter, and disconnect it from his central nervous system.

He poured another half a mug of amber nectar and swallowed it in one. He felt it burn down his throat and into his stomach. That was it. It was over now. No way back. He knew. He'd lost. So many battles, and now he'd lost.

So many rounds. Punch-drunk and soon-to-be-drunk for real. He almost relished the wallowing to come. It was his natural state, he thought. Nothing mattered—really—did it? Nothing in the end *really* matters. We just pretend it does. Rightly so.

Why would you want to go on believing in that? Believing in nothing. His life had been pulled into a black hole and crushed into nothingness. Helping people was for suckers. He was the biggest sucker of them all.

He flicked open the cylinder and pushed the bullet in. He used the palm of his hand to push it closed and heard it click. He set the gun down next to the bottle once more.

Just then a thought—the flash of a thought—the inkling of an idea entered his mind. He saw Zimmer sitting there, smiling cruelly, and Carver wondered for the briefest instant, what the killer priest would make of it all.

He'd consider it victory, of course. Carver consoled himself. Evil wins again. He looked upon the crucifix on his wall. Had that always been there? He hadn't noticed 'til now. Was he imagining it? The pale, wounded, figurine of the Nazarene—face contorted in pain—looking down on him.

Sacrifice. Wasn't it? Giving of oneself so others may see the truth. It was enough to spur an entire religion of followers. The ultimate sacrifice. He could. Couldn't he?

Carver picked up the revolver and put the barrel in his mouth. He felt the cold metallic sensation on his tongue and the brutal stiffness of the steel against his teeth. His pulse pounded in his neck and he felt blood whooshing in his ears.

Do it you goddamn coward. *Do it.*

UNDERWOOD, Hornigen, Fox, and Maudmont had walked out of the rain and into a dive bar near the field office on Grant Avenue called The Philly Tavern.

"What is this place," Fox said as she removed her hood and looked around the joint.

"Cop bar," Hornigen said as he closed his umbrella and tapped the end on the rug at the entrance to dry it off. "Shouldn't get no trouble in here."

"Umbrella, huh?" Underwood said disparagingly.

"What?" Hornigen replied. "It's raining and it keeps me dry, what's the problem?"

"Only Brits use umbrellas, Frank," Maudmont said and gave him a little pat on the back. "There's a table over there, I'll go get it. Toby, why don't you make yourself useful and buy us a round of drinks."

"Me?" Toby protested. "I thought it was Rachel's round."

"Don't be a tight ass, Toby," Frank said. "Make mine a small white wine."

Underwood scrunched his nose up and said, "Really?"

. . .

THE FOUR OF them sat around a high table, quiet now, staring at their drinks, looking at one another, all thinking the same thing, no one willing to put themselves out there first. Then Underwood, ever reliable, took a sip of his beer, smacked his lips and said, "So what did y'all make of the meeting we just had?"

They looked at one another. Fox took a sip of her Coke.

"Actually, what I'd like to know is what we're going to do …"

"About what?" Maudmont asked and picked up her glass of red wine.

"About the case," Hornigen said, "About trying to save the girl."

"Wait a second," Underwood interrupted. "I thought you said that we should follow orders and that we need to make sure it's none of our business."

"I never said we need to make sure it's none of our business," Hornigen said.

Fox lifted her chin and spoke loudly over them.

"It's just … you're a company man," Fox said, "Toeing the line, right? Hate those."

They all stared at her.

"Sorry," she said and lifted her drink to her lips. They all laughed.

"Cheers," Maudmont said and lifted her wine glass. They all clinked glasses.

"It should feel more like a win, right? It should feel more like we helped solve the case, but I feel like … well, we didn't. I, for one, was hoping for a bit of redemption," Underwood said. "You know, after how I got sent to Grant Avenue for accidentally—"

"We know, Toby! *Jeez.* You've told it like sixty times," Fox said a little too loudly again.

"Slipping information to a suspect, right?" Hornigen asked, tongue in cheek.

"A serial killer, wasn't it?" Maudmont asked and winked at Underwood.

Underwood didn't reply, just took a sip of his beer.

Hornigen said, "I feel sorry for Caitlin. She took it worse than any of us."

"She finally confessed," Maudmont said.

"We never did find out why you're in Manassas with us, Frank, did we?" Fox asked.

"Nope, and I sure as heck hope I never mentioned it," Hornigen said.

"Isn't it about time he told us?" Fox asked the others.

"Maybe," Hornigen answered.

They all waited in silence, looking at him.

"Now?" he asked.

"Yes, now!" Fox joked. "Can't you see you have us on your hooks?"

"Your hooks?" Underwood asked.

"What's the expression?" Fox asked.

"Tenterhooks," Maudmont said.

"Tenterhooks," Fox repeated. "What the hell are tenterhooks?"

Maudmont shrugged.

"Kind of a rough story," Hornigen said. "I was doing an investigation into a presidential candidate, his finances and whatnot, typical forensic accounting investigations for the Secret Service, you know? I was under a lot of pressure. A *lot*. Emily was diagnosed ..."

He left the sentence hanging. They all waited.

"I sent the report to the candidate, the man I was investigating, instead of my supervisor. Accidentally, obviously. Ended up being a big poop storm. My bosses got in real trouble and—as you know—it rolls downhill so ... here I am.

They probably took pity on me because of Emily instead of firing me."

"Sorry about that," Maudmont said.

"Damn emails and fat fingers," Hornigen said, trying to laugh it off.

"Nobody knows why I'm here, right?" Fox asked.

They all shook their heads and waited for her to say.

"Why are you here?" Maudmont prodded her.

"Oh, no, I was asking if anyone knew. I have no idea. No idea why they sent me. I do this computer stuff in my sleep. Probably best in Bureau, right? So why don't they want me in HQ? No idea."

The silence grew awkward. Each of them felt like they knew the reason Rachel Fox was in Sofa Squad. No one was going to bring it up now, though. She didn't need to know. Probably better if she didn't. They took a sip of their drinks and looked around.

"Busy in here," Maudmont said.

"So what're we going to do?" Hornigen asked.

"We gotta save the girl, right?" Underwood said. "My wife already can't bear to look at me. No way I could live with myself if we let her down too ... the girl, I mean."

"I'm in," Fox said. "Sure. Why not? Screw the patriarchy."

Maudmont shrugged. "I suppose if we can save a life, it would be mitigating circumstances, wouldn't it? Might even mean a commendation and a place back in the real world?"

"What do you say, Frank?" Underwood asked.

Hornigen lifted his white wine to his lips and took a sip.

"Screw the patriarchy," he said and smiled and lifted his glass.

Fox smiled and clinked her glass on his.

"I guess we're doing this then," Underwood said.

"Yeah, but how?" Maudmont asked.

"Another round?" Hornigen asked. "My treat."

"What do you mean?" Maudmont said. "We can't stay and have another drink, we need to get back to the office and work out how we can solve this thing!"

"'Course, you're right," Hornigen said. "What was I thinking?"

"Come on all, let's go," Underwood said.

"But I haven't finished blowing bubbles into my Coke," Fox said and used the straw to blow a bubble.

"You know you're supposed to drink it, not spray it over the table, don't you?" Underwood said as he put his coat on.

SANDLING WAS DRIVING NORTH. Fast and out of control. She had a vague notion that it was raining. The water hammered the roof of her car. Windshield wipers jarred back and forth thumping against the wind. She was crying as she drove and swerved erratically. She found herself on back roads. Didn't care where she was going. Only wanted to get away.

She felt rage. She felt disappointed. Guilt. Contempt for herself and for Carver. And for Zimmer but, strangely, less ill feeling toward him. Even though he'd killed her father. He was only doing what he was programmed to do. It would be like being mad at a wild animal for killing a newborn calf. It was its nature.

Mostly she was mad for letting herself be put in this position.

How could she have been so stupid? Of course he was using her. How could she have let her guard down so soon and seen another man dominate her? No one gave a damn.

"No one gives a fuck!" she yelled out at the top of her lungs and slammed her hands on the steering wheel. The car veered dangerously to the right. She pulled it back and screamed, "Fuck you!"

She took a large lung full of air and made a loud grunting sound as she exhaled. She didn't know how long she'd been driving. It was getting late. The road was unfamiliar. She entered a dark, wooded road, going down a steep hill.

She pressed the brakes but the rain made the rear end slide. She panicked and swerved and saw truck lights coming toward her. She screamed and locked the wheel the other way. The truck's horn sounded as it raced past and clipped her mirror. She went into a slide and the car started to spin. She slammed the brake and stopped with a thud into a ditch and hit the embankment. All of the loose items in her car—tissues, papers, and empty takeout cartons—went flying.

She sat for a moment taking deep breaths and trying to calibrate what had just happened. Her chest heaved up and down. She looked around—rain—all she saw was rain coming down onto the car.

She put her hands together on the steering wheel and groaned. She rested her forehead on her knuckles.

"Oh, God, what am I going to do now?"

She checked her cell phone. There was barely any signal. At least she didn't have any broken bones, she thought.

She felt for the overhead light on the ceiling and pressed the button. A low yellow glow lit the inside of her car, now strewn with the trash she'd always meant to clean out.

On the passenger seat next to her was Jessica Webb's profile of Augustine Carver and his family. Including quotes from his wife. Details about their new life in Tennessee. A photograph of Bethany Carver and their son in the backyard. The Smoky Mountains in the background. Sandling picked it up and held it close to her eyes. She looked at the message from Zimmer again.

It was included as a block of text at the bottom of the profile piece in the paper. 'Solve this puzzle to win a prize' - more advert than anything, she'd thought at the time. Now she read it again with fresh eyes:

7:1-450, A mask for Krampus

A cutting glance that pierces the night's veil,
Blood whispers, echoes of a hallowed gale.
Dance in the shadows, where misty mountains bend,
In my dreams, town's folk lives must end.

Leaves from green to gold then fade,
Jay's whisper, his son's secrets under glade.
To those who travel in the dark, listen,
For the truth, in starlight, glistens

Like black blood on marble skin,
Stories of immortality begin.
Journey through a black disk, rivers wind north,
In the shadow of the smoke. There is a croft
In it shines, a single Night-light in the loft.

"Hmm," she said to herself. She dropped the paper into her lap. "Zimmer was sending a message. But what?"

As Carver sat there in the dark with a gun in his mouth, rain beating against the window, he felt his heart drumming against his ribcage, he realized something—for the first time in his life—his mind was completely still.

Not a single thought in his head. Just nothingness. Nothing at all.

Complete and empty peace. He didn't feel pain in his body for once. He didn't feel pain in his soul. His mind was totally free and empty and then, like a glow starting in the middle of his brain and warming outwards, he had an epiphany.

It was, this is what death feels like. He didn't exist. He's already dead. None of this matters. If he was already dead even an uncertain outcome was irrelevant. Therefore, his mind told him, he should trust his plan.

He took the gun out of his mouth and said, "You can still save them."

If he couldn't rescue Minny, he was going to rescue himself and get his family back. He would rescue the person who needed him most.

After all, why should Zimmer win out?

He didn't waste any time. For once everything was clear. He stood up, picked his keys up and shoved them in his pocket, gulped the last of the whisky from the mug, and walked to the door.

He unlocked it and put his hand on the knob. Before he twisted it, he looked back at his desk. Bottle and sidearm were sitting there. He went back and picked up the Talisker and left his office, his career, and his life, behind.

The revolver stayed on the desk. Wouldn't need it where he was going. He stepped outside into the rain. He got in his car and headed for the airport.

43

Oʜ, God, Sandling thought and picked the paper up off her lap. She looked closely at it in the low light again. She had to warn Carver. There was no time to waste.

Sandling simply *had* to get hold of him. She checked her cell. No signal. She started the engine and tried to gently get the car out of the ditch. The wheels spun but the car didn't move. She pressed the accelerator harder and the engine revved higher. She could see smoke coming from the back. The tires just kept spinning in place. She felt like she was slipping further down the bank the more she tried.

She felt frantic now and scared. Her heart was racing. She needed to get out of there and find a phone. Screw it. She pulled the handbrake, unclipped her belt, climbed into the passenger seat, and pushed the door open.

The raindrops hit her arm and splashed into the footwell. Where was Hornigen with his umbrella when you needed him, she thought. Instead, she climbed out and used the newspaper to cover her hair as she looked back up the hill. She'd just come from that direction.

"The only option is down," she said, and it was decided.

So, in the pouring rain, she started shuffling down the

road toward what she hoped would be a town with a pay phone.

She cursed herself. Why're you always so caught up in your own head? She was aware that her perception of her own reality was just a very impressive and difficult-to-shift illusion. Still, it felt real enough, and it still hurt —these old wounds—especially from childhood. She knew, as a psychologist, that childhood trauma was still felt very strongly by people until very late in their lives. She should be able to shift those feelings though, shouldn't she? After all, it had been long enough. Hadn't it?

She wondered if it was because of how strong children's emotions are. They don't develop rational thought until they're almost ten years old. So everything is felt emotionally and those feelings are so strong and so ingrained in young, malleable minds.

She was lost in her own head when she saw a yellow blur of headlights coming toward her through the rain droplets clinging to her eyelashes. She wiped her eyes with the base of her palm as the truck pulled up. The driver wound down his window. He was wearing a tatty ball cap and had a bushy ginger beard and said, "Where ya headed, missy?"

She suddenly felt as pathetic as she looked. Like a drowned cat. The worst part of it was that she'd done this to herself.

"I need a phone," she said, talking over the rain and engine noise. "Something wrong with mine, it's not getting any signal out here."

The driver checked his pockets like he was looking for his cell but he must've misplaced it. "Golly, there may be a pay phone back down 'er in Sudley Springs. Could take ya, if ya want?"

"You're an angel," she said. "The Lord has sent an actual angel to rescue me." She felt it might be true and smiled.

"Hop on in," the man said and signaled over his shoulder. "You don't mind riding in the back, do ya? Hate to get the cab all soaked."

Sandling's face dropped. She stood there for a second eyeing this guy up, considering whether she could take him if she needed to commandeer his vehicle and he tried to resist.

She reached into her jacket and flipped open her ID. "I'm a federal agent, sir, I'm afraid I'm either sitting in the front seat, or I'm going to have to ask you to step out of the car."

There was a moment between them while the wily old farmer held her gaze. Maybe he was a poker player, she thought. Then he said, "Let me see if I can find a rag."

"Thank you," she said.

"For the seat," he replied.

———

THE GUY IN THE TRUCK, turned out his name was Mel—on his way to fetch a ewe from another gentleman farmer—dropped her off at the only lonely old gas station in Catharpin, the next town over from Sudley.

The gas station was flanked by a swimming pool supply store and dive shop, both of which Sandling thought were odd businesses to be paired with a gas station in such a small settlement.

Her cell phone was still useless to her. They didn't have a pay phone but the lady behind the counter let her use the manager's office to make a call. She also brought her some paper towels from the bathroom and gave her a disposable yellow raincoat which Sandling slid on over her clothes. She felt miserable. Like her heart had been stomped on and was now being kicked around like a soccer ball.

As she sat in the cluttered, dusty office, with the smell of gasoline and engine oil permeating the whole place, she wondered why she'd reacted like that. Running out of the office, the same way she ran out of her house when she was a child upon hearing the news of her father's death. She still hadn't dealt with it, maybe? Perhaps this was her chance.

She hesitated about what she knew she had to do next. She needed to try and stop the events she'd set in motion like a runaway freight train. Carver's family was in danger from an active serial killer. She was sure. She just couldn't prove it.

And now, knowing what she knew ... that the man who'd sabotaged the brakes on the train was the same man who'd —not only—killed Carver's baby daughter but had also brutally and mortally stabbed her father through the kidneys, lungs, and spinal cord, rendering him useless, flopping like a landed fish, and suffocating on his own blood.

The thing that hurt most was knowing the last thing her dad ever saw was the thing that she'd been looking at every day in her nightmares too. The sight of Hermann Zimmer staring back at him with that plastic smile plastered on his revolting face. And now she had to ask him for help. She was beginning to get a sense of what Carver must've been going through, needing help from the man who'd taken the most precious thing in his life.

As Zimmer had told her face-to-face when they first met —something she was only now beginning to see clearly— this was a game of power. And no badge, judge, law, or court came up trumps. This was a game of manipulation and control. Maybe she was naive but she'd never really realized before, how some people's minds were always working on ways to manipulate and suffocate another's for their own gain. Or maybe it was simply out of habit. A sadistic pleasure. But now she knew. Now she was starting to see clearly.

The one thing she couldn't do was give Zimmer more power. He couldn't know that she knew what he'd done. Zimmer needed to think he still had the information advantage. The power advantage. That she was playing a deadly game against someone, but had no true idea about who that someone was.

Zimmer must believe that.

She knew she was only useful to him so long as she was useless, weak, and ignorant.

Could Hermann Zimmer feel pity? He'd be more inclined to put someone he felt pity for out of their misery, permanently. He'd probably feel like he'd done the person —and the world—a favor. Bring me your sick, your weak, your tired. Zimmer thought he was sending those people to his God and doing good works.

She took a deep breath, her finger hovered above the numbers, she dialed, got the switchboard, and explained the situation. Now she was on hold. She shivered as she waited for Dr. Forsmith at Patton State Psychiatric Hospital to pick up.

"Hello?" a man's voice said.

"Dr. Forsmith?"

"Dr. Forsmith ain't here," the man said. It sounded like Adrian, the orderly she'd met.

"Adrian?"

"Yes, ma'am?"

"Adrian, it's Special Agent Sandling, Cate, do you remember me?"

"Yes, ma'am, I sure do. It's all Mr. Zimmer has been carrying on and on with. All that carrying on."

"Oh, really?" She was intrigued. "What sorts of things does he say?"

"Oh, you know, this and that, all sorts—"

"Actually, Adrian, never mind," she said and put her balled-up fist to her head. She was shivering from the cold. She didn't need to ingratiate herself with vanity about what Zimmer—a criminally insane person—was saying about her behind her back. "I need to speak to Mr. Zimmer, it's real urgent, Adrian, a girl's life is in danger."

Adrian was silent for a while. Then said, "Gosh, ah, Mr. Zimmer is in lockdown now, Miss ..." he was quiet for a moment again. "There's a telephone he uses to speak with his lawyers. You see, he's back on Ward Twenty now, with the others, but if he will speak with you, I could run the cable all the way down to him and you could speak to him that way."

Adrian was the angel, she thought.

"You're a star, Adrian but please understand very well, he *must* speak to me. Convince him if you can. You may have just saved a girl's life." There was silence. "Do you have a pen?"

"Yes ma'am," Adrian said, just as slow and careful as he had the rest of the conversation. She read out the number at the gas station to him. "You got that?" she asked.

"Yes, ma'am," Adrian said again.

The line went dead.

"Adrian, hello?" Sandling held the receiver away from her ear and looked at it. She could hear the dial tone beeping. "I guess I'll just have to wait then," she said.

44

THE REST of the Sofa Squad were gathered around Fox's computer screen back at the office. Hornigen was leaning forward. He had his elbows on his knees. Underwood was switching between standing and sitting, chewing his thumb, and pacing.

Maudmont was next to Fox at the computer.

"There must be something we can do," Maudmont said.

"First we need to find out where they are with the investigation," Underwood said.

"Just checking the Richmond Sheriff's database files," Fox said. Hornigen looked up, "Who gave you access to the investigation files?"

Fox gave him a sideways look and he immediately understood that Fox had hacked into the system.

"Just don't get caught," Hornigen said.

Fox scoffed and shook her head. "You think I'd be anywhere near this job if I thought they could catch me?" Fox said with a tinge of arrogance.

"Could be one of the reasons you're here," Underwood said. "Sofa Squad—you know—you never know ..."

"No, Toby, I do know. They couldn't track me with a

team of bloodhounds. I'm a digital ghost, and I intend to keep it that way," Fox said.

"Alright, alright," Maudmont said. "Keep it civil. Not civil war, please."

They waited while Fox pulled up the reports, "Here we go," Fox said.

Maudmont scanned them and said, "Right, we know they've identified Ronald Jeffrey Hyatt. They've put out an APB on him. They haven't identified his vehicle yet, but there are at least fifteen possibles that they are tracking from closed circuit television around the antique store during the time window when they might've left. All highway patrol, ports, and airports are on the lookout for two people traveling in a van. Registration number at present unknown."

"Did we get access to the CCTV footage that they were using to cover the area?" Underwood asked.

"What for?" Hornigen asked.

"If we see the footage, maybe we could identify the driver or narrow the vehicle down ourselves?" Underwood suggested.

Fox was tapping away on her keyboard. "Richmond Sheriff hasn't uploaded video snippets of the vehicles. We've just got an unedited video file which," she checked her watch, "Is seven hours long."

"It would take us too long to try and identify the vehicle via video," Maudmont said.

"We can't track him without knowing what specific vehicle we're looking for," Underwood said.

"No shit, Toby," Hornigen said.

"Haven't they identified any vehicles he might have used to escape crime scenes before?" Underwood asked.

"None from Charleston," Maudmont said. She saw Hornigen looking sideways at her. "What?" she asked.

"I'm impressed you remember the reports so well ..."

"Yeah, well, me and Rachel have been working on the data and trying to analyze it for a few days now, I thought it best if I memorized all of the key information."

"Let's go back and look at Augusta," Underwood said. "Carver and I spoke with an eye witness." He snapped his fingers, searching for her name. "I can't remember ... Mrs. something or other. She was a widow. But she remembered him with blond hair. I'm pretty sure we got a description of the vehicle and maybe a partial license plate number, didn't we?"

"Let's check," Maudmont said.

"Already on it," Fox replied.

"Mrs. Henderson," Maudmont said.

"That's right!" Underwood said, suddenly remembering.

"We know," Fox said. "It says so right here in the report." She pointed to the screen.

"Okay, okay, whoa Nelly, whoa!"

"Did you just call me Nelly?" Fox asked Underwood.

"There's nothing in your report to be about a license plate number from a van, but the Richmond County Sheriff's patrolman who took the initial statement said that Mrs. Henderson reported that she thought the partial license plate could start ... might've had a 'D' or an 'O' or an 'E' or a 'B' in it, and that her glasses were dirty so she couldn't be sure."

"Not much to go on," Hornigen said.

"Do we have a list of the suspected vehicles' plate numbers that we could check against?"

"That we do, that we do," Fox said and pulled up the list of suspect vehicles that had been in or around the area of the antique shop. They had make, model, color, and plate numbers.

"Checking, checking," Maudmont said as she scanned the list.

"Wait, what's this," Maudmont said and pointed to the screen. "OBW 1288, early model blue VW California ..."

"What's that a camper van?" Hornigen asked.

"Not really our guy's style," Underwood said.

"Oh, yeah? What's his style?" Maudmont asked.

"I'd say more panel van, worker's van, something that you could put swimming pool cleaning equipment in or, in this guy's case, a dead body. You know, something like the A-team drove."

"Never saw it," Fox said.

"You never saw the A-team? You have to," Underwood said. "I pity da fool."

"I pity you," Hornigen said.

Maudmont laughed and Fox said, "Burn!"

"Come on guys, this is serious," Underwood said, trying to deflect attention away from himself.

"What about this one," Hornigen said. "DER, 767."

"South Carolina plate," Maudmont said. "But it's an older model. A nineteen-ninety-five Ford Transit in blue."

Hornigen and Underwood glanced at one another.

"DER?" Fox asked.

"Yeah."

"No, I mean, the letters, didn't he call himself Edward Derange?"

Hornigen was a calm man. He still had a resting heart rate in the low fifties, same as he'd had when he was running alongside presidential limousines in the Secret Service. He prided himself on never losing his cool, never letting his temper get away from him, and never showing his hand too early. But his heart rate picked up significantly and very quickly, like a shot of adrenaline in the arm. He was suddenly very alert, and the hairs on the back of his neck stood up.

"That's gotta be him," Hornigen said. "Can we pull the CCTV?"

"Checking," Fox said.

There was a nervous energy amongst the team now. High sense of anticipation. Were they actually going to be the ones to catch this guy?

"No time to lose, Fox!" Underwood said.

"Let her work," Maudmont said.

"Thanks, Penny," Fox said as she typed.

"Just trying to be supportive," Underwood said like he was feeling hurt from the rebuke.

"Take a look," Fox said and played the grainy video. "Looks like it was taken from a side street. Less than a block from the antique store."

It was low-grade quality and they all leaned in to see. Hornigen couldn't make out the driver, or anything else about the vehicle, but it was a blue Ford Transit with the right registration number.

"Which direction is he heading?" Hornigen asked.

"Looks like he's heading south," Underwood said and checked it against a map.

"South," Fox said, confirming.

"Okay, so we need to let the Richmond County Sheriff know that that's the right vehicle, or at least point them in that direction. Don't we?" Hornigen said.

"Yeah, but we've been taken off the case," Underwood said. "You know, not to be a stickler or anything, but how do we let them know that that's the vehicle without overriding a direct order from Deputy Gibson?" Underwood asked.

"Don't be such a nerd," Fox said.

"That's rich. And I'm not! I'm looking out for all of our best interests here, remember?" Underwood said.

"A girl's life is at stake, Toby."

"It was just a thought, all right?" Underwood said. He

was defensive. "Carver wouldn't want us getting caught or getting him in trouble, would he?"

"I don't think Carver gives a damn, frankly," Maudmont said.

"He does," Hornigen said quietly. "Rachel, is there any way to track it?"

She cracked her knuckles, "Give me five minutes."

Hornigen was pacing back and forth at the rear of the office, near Carver's door, while Fox worked her magic trying to ascertain whether Derange's vehicle had been picked up on any private or state CCTV cameras. Not only was it highly illegal without a warrant, but he wasn't sure it would work.

"Got something," Maudmont said. "We've got something!"

"Here," Maudmont said pointing to the screen as the team gathered around the terminal again. "This is Derange."

Hornigen watched as—stepping out of the Ford Transit on another grainy image from above—a wiry, darker-skinned man in a baseball cap headed into the gas station. They couldn't see anything inside the van.

"That's definitely him?" Hornigen asked.

"As close as we can tell," Fox said. "It's his car."

"And where is this?"

"Heading south on the twenty-five into Waynesboro."

"We've got to tell the Sheriff's office, they need to get a car down there now," Maudmont said.

"This was three hours ago," Underwood said. "He could be anywhere by now."

"Where did he go after this? Did he keep going south or was he heading into Waynesboro? And if he was heading into Waynesboro, what was he doing there?"

"What would you do if you were a wanted killer on the run with a hostage?" Underwood asked and tapped his chin.

"What every criminal does," Fox said.

"Which is?"

"Get a new ID and travel money."

"A safe house," Hornigen said.

"Or self-storage garages?" Maudmont suggested.

"Pull up any self—" Underwood started to say.

"Already did it," Fox said. "There's only one in Waynesboro—Secure Self-Storage." She pulled up an image of the place. "Looks like a bunch of garages."

"Perfect for hiding out," Hornigen said.

"Do they have CCTV?" Underwood asked.

"We can find out," Fox said.

After what seemed like an hour but turned out to be around fifteen minutes, still enough time for Hornigen to chew the last remaining bit of his nails down to the soft pink skin underneath, Fox had some bad news.

"I managed to hack into Secure Self-Storage's router but they don't have a digital hard drive," she said.

"What does that mean?" Maudmont asked.

"It means we can't get into their security cameras," Underwood said.

"Yes," Fox said.

"So now what?" Maudmont asked.

The team was quiet. Resigned. Contemplative. No one had any ideas. Time was ticking away.

"Come on guys, we need to think of something," Maudmont said.

"What about, ah," Hornigen said and hesitated. Everyone turned to look at him. "What about a bit of forensic accounting?"

"What do you mean?"

"Well, ah, we're assuming he's going to the self-storage, right? That must mean that he's had that on layaway for a while."

"He pays for it," Underwood said.

"Yeah, I mean, if he has it as his escape route, then someone pays for it," Hornigen said.

Fox spun her chair back toward the keyboard and typed again. "Searching," she said.

The team waited anxiously. She shook her head. "No hits for Edward Derange," Fox said.

"What about Ronald or Jeffery Hyatt," Hornigen asked.

"No hits for those either," Fox said and shook her head.

"What other aliases could he use?" Maudmont asked.

"Wait," Underwood said. "Didn't Caitlin say something about Derange being related to *what was his name, the* photographer guy?"

"Bastien Dufresne," Maudmont said.

"He could have gotten access to ID documents or bank paperwork," Hornigen said.

"Boom!" Fox said and smashed the spacebar on her keyboard. "Damn, I'm good. E-9, number 112."

"You found it?" Underwood asked.

"Bastien Dufresne," Fox said, reading from the screen. "Opened his account about eighteen months ago. Pays weekly by wire transfer. Never missed a payment."

"That's it," Underwood said, "We got him, right? He's in that storage facility."

"We need to get ahold of Carver," Hornigen said. "He needs to tell Deputy Gibson and notify the local police."

"I was trying Carver earlier on," Maudmont said. "His phone is switched off, he's not answering."

Underwood lifted his cell phone to his ear and glanced at Hornigen.

"What're you doing?" Hornigen asked.

"Making a call," Underwood said.

"To who?"

"Hello," Underwood said. "Is that Lieutenant Davies?"

Everybody was watching Underwood now and he turned away from them. "Lieutenant Davies, hi, this is Special Agent Toby Underwood—we met at the Augusta crime scene with Gust Carver, do you remember?" Underwood turned back and half-nodded to them, confirming that Art Davies remembered him. He lifted his hand and rubbed his forehead. "No, yeah, listen, and that's why we're coming directly to you. We think we have a handle on where the suspect—Ronald Jeffery Hyatt—the Skinwalker Killer is hiding."

Underwood was quiet for a while, listening to Davies.

"Of course, do you have a pen?" he said.

The team could barely contain their excitement.

"We got him," Maudmont said and gave Fox an awkward high five. "We got him! They're gonna catch him and get the girl, she's gonna be safe."

45

SANDLING FELT FREEZING COLD. Her teeth were chattering. The black plastic phone on the gas station manager's desk trilled loudly. She jumped with fright.

She snatched at the receiver and said, "Hello?"

"Special Agent Sandling?" Adrian said.

"Yes."

"Hold for Mr. Zimmer."

There was a click and a shuffling sound and then Sandling heard Zimmer's breath. He was blowing into the microphone. She could picture him, holding the phone in both hands, close to his mouth, one good eye darting over the wall as he waited patiently for her to speak first.

"Hermann?"

"Hello, Caitlin," Zimmer said.

His accent sounded somehow different. A bit stronger now that she wasn't in the same room with him but, somehow, she felt even more insecure - all alone in the office a few thousand miles away. He was speaking slower, more intentionally.

"You got me out of bed and disturbed my quiet time. Adrian's had to promise me a lot of little *tidbits* and *extras*, including a subscription to my favorite dirty magazine—so why don't you go ahead and get this over with so I can get back to bed," Zimmer said.

"Thank you for speaking to me," Sandling said. She felt like crossing herself and saying a prayer.

"Caitlin, is that really you? You sound so different. Is something the matter?"

"Funny you should ask," Sandling said, "I've just been caught in the rain and I'm shivering cold."

"Well, I wouldn't want to keep you from a hot bath and a warm fireplace," Zimmer said.

Sandling laughed whimsically.

"You think I'm funny?"

"Just the idea that you think I have access to a hot bath and a fireplace, Hermann," Sandling said, and forced a smile.

She felt him grin on the other end of the phone. Maybe it was a grimace.

"What is it I can do for you, Special Agent Sandling?" Zimmer asked. "I really have the right to know, because everything is so beautiful."

"It is?"

"Yes."

"Like what?"

"Enough chit-chat, let's get on with it," Zimmer said.

"You sound frustrated, Hermann. Are you?"

"Don't try your clinical psychology *mumbo jumbo* on me, Jane. Me Tarzan. You ape."

Sandling was wondering if Zimmer had been given some medication she wasn't aware of because he seemed stranger than usual, although it was hard to tell. Maybe it was just the difference of communicating with a madman over the phone; did the distance make a difference to his sanity?

"The poem you wrote me ..."

"Oh, you're intrigued by it?" She could hear the excitement in his voice. "What happened? Did somebody solve the riddle?"

"So it's a code?" Sandling asked. Zimmer was quiet for a moment. "Hermann?"

"Of course, my dear, it's a code. What of it?"

"Could you share the key to unlocking it with me?"

"And why would I do that?"

"So we can get what we want, what we *both* want."

"What is it that we want, my dear Cate?"

"To catch the Skinwalker."

Now it was Zimmer's turn to stifle a laugh.

"To catch him? Whatever made you think that we wanted to catch him?"

"If we weren't trying to catch him, then what were we trying to do?" She asked it innocently, hoping Zimmer took the bait.

"We were trying to lure him out of the shadows," Zimmer said. "And influencing the way the cards fell."

"I see."

"Do you?"

"Yes."

"Are there any others with such powers, hmm? Did we lure him out of the shadows then?" Zimmer asked.

He couldn't hide his curiosity. This was the second time he'd asked. He was as intrigued about whether his little ploy had worked as she was.

"That's why I'm calling you, Hermann, I have some news. It's rather unpleasant, something bad has happened."

"Has it ..." Zimmer said. He didn't sound surprised.

"I would tell you, but first you have to help me with something."

"I thought I was already helping you," Zimmer said.

"What more can I do? Do you want me to write you a map and directions too?"

"To where?" Sandling asked.

"That's something that you'll have to try and figure out, I suspect."

"Is that what you gave the Skinwalker?"

"You haven't identified him yet?" Zimmer asked.

Caitlin didn't reply.

"Ah, so you have identified him, but you haven't caught him. I see ..."

"I'm not at liberty to discuss the particulars of the case, Hermann, you know that."

"I'm like the little Dutch boy, aren't I, so far as I can tell," Zimmer said, "But I only have ten fingers, so it'd be nice to know which gaping holes you have filled."

"You recognized the Skinwalker's code from the 911 call, didn't you?"

Zimmer was quiet for a second and then confirmed. "As soon as you played it for me, I knew what it was."

Too proud not to gloat.

"What was it?" Sandling asked.

"How's your Greek mythology?" Zimmer asked. "Not good I imagine, knowing the American school system."

"You'll have to remind me."

"Oh, these games were so much more fun to play with Augustine, although I suspect I'll be seeing him soon. Haven't you ever heard the legend of Jason and Medea? It's an iconic story of revenge."

"I haven't ..."

"It's one of my favorites. It has it all: spells, curses, love, betrayal, and, of course, some of the juiciest and bloodiest revenge. Do you know the story?"

"No."

"Jason betrayed Medea, even though the gods made her

love him, and so she enacted a terrifying revenge—*terrifying* —including killing Jason's new bride and Medea's own children ..."

"Sounds lovely."

"It is. Truly it is a classic. You really should brush up on your classical Greek education."

How nice, Sandling thought, being talked down to by a serial killer. She shook her head at the whole state of play. Where had it all gone wrong? She had so much vibrancy and so much hope once upon a time.

"Is that what was in the Skinwalker's code?" Sandling asked. "In the dial tone to 911? Was he referring to Greek mythology?"

"No," Zimmer said, "He was referring to a book, a very old book."

He was relishing telling her his secret. He was relishing being in control. Showing her how clever and powerful he was, she thought.

"As soon as I heard the numbers I knew what it was. But of course, the infamous *eff-bee-eye* didn't have a clue."

"No, you're right, Hermann, you're far more intelligent than we are. It's a pity you just weren't intelligent enough for us not to catch you."

It was a dangerous game she was playing now, trying to rile him up. He would interpret it as sour grapes and weakness on her part, she knew. This time Zimmer let out a billowing, guttural, strained screech of a laugh that Sandling felt became real at some point as he was making the noise.

His grotesque laughter trailed off and Zimmer said, "Yes, maybe your boss got lucky when he managed to stop me ... But it's not like he figured it out, is it? It's not like he worked out who I was before I tried to exact my version of Medea's revenge on him and his kin."

"And yet, there you are talking to me from a prison telephone."

"Prison? No. I'm in hospital, Cate, remember? And soon I'll be walking free."

"Hermann, come on …" She said it like she was trying to make a toddler see sense. An impossible task.

"What are you trying to say, Cate? Trying to get under my skin—so to speak—see if I'll tell you more than I should?"

"I don't know. Is there something else for you to tell, Hermann? A joke is only as good as the punchline, you know. A trick—even a magic trick—only works if you can make the rabbit come back, doesn't it?"

"*Touché*," Zimmer said. "What is it that you want to know to make the bunny bounce back?" he asked.

"Did you send the Skinwalker to find Carver's family?" Sandling asked plainly this time. Zimmer was quiet. "Hermann, did you know who the Skinwalker was?"

"That I did not."

"But you knew after I played you the 911 tape …" Zimmer was silent again.

"I suppose this is one of those times where it's best to leave a little mystery," Zimmer said, making it sound like he'd said as much as he cared to.

She was losing him and he hadn't told her what she needed to know.

"Just tell me one thing," Sandling said in a hurry.

"Try not to sound so desperate, Cate. You know? You really do yourself no favors with your *whining*."

"One thing, Hermann."

"What's that?"

"Is the killer on his way to Carver's family?"

She could feel Zimmer thinking. She could imagine him checking his watch or asking Adrian for the time. When he

354

came back on, he was serious and talking low into the microphone again, heavy breathing.

"Whatever I tell you now," Zimmer said. "Carver's out of time. The only thing I'll say further is ... I always loved nighttime at the Carver residence. There was such a wonderful red glow visible in the highest reaches of the house. I used to see it from the street. I still picture it sometimes."

The line clicked dead. Sandling felt dread in her gut.

"Hello? Hermann, hello?"

She looked at the receiver. He'd hung up on her.

Sandling pulled the scrunched-up bit of newspaper she'd torn out and unfolded it. She held it close to her face to read the poem again.

She said the words out loud to herself. "In the shadow of the smoke. There is a croft / In it shines, a single Night-light in the loft. Oh my god," she said and immediately dialed Carver's number from the office phone.

She had no other thoughts than she had to warn him. She was certain now. She'd unwittingly given Ronald Jeffery Hyatt—also known as Edward Derange, also known as the Skinwalker Killer—Bethany Carver's home address.

Carver's phone went to voicemail. She left one, "Gust, it's Sandling. *Please*, you have to call me as soon as you get this ..." she checked her cell phone. Still not working. "My phone is—just call me as soon as you can!"

She knew she had to get to him to warn him.

She ran out of the gas station shop and yelled, "Thank you!" to the cashier and went out onto the front. She saw a young guy in a vest filling up his lime green muscle car.

"Screw it," she said and pulled out her badge. She held it up and yelled, "FBI, I'm commandeering your vehicle."

"Oh no! Ain't no way, lady," the young punk started to say.

Before he could do anything, she'd jumped into the front seat and started the engine. The guy panicked and tried to run around the front. She floored it and the tires screeched and she checked the rearview mirror. He was getting up off the ground.

"You'll live," she said and sped off in the direction of Manassas.

46

SANDLING SWERVED the lime green muscle car into a double parking bay in front of the Grant Avenue offices and jumped out. She sprinted up the stairs, water dripping off her, as she climbed the stairs two at a time. She was still soaking wet wearing the see-through plastic yellow raincoat.

She burst into the office assuming it would be empty. Instead, she found the whole team, minus Carver, in various poses huddled around Fox's computer.

They barely noticed as she walked in, glued to the screen. Underwood looked at her, back at the screen, and did a double take.

"Where the *hell* have you been?" Underwood asked.

"Leave her alone," Maudmont said. "She's emotional."

"I don't have time for this, Toby," Sandling said. She was out of breath, in a rush, and more than a little frazzled. "What the hell's going on? What are you guys doing here?"

"*Shhhh*," Fox said and turned the volume up.

"What's going on?" Sandling whispered.

"We've got the headcam feed from the Richmond County Police special weapons and tactics team," Fox said.

"SWAT? What're they doing?"

"We're about to watch the bust—live—of where we tracked Ronald Jeffrey Hyatt to. And I *hate* people talking during a movie, so if you'll please let us watch in silence?"

Sandling leaned in closer to see. There were flashing lights, darkness, and she felt a sense of foreboding. They were viewing the feed from the chest rig of one of the operators with a view down the barrel of his submachine gun.

One of the team leaders, at the back behind the ring of cars, had a bullhorn and was telling the suspect to come out with his hands up.

"Wait, is this happening live?"

"Yes," Maudmont said. "We managed to track him—well, actually Frank and Fox managed to track him—with CCTV and some clever accounting to this storage facility in Waynesboro. He's holed up in there with the hostage."

"And they're going in like that?" Sandling asked, referring to the SWAT team stacked up on either side of the garage door, ready for an explosive entry.

"Seems like it," Hornigen said. "A state judge's granddaughter is in there. I don't think they take kindly to that sort of thing in Georgia. Anyway, it's not our operation, we just gave the details to Art Davies down in Augusta."

"He's not in there," Sandling said.

She surprised herself with how confidently she'd said it and glanced at Underwood who furrowed his brow and pulled the face like, 'What do you know? What do you mean he's not there?'

"We literally watched him at a gas station, on their CCTV, and we have the payment records from his account … it's the only place he could've gone," Underwood said.

"He's not there," Sandling said again. "I just spoke to Zimmer. He was pretty much *this* close to confessing that he put a message in the paper for the Skinwalker directing him to Carver's family home."

"What, to his wife's home?" Hornigen asked.

"I think so. I've got the poem here, just no cipher to decode it but he was pretty adamant that the Skinwalker was headed to take out Carver's family."

"Have you warned Carver?"

"His phone's off," Sandling said. "I came to find him."

"He's not here," Maudmont said. "We also can't get hold of him." Sandling glanced at Carver's office. It was dark. "We haven't seen him."

"Let's hope you're wrong, Cate, and the suspect is in the storage ..." Underwood said.

The team was distracted watching the SWAT team preparing to enter the double storage garage. Sandling left them and went to Carver's office. They'd said he wasn't in there but she tapped on the glass anyway before she went in.

She was never going to get used to the smell. She saw the signs of the earth that Carver had left. She lifted the mug on the desk and took a whiff. Booze. This was bad. Carver didn't drink.

There was a brown stain where the bottle had been resting on his unused desk calendar. She had a sinking feeling when she saw the revolver and thought about picking it up to check if it had been fired. She reached her hand out and hesitated. She could barely even touch a gun let alone try and fire it.

Instead, she walked around Carver's desk and opened the drawers. She heard the clinking sound of brass bullets and pulled out the box. She put them on the desk next to the revolver, then picked up the revolver while trying to remember her training. She opened the cylinder and saw that there was a single round in there. She tipped the gun toward herself so that the barrel was facing the ceiling and jostled the round out of the chamber. She snapped the cylinder shut and set the gun back on the table.

"Come here, Sandling," Underwood called to her. "You're going to miss it. They're about to blow the doors."

The Skinwalker is not in there, she thought, but left Carver's office anyway and went back to be with the team. All she could think was that she needed to get out of her clothes. She left them standing watching the monitor and went to her desk.

She always kept her gym clothes and running gear in a gym bag in her desk drawer, which she'd never once used since she started her time at Grant Avenue. It was a just-in-case scenario and persistent reminder that she could—theoretically—go out for a run to pass her basic fitness tests if she wanted to. Now those sneakers and running clothes were finally going to come in handy. That's if she didn't already have pneumonia, she thought.

Sandling went behind her desk and started to change out of her wet clothes. She kept an eye on Underwood who was standing furthest back of the team watching the screen. One, to see whether he would chance a peek at her getting undressed. And two, to see what his reaction was to the SWAT team's explosive entry.

Obviously, it was possible, she thought, that Derange was in the self-storage unit, but from what she'd seen it just wouldn't make sense.

"What's going on," she asked while looking at Underwood.

He half glanced at her, not wanting to take his eyes off the screen.

"They're just about to blow the doors," Underwood said.

Sandling heard the thud of an explosion and leaned over her desk to get a better view. There was gray smoke billowing in the bright white lights and the sound of men shouting. Black-clad SWAT team members stormed into the garage. Lots of shouting and yelling.

"What's going on?" Maudmont asked. "Did they get him?"

Sandling, with her top now changed, couldn't hold her anticipation in check anymore and went around to join them.

"Feeling better?" Underwood asked out of the corner of his mouth.

"Much," she said looking at the screen.

The SWAT team radio chatter crackled. "Clear, all clear," they heard. "There's no one here."

Fox turned around with a confused look on her face.

"Wait a second. He's not in there," she said to Sandling. "How did you *know* he wasn't going to be in there?"

"*What*? They're saying they didn't find him?" Hornigen asked.

Derange's van was in there. They could see the back doors were open from the video feed. They found a corpse and a snake. And all sorts of scrawls and spray paint and drawings were all over the walls. A notice board pinned with pictures and a carpenter's work desk. The camera panned down.

"Look at this," one of the SWAT team said. "Tire tracks and a tarpaulin."

Fox was still staring at Sandling. "How did you know?" Fox asked.

47

MINNY WAS in the trunk of a car. She could smell the gasoline fumes coming in and she felt nauseous and quite ill in the cramped space. At least there were no poisonous snakes or decomposed human bodies, she figured.

Just a very uncomfortable bumpy ride and the uncertain anxiety of not knowing where she was going. She forced herself to stay alert and stay aware and hoped for any opportunity to get away. Wasn't that what victims in her situation were supposed to do, she wondered? She needed to be alert to any opportunity for her kidnapper to get distracted, or take his eye off the ball, then try and get a message to someone, or communicate, or *something*.

To keep herself occupied, she tried to think of all the details she would tell the police when she finally saw them. How Edward had opened the back doors of the van, how they'd been in a brightly lit, concrete-walled garage.

For a moment, she was terrified he was going to leave her all alone, trapped in that concrete room but, instead, he'd pulled her out of the van and made her sit on a stool while he switched vehicles.

Much to her distaste at the thought, she'd been

impressed by his preparation and organization. There'd been a dirty sort of green canvas tarpaulin covering a different car. He pulled it off and a cloud of dust lifted into the air. It must've been there for some time. She didn't really know what sort it was, just that it was an old car. One of those really big, wide ones. Something like a Cadillac or one of those cars you see in the movies sometimes. A proper cruiser, something like her grandfather might have driven, she thought.

Was it a Lincoln Town Car, she wondered? Remember every detail, she told herself, so that she could tell the cops. She planned to live.

She planned to escape. No way she was going to let this sicko take her life away. She still had too much she wanted to do. Telling her grandmother she was safe was one of them.

She vowed to see her again.

She'd watched Edward as he quite meticulously sorted things. He'd been much more concerned with the welfare of the snake, which he transferred into a different terrarium, turned red lights on, and dropped a few dead mice in for it. He'd also taken some items, including a wig and some other weapons, which he'd put into a duffel bag.

She was feeling faint now. She hadn't had anything to eat for hours and hours, she couldn't even remember the last meal that she'd had, which wasn't like her. She loved her food. She was dreaming of a fat, juicy burger or a few slices of extra-cheesy pizza.

The other thing she desperately needed was to use the toilet. Edward hadn't let her go since they'd left the antique shop. She was sure she was going to pee herself. In fact, he'd encouraged her to pee herself saying she *wasn't gonna be able to smell anything at all very soon*. So even if she did end up peeing herself, the smell would be something she should cherish. One of the last things she'd ever smell on earth, he'd said. He was *so* charming. She had no doubt that he planned to kill her. It was just a matter of when.

———————

"HOW DID YOU KNOW?" Hornigen asked, reiterating Fox's question. Sandling went back to her desk and found the torn bit of newspaper.

"This," she said, unraveling and holding it up for the team to see.

"What is that?"

"It's what I said. It's the poem that Zimmer got me—forced me—to publish along with the article on Carver's family."

"Wait, you did what? You let Zimmer give you something to publish?"

"Carver told me to do it."

"Bullshit," Underwood said. "You were seduced by the madman, weren't you? You thought you were going to be the hero in all this and that Zimmer was actually going to help you."

"Don't give me that crap, Toby. You would've done the same thing in my position. You also wanted redemption out of this mess, didn't you?"

"Okay, okay, guys, let's not fight," Maudmont said. "We just need to work out what we can do."

"The suspect got away and we don't know where he is. We don't know what vehicle he's in, and we don't know where he's headed," Underwood said.

"I think I do know where he's headed," Sandling said.

"How?" Underwood asked.

She looked at him for a second, checking his tone, and

decided either to let it slide, or that he was genuinely just asking.

"I think Zimmer planted a message in this poem that only the Skinwalker Killer would understand."

"How do you figure?" Hornigen asked.

"Zimmer knew the cipher that Derange, or the killer, was using," Sandling said. She closed her eyes, to remember. "He kept going on about Jason and Medea, and talking about Greek philosophy, and I'm sorry but my knowledge of Classics isn't great."

Fox started typing into her computer again. Sandling opened her eyes.

"Could it be *The Metamorphoses*?" Fox asked.

"What's that?"

"Ancient collection of Greek mythology and lore," Fox said.

"It could be," Sandling said and shrugged. "But that was just to tell the killer that he understood. That he *knew*. The more important thing is the message hidden in the poem from Zimmer to Derange."

"What does the poem say?" Hornigen asked.

Sandling read it to them.

A cutting glance that pierces the night's veil,
Blood whispers, echoes of hallowed gale.
Dance in the shadows, where misty mountains bend,
In my dreams, towns folk lives must end.

Leaves from green to gold then fade,
Jay's whisper, his son's secrets under glade.
To those that travel in the dark, listen,
For the truth, in starlight, glistens

Like black blood on marble skin,
Stories of immortality begin.
Journey through a black disk where rivers wind north,

In the shadow of the smoke. There is a croft
In it shines, a single Night-light in the loft.

"Zimmer wrote that?" Underwood said. "That's impressive for a madman."

"It's impressive, period," Maudmont said.

"More impressive is that there's a hidden message somewhere in there," Sandling said. "Something only the Skinwalker would understand."

"What did the article say about where Bethany lived?" Hornigen asked.

"Somewhere in Tennessee," Sandling said.

"Where misty mountains bend," Hornigen said. "Smoky mountains."

"He mentions smoke somewhere there too," Sandling said. "Journey through the black disk, where river's wind north / In the shadow of the smoke."

"Could he mean in the shadow of the Smoky Mountains?" Maudmont asked.

Fox was suddenly very animated. "Ciphers are revealed by patterns. It had to be simple enough for the suspect to decipher. We can look at the first and last words of each line, or another pattern, that reveals a message," she said. "For instance, if we take some of the first and last words of each line, we'd get: *A veil whispers gale. Dance bend, towns end. Leaves fade, Jay's glade. To listen, starlight glistens. Like begin, immortality skin. Journey north, rivers forth. In croft, Night-light loft.*"

Underwood crunched up his face. "Doesn't make much sense."

"Well, he can't just come out and say it, can he?" Sandling said.

"Towns end?" Hornigen said. "He means Townsend. Townsend, Tennessee."

The team scrambled for a map.

"Townsend is in the shadow of the Smoky Mountains," Maudmont said.

"Holy shit," Underwood said. "You're right, Caitlin. I think you might be right."

"What about those last two lines?" Sandling said.

"What about them?" Maudmont asked.

"When I spoke to Zimmer, he told me something about Carver's son, Ryan, how he used to sleep with a night-light on."

"Did he?"

"Well, Derange—or Hyatt—doesn't have a house number, right?" Underwood said.

"Right."

"But maybe Zimmer is betting they still leave the night-light on in the attic room ... either for Ryan, or maybe as a memory or commemoration to his daughter," Sandling said and swallowed. "Zimmer killed her. It would be a gamble on Zimmer's side, but what does he have to lose? Nothing."

The team was silent. The weight of it bore down on them.

"Townsend, Tennessee," Underwood said, biting the inside of his cheek.

"It has to be directions," Sandling said, "Right?"

It was a huge call.

It was also a guess. They only had this one shot to interpret the poem correctly and get to the house before it was too late for Carver's wife and child.

"What if we read it like that," Fox said. "A gale whispers in the bend of Townsend. Leaves in Jay's Glade fade and listen as starlight glistens. Begin, like immortality on skin, journey north where rivers go forth. In the croft, a Night-light in the loft."

"What does it mean?" Underwood asked.

"It means ... do this for *me*. Zimmer has a dream of finishing what he started," Sandling said. "And is trying to tell the Skinwalker Killer that he sees himself in him. He's telling him to go to Townsend, find Carver's family, and kill them, and he'll become immortal. Not only that, but *croft* means some sort of farm or smallholding. He's telling him to go at night, and to head north. So, that's what we've got to do." Sandling's eyes were wide with realization.

She ran to her desk, pulled off her wet skirt, and put her running tights on. The team were looking at one other, confused.

Sandling grabbed her lime-green muscle car's keys and was about to run out the door when she stopped and turned. She was looking back toward Carver's office.

"Hey, Caitlin, what are you doing?" Hornigen asked.

"Yeah, shouldn't we talk about this some more?" Maudmont said.

"No time," Sandling said quietly and ran to Carver's office. She kicked open the door and grabbed the revolver and the sleeve of bullets from the desk. She tucked the revolver into her yoga tights and walked with brisk, determined strides toward the team.

"Hey, where are you going?" Underwood asked as she went past him. She reached up and grabbed his phone out of his hands and started running.

"Hey! My phone... what are you doing?"

"Mine is broken! Going to find a night-light in a loft!" Sandling yelled over her shoulder.

48

BETHANY CARVER STOOD at the kitchen sink absentmindedly rubbing a dish with a cloth. She'd missed a call from her husband, Augustine, and was wondering what it might've been about. He didn't leave a message. He never did. The truth was she missed him. As she thought about him, she looked across at their son, Ryan, playing with his train set in the living room.

Her eye was drawn away and she looked out of the window. She half expected to see her husband's headlights coming down the road. She'd let Ryan stay awake a bit longer than usual without telling him why, because she loved seeing the look of surprise and joy on his face and hearing him squeal and run and jump into her husband's arms as he walked through the front door. Something Gust hadn't done in so many weeks.

She found it hard, all alone most of the time with their child, still suffering the pain and fear from the loss of their daughter. She questioned herself every day about whether sending divorce paperwork to Gust was the right thing to do.

An attempt to get him to react or show some—sign—of wanting to keep the family together. She realized he was hurting too and needed his own form of closure. But she didn't want to just keep going through the hoops and loops, doing the same things over and over, stuck in the kind of rut they were in after the trauma they'd suffered.

She'd sought counseling and had been speaking to someone for some time, trying to understand her feelings and get her thoughts straight. She was hoping that the paperwork from her lawyer might just jolt Gust into remembering what he had and deciding he wanted to keep it.

She realized that she'd been rubbing the same, very dry, dinner plate for six or seven minutes. She glanced across at Ryan again and he gave a big yawn which showed off his missing tooth that the tooth fairy had come and taken away. She didn't even know if Augustine knew that he'd started losing his milk teeth.

She *so* wanted Ryan to see Gust come home but he was also falling asleep where he sat. She decided not to live in mere hope. It was time for bed.

CAITLIN SANDLING SPRINTED down the stairs and out of the front door. She unlocked the lime green Mustang and started the V8 engine. She found Fox's number in Underwood's phone and called her desk.

"Hello?" Fox answered.

Sandling jammed the muscle car into first gear and pulled off with a judder.

"Gosh, sorry, hold on one second, Rachel. This is a stick and I haven't driven one since I was a teenager."

"Who is this?" she heard Fox ask.

"Rachel, it's Caitlin—Cate—from the office. I literally just left."

"I get that, I just don't know why you're calling me."

"Okay," Sandling said. "This is why ... I need you to check personnel records and see if Carver's next of kin is listed and what their phone number is. I have to call and warn them."

"Okay, give me a minute," Fox said.

"I'll call you back." Sandling dropped the phone into her lap. "Wait! One more thing," she said loudly, hoping Fox would hear. "Send me Deputy Gibson's personal number too. It's urgent!"

She took the corner sharply and accelerated out of town heading north. She sped along and swerved between cars to overtake. It was reckless and people honked at her.

She didn't care and pressed the accelerator. The engine revved and pulled. She was quite enjoying driving this hunk of metal with all its grunt and power. She just hoped that she would be able to get to the Carvers' home before the Skinwalker did.

Holding the steering wheel in one hand, she picked the mobile phone up from between her thighs and scrolled for Carver's number while glancing at the road. It was a dark night and her headlights lit up the black asphalt. The countryside *whooshed* past and she found Carver's number and dialed it. She held the phone close to her ear and said, "Come on, come on, Carver. Pick up, pick up, pick up—*please*—pick up, pick up ..."

RACHEL FOX HUNG up her desk phone and Underwood asked, "Who was that?"

"It was Cate," Fox said, in a tone that implied that Underwood should already have known that.

"Well, what did she want?" Underwood asked.

"She wanted me to ... none of your business," Fox said. "I'm busy."

"Hey, listen, we're all on the same team here," Underwood said.

"Hold on, Toby. Looks like Rachel has something that she needs to do, so why don't we let her do it?" Maudmont said.

"Thanks, Penny," Fox said, quietly under her breath.

"Well," Underwood looked at Hornigen, who was sitting with his elbows resting on his knees. "Well, what do you think, Frank? I mean, we should go after her, shouldn't we?"

"We don't know where she's headed," Hornigen said.

"We could call and ask."

"Yeah, we could."

"Someone needs to stay here and man the phones in case Carver comes back," Maudmont said.

"Don't worry, Penny, we don't expect you to actually go into the field and do anything," Underwood said.

Frank stood up and put out his hand to calm him down.

"That's a bit uncalled for. Penny has played a big role already. She and Fox managed to track down the suspect and find a profile for the unsub, which, you know ..."

"We would have had that anyway because the police found the antique shop and his hideout," Underwood said.

"Yeah, but if the police hadn't," Fox said as she typed into the database looking for Carver's personnel file. "You'd still be picking your nose having let another serial killer off the hook. Didn't you visit a victim an hour before she was killed?"

Underwood was standing with his hand on his hips and an open mouth looking like he'd been struck dumb.

"That's harsh, Rachel," Underwood said.

"You kinda deserved it," Maudmont said.

"Come on Frank, let's go and find Caitlin," Underwood said.

Frank took a deep breath and looked at Fox and Maudmont. "Are you guys okay to stay here and help us with any information requests and man the phones?"

Maudmont and Fox glanced at one another and nodded. Maudmont looked at Frank and said, "We can do that, Frank, we'll be on call, just let us know what you need."

"By the way," Fox called out as the two men were leaving. "Tell Caitlin, when you see her, that there's no record of Carver's next-of-kin, nor family address on the system, and no telephone number. Hasn't been updated or that information is not available."

"Noted", Underwood said, "We'll let her know, but you should try and tell her in the meantime, right?"

IN THE PARKING LOT, Hornigen got into his minivan and gently turned the key. The small, efficient engine turned over, and the minivan started. "Right, where are we headed?" He asked.

"Tennessee, I guess, just head generally southwest. We'll try and get hold of Cate when we know more."

"Sounds like a dubious plan," Frank said and pulled away smoothly. "It's ten hours to get there and we don't know where *there* is."

"Not ten, more like eight, if you put your foot down."

"Eight? The show'll be over in three."

"So what do you suggest?" Underwood asked as Frank waited a long time to turn out of the parking lot, with his indicator flashing, and no cars anywhere in sight.

"We're not really taking your car there, Frank, are we? We're never going to catch her in this."

"Well that's what I was trying to tell you," Hornigen said

and turned into Grant Avenue. "No way Caitlin is driving anyway."

"So what's she doing then?" Underwood asked.

AUGUSTINE CARVER WAS ALONE. He was slumped, motionless, resting his chin on his chest, in an uncomfortable rocking chair in the back corner of a room. He sat in darkness facing the front door.

The wind was blowing outside, he could hear it *swish* through the trees as they creaked and swayed. The yellow glow from the streetlights glistened off the wet stones and gravel outside and shone through thin net curtains.

Next to him was a third of a bottle of Talisker set on a small side table. He'd had some on the flight and some in the taxi and some while he'd been waiting for his caller to arrive.

He was in a foul mood. A drunken stupor. His tongue was numb. His lips stinging from the Scotch. His eyes swollen and drooping. A sad end to a sad state of affairs.

He had had only one card to play, and he'd played it. Now he waited alone in the dark for the dealer to turn over the cards and show him his hand. He was a poker player waiting to hit a straight on the river. All the odds were stacked against him. He was stuck in the sense of suspension waiting for fate to reveal its hand. How would it all play out?

He hadn't been able to get the image of the crucifixion out of his head. The quiet nobility in sacrifice. An undercurrent of appreciation when putting others before oneself. Not an easy human drive to overcome, he thought. The drive for survival was strong. It made making a sacrifice for the greater good even more difficult to achieve.

That sense of love for one's fellow man was a hard thing to comprehend. Like those stories of heroes who'd dived on hand grenades to save their comrades. Bravery they called it. But what must they have thought of themselves to feel that someone else deserved to breathe air more than they did?

He didn't think he was making much of a sacrifice. In fact, he was sure they would all be better off without him. What a thing to do, though, especially in war. And he had no doubt this was a battle. Maybe not of states, but of wits, sensibility, and fairness. Order versus chaos. What Zimmer and Derange were doing, to Carver, felt immensely unfair. Could there be any victory? Not as long as Zimmer was breathing.

RUTH MINNESOTA LAY in the trunk of the old Town Car.

Her ears were being blasted by the overwhelming road and tire noise. Her head ached. She tried to stay conscious and not close her eyes. It was hard. She wanted to cry and scream and kick and yell. Instead, she'd listened to Derange. She didn't want to get him mad and make him kill her before she'd tried to escape. For that, she needed an opportunity.

She could sometimes see light in the corners and gaps of the trunk. She thought it was street lights as they drove through towns or rest stops. They'd been driving for a long time. Her body was really sore and she kept trying to shift her weight off of her shoulder and hips but it was no use. She was trapped snugly in the back of Derange's getaway car. Then she heard what sounded like a single blast of a police patrol siren.

She could just about make out the blue and red flashing

lights behind them. At first, she thought it must be a car trying to get by because Derange didn't seem to react at all.

But the lights kept following.

Then she saw the orange blinking turn signal and Derange moved slowly over to the side of the road. He's being pulled over, she thought and was gripped by a sudden excitement. Oh, thank God. I'm saved. It's over, she told herself. It has to be. She was dizzy with hope. She tried to change her body position again. What was she going to do? She took some deep breaths.

I'll wait, she decided.

EDWARD DERANGE SAT silent and still and watched the Tennessee highway patrolman in his side mirror. He could make out the silhouette of the cop's forest green campaign-style wide-brimmed hat behind the headlights. When he was sure the cop wasn't watching him, he took his pistol and wedged it under his left thigh.

He'd pulled over on a dark, quiet stretch of road.

He'd driven until he was in a blind spot on the curve of a bend and made sure trees covered them from view. It was secluded. Something he liked. Come now little piggy, Derange was thinking. Come and get your dinner. The car wobbled a little as the fat thing in the back rolled over. He gritted his teeth. He'd almost forgotten about her. That's how useless she was to him, he thought.

He turned his head to the side and said, loud enough for her to hear, but without moving his lips, "Listen to me, little girl, if you so much as breathe too loudly, I'll kill you and I'll kill this cop and there's nothing you can do about it, do you understand? Stay still, stay silent, and don't make a peep until I say so ... or *else*."

She'd stopped moving.

He turned his head forward and hunched down a little in his seat to better see the patrolman. The dirty cream-colored Tennessee Highway Patrol vehicle's door opened and the traffic cop stepped out.

CAITLIN SANDLING HELD the phone to her ear and swerved past a slow car with one hand on the wheel.

Deputy Director Gibson answered. "Who is this?"

Sandling had to talk over the engine and road noise, "Hello ma'am, it's Special Agent Sandling in Gust Carver's team from Grant Avenue."

"Oh, *you*," Gibson said with a downward inflection. She sounded like she was bored, or worse—disappointed—to get a call from Sandling. "How in the hell did you get this number?"

A very socially awkward but super high-technical IQ colleague, Sandling thought. And before she could answer, Gibson followed up, "Please tell me you're not driving and calling me."

"Actually—I am—deputy director, you see I'm on my way to the Quantico airstrip."

"Listen, it's late, Sandling. I'm about to have dinner."

"Yes, ma'am, it's just that, wait, hold on," She swerved to overtake a lane hogger, "This is really urgent," Sandling said. "It's about Carver's family and about ... it's about catching Edward Derange. The Skinwalker Killer, who—we believe—is on his way to Bethany Carver's house as we speak."

There was a moment's silence. Gibson was digesting what she'd said.

"Ma'am?"

"Who's we?" Gibson asked, and Sandling thought she sounded like she was moving now. Pacing. Either way, she was paying more attention.

"Well, just me."

"Sounds thin," Gibson said. "You expect me to just trust your *instincts*? Ain't gonna happen."

Sandling was furious. The gall! The presumptuousness. The lack of teamwork and trust.

Thinking for a second, she said, "You trusted Carver, didn't you? I mean, you brought him back into the fold to get to Zimmer ... isn't that right?" Gibson didn't reply. "You trusted Carver, and Carver trusted me. So trust me now." Still Gibson said nothing. "Ma'am, Carver's life—the life of his family—is at stake. Are you really going to be able to live with yourself if I am right and the killer is on his way there?"

"I'll live with myself," Gibson said.

"It'll go into my report ma'am. You might be the new head of the Sofa Squad."

"The what?"

"Grant Avenue, ma'am."

"Grant Avenue's been removed from that case, Agent Sandling, you're aware, aren't you?"

"Yes, I am, but the suspect escaped the Richmond Sheriff's office with the hostage and there's no known location."

"Except for what you *think* you know," Gibson said. "What makes you think they're on their way to Carver's house?"

"Something Zimmer told me—it's a long story—but he indicated, we believe he indicated, to the killer, the location of Carver's family."

"And how would he have got that information?"

"Ma'am, there's really not a lot of time for me to explain right now. I'm heading to Quantico, it's the only way I'm going to get to Townsend, Tennessee in time."

"How did you find out Bethany's location? I thought it was protected info."

"I cracked the code Zimmer sent to the Skinwalker, ma'am. We're able to do—some—things right down in the Manassas office."

Gibson was quiet and then harrumphed. "Townsend, you say ... hmm."

"Yes, ma'am. I just need authorization for a flight from the Quantico airfield. Departing immediately."

"What if you're wrong?" Gibson asked.

"But what if I'm *right*?" Sandling said.

Gibson was silent, then said, "Okay, I'll make the call."

"Thank you, ma'am."

"And, Agent Sandling."

"Yes."

"I'm putting Knoxville SWAT on alert but we'll need visual confirmation before we can deploy, do you understand?"

"Yes."

"I need confirmation."

"Understood."

"There'll be a car waiting for you at McGhee Tyson."

"Yes, ma'am," she said and hung up.

Strong confident woman, she thought. Handled that well. Hang up as soon as you get the answer you want. No point waiting around. Her Daddy taught her that.

BETHANY CARVER CARRIED her son from the bathtub wrapped in a fluffy white towel and said, "Gosh, but you're getting heavy, baby. Soon I'm not going to be able to pick you up!"

Ryan thought about it for a second before he said, "But Daddy will still be able to pick me up, won't he?"

"Oh yes, I'm sure he will …"

"Because Daddy's strong, isn't he?"

She put him on the bed and used the towel to dry his damp brown hair. He wriggled and fussed as she put the towel into his ears and dried under his earlobes.

"Yes, Daddy is very strong. Now, which PJs do you want to wear tonight, pal?" she asked as she went to his dresser. "Spiderman or Looney Tunes?"

Ryan lifted his finger to his mouth, thinking, and said, "Looney Tunes! No wait, no, Spiderman! Spiderman."

She smiled at him and brought the fresh, soft, cotton pajamas to the bed and helped him get dressed.

Ryan got under the covers, and Bethany lay next to him, resting on her elbow. She half-rolled over to reach for an old copy of *The Hobbit* from the bedside table and opened it to the place where they'd stopped reading the night before. It was something about goblins in the forest, and she'd skipped over the bits that she thought might give her, now only child, nightmares.

"This is Daddy's book, isn't it?" Ryan asked as she tried to find her place.

It was. It belonged to Augustine when he was a child.

"You know it is, pup. Why do you ask?"

"I don't know. I just like reading it because sometimes I think Daddy used to read it too. He might know that we're reading it and might want to come and read it with us."

"Oh, sweetheart. Your Daddy loves you, you know, right?"

Ryan nodded. "He never comes."

She kissed him on the head. She felt the lump in her throat and squeezed her eyes closed. The last thing she wanted was for Ryan to see her crying. She took a deep breath and said, "Where were we?"

"Bilbo was escaping in the forest!"

"Oh, yes, that's right," she said and cleared her throat.

Ryan looked up at her. He sucked his bottom lip and said, "Everything is gonna be okay, mama."

"I know, sweetie. I know."

She started to read, and after some time, she glanced at her boy. His eyes were closed and his breathing shallow. She closed the book and put it on the bedside table. She climbed carefully off the bed, crept across the room, and stepped out. As she pulled the door shut, Ryan said, "I want Night-light."

Night-light was the name of their ambient glowing lava lamp that she'd used since they were babies. Ryan hadn't asked for it in weeks.

"Why sweetheart?"

"It reminds me of Madeleine and lets me know she's safe. Also so she can find home if she wants," he whispered.

Bethany, choking back the tears, went over to the window and switched it on.

The red glow was meant to remind babies of being in the womb and comfort them. It was still comforting her sweet, sensitive son.

"Sleep dreams, baby," she said quietly and closed the door.

EDWARD DERANGE'S mind was like a black swamp, a primordial soup of infestations and bacteria and viruses out of which life sprung during the harsh, volcanic period of the planet's evolution.

He'd never known anything else or experienced anything

else, and if he had ever stopped to consider it—which he hadn't —he would have assumed that everybody else's mind was just the same. A writhing, twisting, intertwined pit of snakes.

He sat and watched the Tennessee Highway Patrolman approach his vehicle. Even though it was already dark, the patrolman was wearing Ray-Ban sunglasses, and they reminded him of something out of a film. He smirked as he watched the man saunter toward him. "Come on closer, little piggy piggy, come on a little closer," he sang quietly to himself.

He already knew what he was going to do.

The cop pulled out his flashlight and tapped the base of it on Derange's car window. *Tick, tick, tick.* Derange smiled and looked down at his lap as he wound the window down. The cop flipped his flashlight and pointed it directly in Derange's face and turned it on.

"License and registration," the patrolman said.

Without looking up, Derange said, "Good evening, officer. How are you doing? What seems to be the problem?"

Derange heard him roll his tongue around his mouth, as he considered the relatively polite question, and how he was going to react.

"License and registration," the cop said again.

"Yes sir, of course," Derange looked up at him for the first time and squinted into the brilliant white light. "If you don't mind, sir, would you mind switching your flashlight off? It's really blinding me and I'm worried about driving in the dark after staring into your high beam."

After a pause, the cop clicked his flashlight off and put it into its holster on his black leather belt.

"Much obliged," Derange said.

"Where you headed?" the cop asked, "What are you doing out here on this stretch of road tonight?"

Derange looked at the man's face and forced a smile

without showing his disgusting teeth. He thought about the answer because he considered it a strange question. After all, what difference did it make whether he was out here on this stretch of road or not? And, what business was it of this *bacon-smelling* pig?

"Gee, I dunno, sir, I-ah, I'm just headed over yonder to the Smoky Mountains," Derange said, doing his best impression of what he thought a Tennessee country hick sounded like in his psychologically disturbed way of trying to win the officer's trust.

"Oh yeah? That's a long way to go with a busted tail light, isn't it, son?"

Derange feigned surprise and turned his head over his shoulder to look at the back seat as if he were looking back to see what he'd tripped on.

"A busted tail light officer, really?" Derange said and looked up at him again. "Oh my *gosh*, I'm so apologetic about that. I swear I'll get it fixed as soon as I can!"

"You didn't use your turn signal when heading out of town a few miles back and I noticed you driving a little care-ful-like. Something about this whole situation just doesn't seem right to me, boy," the cop said, thinking out loud.

Derange found it odd because he'd been driving care-fully to avoid attention and instead had inadvertently drawn it to himself. The universe works in mysterious ways, he thought, and it's put another challenge in my path. This won't stop my quest. A challenge was to be overcome.

"Yes, sir, I'll get it fixed right away. If I'm okay to just get on my way, it's so late, and I wouldn't want to fall asleep at the wheel."

The cop sucked his tooth. "You're driving tired?"

"No sir, not tired. I've just been on the road since Augusta. No, I just look forward to my motel room pillows.

You know what I mean? Sure you do," Derange said and smiled and winked at the pig.

"No, I'm afraid I don't and I'm also fairly certain, I don't want to know." The patrolman's radio squawked. "One sec," he said and held up his index finger and stepped to the side, behind Derange.

Derange didn't like this. No doubt he was checking the registration with his switchboard operator back at the station.

The car had been registered in his father's name— Bastien Dufresne—which was a problem for Derange because his driver's license was stolen from a man he'd stabbed in an alleyway a few years ago, and he didn't have insurance.

"Roger that," the cop said and Derange heard him unclip his holster. "Sir, I'm going to need you to step out of the vehicle and put your hands behind your head." The cop stepped closer, just behind Derange's left shoulder, and started to yell the instructions again.

Then, Derange gasped. He heard the strained, screaming panic of Minny Minnesota kicking and hollering in the trunk. There were loud thumps and bangs and the whole car swayed as she jumped up and down and tried to get the cop's attention.

Derange and the patrolman's eyes locked. He saw the surprise and fear in those wide, blue eyes, like some sort of angel seeing death for the first time.

The patrolman immediately reached for his sidearm but before he could pull it from his holster, Derange had his pistol out from under his thigh and pointing directly at the cop's chest. The patrolman's face changed instantly to a look of horror as he realized what was about to happen. Derange smiled as he pressed the trigger three times.

He hit the cop in the heart with at least two of the shots.

The cop fell on his butt in the middle of the street. He had a stunned-dumb look on his face. Derange watched him for a second hoping he'd be able to remember the man's reaction to the realization that he was going to die in the next few seconds. The car was still now. Minnesota had stopped screaming.

He then wished he had something smart or insightful to say. He couldn't really think of anything so he simply said, "You asked where I'm headed, piggy? I'm on my way to put out a night-light."

Derange thought that was a pretty good thing to say as he wound the window up, started the car, and pulled smoothly away.

AUGUSTINE CARVER SAW the flash of headlights.

Usually, when cars drove past in the evening, he would see the lights brighten and intensify; beams of light would penetrate the dark room, before disappearing. This time, the headlights came past very slowly, stopped just before they should've gone away, and came gradually back again.

Carver closed his eyes and tilted his head back. He could hear the low rumbling of a gasoline car engine. The timing was out. Suggested an old car, badly maintained.

The headlights switched off and so did the engine. He's here, Carver thought. It had to be him. It was him paying me a visit. He felt his pulse quicken. His breathing became more focused and intense. The front of his brain tingled.

This was it.

Ruth Minnesota was sobbing into the crook of her right arm. She was so sore and in all sorts of physical and mental anguish.

She wished it would end. She'd decided she wasn't going to let this madman get away with what he was doing - to her or anyone else.

Just when she was losing all hope that it could be over, she felt the car slow and the brakes squeal and they came to a stop. She heard Edward saying something to himself from the front seat.

He sounded excited. And then the engine cut. She finally had some relief from the grumbling vibrations she'd felt for the last few hours. Her ears were buzzing and now she felt a heightened sense of anxiety over what was to come.

She whined and got into a fetal position when she heard Derange's car door creak open. The pain and the fear and the anxiety were just too much. She couldn't hold onto it anymore and let herself go. She felt the warm, yellow liquid slide down her thighs.

She sobbed in embarrassment and in pain. Then she heard a key scrape into the lock. The trunk opened and revealed Edward Derange.

Her eyes went wide as she stared up in fear and awe. It wasn't Derange like she knew him. It was a monster. She could hear him breathing through the mask. He was peering down at her. His dark eyeballs embedded deeply under some kind of mask. He was wearing—Oh my god— he's wearing someone else's skin on his face. She lost it. She started to scream but Derange smacked her hard on the temple with the butt of his pistol and she went quiet, dazed by the blow. Whimpering now.

"Shut your mouth," Derange said, his voice muffled by the human skin mask covering his face. He bent to pick her up by the arm and then recoiled. "You—for Christ's sake—you've actually gone and soiled yourself. You stink. You disgusting dirty pig," he hissed. Then said, "Good thing this'll all be over soon."

He bent down, put his hand under her arm, and lifted her up. "Climb out," he said quietly. "And if you so much as hum a lullaby, I'll cut your eyes out and feed them to the pigs so your DNA can be back with its own kind."

She sniffed and nodded and put her leg over the back of the car and felt the sticky, slimy sensation of urine running down her legs.

"You disgust me," Derange said. "Now walk."

He pulled her by the arm across the street toward a large, dark house. Her eyes were drawn to a single pink night-light on in the attic window.

Caitlin Sandling's phone buzzed and she answered it as she drove, "Hello?"

"Sandling, it's Gibson. They told me you landed and took a car. What's your situation?"

Sandling held the phone to her ear and leaned forward as she peered through the windshield looking at the large houses that lined the road in Townsend.

"I'm looking for the house," Sandling said, and added, "And I'm a little busy right now."

"Watch your tone with me, Special Agent Sandling. You're already skating on thin ice ..."

Sandling said nothing but scanned the houses along the road. Her eyes were darting and she felt like she was late for an important appointment.

"I wanted to share some information with you, Miss Prissy."

"I'm listening," Sandling said, only half paying attention.

"We've heard a report of a traffic cop with gunshot wounds on the 411 heading north toward Townsend."

"When did this happen?" Sandling asked.

"An hour ago, maybe more."

"So he could already be here," Sandling said.

"Yes."

"Is he dead, the cop?" Sandling asked.

"Miraculously, no, but he is in critical condition."

"A .22 caliber?"

"Yes."

"From the vague description he could manage, it sounds like a man who could fit your killer's description."

"Got it," Sandling said. "Anything else?"

"He was driving a nineteen-ninety-five—"

Sandling cut her off. "Lincoln Town Car, in maroon, with whitewall tires and a busted tail light."

"Yes—how did you—my report says 'rust' colored," Gibson said.

Sandling pulled a little further forward and craned her neck to see above the hedgerow in front of a big country house. She saw a red glow coming from the top-floor window as she spoke.

"It does have a lot of rust on it," Sandling said. "I'm looking at it right now. I gotta go," she said and went to hang up.

"Wait, Sandling!" she heard and put the phone back to her ear. "We need confirmation, you hear? *Visual* confirmation."

"*Jesus*! Gibson, if you were any more on the fence you'd have a white picket up your ass!"

Gibson said nothing. "Sorry," Sandling said and calmed herself.

"No, you're not. Now go get eyes on, that's an order."

"It'll be too late by then."

"Then that's on you. This is your case."

Fine, Sandling thought. But you took us off it, remember?

"All right," Sandling said. "But it's him. I'm telling you it's him. Now send the SWAT team before it's too late. Carver's family is in danger."

She hung up. She couldn't breathe. She couldn't think.

"Think, think, think, *think* Caitlin," she said.

She pulled over and switched the car off. She sat for a second and realized she was biting her tongue *really* hard. She unclipped her seatbelt and opened the car door and felt the cool, crisp night air and saw the dark, clear sky above. White stars and a bright full moon.

It was a beautiful evening. A dog barked in the distance. She went to close the car door and, before she did, thought of something. She leaned back in, opened the glove box, and took out Carver's revolver. Holding it close to her face, she opened the cylinder, slotted a bullet into each chamber, and clicked it shut. She was ready.

AUGUSTINE CARVER, even though he was drunk, suddenly felt very alert and got an attack of anxiety. He'd heard the engine noise cut off and now he could hear two pairs of footsteps crunching over the stone gravel at the front of the house.

He was prepared, he told himself. He was ready. He'd worked for this moment. He had no doubt now that Derange was on his way to the front door having followed the Hansel and Gretel-like breadcrumbs Carver had laid so carefully.

Then he saw it. A shadow cast on the net curtain which

hung on the front door. There was some shuffling and the visitor tested the doorknob, which turned, and the door opened.

From his position at the back of the empty living room, Carver could see one silhouette of a taller, thinner man holding a gun to the head of a shorter, overweight woman. Carver did a quiet intake of breath. His heart raced like crazy. A sudden rush of thoughts flooded into his mind. So many different possibilities. Derange could simply shoot him where he sat and Carver would be none the wiser. So long, world.

The visitors stepped over the threshold and Derange reached out and ran his gun hand along the wall. He found the plastic housing and flicked the light switch. Nothing happened. Carver had cut the power and there was no electricity supply. Something he'd hoped would work in his favor.

Derange was hissing in Ruth Minnesota's ear. Instructing her and berating her. Carver was sure Derange would sense his presence. He hadn't reacted yet and Carver sat dead still on his chair in the shadow of the back corner. A fly welcoming in a spider.

Nothing he could do now. This was it. End game.

Derange took a few steps forward. Carver froze and held his breath. The killer was standing in the middle of the room, stationary, and seemed to be looking directly at him. But didn't say anything. Carver could hear a high-pitched whistling sound coming out of Derange's nose when he breathed.

Carver let out a sigh as Derange pushed Ruth Minnesota's arm and they moved through an opening that led to the kitchen. The shadow disappeared from in front of him and Carver heard Derange trying the light switch in the kitchen and swearing.

Carver took a deep breath and quietly cleared his throat. He wanted to sound confident, even though he was afraid.

"Hey, *Edward*, in here. Don't bother with the lights, someone—the old ball and chain I'm guessing—forgot to pay the utility. Why don't you come in here and talk?"

For a moment there was no sound, and Carver realized he'd caught Derange off guard. The visitor had his back to where Carver sat and was probably feeling a little hesitant.

"I've got a gun to her head, Augustine."

"That's not very polite, is it?"

"It means, I do the talking,"

"So talk, friend. What do you want to talk about?"

"Bethany and Ryan, go fetch 'em. Or we're gonna turn this place upside down."

"They're not here," Carver said loudly. "You can search the place."

"Yes, they are!"

Derange came back into the living room. His hostage held close to him, his arm around her neck. She stumbled as Derange stepped on her heel and she made a sound to express her pain.

"Shut up!" Derange said into her ear.

"It's just me, *Edward*, no one else."

"Don't call me that."

"Why not? Daddy didn't like it?"

"You're crazy," Derange said.

Carver let out a single laugh. He hadn't meant to but he couldn't help it. A serial killer, holding a loaded weapon to a victim's head, calling him crazy. Hell, he was probably right.

"This is how this is going to go—" Derange started to say.

"How is your Daddy?"

"What?" Derange said, incredulous. "Shut up, Carver, I'm doing the talking." His voice was higher pitched than

Carver expected. "Stand up. Open up your jacket. Show me your gun."

"I'll stand," Carver said. "But I'm unarmed."

"Bullshit," Derange said. Then, more to himself, "They're all liars, Edward. You can't trust 'em."

Minnesota whimpered.

"Shut up," Derange said into her ear, then "Stand up!" he shouted at Carver.

Carver did, slowly. He held his jacket open and did a twirl. He nearly lost his balance.

"Too dark in here, Augustine. Turn on the light, will ya?"

"No lights in here, Edward. We'll have to do this in the dark."

"I tell you how we do this."

"Yes, you're in charge, *Edward*."

"Stop that. You've called the cops, haven't you?"

"No one is coming, I guarantee it."

"How did you know I'd come here?" Derange asked, suspicious.

"Do you like Faust?" Carver asked.

"What?"

"I'll make you a deal. A deal with the devil. It's called a Faustian bargain."

"Who's the devil here? It sure ain't me," Derange asked.

"I'll trade places with the girl. So you'll get me for the price of her life but ..." Derange was listening. "You need to tell me why you did it."

"Did what?"

He asked the question like it wasn't apparent what Carver was talking about. As if it could be any number of things. Carver didn't know what to say. He raised his eyebrows and shook his head slightly.

"Did all of this, Ronald."

"So you know who I am."

"We found your attic."

"Oh, yeah? What did you find?"

"We know the real you."

"You don't know nothing."

"So help me understand," Carver said. "That's the deal. Me for her. You get to do what Zimmer never could. You get the bad guy. Your pursuer. You get the glory. All you have to do is just tell me why you did it."

"What difference does it make? You'll be dead. No one will care."

"I care. So help me understand. Why not?"

"You can't understand. *No* one can. No one has been through what I've been through."

"That's right. You're unique. Listen, why not let her go? She's obviously terrified."

"See, even the pig thinks you're a *pig*," Derange said with venom into Minnesota's ear. She whimpered again. Carver could hear Derange breathing heavily, his nose whistling.

"So it'd just be you and me?" Derange asked him.

"Yes," Carver said and nodded. "The predator becomes the prey. I'll be at your mercy."

"Why shouldn't I just kill you both right now?"

"You could try—*Ronald*—but how good are you with that gun, hmm? Think you'd get two decent shots off before I got to you?"

The legend of Carver getting to Zimmer with his entrails dragging along the floor was well known. It was the one bluff Carver had in his hand. Enough to make Derange think twice about the cards he was holding.

Derange thought about it. "You a man of your word, aren't you?"

"Scouts honor," Carver said. "I'm ready. Anyway, with a man like you, she won't get far, will she? You'd probably pick her up round the next corner, easy."

Derange scoffed but seemed to warm to the idea. He'd probably never had a compliment in his life, Carver thought. Definitely not about this, his *hunting* skill.

"Okay, Augustine. I'll play. But I want to see how the game progresses before I let her go."

Carver was disappointed but not yet defeated. There was no point arguing with a madman and a gun. Certainly you couldn't turn your back on one.

"You can remove your mask if you like," Carver said. Derange's voice sounded muffled through it, like a kid's costume on Halloween.

"Mask stays."

"Okay."

"Where's your wife, your child?" Derange asked.

"Why," Carver asked. "Did Zimmer tell you they'd be here?"

Derange was quiet.

"Worried he set you up?" Carver asked.

"Don't play *games* with me."

"Isn't that all this is, *Ronald*," Carver said. "A game. Cowboys and Indians. Cops and robbers."

"Those are children's games."

"And this is adult stuff?"

"That's right."

"It's a lot more serious, I'll grant you that," Carver said. "But in the end, we're all just children inside our aging bodies. Nobody really grows up, do they? We're all Peter Pan."

"Then I'm Captain Hook," Derange said,

"No," Carver said. "You're just one of The Lost Boys, crying for his mommy. Or is it your daddy? Bastien ..."

"So he *is* my father ..."

"You didn't know?"

Derange was silent, then said quietly, "I suspected."

"Is that what all this is about?" Carver asked.

"I saw you that day," Derange said. "I couldn't believe that it was really you, *the* Augustine Carver, and your useless sidekick chick, but there you were ..."

He was confused about what Derange was talking about. Then, his mind clicked. The disparate pieces of the puzzle like a Tetris game, fell into place.

"It was you ..." Carver said, with more wonderment than he'd meant. "You were there the day we visited the Dufresne's. You were cleaning the pool. You were *cleaning* the pool."

Derange's voice rasped and he sniffed. "Yes, that was me. It was such an excitement seeing you and thinking how close you were. And I realized people were tuning in."

Carver had to keep himself from arguing with this killer. His emotional response was to want to scold him and yell at him and tell him that what he'd done was wrong, but none of that would make sense to a mind like Derange.

Everything he'd done was for some specific purpose, even though that purpose was out of the realm of understanding for normal people. Out of the corner of his eye, Carver saw a shadow at the window to his left. Derange didn't react. He didn't see it, Carver thought. In all, Derange came across as remarkably calm. Angry and hell-bent on destruction, but calm.

"So what happens now?" Derange asked.

I thought you said *you* were in charge, Carver thought.

———

Caitlin Sandling had run along the neighbor's low brick wall, to avoid alerting Derange by moving on the gravel, jumped down at the side of the house, and snuck up to the window. She was freaking out. Holding the revolver in her right hand. Keep it together, she told herself. Somehow. Keep it together.

The moonlight glowed down from above her and Sandling shivered thinking her shadow may be being cast into the room.

Through a gap at the edge of the net curtain she could see dark figures inside. Clouds were moving fast overhead and there was enough light to see Derange in a strange, human-skin mask, holding a shaky, terrified-looking Ruth Minnesota.

Sandling dipped her head below the windowsill and moved along under it in the other direction. She couldn't see Carver from her vantage point but felt he must be there.

She inched her eyes up toward the edge of the sill and caught a glimpse of Carver standing there holding his jacket open.

The look on Carver's face ... she'd never seen it before. He usually had a quite forlorn look of sadness in his eyes. Now, they were hard, clear, and determined.

What an agent he must've been in his prime, she thought. But Derange was going to kill him. Carver was unarmed, and *that* look—that look of defiance—she just knew he was staring into the abyss. And the abyss was also staring back into him. She had no doubt.

Her breathing was shallow and forced, and she started to hyperventilate. Need to call Gibson, she thought as she sucked in air, and began sneaking back the way she'd come. Once she hopped off the wall, she ran back to the car and dialed Gibson's number.

"Gibson," the deputy director quickly answered.

Sandling realized she was very out of breath, more than she should have been, and the adrenaline was pumping.

"It's Derange," she said breathlessly. "Ronald Jeffrey

Hyatt. Carver is there. He's got a gun. And Ruth Minnesota by the neck."

"You've seen this?" Gibson asked. She sounded suspicious.

"I've just seen it. They're standing in the house."

"Okay, text me the address," Gibson said. "I'm sending a SWAT team."

"They'll be too late!" Sandling said. "You haven't sent them already?"

"We were waiting for confirmation, Sandling. You know that."

"It's gonna be too late," Sandling said again and looked out of the window toward the house. The glow from the night-light now an ominous beacon.

"You've got a choice to make," Gibson said. "Don't you have your service weapon?"

Sandling looked down at the revolver. She felt nauseous even looking at it and started to hyperventilate again. "I have a handgun," Sandling said.

"So use it," Gibson said. "I can't be there to wipe your ass, special agent. Use your judgment and make the right call. That's all."

"But I don't have my firearms proficiency."

"You're worried about paperwork?" Gibson said. "Don't worry about paperwork, Caitlin. Let *me* worry about that. Worry about the life of the judge's granddaughter. Worry about the life of your mentor. Worry about *your* life if you don't do something about this!" Gibson said and hung up.

"Hello?" Sandling said and looked at the phone. "Bitch hung up on me," she said. Now what? she thought.

Augustine Carver glared at the criminally insane individual standing opposite him with as much contempt as he could display, and said, "Think about what you want, Ronald," and thought, *You goddamn clown*, without saying it.

He wanted his words to penetrate Derange's dull mind.

"If you try and kill us both, you're going to get caught. You're no better than any other killer out there. I'll have caught them all. You know what I did to Zimmer, and you know that I'm not going to stop and just *let* you do it. You know that, right? You have leverage because you have the girl, yes." Derange's head darted around. Now he seemed more shaken and unsure. "Let her go," Carver said. "And in return, you get me. You get to do what Zimmer never could."

"Yes, yes, you've said all that," Derange said. He sounded frustrated and stressed. The calmness had gone. "Where is your family? I'm here for Bethany and Ryan, why you say they're not here?"

"I'm here, though, *Ronald*."

"Stop calling me that!" Derange shouted and pointed the gun at Carver's face.

"Focus on me," Carver said and showed Derange his palms. He was no threat. "I'm the one that you want."

"No! You're not," Derange yelled. "Stop telling me what I want! You know nothing. *You* are not what Zimmer and I agreed."

"Oh, you've spoken with him?"

Derange sighed with the frustration of a teenager and lowered his weapon, waving it instead like a prop as he spoke.

"You will *never* get it, Augustine. You'll never understand. Zimmer and I share a connection beyond anything that you can imagine."

"What are you talking about?" Carver asked. "Telepathy?"

"We operate on a different plane of existence than you. We are immortalized by our deeds."

"This ain't some Greek tragedy, *Ronald*," Carver said. "Especially with a name like *Ronald*. But you are a clown. Aren't you?"

"A killer clown."

"You do wear a mask."

"We all wear masks, Augustine. Mine just happen to be handmade. And you're right, it's not a Greek tragedy, but it is an American tragedy—the American century—and we're all doomed," Derange said.

"How grandiose," Carver said. It was dismissive. He wanted Derange off balance. "How wonderful for you. And yet, all you are is a killer of innocent people."

"Innocent, innocent. All I hear is this word, *innocent*. Who's innocent in this? People deserve everything that they get, especially if they unleash forces on the world as powerful as me."

"You think that if you want. Obviously it doesn't change the fact that you're just a shit stain on the toilet bowl of society. Always have been and always will be."

The girl squealed and tried to pull at Derange's forearm. Carver realized the madman was choking her.

"She dies, *you* die, Ronald. You got that, right?"

"I'm the one with the gun," Derange said through gritted teeth but eased the vice grip around her throat. Minnesota fought for air through her nose.

"She's a judge's granddaughter," Carver said. "They'll never stop coming for you. This way—the way I'm offering —you get to escape. After all, if you let her go, that's gotta count for something, right?"

Derange seemed to relax. "Your words are venom, Augustine."

"You would know," Carver said.

CAITLIN SANDLING WENT around the other side of the house. If Carver had really wanted the murderer to find him—and kill him—she figured he'd have left any available option open for Derange to get into the house. Back door. Side window. She could try and sneak in.

Hell, she thought as she breathed hard and kept her mind running, even if he hears me maybe it'll draw him away. Maybe it'll at least save the girl. Who knows? It might work, right? Carver might be able to subdue him. I might not even have to fire a shot. That'd be something, wouldn't it?

Deep down she knew it was an impossible dream. They were more likely to lose at least one of them. She knew the odds and she knew the risks. Maybe that was why she couldn't bring herself to overcome her fear and fire a weapon. Nope. She knew why.

It was because someone—a bully—had told her when she was five that her father was *shot*. He'd said it in grotesque detail. She spent many hours every day imagining what it would have felt like. How he'd suffered. She'd started studying pictures of what gunshot wounds looked like. Imagining what it made her dad look like. It became so real for her—this imagined end to her father's life—that it was as if it had *really* happened to her.

Ever since, even seeing a shootout on television made her gag. And you joined the FBI, she thought. What the hell did you think it would entail? Again, he was there. In her thoughts. On a loop. Daddy. Always. Daddy.

She pulled the screen door open slowly and put her hand on the backdoor's brass knob. Come on, Carver, *please*, she thought and held her breath. She turned it ever so gently and pulled very lightly and the door opened.

Thank goodness, she breathed. She stepped in like a cat burglar, over the threshold, and cushioned the screen door closed. She removed her shoes. She would pad across the house in her socks. Her eyes adjusted to the darkness. She could hear angry voices off to her left. She took exaggerated steps and moved across the old wooden floor.

AUGUSTINE CARVER WATCHED Edward Derange glaring at him from behind his human-skin mask. "I've had just about enough of this," Derange said and pushed Minny down onto her knees. He pushed his .22 caliber pistol into the base of her skull and she started sobbing.

"Wait!" Carver shouted. "Let me make it easy for you," and slid down onto his knees. "Here, see? I'm on my knees. I'm making it easy for you." He had his hands up by the side of his head. "Come over and give me a clean death. Let the girl live."

"First I'm going to kill her and then I'm putting you out of your misery." Minny whined as he said it. "Next, I'm gonna find your family and then maybe I'll take a break and find some place where people don't mind people being different."

"Different? Hell. I'll say. Did you ever stop and wonder," Carver asked. "Why are you the way you are?"

Derange pressed the barrel into Minny's head and said, "I'm a special one."

"You're full of hate."

"If I am, it's because of what they did to me."

"And who was that, Ronald?"

"Did your father screw your underage mother, only to hide her away, deny her existence, and forsake his only son?" Derange's voice was breaking. It was high-pitched and strained. He was angry. His hand was shaking. Carver was sure he'd pull the trigger any second.

"Did he even know who you were?" Carver asked.

Derange sniffed and used the back of his gun hand to wipe under his nose.

"He will know soon enough. He'll be able to see me for the first time. His son. And it'll be glorious. The one who took away his girls."

"Were you punishing your father, Ronald? *Why* were you punishing him?"

"To make him see."

"See what?"

"Me."

CAITLIN SANDLING COULD HEAR Derange's voice strained and clear. He was on edge. About to snap. She was scared. She tried to control her breathing and work out what to do.

She was in the kitchen. Fifteen feet—or less—from the serial killer.

Creak. She'd stepped on a floorboard. *Fuck me*, she thought and froze.

"What was that?" she heard Derange say. "You said no one was here! You lied! You're dead!"

Sandling saw the electrical panel on the wall and dove toward it.

She found the main gray breaker and flicked it up. There was a loud beep and the lights flashed on. Out the corner of her eye she saw Derange standing behind Ruth Minnesota with his weapon raised and pointed at Carver.

Derange was momentarily blinded by the bright lights. Sandling didn't think, she just reacted and took her chance.

Augustine Carver was on his knees. A madman was yelling and pressing the trigger of a handgun that was pointed at his head. Carver jumped to his feet a second before Derange fired. It was a wild shot. But he felt a hard punch in his left shoulder. He kept moving forward. Carver was charging at him. He saw the fear in Ruth Minnesota's eyes. Derange grabbed a fist full of her hair and dragged her backward toward the door. She was struggling and fighting him. Base instinct for survival. From everyone.

Carver saw her reach back over her head and dig her nails deep into Derange's forearm. Derange cried out and fired again and Carver flinched. The bullet smashed into the wall behind him.

Caitlin Sandling burst in. It was chaos. Flailing arms and shouting. The smell of cordite in the air. Derange had fired once and had just got off a second shot. He was swearing and his feet were sliding under him as he scrambled to get away.

For a split of a second Sandling's eyes locked with the killer's. She could see they were dark brown and swirling like a whirlpool. Derange sneered from behind the mask and turned his pistol on her.

Time slowed down. Seconds became minutes. She was moving in freeze-frame. Sandling was totally self-aware, watching herself from above. Like someone else was in control of her body.

She felt the weight of the gun like a mallet in her hand. It was difficult to lift. Like in a dream. Heavy because of the burden attached to it. Heavy because of the fear that filled her lungs and choked her breath. Heavy because of what it represented.

It was heavy because she didn't know if she was capable of doing what was required.

Derange released his grip and Minnesota got free and dropped to the floor. The killer was cornered now and pressed the trigger again.

At the same moment, Sandling fired. She felt the heat from Derange's bullet go past her left ear and she flinched. Time suddenly sped up. Sandling's ears were ringing. Everything sounded tinny.

Derange took a stumble backward and stood there, handgun dangling by his side. He looked down at his left arm and Sandling saw a red patch of blood begin to spread from the gunshot wound in his chest. He dumbly took another step back and tried to lift his weapon but he couldn't do it. Drool ran from his mouth and he slumped down onto the ground. He sat there like an infant who'd woken up in the night. Confused and unsure.

Sandling was aware now that she was screaming at him. "Drop your weapon! Put your hands behind your head. You're under arrest!"

She had him covered with both hands on her weapon and moved forward and kicked the gun out of his hand. It went spinning across the room. While covering Derange, Sandling put one of her hands on Minnesota's shoulder and asked, "Are you okay? Are you okay?"

Minnesota was crawling away from her on all fours and crying, trying to pull the rest of the duct tape from her face.

Derange looked up at Sandling from the floor, reached up, and pulled the mask off his face. For the first time, Sandling saw the man who'd taken up so much of her energy. The man who Zimmer had sent to kill Carver's family.

He looked like a demon. She could see his features clearly. Sharp bone structure, his thin, stretched skin the color of milky tea. He had the most opaque hazel eyes.

"Where'd you come from?" Derange gurgled.

He was mixed race, but so fair-skinned it was no wonder witnesses thought he was white. The ultimate chameleon. Someone who could move through racial boundaries with ease. In a world so used to putting people into categories, he just didn't fit. And he used his ability to slip through to murder women.

Sandling heard a groan and turned and saw Carver lying on his back, spread-eagled and staring at the ceiling. There was a pool of dark blood next to his body.

"Gust!" Sandling yelled and ran to him. She knelt by his side and touched his face. He looked at her.

"It's okay," he said. "It's okay."

"You're hurt."

"Yes," he said and closed his eyes.

He had a thin, content smile on his face.

"Don't you die on me, Augustine!" She put her revolver down, put both hands on his gunshot wound, and pressed her body weight into it.

"Why not," he croaked. "I'm going now."

Sandling applied pressure and began to sob.

"Why are you crying?" Carver asked.

She looked at him through a blur of tears.

"What do you mean?" she sniffed.

"Don't cry," he said, voice barely above a whisper. "End of the day, we have no control. Only thing we control in this life is our thoughts. Our own mind. Everything else ... whatever will be, will be. That's the discipline."

"Have you been drinking?" Sandling asked. She could smell it on his breath.

"Maybe a little," Carver said hoarsely. "I figured, last night on Earth - might as well have a taste."

She felt so angry with Carver all of a sudden.

"Don't you dare leave me," she said.

She felt something like hate toward him. She realized that Carver was willing to leave her. Leave her just like her father did. Carver was willing to sacrifice himself without even telling her. She realized that if she hadn't come to warn him, and he'd been killed, she'd have spent the rest of her life questioning herself and her actions. That wasn't fair.

"Don't be upset with me," Carver said. He was looking deep into her eyes.

"I'm not," she said.

"*Yes*, you are," he said quietly. He had a knowing smile on his face.

"You're just delirious," she said and pressed down harder.

Carver winced and said, "*Ouch!*"

49

SPECIAL AGENT SANDLING walked up to Carver. She'd been checked over for any injuries and was wearing one of the EMT's heavy jackets. Carver was lying propped on a gurney. Left arm in a sling and despondent look on his face. The reflection of the blue and red lights swirled around them. Lots of people rushing past. A small group of neighbors and photographers were being kept at bay by a cordon of local police.

"Better late than never," Sandling said and forced a smile. "How's the arm?" she asked. Carver didn't respond.

WHILE SHE'D BEEN APPLYING pressure to his wound, Gibson's SWAT team had burst through the door and secured the premises. Better late than never, Carver had said. They were followed by ambulances and emergency response teams. Ruth Minnesota was shaken but safe. She was taken into protective custody, and her parents were at her side having arrived shortly after the ambulances. Called by Deputy Gibson, no doubt, to make sure she was in the judge's good books.

Edward Derange—Ronald Jeffrey Hyatt—had succumbed to his sucking chest wound and left the earthly plane, slipping out of consciousness and destined for whichever alternate universe, Sandling didn't know. She was just content that he was no longer in this one. She hadn't been able to pick the weapon up again. Her hand shook at the thought. She'd overcome her phobia when it mattered though.

STANDING in front of Carver now, on his hospital gurney, she looked at him and said, "You owe me an explanation." She thought she saw a slight glint in his eye.

"You saved my life," he croaked and winced.

"Carver, you owe me."

"Yeah, I know. I'll buy you a beer."

"You shouldn't be drinking."

"Okay."

"Tell me," she said.

"What?"

"How'd you figure out Derange's 911 code?"

"Do we have to do this now?" Carver asked and closed his eyes.

"You might not be with us much longer ..."

"Ah, well, you know, when you've been doing this as long as I have these things come naturally."

"I'm serious, Carver. How did you know to look out for it? There's something you're not telling me!"

Carver was quiet a moment. He opened his eyes and stared into hers as they welled up again and she tried to keep it together.

"Why won't you tell me?"

"Because I am worried about what it will do to us ..."

"Wha— What do you mean? You never cared about anyone or anything ..." Sandling said.

"That's not true," Carver said and leaned forward. He was trying to be gentle and calm her. She didn't need it. She wanted to know. Sandling clenched her fists to control her tears and set her jaw.

"Tell me," she said. "Please."

Carver sighed. "The Peninsula Killer."

"What about him, Carver?"

"That's how I knew Zimmer would recognize it. The 911 code."

"How?"

"He just has a knack for it. It's like his parlor trick. His father had been a signaler in the army and taught his son— Hermann—Morse code. They used to do ciphers and puzzles all the time. Zimmer is obsessed with them. When you told me how he reacted after you played Derange's dial tones ... I don't know, I just *knew* he knew."

"How did you know that about Zimmer's father?"

"Yeah, well," Carver cleared his throat. "Look, I'm sorry, all right? I was wrong to do it, okay? When I said I didn't know your dad that wasn't exactly true."

Excuse me? Sandling thought. "How *not exactly true* was it?" she asked.

"I knew him. Well enough," Carver said. "Jim Braddock. I knew your dad. I worked with him on the case. The Ray Ridgeway-Kraft case."

"The Peninsula Killer," Sandling said, stunned. "*You* caught the Peninsula Killer?"

"Me and your Dad."

"What the hell." She shook her head. It felt like a dream. Her ears were ringing. She was checked out. It was too much for her. Then she opened her eyes wide in realization and said, "Oh my God, *you* shot him. Ray Ridgeway. You shot him. You killed Zimmer's father. You're the one who tried to save my dad." She was astonished.

Carver nodded. "The man he *believes* is his father." Sandling was staring at him. "I'm sorry," Carver said. It came out like a whisper.

"Did Zimmer really know Jim Braddock was my dad?"

Carver shrugged, "I don't know for sure. It's possible. Likely even. He could've put two and two together."

"So that whole time—" She choked up. "The whole time I was interviewing him, trying to use *him*—the whole time —he knew exactly who I was and what he'd done to me."

Just then it clicked for her. Carver's role in all this. He'd been moving the pieces around the chessboard from minute one. Using her to get Zimmer to lure the Skinwalker into a trap.

"Why didn't you tell me?" Sandling asked. "What were you hoping - that you might get some leverage out of Zimmer if he thought I didn't know? You were playing me."

"Caitlin, no, I—"

"Yes. Just *admit* it," Sandling said.

"No, listen. *Ouch*," Carver flinched as he tried to get up. "I didn't tell you because I didn't know how you'd react. We needed you. We *need* you. I needed you on this, okay? If I told you that Zimmer killed your dad, you wouldn't have been the same with him, it would've thrown you off."

"You sent me in there—in with a monster—alone and unarmed because you were *hoping* Zimmer might use it to his advantage."

Carver shook his head and looked at her with pain in his eyes.

"I'm sorry, kid, okay? I am. Was it wrong? *Yes.* Should I have handled this better? *Yes.* Would I do it again if it meant catching the killer?" Carver left it hanging.

"Absolutely," Sandling said answering for him. She

pinched the bridge of her nose and shook her head. "I trusted you, do you not understand?"

"I do understand," Carver said. "And I know it's hard for you to trust after your dad and all, okay? But *look*, we got him. *You* got him."

"No, Carver. *You* caught him. You laid your plan, using the rest of us as bait, and you caught him."

"I was the bait," Carver said. "Don't forget. He thought it was my family. So yeah, don't go thinking you're the only one who's suffered because of monsters. The bogeyman wasn't under the bed in my daughter's bedroom. He was in the cupboard. He was walking around my home with a butcher's knife and he killed her in front of me, so don't talk to me about loss, all right? This is the job. You know where the door is if you think it's too much to take. I will sign a release and give you a glowing recommendation for any job in the Bureau you want. Okay? I'm sorry but it *had* to be done."

"So you killed Zimmer's father," Sandling said. She still sounded amazed. "That's why he killed your daughter."

Carver didn't say anything.

"I was beside myself with worry," Sandling said. "I thought Bethany and Ryan ... You *made* me believe I'd put their lives in danger. And then you didn't answer your phone! What the hell were you playing at, Carver?"

Sandling felt that, although Carver had risked his life to save Minny, he was also incredibly selfish for letting her believe she'd put his wife and child in danger.

"You're right, Caitlin," Carver said. "You're right. I know it. I'm sorry."

"So?" Sandling asked.

"So what?"

"Where are your wife and child, Carver? Are they safe?"

"Yes, of course they're safe. I would never put their lives in danger ..."

"Except by trying to commit suicide by serial killer," Sandling said.

Carver was silent, contemplative. When viewed in retrospect, she was making sense, and maybe he didn't like the sound of it.

"So where are they really?"

"Massachusetts. Near her family."

"What is this place?" Sandling asked and gestured over her shoulder toward the farmhouse.

"This is the first place I was happy," Carver said. "This was my first home. My adoptive parents, Ben and Melinda Moats, lived here." He looked at her dead on. "I'm adopted, in case you didn't know. They were older. I stayed with them for a couple of years until they got *too* old. After they died, I bought it and kept it. Sentimental reasons, I guess. The only heirloom I have of my childhood ..."

Sandling just listened now. She didn't know what the right thing to say was. "What will you do with it?" she asked.

Carver lowered the corners of his mouth and shook his head slowly. "I don't know, maybe burn it down? Seems like it would be fitting."

Sandling just stared at him.

"Can I use your phone?" Carver asked.

"Why? Where's yours?"

He reached into his pants pocket and pulled out his cell phone. It was cracked into two pieces, "Took a direct hit," Carver said. "Bullet struck it and ricocheted into my shoulder."

Sandling scoffed. "You're one lucky bastard, Augustine, you know that? One of these days it's going to catch up with you."

"Don't I know it," Carver said. "But for tonight I am still at the roulette table and the balls are still spinning."

"Some balls."

Sandling took out her phone and put it in Carver's palm. "Call them, Augustine, and make sure they're safe. You owe me that much."

A pair of paramedics came to either side of his gurney and flicked the latch and lifted him into the back of the ambulance. Carver and Sandling stared at one another as he was hoisted in. She was trembling. Maybe it was the adrenaline. Carver had a look of shame on his face and pity in his eyes. The physical wounds would heal, she was sure, but the psychological and emotional ones? Right now she had no idea.

———

BETHANY CARVER STOLE SILENTLY with exaggerated steps into her sleeping son's bedroom and walked to the window to turn off the glowing pink night-light. She glanced back at him to make sure he was asleep and catch a final glimpse of his angelic face before she turned the light off. For an instant, she was in complete darkness. Her eyes adjusted to the light of the moon that shone through the window. She looked out into the night and wondered about her life, about her husband, and about what they were doing to one another. Just then she heard a noise. Her cell phone ringing and vibrating downstairs. She pulled the curtains a little closer together to block the moonlight and hurried out of the room and down the stairs to get her phone. She had a terrible sinking feeling. A strange sensation that she'd felt all night and couldn't put her finger on. She was sure that something terrible happened and was praying that it was

Augustine calling to tell her everything was okay. Deep down she knew it wasn't.

She reached for her vibrating cell phone on the countertop and picked it up. An unrecognized number.

"Oh my god," she said out loud. It was the moment she always dreaded. It was the moment she always felt was coming. A strange call in the middle of the night from somebody in the Federal Bureau of Investigation whose job it was to notify the next of kin. Every time she'd sent Carver out the door and watched him leave for work she wondered if it was the last time she was going to see him. Now her heart sank and she braced herself for the inevitable news that was coming.

She closed her eyes and put the phone to her ear and answered, "Hello?"

There was a *whooshing* sound in the background like somebody was driving.

"Augustine?"

"Hello, my love," she heard Carver say.

"Oh my God, you're alright. I can't believe it. I thought something terrible had happened."

"No, no sweetheart, I'm okay. We're okay. Everything's going to be okay." He sounded in pain.

"Where were you? Augustine, why didn't you answer your phone?"

"It's a real long story, Beth, but everything's going to be all right. You and Ryan are safe. And I realized something."

His voice sounded different to her. It sounded more serene and more calm, like he'd faced down his fears and overcome some terrible demon.

"You sound different," she said.

"I feel different but it might just be the morphine."

"Morphine? Wait, is that a siren that I hear? Where are you, Gust? Are you okay?"

414

"I'm in the back of an ambulance, Beth, but I'm going to be okay."

"Oh my God, what happened?"

"I've been shot, but it's not life-threatening, and we managed to save someone. We managed to keep them alive."

"Oh my God, Gust. Where are they taking you?"

"I'll send you a message. I'm in Tennessee right now."

"Tennessee? We'll come and see you."

"No, don't. Don't. I'll get moved back to Virginia, and I'll arrange to come home."

"We'll come to Virginia, Gust."

Carver was silent. One of the big issues in their relationship was constantly moving the family for the job. Bethany felt that it wasn't good for Ryan, and Carver just became too fixated on the job.

"Really?" he asked. "I thought you didn't want anything to do with the Bureau anymore."

"I don't, but I think I still want there to be something between us. I don't think I'm ready to give up."

"Me neither," Carver said. He sounded emotional. "I'm sorry. It's been a hard couple of years, Beth."

"We can work it out," she said. "I'll come and see you in the hospital. I'll come and look after you, and while I have you laid up and recovering, maybe we can talk. You won't be able to run away this time."

Carver laughed, then winced. "Maybe you can bring Ryan too?"

"Absolutely, he'd love to see his dad."

"Beth?"

"Yeah?"

"I love you."

"I love you, too. God, I thought I'd lost you."

"Me too."

"I want to try again," she said.

There was a moment of silence.

"Me too. I've got to go," Carver said and hung up.

He wasn't one for long goodbyes.

50

A FEW MONTHS LATER

CAITLIN SANDLING STOOD at the back of the large auction room. There were rows and rows of people. She was looking at the back of their heads. The gallery was full, including a bank of buyers on the phones. It was a spectacle. It felt surreal. Up for auction was a collection of Edward Derange's works of art; what they were calling art, anyway. They were his creations.

She'd flicked through the catalog. There was the body of a Chesapeake blue crab, attached to the head and torso of a baby sloth. The grimace and look of pain he'd captured on the sloth's face was disturbing. People couldn't get enough. There was a whole collection of Derange's oddities up for sale. One was an unholy mix of the top half of a black rooster in mid-crow attached to the body of a goat on its knees like it had just been born and was trying to stand. Another taxidermic sculpture was a double-headed swan on the body of what appeared to Sandling to be a small gazelle.

She shook her head. It was too weird. People wanted to collect the creations of a sick man and a sick mind. Supposedly the proceeds would go into a fund to help the families of his victims. That must have taken away the distaste of the whole affair for the people buying this stuff.

She was there to witness the depravity of fascination that permeated through society at the outing of a serial killer. It was a circus freak show dressed in tailor-made suits and smelling of fancy cologne. Edward Derange had been headline news. A sensation. The press wanted profiles of everyone involved. And the people wanted as much as they could get.

Ruth 'Minny' Minnesota appeared on one daytime talk show after another. Dabbing her eyes with tissues whenever she spoke about her ordeal. Sandling heard there was a book deal in the offing. Minny had become a minor celebrity. The antique shop was a major tourist attraction for people wanting a glimpse of the Skinwalker's hideout.

Some outlets delved deeper into the story too. They tracked Derange's family. Reporters hounded the Dufresne's. They had Freja Silvstedt's parents on camera in tears. They managed to piece together the timeline and story behind it. How did this monster ever get created? Was he born, or was he made? And who will be next?

Ronald Jeffery Hyatt was the illegitimate son of fashion photographer Bastien Dufresne, they alleged. Something Dufresne denied in statements from his lawyers and through his PR agency's crack crisis communications team.

A lot of people, particularly the public and the media, wanted to know and understand the motive for the killings. As if there was such a thing. Why would somebody like Edward Derange carry out these horrendous crimes?

As Carver often said to the team, the challenge is that these sorts of sexual murders are *motiveless* crimes. They are for their own sake. It's the nature of sex crimes. The twisted logic of a sick mind is enough. The only human emotions that translate are power and greed in this case, Sandling concluded, but she also felt there might be more.

In her investigation into Derange's state of mind and trying to put together an analysis of his behavior and his background, the one thing that Sandling kept coming back to was his obsession with the women his father had selected to be with.

Derange, in his twisted mind, was driven by a desire to be the apple of his father's eye—as we all are—and Sandling believed that he saw the girls his father was taking advantage of, and being promiscuous with, as a personal insult to himself.

In Derange's eyes, Dufresne was choosing these other women over his own mother. And this created a deep-seated hatred—misguided though it was—because of the way that Bastien Dufresne had turned his back on him. At the same time, he wanted what his father was giving them, his attention. And in Derange's slithery mind, Sandling's profile posited, he felt that if he could *only* become what they were, he might get what he craved more than anything. His father's affection. And so, he wore their faces and used their beauty products to be more like them in the vain hope of attaining approval. Oddly, in a twisted way, it worked, Sandling thought. Bastien Dufresne definitely knew who he was now. And he'd never forget him.

Although it was difficult for her to empathize with somebody so brutal and sadistic, on one level she could see it as a cry for help from a very disturbed person. Trying, on one hand, to punish his father for his indiscretions by taking the things that he valued—his models—away from him. At the same time, he was seeking a way to gain his attention, if not his affection. Derange wanted acknowledgment and love. Two things he'd never had in his life. And in his disturbed, psychotic brain this was a legitimate way of satiating that need.

The press made all the connections too. Derange's unhappy childhood. He was abused and taken advantage of by his *evil* mother.

Obviously, they picked up on the racial element the way Derange had, because of his light complexion, he'd been able to flit between races. He could blend in or show the world a different face, depending on his needs. He used his skin color as a weapon against a society that was fixated on it, and it allowed him to remain unseen, and on the loose for far longer than he otherwise might've been.

Someone also leaked details of his leather-bound copy of *The Metamorphoses* and his drawings, photographs, and annotations, along with the link to Hermann Zimmer. Of course, Augustine Carver was mentioned.

Sandling had shied away from the newsreels. She gave one interview to the cameras on the night she shot Derange, standing in her gym clothes, in the blinding spotlight trying to get her hair out of her face. She cringed every time she saw it, or thought about it, which was often.

Derange had learned to sew, cut, and stitch animal trophies in state correctional facilities. So much for *rehabilitation* or becoming a functioning member of society. Details of his disfigurement at the hands of the hoodlums in juvenile detention were kept confidential. His fascination with snakes was put down to his obsession with Medusa and Greek mythology.

Sandling replayed her interviews with Zimmer the Ripper over and over in her mind. So much of what Zimmer said to her seemed like it was the incoherent rambling of a sick individual but when she reviewed it—and only in retrospect—much of what he said was a hint wrapped in a riddle. He'd been toying with her and with Carver. He'd thrown her off the scent by mentioning Carl Jung and the ancient Egyptian funeral texts, but his allusion to Greece and *katharos* and even quoting from *The Metamorphoses* itself meant he knew more than he let on.

Sandling learned during the analysis of Zimmer's poem, for example, that his use of the numbers 7:1-450 in reply to Derange was a direct reference to the story of Jason and Medea - that she and Zimmer spoke about during one of their interviews. It made her mad that she didn't see it. It made her mad that Zimmer had blinded her with her own ambition and need for validation. It was something she would work on to fix.

The code itself was a reference to book 7 of Ovid's *Metamorphoses* and lines 1 to 450, which is the section that includes the murder of Jason's bride and their own children. Sandling could clearly see—in retrospect—how Zimmer painted a very clear picture of what he wanted Derange to do for him.

In fact, the solution of Derange's 911 dial tone code, and one of the reasons Zimmer could identify the cipher, was also something he'd said to her during their interviews. "All things are subject to eternal change," Zimmer told her. He'd given her the answer, she simply didn't know it. It was a line from Ovid's epic poem and something he'd been recorded saying in his tent revival sermons many times. The investigating officers had found a VHS of Zimmer preaching amongst Derange's items in the storage garage.

Derange's calls to the police, far from being attempts at communicating with them, turned out to be messages from a madman sending signals out on the airwaves in the hope that Father Zimmer would snatch them out of the air. He willed it and it happened, with a little help from the Sofa Squad and Sandling's own insecurities. "At least we lived up to our reputation," Sandling thought at the time, once she'd put the riddle together.

Because Zimmer had reemerged into public consciousness, he also became a political sore point. The link between Carver and the FBI working with Zimmer wasn't widely known or reported on but *someone* leaked details of the medical review board. There was a public outcry. Once Derange's body was cremated and the dust from his remains scattered near a turnpike, the sensation died down and the next bit of celebrity gossip took over the news cycle. Normalcy was restored. People went back about their business. No one was whispering in coffee shops about beautiful faceless corpses anymore.

After Zimmer's involvement in sharing information with Derange came to light, he became an accessory. Deputy Director Bronwyn Gibson went personally to inform Zimmer that his medical review was being dropped. That he was being moved to a different facility. Something much less accommodating.

Upon hearing the news that Edward Derange failed in his mission to finish what the Ripper couldn't, Zimmer smirked and told Gibson, "Good help is hard to find," as they put shackles on him. Before they gagged him he asked Gibson to, "Pass on my warmest regards to Saint Augustine and his family."

Zimmer was moved. Sandling didn't really care where. She just wanted to know she'd never have to deal with him again.

Their main salvation turned out to be Carver's intimate understanding of Zimmer's sick and meddling mind. Carver's ability to intuit the moves the killer priest was making before he made them. It was a high-risk strategy. What other option did he have? And it worked too.

For now, Sandling was just an observer. She was trying to process everything that had happened. She started therapy with a specialist who was used to seeing and working with cops. She was starting to open up and understand more about her own place, psychologically. She was starting to heal. Although, she still gagged at the thought of holding a gun. It seemed to her now that it must have been someone else who shot Derange.

As the bidding for the first of Derange's freak animals started, she decided she'd seen enough. He would be consigned to fan forums and documentaries for people to pore over. He was just a footnote in the long line of depraved serial killers. She doubted she'd ever forget looking into his swirling brown eyes as he lay dying in Tennessee.

51

ı

CARVER WAS STANDING on the deck of a yacht in the Quantico Marina and he saw Jessica Webb coming before she saw him. He waved and she saw him and did a little jog to let him know she was hurrying. She walked down the wooden slatted dock with an amused grin on her face. He could tell that she thought Gust Carver was not the type of man she'd ever expected to see standing on a sailboat. He wasn't the type of man he'd ever thought would be seen on a yacht either.

When she got up alongside, she knocked on the hull and said, "Hey, Gust! Nice yacht."

"Oh, hey, Jess. Thanks."

"You goin' sailing?"

Carver looked up at the top of the mast and saw the ropes slapping against the pole. "I don't sail," he said looking back at her. "Besides, weather seems a bit *iffy* to me. How you doing?"

"Actually, I was really hoping to find you."

She sounded serious. Like she had something to get off her chest.

"Oh, yeah? How come?"

"Yeah—um—they told me where I might find you and ... here you are!" she said with a laugh. Carver gave her a half-grimace, half-smile and waited for her to get to it. "Um, anyway. Are you living here now?"

Carver could tell she was stalling. He picked up a rope from the deck and started looping it around this arm and wondered what she was thinking. She looked uncomfortable.

"Just until I find somewhere permanent," he said.

"Family joining you?"

Carver didn't reply. She opened her mouth to speak again and Carver said, "Hey, Jess, not to be rude but I'm a little busy getting my sea legs here ... is there something I can do for you?"

"Do you mind if I come aboard? I really need to speak to you."

"Sure," Carver said. "Come on up." And helped her up the small ladder and over the side. "Come into the galley and I'll make you a cup of coffee. Folgers all right?"

"Sounds great."

Carver moved around the narrow galley kitchen, lit the stove, and put the pot on. She wedged herself into the small seating booth that doubled as the dining table. The pot whistled loudly and Carver poured the water into the cups. He didn't stir.

"Hope you like it black," he said. "Haven't gotten to the supermarket yet."

"Thanks," Webb said and took a sip. She wrapped her hands around the mug and smiled at him.

Craver winced and pumped his fist and rolled the shoulder of his left arm.

"Gunshot wound still bothering you?" she asked.

"Yeah, it is," Carver said. "I'm starting to wonder how long this is going to take, but I'm still doing rehab and it's getting better."

"How long were you in hospital for?"

"Not too long," Carver said, "But I had help."

"Bethany came down to see you?"

"She was great. She was with me every day. It really helped bring us together again, you know? And trust each other again. We spoke a lot while I was laid up. It helped."

"With nowhere to run to," Webb said with a hint of irony. "I know the feeling."

"That too," Carver said. "Strange how things work out."

"What's happening with them now?"

"We're just looking for a place and Beth is going to come down and stay with us. We'll try again. She's trying to find Ryan a new school, you know, it's a whole process."

Webb nodded and lifted the mug to her lips. The silence dragged out. Carver sat patiently waiting for her to speak. He took a sip of his coffee and looked over the top of the mug at her. He nearly gagged at the taste and put his mug on the table.

"So, what brings you—"

"My sister was Elizabeth Webb," she said. She looked a bit shocked at the words that had come out of her mouth. "Sorry."

Carver smiled at her expression and thought, *okay*, is that supposed to mean something to me?

"Wait, *was* your sister?"

"Yes," she said. "She died the night of the nineteenth of August, two years ago now."

Carver's mind was working.

"Does that date mean anything to you?" Webb asked.

"Yes, it does," Carver said and swallowed. He had a lump in his throat and furrowed his brow. What was this about? How did she know that date meant something to him?

Webb took a deep breath and asked, "Does my sister's name mean anything to you?"

"As in, recognize it?" Carver asked and shook his head. He didn't think so. He was watching her expressions closely. "Not really," he said. "Should it?"

JESSICA WEBB WAS uncomfortable being there. She pushed her coffee away. She wasn't sure of herself. Was Carver really the right man to help her? He had his own problems. But it wasn't like she had any other options. Most of her contacts and informants in the police force–usually she called them sources–had, if not quite laughed her out of the building, taken her aside and held the top of her arm, leaned in closely, and given her some 'friendly advice'. Something along the lines of 'Listen here Jessica, speaking as a friend,' they'd said different ways. 'You ought to leave this alone. You know? Try and move on. I know it's hard to deal with, but the fact is, and I'm sorry to say it like this, she killed *herself*.' She was sick of it. Walk away. Forget about it. Move on with your life. No.

"I need your help, Carver."

"Okay," Carver said. His expression changed. Now he could tell it was something important.

"It's about my sister, Gust."

"Okay."

She didn't really know what to say, so she said, "You have her kidney."

Carver just looked at her unblinking. She took a deep breath. She had his attention now.

427

"The night you were brought into the ER, you know, the night Zimmer—"

"Cut my internal organs out and murdered my daughter. Yeah, August nineteenth. I remember."

"That night ... That God-awful night. My sister—my twin sister—was brought into the ER a little before you. She was alive apparently, but barely. And they couldn't save her."

"I'm sorry," Carver croaked and lifted his hand to his mouth and cleared his throat.

"You were also there," Webb said. "You'd come in alive too, but barely. And it turned out you were a match. She's your ..."

"My what?"

"Your organ donor."

Then Webb felt the tears coming. Her eyes welled up and she was just crying and Carver was holding her. They embraced and she sobbed into his shoulder.

"I'm sorry," she said as she pulled back from his embrace and sniffled and reached into her handbag for a tissue.

Carver asked, "Your sister saved my life?"

She smiled through the tears and nodded. "I signed the papers. She donated her organs so you could live. It was ... the least we could do."

"How did she–ah–you know...?" Carver asked.

"They ruled it suicide or attempted suicide but ..." she said and looked apologetic.

"But you don't believe them."

Webb shook her head. "No. I don't, Gust. I've been working on it a lot these past two years. I know it might sound like grief or denial or both, but I'm telling you, there's no way she'd have done that to herself."

"Okay. So, what then?" Webb gave him a look of *c'mon.* "You think she was murdered," Carver said.

"Yes. A hundred percent."

Now it was Carver's turn to give her a look.

"Fine, maybe not a hundred percent 'cause we don't deal in certainty, right? We deal in probability. So, I'll say ninety-five percent. But it's a hundred, you know? Will you help me?"

Carver half shook his head before saying, "Uh, Jess ... *jeez*. You know. What do you think it is I can do?"

"Hell, I don't know Augustine, put some of that magic stardust of yours to good use and help me bring her killer to justice."

She could feel that Carver didn't want to say 'no' but getting involved in something so personal and being responsible for her grief wasn't something he was comfortable with. Nobody was. She wasn't going to accept that.

"I'm not in the field anymore, Jess, you know?"

She sat staring at him. Her eyes burned holes in his head.

"I'm more focused on the management of the team at Grant Avenue now."

"Oh, yeah?"

"But don't think I haven't forgotten what you did for us."

"I'm starting to feel like you *have* forgotten. You *owe* me, Gust. Are you going to ignore the story I planted? I helped you lure the Skinwalker out. I put my neck on the line for you. This is my *sister* I'm talking about."

"I know what it's like to lose family."

"Why won't you help me then?"

"It's not as simple as that."

"Why not?"

"It's police business. There's a process."

"My sister gets brushed under the carpet while what, you do paperwork? She deserves justice, Augustine, not just a file in a drawer."

"It's not that simple and you know it."

"I helped you out when no one else could, Carver. I need to cash in my chip now. I'm not asking you to go rogue, just ... just *look* at it. That's all I'm asking."

"Jess, I ..." Carver stopped.

"No, Augustine, *you* listen. You once told me we do what we must to catch monsters, remember? Well, there's a monster out there, and he took my sister. I'm asking you, no, I'm *begging* you. Help me catch this monster. *Please*."

"What makes you so sure?" Carver asked carefully.

She could tell that he didn't want to be one of the dozens of people who'd disregarded her out of hand.

"I've looked into it," she said. "A lot. It's one of the reasons I work freelance, 'cause I need the time to do my own research."

"Okay. What did you find?"

She paused for a moment and looked directly into his eyes. "I think we're dealing with a serial killer."

Carver didn't say anything. He had kind, remorseful eyes. He was thinking. But *what* was he thinking?

"Who else knows about this?" Carver asked.

"You and me," Webb said.

THE NIGHT CRAWLER

What if your vital organs once belonged to the victim of a brutal serial killer?

Senior detectives with troubled pasts. Apparent suicides and unsettling connections. The police see only coincidences. One relentless investigator sees the hand of a meticulous killer.

When Carver discovers that his organ donor was a victim of a methodical and maniacal murderer, the hunt becomes personal.

As the body count rises, can they stop the Night Crawler before they're trapped in his deadly game?

Grab it now: The Night Crawler

ALSO BY STEWART CLYDE

Discover the Stirling Hunt thrillers:

Printed in Great Britain
by Amazon

59225586R00249